INSIDE LIA'S HEART

Lia sat facing Moses as the ambulance backed up, found a place to turn around, and headed down the hill. She could tell that Moses fought to keep his eyes open. They must have given him something for the pain that made him drowsy.

"I like tall girls," he said, letting his eyes close, as if he were unable to keep them open for one more second.

He might like tall girls, but he wouldn't marry one.

Lia held her breath as a wave of pain washed over her. She loved Moses Zimmerman. She loved his kindness and his cheerful spirit, and yes, even though appearance shouldn't matter, his handsome face and tall, strong figure. She couldn't imagine ever wanting anyone but Moses. No one else would measure up—literally.

It didn't matter that he didn't want to marry her or that he favored her sister or even that Lia was too plain to dream of such a match. She loved him. Her heart broke even as she realized how completely it belonged to him . . .

BOOK YOUR PLACE ON OUR WEBSITE
AND MAKE THE
READING CONNECTION!

We've created a customized website just for our very special readers, where you can get the inside scoop on everything that's going on with Zebra, Pinnacle and Kensington books.

When you come online, you'll have the exciting opportunity to:

- View covers of upcoming books
- Read sample chapters
- Learn about our future publishing schedule
  (listed by publication month and author)
- Find out when your favorite authors will be visiting
  a city near you
- Search for and order backlist books from our
  online catalog
- Check out author bios and background information
- Send e-mail to your favorite authors
- Meet the Kensington staff online
- Join us in weekly chats with authors, readers and
  other guests
- Get writing guidelines
- AND MUCH MORE!

Visit our website at
http://www.kensingtonbooks.com

Huckleberry Hill

JENNIFER BECKSTRAND

ZEBRA BOOKS
KENSINGTON PUBLISHING CORP.

http://www.kensingtonbooks.com

ZEBRA BOOKS are published by

Kensington Publishing Corp.
119 West 40th Street
New York, NY 10018

All Kensington titles, imprints and distributed lines are
available at special quantity discounts for bulk purchases
for sales promotion, premiums, fund-raising, educational
or institutional use.

Special book excerpts or customized printings can also
be created to fit specific needs. For details, write or phone
the office of the Kensington Special Sales Manager:
Attn. Special Sales Department. Kensington Publishing
Corp., 119 West 40th Street, New York, NY 10018. Phone:
1-800-221-2647.

ISBN-13: 978-1-4201-3356-1
ISBN-10: 1-4201-3356-X
First Printing: January 2014

eISBN-13: 978-1-4201-3357-8
eISBN-10: 1-4201-3357-8
First Electronic Edition: January 2014

10 9 8 7 6 5 4 3 2 1

Printed in the United States of America

Chapter One

Anna Helmuth eased herself into the wooden rocker where she once cuddled each of her thirteen babies and took up her needles. "Moses is miserable, absolutely miserable. We must find him a wife."

Felty lowered his newspaper just enough to spy his wife over the top of it. "You mean Moses, our grandson? He doesn't seem miserable to me."

"He won't know how miserable he is until he meets the right girl," Anna said, peering through her thick, round glasses.

"Then we must make certain he never meets the right girl. Ignorance is bliss."

Anna clicked her knitting needles with blinding speed. "Now, Felty, don't tease me. Our grandson's happiness is at stake."

"Let the poor boy make his own hay. What young man wants two eighty-year-olds picking his future wife? Besides, I don't know who is good enough for him. He's a catch, that one."

"He takes after you, Felty, except I think you are the handsomer."

Felty lowered his paper to his lap. "Oh, Annie Banannie, I was never that handsome."

"Pretty Felty. The handsomest boy in Bonduel. That's what we girls called you behind your back. I was lucky enough to snag you before Rosie Herschberger did."

"Rosie Herschberger can't hold a candle to your fried chicken. It never would have worked out."

Anna smiled but didn't look up from her knitting. Already March, and Felty didn't have one new scarf to wear to ward off a change-of-weather cold. Surely any Amish wife worth her salt would knit her husband at least seven spring scarves, one for each day of the week, to last until the weather warmed up. "All I'm saying is, it is about time."

"For Rosie to learn to cook?"

"For Moses to find a wife. And we must help him. The grandparents are always in charge of making the matches."

Felty shook his finger. "Annie girl, you are making that up."

"Now, Felty. Why else would the good Lord grant us years to sit in our rockers if not to scheme and plan other people's lives?"

Trying to fold *The Budget* neatly on the crease, Felty managed to buckle the thin paper until the fold crumpled in his hands. "We reached this age by keeping our noses out of other people's business."

"Not me. I like to stick my fingers into other people's pies. It's my birthright as a woman."

"Moses won't go along easy. That girl broke his heart something terrible yet," Felty said.

"Three years ago, and the whole rigmarole turned

out to be a blessing. She left the church, and Moses, bless his heart, wouldn't follow her."

Felty gave up on his paper and wadded it in his lap. "Smart one, that boy."

"It's high time for him to get busy."

"What makes you think you can help him to a good wife? His *mamm* has tried to match him up with every girl in Wisconsin plus four or five from Ohio and even one from Canada."

"And she has fallen short on her duties. We are Moses's only hope. Do you remember that family we met in Wautoma when we went for Bishop Glick's funeral?"

Felty furrowed his brow. "Bishop Glick passed away?"

"In October. Don't you remember?"

"I remember getting old."

"There was a lovely family who took us in overnight."

Felty brightened and threw his ball of newspaper into the air, but it got away from him and floated to the floor behind his overstuffed recliner. "The Shetlers. With several grown boys and two girls at the tail end."

Anna grinned at her husband. "I knew you would remember."

"I still don't remember about the bishop. But the eldest Shetler daughter was tall and pretty."

"Just the thing for our Moses."

"A sweet girl. She helped me when I sank into that sofa and couldn't get out. We took hands, and I got about halfway up before falling back into the cushions. I grunted, she snorted, and we laughed so hard I think I sprouted a hernia."

"She baked us goodies for the trip home."

"A sweet girl. I remember the pumpkin whoopie pies." Felty stroked his beard. "You could send Moses to Wautoma to fetch her, but I don't think he would agree to go without a taste of those whoopie pies first."

"Moses will take some buttering up. We must bring his bride to Huckleberry Hill."

"Annie, leave the poor boy be. When he's ready, he'll find his own wife."

Annie rested her knitting needles in her lap. "Now, Felty. We can't leave something this important to a man. What man has ever known his own heart?"

"When I first laid eyes on you, Banannie, I knew I wanted to hold on to you for the rest of my life."

"Well, you're stuck with me."

"And you're stuck with me."

"*Gute.* I'll write the Shetlers tonight."

"And I'll hitch up the buggy and go warn Moses to beware of old women with knitting needles."

"You'll do no such thing. We will catch him by surprise. When I am determined to do something even the angel Gabriel himself can't stop me."

"Oh, Annie, *that* I know from years of experience."

Chapter Two

Moses Zimmerman whistled a lively tune as he unhitched his horse from the buggy and led him to the barn. Letting his eyes adjust to the dimness, Moses made a mental note of what needed to be done for *Mammi* and *Dawdi* today. Pull bales from the loft, pitch hay, milk the cows. Thin peach trees, chop firewood, haul coal. If he weren't so busy with his cheese factory, he'd get up here more often. Dawdi had sold his sixty-acre farm to Uncle Tim over a decade ago and moved to Huckleberry Hill where Dawdi tended peach trees and gathered huckleberries and maple sap from the woods. Uncle Titus and three of Moses's married cousins occasionally helped on Huckleberry Hill when they weren't busy working their own farms, but in Moses's mind, it never seemed enough.

Huckleberry Hill sat west of Bonduel, making it a remote place in a remote Wisconsin settlement. Dawdi had plowed two acres for a garden and some fruit trees, but otherwise the hill grew wild with sugar maples and thick stands of huckleberry bushes. Early spring harvest kept the family busy collecting sap, and in late summer, they gathered baskets full of reddish-purple huckleberries.

Moses heard Dawdi's rich bass voice and poked his head out of the open barn door. Dawdi, carrying a bucketlike container, attended to his chores like he always did—singing at the top of his lungs.

"Life is like a mountain railroad, with an engineer that's brave, we must make the run successful, from the cradle to the grave." He stopped singing when he laid eyes on Moses. Smiling in his grandfatherly, protective way, he shook his head. "My boy, there's trouble brewing."

Moses took the container from Dawdi's hands and gave him a stiff hug. "What kind of trouble?"

Dawdi pointed in the direction of the house. "Just keep in mind how much your mammi loves you, and there won't be no ill will." He smoothed his beard. "In this case, it might turn around all right. She's a pretty little thing with a heart a gold. I could tell right off."

Moses hadn't a clue what his dawdi was talking about. "Has Mammi been trying out a new recipe?"

"All's I'm saying is, don't lay no blame to my charge. When your mammi gets a notion into her head, she won't go back."

Moses nodded as if he completely understood and decided to change the subject. He lifted the container in his hand. "What kind of bucket is this?"

Dawdi lit up with enthusiasm. "Ain't it something? It's my new chicken feeder. You turn this crank and the feed shoots out here. It spreads the feed without hardly lifting a finger."

"Can I carry it to the coop for you?"

"I'll take it." Dawdi winked. "You got bigger fish to fry. Go look in on Mammi."

Dawdi disappeared around the barn as Mammi

and her curly-haired dog, Sparky, burst out the front door. Sparky sported a green doggie sweater with a black stripe running all the way around Sparky's midsection. Mammi's sweater was made from the same yarn as Sparky's, without the black stripe.

Mammi's favorite hobby was knitting. She could knit a pair of mittens for every one of her grandchildren in twenty-four hours flat.

Mammi threw out her arms, and Moses couldn't help smiling as she hopped down the steps like a much younger woman. Her hair, the color of billowy clouds on a sunny day, blended in with the white of her *kapp*. Her blue eyes twinkled persistently, as if every day were Christmas.

"Moses!" she squealed as she wrapped her arms around his waist. She couldn't reach her hands high enough to get them around his neck. Moses had not inherited his height from Mammi's side.

"My favorite day is when you come to see us," she said.

Moses squeezed his mammi tight and planted a kiss on the top of her head. "What do you need done today?"

"Plenty of time for that. I have two surprises for you."

"Two?"

"I made your favorite cookies, but I had to hide them because Felty won't stop eating them. I wanted to save some for you."

Moses grinned. He had never had the heart to tell Mammi that her ginger snaps could break a tooth if they weren't soaked in milk first. And "ginger snaps" was an apt name for Mammi's personal recipe. The heavy ginger made people snap their heads back and look frantically for a drink of water. But it warmed his heart to please Mammi with how much he loved her cooking, so he always gobbled up four or five cookies for her sake.

"What is your other surprise?"

Mammi sprouted a twitchy grin and clapped her hands in delight. "I have found just the girl for you."

Moses became a wrinkly, deflated balloon. He resisted the urge to slump his shoulders. Dawdi had warned him. *There's trouble brewing.*

Since Moses's nineteenth birthday seven years ago, a host of well-meaning relatives and friends had done their best to marry him off. Up until now, Dawdi and Mammi's house had always been a safe haven. His grandparents were his only blood relatives who had never admonished him about finding a wife.

It seemed that their patience had finally worn thin.

Moses had tap-danced around so many requests that he didn't even have to think about his response. He managed a weak smile, which considering his sudden change of mood was quite admirable. "If you like her, Mammi, I'm sure she's a peach. But I don't think I'll get the chance to meet her. Things at the cheese factory are mighty busy."

Being conveniently busy proved a wonderful-gute way to avoid desperate girls and their equally eager mothers.

"Not to worry. I knew I'd have to bring her to you."

"I'm too busy to have visitors at the factory."

Mammi smiled smugly as if she had bested him in a game of cards. "No, my dear boy. She's here. In the house. She's from Wautoma settlement and will be staying with us all summer. You'll have plenty of time to get to know each other."

Moses wanted to throw his hands in the air and run screaming down the hill. Instead, he fell silent as his mind raced. Mammi had done her own dance around his bucket of excuses.

What now?

No escape. He'd have to buck up, meet this girl, and get it over with, although he dreaded the introduction almost as much as he dreaded that root canal last year. He pictured the kind of girl Mammi would choose for him. Probably some woman fifteen years older than he with sunken cheeks and a glassy stare from working at her knitting too long. Or perhaps she was one of those empty-headed schoolgirls who couldn't put two sentences together without giggling. Old ladies like Mammi thought youth was the only thing a female needed to make her attractive.

His own mother said Moses was too picky, but not even Mamm seemed to understand that Moses didn't want to find another girl. Barbara would be back, and he intended to wait for her. When he told people this, they thought he was *deerich*, foolish, holding out for a girl who'd left three years ago.

He wanted astonishing, and he'd only found astonishing once. He would wait for Barbara.

Mammi wrapped her arthritic fingers around his wrist. "*Cum reu*, come in."

Moses had no choice but to follow. Shuffling his feet, he tromped up the porch steps and into the house.

Mammi handed him three rock-hard cookies in a napkin. "I just know our plan is going to work out wonderful gute. I just know it."

Our plan?

Moses refused to claim any credit for such a plan.

She looked up at him expectantly. "You'll find her in the cellar."

Determined to be grumpy about it, Moses sighed inwardly, surrendered to the inevitable, and opened the cellar door. At six feet five inches tall, he had to stoop all the way down the stairs to avoid scraping his head on the ceiling. He heard a crash and set foot on the bottom step in time to see a girl kneeling on the floor, carefully gathering shards of a broken canning jar.

She turned her face to him, and he almost fell over. He had expected a girl and he had expected Amish, but he hadn't expected beautiful.

Chapter Three

Blast!

Lia sank to the floor and surveyed the pieces of what used to be a bottle. Her first day at Helmuths' and she had already burned the pancakes, snagged a hole in her stockings, and broken an innocent canning jar that had probably never done harm to anyone in its entire life.

As she reached out to retrieve the biggest piece, her hand grazed a shard protruding from the broken base of the jar. She gasped in pain and watched as droplets of blood appeared in a nice straight line across her palm.

Blast!

One more mishap like this and she wouldn't blame the Helmuths if they sent her packing. But, oh, how she wanted things to work out here on Huckleberry Hill! This was the first time in her life she'd left home. It was bound to be an exciting adventure, even though her sister, Rachel, kept reminding her that she was only going to tiny Bonduel from just-as-tiny Wautoma to work for "two boring old people."

Still, Lia had been almost giddy with excitement.

Back home she had so many people depending on her for their happiness. Some days the weight of her responsibility felt like it would suffocate her right quick. Huckleberry Hill seemed like a place where she could take a deep breath.

She heard footsteps on the stair and quickly brushed her bleeding hand across her apron. Not even enough blood to worry about, and she didn't want Anna to fuss about it.

Lia looked up, expecting to see Anna, who could take a set of stairs like a twenty-year-old. Instead she saw an exceptionally tall young man. She estimated he stood taller than she by a good five inches—didn't see that every day. But his height wasn't what made her look twice. His lips curled into a half smile, revealing a charming dimple on his left cheek. His eyes, so intensely blue they almost glowed in the dim light of the cellar, studied her face with a mixture of surprise and annoyance. Annoyed or not, he looked unnervingly handsome.

"Oh my," she said out loud before clapping her good hand over her mouth.

He didn't seem to notice that she'd made a fool of herself. "I'll get the broom," he said.

Stuffing a handful of cookies into his pocket, he bounded back up the stairs. He had to stoop to avoid hitting his head. Lia hadn't even had to do that.

A thrill of pleasure ran down Lia's spine before she squared her shoulders and returned to her task of picking up broken glass. Tall didn't make a difference. Years ago she'd quit sizing up any man as a potential suitor. Dat reminded her often that no man wanted a tall, homely wife with a scarred hand—and she knew he spoke the truth. Lia smiled to herself. What man striving for humility wanted his wife towering over people like the Statue of Liberty?

The young man returned as quickly as he had left with a broom and dustpan in one hand and a small white box in the other. His eyes still held that glint of annoyance, but he smiled pleasantly and propped the broom against the wall.

It shouldn't be allowed in the Ordnung to be that handsome. His good looks would be thoroughly distracting at church.

Still kneeling, Lia slipped her right hand into her apron pocket. She'd hidden her hand so often, she almost didn't realize she was doing it.

The young man squatted beside her and held out the box. "I brought a little first aid."

Blast! He'd seen the hand. She balled her fist and buried it deeper in her pocket. "Oh. No need. It's no worse than a paper cut."

He opened the box and rummaged through the contents. "Paper cuts are nasty. I got one on my toe once and couldn't walk for three days."

Lia felt the corners of her mouth curl up. "How did you get a paper cut on your toe?"

"I tried to read a book with my feet."

She couldn't help the laugh that escaped her lips. "Maybe you should wear stockings next time."

The dimple became more pronounced. "I never thought of that." He stared into her eyes for a moment before clearing his throat. Then he seemed to recollect his annoyance. "I should tend to that cut."

Lia kept it safely inside her pocket. "No need."

He raised an eyebrow and held out his hand. "Cum, let me see."

She couldn't kneel there forever, her hand stubbornly balled in her pocket, without looking foolish.

Again. Embarrassed, she slowly pulled her hand from her apron and held it open for him to see.

If the burn scars that covered the back of her hand repulsed him, his expression remained neutral. He took her fingers in his and studied the palm lightly smeared with blood. After shuffling through the box, he dabbed the cut with an antiseptic wipe. "Does that hurt?"

"A little."

"A bandage all the way around will at least keep it from hurting worse when you use it. What do you think?"

"Um, *jah*, that would be a gute idea."

He quickly fashioned a dressing from a sterile pad and some stretchy tape. She tried not to blush as his fingers brushed across her bumpy scars. He'd seen every hideous mark, and she found herself wishing Anna had been the one to doctor her cut.

"Good as new," he said, closing the first aid box and standing up. "Well, as good as I can do. You can rewrap it later when I'm not looking." He said it with a raised eyebrow, and Lia cracked a smile. She liked a man who could laugh at himself.

He held out his hand and pulled her to her feet. Lia recognized the look of surprise that popped onto his face when she stood up, the same reaction most people had when they saw her towering height. But this was one of those rare instances when she didn't have to look down on the person staring at her. She rather liked looking up.

"Oh, *sis yuscht!*" he exclaimed, his eyes wide. "You are tall."

Why did his words feel like an icy hand slapping her in the face? She'd seen the same reaction so many times it should have made her laugh. But this time it didn't amuse her. It hurt in the corner of her heart that she usually kept tucked away.

His annoyance seemed to increase, and he backed away and plopped himself on a step. "Mammi thought of everything."

She had no idea what he was babbling about, only that a spot deep inside her ached, as if she had the wind knocked out of her. At home when people commented on her height, Lia's dat would chuckle and say, "Jah, Lia is our beanpole. But my other daughter, Rachel, is a wisp of a thing with golden hair. Like her mamm." Then he would praise Rachel's virtues so people would know that he had at least one daughter of whom he need not be ashamed.

Not of a disposition to wallow in self-pity, Lia took a deep breath and huffed the irritation out of her lungs with the air. She threw away the shards of glass still in her hand and reached for the broom.

The young man leaped to his feet as if the step suddenly got hot. "Please, let me do it. You should nurse that hand for a few days."

"No need. I am gute at sweeping. Even with a handicap." Lia turned from him and swept insistently while the young man stared at her—probably puzzling at how such a tall girl could reach the ground with a broom. As he watched, he squeezed his eyebrows together as if working out a very difficult arithmetic problem in his head.

She almost asked him if there wasn't somewhere he'd rather be, when he said, "I don't mean to hurt your feelings, but I'm not looking for a wife."

Surprise tied Lia's tongue into a knot. She stopped sweeping altogether to study the young man's face. Surely he was teasing or was perhaps just painfully awkward around girls. But this young man didn't seem the awkward type. With growing confusion, Lia concluded that he was completely serious. The sincerity that washed over his handsome features smacked her funny bone, and she couldn't help it. She burst into laughter.

His frown deepened and his eyebrows moved so close together they were almost touching.

She couldn't keep her amusement in check. "Did you think I was about to ask you to marry me?"

He took a step closer. "*Nae*, what I mean is—"

"I still try to let the boy do the asking. I am not quite that desperate yet." Lia punctuated the "yet" with a raised eyebrow and renewed vigor in her sweeping.

"I said nothing like that," the young man protested, taking two steps closer and holding out his hands in surrender.

"Have you judged that my sweeping skills are lacking and decided I would make an unsuitable wife?" Smiling to herself, Lia swept around the coal bin nowhere near where the glass had shattered.

His voice filled with compassion, even as the annoyance etched itself on every line of his face. "I'm sorry. Now I've embarrassed you. I don't know what my mammi has told you or what your expectations are, but this is what I tell all the girls. I am not looking for a wife. It is best not to get your hopes up."

Lia had to clench her teeth together to keep her jaw from falling to the floor. Was she really having this conversation with a complete stranger in Anna Helmuth's basement? "You think I want to marry you?"

"And I'm not interested."

Absurdity always made Lia laugh. Her amusement skipped out in deep, throaty spasms. "Is Anna your grandmother?"

He nodded.

"I don't know what your mammi told you, but I never even knew you existed until five minutes ago. Are you so arrogant as to assume that every girl you meet wants you for a husband?"

She must have caught him off guard with her bluntness. His face bloomed into a grin. "According to my *mamm* and *dat*, every girl would choose me."

"I wouldn't."

He showed all his teeth as his smile widened. "It is nice to meet a girl with a bit of gute sense." He fingered the stubble on his chin. "So this is Mammi's scheme, not yours?"

"I don't know what scheme you are talking about."

"The scheme to marry me off." The young man held the dustpan as she swept the last bits of glass into it. "Everyone thinks I'm dawdling."

"It is none of my concern whether you want to dawdle or not."

He dumped the dirt and glass into the trash. "Gute. We might be seeing a lot of each other over the summer. I won't have to pretend to be interested, and you won't have to try to be agreeable."

She took the dustpan from him with a mischievous grin. "I'm relieved. I dislike being agreeable. I'd much rather make myself unpleasant."

"This works out well for both of us, then."

"It wonders me what you will tell your mammi."

He rubbed his hand across the back of his neck as if he had a sudden headache. "That she has very gute taste in young women."

"You do not have to lie to your mammi for my sake."

"I would never lie to my mammi." He took a small shovel from a hook on the wall and buried it into the pile of coal. "I'll be right up with a bucket of coal in case Mammi needs it."

He turned his back on her, and Lia was left scratching her head at the strange young man who declared his intentions, or lack thereof, before she even knew his name. She marched up the stairs and started chuckling all over again. Pulling her shoulders back, Lia stood up straight so the young man would see she didn't have to stoop to avoid the ceiling. She wasn't as tall as some people.

Anna stood at the top of the stairs with a wide grin and a plate of ginger snaps. "Have a cookie."

Smiling, Lia chose a cookie from the plate and took great care putting it into her mouth. She'd made the mistake earlier of taking a hearty bite, and she'd almost cracked a tooth.

"How did it go with Moses?"

"Who? Oh, uh, the young man downstairs?"

Anna lifted her eyebrows in indignation. "He didn't even introduce himself? No wonder he doesn't have a wife." She deposited her plate on the table, propped her hands on her hips, and called down the stairs. "Moses, will you come up here?" She spoke it sweetly enough, but Lia suspected Anna's tone was meant to lure Moses upstairs for a scolding.

Moses appeared carrying a bucket of coal, unprepared for an attack. Coal dust tinted his fingers black. "I brought more coal."

"Moses Zimmerman," Anna said, "you did not even introduce yourself to our guest. Where are your manners?"

Moses did not miss a beat. "We got to know each other quite well. I proposed marriage, and she refused me. I think that's enough for one day."

Chapter Four

Moses folded his arms across his chest and chuckled. Mammi's pretty friend didn't even flinch, but he caught the sparkle of mischief in her eyes along with a hint of scolding for trying to deflate Mammi's hopes.

Mammi's expression was worth a whole gallon of whipping cream. Her eyes popped wide like shutters as she groaned in exasperation and shook her finger at him. "What a tease you are, Moses Zimmerman. I have better things to do than put up with your nonsense." She picked up her plate. "Have another cookie."

He already had three knocking around in the bottom of his pocket. "No, *denki*, Mammi. I am full."

"Don't be shy. Have another cookie. I know how much you like them."

"May I have another too?" the girl said.

Moses stifled a grin. Anyone who watched out for Mammi's feelings had his approval.

Mammi beamed in satisfaction and held out the plate. "Moses, if you are not careful, Lia will eat your share."

Moses grabbed a cookie. "Lia. Nice to finally learn

her name. Mammi, why didn't you introduce us? Where are your manners?"

Mammi patted Moses on the shoulder. "What a tease you are."

"I will thin the peaches and muck out the barn this morning," Moses said, "and see what else Dawdi needs me to do."

Mammi nodded. "Lia, will you help Moses thin peaches? There is plenty of trees for both of you."

"Of course," Lia said. "I would be happy to do anything that needs doing."

Mammi might have just heard the news of twenty new grandchildren for as happy as this made her. She bustled to the front closet and pulled out two long pieces of knitted yarn. "Early June is still a bit chilly. I made a scarf for each of you."

It wasn't all that chilly today, but Mammi never felt so happy as when people wore her creations.

She hung a chocolate brown scarf over Lia's shoulder and handed Moses a bright red one. Lia ran her hands over the length of scarf that looked like a furry dog after a bath.

"I used a new kind of yarn," Mammi said. "Soft, isn't it?"

Lia nodded and tossed the scarf around her neck with a graceful sweep of her hand that Moses found surprisingly charming. He wasn't trying to pay particular attention to Lia but found himself intensely aware of every move she made, every tilt of her head or curl of her lips. Tightly snuggled up against her chin, the color of the scarf accented the brown of her intelligent eyes, which were framed by impossibly long lashes.

The irritation bubbled inside him like a pot of oatmeal left too long on the stove. He refused to let himself be taken in by something as superficial as beauty. Attractive meant nothing to him. Pretty meant nothing. Even tall and graceful meant nothing. Mammi had outdone herself, but he refused to let Mammi pick a wife for him. He stood determined to wait for Barbara, to prove the strength of his commitment.

Moses studied the cherry red scarf in his hand. He already owned three other scarves and two pairs of mittens made by Mammi, not to mention an assorted collection of beanies and pot holders. Knitting was more of a calling than a hobby for Mammi.

"There is a ladder and gloves in the toolshed," Mammi said.

Moses secured the bright scarf around his neck. At least any deer hunters who happened by wouldn't mistakenly shoot him. He could be seen in the better part of three counties.

The early June air was pleasantly warm, especially with a hint of sun peeking through the clouds. Newly planted red petunias huddled at the foot of Mammi's front porch. A fine day to be outside. When they were out of sight of the house, Moses loosened his scarf and let it hang around his neck.

Trying his best to suppress his fascination with Mammi's chosen bride, Moses led the way to the small grove of peach trees behind the house. Moses had pruned in March but hadn't yet had time to clear away the dead limbs from beneath the trees. He had left the ladder in the shed, figuring they both were tall enough to reach the fruit of the stubby trees without one.

Moses didn't want Lia to suspect that she had an unnerving effect on him, so he made only brief eye contact when he spoke. "I'll show you how to thin on this first tree."

Lia took off the coral pair of mittens, also knitted by

Mammi, that Mammi had insisted she slip on before leaving the house. They matched the blush of her creamy cheeks. Moses quickly looked away. His reaction to a girl he'd only just met bordered on ridiculous. He chastised himself for letting superficial beauty sway him. His loyalty was squarely fixed on Barbara.

Lia propped her hands on her hips and tilted her head as if trying to get a better look at him. "Are you annoyed with me specifically or just a generally irritable person?"

Moses tried to swallow his surprise. She might have been pretty, but he wouldn't want to marry a woman so blunt. He sighed in amusement before a troubling thought pulled him up short. Most women thought men should read their minds. That guessing game kept many a husband tiptoeing on eggshells. When Moses really thought about it, he couldn't think of anything more attractive than the plain, unsugarcoated truth.

"There it is again," she said. Her lips curled slightly, almost as if she were teasing him.

"What?"

"That look my dat gets when our horse throws a shoe for the third time in a week. Exactly what bee do you have in your bonnet?"

Moses chuckled in spite of himself. "I ain't never worn a bonnet in my life."

"So you're annoyed with me specifically."

I'm annoyed that you are so pretty.

He couldn't very well be equally blunt. "On the contrary, I am glad for your help. You are the only girl I know who can help me thin peaches without a ladder."

That wasn't the answer she wanted. Her face immediately clouded over, and she cast her eyes to the dirt.

"I'm aware of how tall I am. You don't have to keep rubbing it in."

Moses raised his arms as if he were guiding a semi truck into his loading dock. "Whoa, whoa, whoa. You took that as an insult?"

She forced her lips into an unconvincing smile. "Not on purpose. I know you didn't mean it on purpose."

"Since when has being tall been something to be ashamed of?"

Her gaze pierced through his skull. That's when he noticed the specks of gold in her chocolate brown eyes.

"It doesn't bother you that I'm tall?"

"Bother me?" He took off his hat and stepped so he stood directly in front of her. He placed his hand flat on the top of his head and then moved it down to Lia's head. Up to the crown of his head again and back to hers. "Me. You," he said as he moved his hand up and down. "Me." Hand up. "You." Hand down.

Lia surrendered a grin at his dramatics.

"Haven't you noticed that I'm taller?" he said.

Lia sighed in resignation, but she didn't look unhappy anymore. "You're not a girl. Nobody likes a tall girl. I'm almost six feet."

"They tease you?"

"They disregard me."

"Wouldn't it be more fitting to say that they overlook you? Or better yet, you overlook them." He raised his hand to the level of her eyes and drew an invisible line. "You know, over-look."

Lia groaned in mock pain. "I truly thought I'd heard all the tall jokes."

"So you don't like being tall? Not even when you can reach things on high shelves?"

"Especially not then. It seems like it's the only thing

I'm good for—reaching bottles—because Mamm can't be bothered to pull out the step stool."

"I love being tall."

"You're not a girl."

Moses's voice rose with his enthusiasm. "But I love tall girls." He cleared his throat. "I don't mean love—"

"I know. You don't want to marry me."

"I mean, I get tired of looking at scalps all day. I've seen dandruff that would make your toes curl in disgust."

"And shiny bald heads."

"Folks get sore necks looking up at me for a simple conversation, but I can talk to you without straining my neck or yours. You are one of the few people who doesn't have an unflattering view up my nostrils."

Lia cracked a smile before pressing her lips into a tight line. "But most people don't consider my height a blessing."

"You let other people determine your happiness?"

She furrowed her brow. "Not usually. I've been told so often that I am too tall. . . ." She studied his face. "I suppose I have always believed that my height is an affliction, just as sure as I know the sun will rise every morning. Dat says I am naturally prideful because I tower over other girls."

"As if you had any control over that! God made you the way you are. 'I have learned, in whatsoever state I am, therewith to be content.'"

Lia sprouted an exasperated half smile. "My *fater* quotes that scripture to me often when he admonishes me to be content that I will never marry."

At that moment, Moses wished Lia's fater were standing next to him so he could chastise her dat for saying such an unkind thing to his daughter. But he let his indignation pass like a summer thunderstorm and raised his eyebrows mischievously. "The only thing that will keep you from marrying is that you reject perfectly good marriage proposals."

Her face popped into a full smile. She had brilliantly white teeth. "You didn't propose."

"Of course not. You said you wouldn't have me."

"I won't marry someone arrogant enough to assume I want him to propose."

"I can't help being arrogant. Who wouldn't be proud to be this tall?" He looked at the peach trees and propped his hands on his hips. "I'll fetch the ladder if you want to pretend you need it. Will that make you feel better? Less proud?"

A laugh bubbled up from her throat and could not be stopped. "My one comfort is that I am not as proud as you are."

"Not until you grow about six inches. Then you could look down your nose at me all you want. Until then, I get to look down my nose at you—nostrils and all."

"Have you ever considered trimming your nose hairs?"

Moses laughed until tears sprang to his eyes. "That bad?"

"Nae. I am just trying to pull your pride down a notch or two."

"Do anything but joke about my facial hair. I'm very sensitive."

Chapter Five

By the middle of June, spring gave way to summer. Old sugar maples were thick with young leaves, wildflowers blanketed the field behind the house, and a hundred varieties of birds kept up a lively conversation as they tended to their nests.

Lia helped Anna put on her sweater as they stood on the front porch.

Anna thanked her with a motherly pat on the arm. "You've taken such good care of us since you've been here. I can see why you want to be a midwife. You have a talent for seeing a need and filling it."

"I don't think I'll ever be a midwife. My dat thinks it's a waste of time." Lia deftly fastened the last of Anna's sweater hooks. The azure yarn accented her twinkly blue eyes.

"I knitted this sweater last spring," Anna said. "A new pattern."

"It's beautiful."

"My hair is so white, my head looks like a cloud floating in the sky of my sweater."

Anna wore her lavender dress and black bonnet. Lia had on the spinach green dress that she'd worn the day she met Moses. A boy at a *singeon* once told her the green made her eyes look like black-eyed Susans. She didn't know if he meant to be flattering, but he had an unexpected look of admiration on his face, so she decided to take it as a compliment.

They heard Moses's buggy rolling up the lane before it appeared from behind the leafy trees. The ancient, secondhand buggy he used to drive had finally busted an axle two weeks ago. In its place, Moses had purchased what Felty called "a newfangled contraption" a far sight too fancy for Felty. But some of the families in the settlement had such buggies, and the bishop consented to the improvements. Three chickens scooted out of the way of the wheels.

Moses leaped from his buggy with a grin as wide as a country mile. "Is everybody ready?"

Lia ignored the little flip her heart did when Moses smiled. She'd been here two weeks and already seen him three times at Huckleberry Hill and once at *gmay*. Anna finagled choring so that they often worked on a project together. Moses was a pleasant man to be with. He might even consider her a friend. Her heart shouldn't do a somersault when seeing a friend.

Lia ducked into the kitchen and picked up the two pies she made for bakery.

Moses followed close behind looking as handsome as ever but doing his best to avoid her eyes. "Mammi says there's a box of pot holders to bring."

"On the table."

Moses stuffed the shoe box full of Anna's knitted creations under his arm. "I am to fetch Dawdi too."

As if waiting for an introduction, Felty ambled down the hall with hat in hand, singing softly. *"Life is like a canyon railroad with an engineer that's brave—"*

"Ready, Dawdi?"

Dawdi gave Moses a quick embrace. "Are we riding in that newfangled contraption?"

Moses's dimple appeared. "As sure as you're born, Dawdi."

Dawdi raised an eyebrow. "Does it come with seat belts? You might lose your head and get to going along too fast."

Moses helped Dawdi on with his jacket. "We'll take it nice and slow for you."

"Not too slow," insisted Felty. "I'd like to make it to the auction before nightfall."

They paraded out the door, and Moses took Anna's arm to help her down the steps. Anna patted Moses reassuringly. "No need, dear. I can do stairs just fine."

With his box still under one arm, Moses released his independent grandma and took hold of Lia's elbow. "I'll help Lia. She is lugging two pies, and if she falls, it's a long way down."

Lia's heart skipped around her chest like a skater bug. How did Moses make a teasing comment sound like admiration? She huffed in mock indignation and nudged Moses away from her. "If you fall, you'll take me with you."

"I want to protect the pies," Moses said. "We might as well leave them here because I plan on buying both of them."

More heart somersaults. "My pies are plenty expensive, Moses Zimmerman. How much are you prepared to pay?"

Anna insisted Felty sit in front with Moses while she and Lia sat in the backseat. Lia had never seen such a spiffy buggy. The wheel spokes glistened with black paint and shiny lacquer, and the seats were upholstered in deep midnight blue.

Once they and the pies were securely settled, Moses

took up the reins and guided the horse down the hill. "Look at this electric control panel, Dawdi. I can turn on the battery-powered headlights and the signals from here."

"It sure is fancy," Felty said. "The bishop has got strange notions about what's plain and what's not."

"We're less likely to be hit by a car," Moses said, not the least bit ruffled by Felty's reproof.

"It wonders me what the bishop would say if I came to gmay in my skivvies next Sunday."

Anna leaned back and pushed her glasses in place. "Now, Felty. Remember what the good Lord said, 'Some folks choke on a gnat and swallow a camel.' Moses is a godly man who takes fine care of his grandparents. He is not on the road to hell in this buggy."

Felty, not apt to be grumpy, threw up his hands in resignation. "The road to hell is paved with good intentions, but I don't know what vehicle people take to get there."

Moses threw a sideways grin to Lia. "I think they walk."

Once down the hill, Moses eased the buggy onto the paved country road. The trees formed a canopy of green so thick, it looked as if they were in a tunnel. A car inched up behind them and slowly passed when the way was clear.

Felty's eyes lit up like a propane lantern at midnight. "Texas. I don't have that one yet."

Anna patted Lia's hand. "Felty plays the license plate game with himself every year."

"The license plate game?"

Felty took out a small spiral notebook and a stubby pencil from his shirt pocket. "I start in January and try to find all fifty state plates before the end of December."

Lia saw him write "Texas" below the names of seven other states.

"Not many out-of-state cars come through here. In summer I see more. Last year I got all but Alabama and, wouldn't you know it, on Christmas Eve I spied an Alabama coming out of the parking lot at Lark Country Store. The best Christmas present I ever got."

"Why folks from Alabama would want to be in Wisconsin at wintertime is a mystery to me," Moses said.

Felty nodded solemnly. "A Christmas miracle."

True to his word, Moses took the trip nice and slow, but fast enough to get them to the auction before dinnertime.

They found a spot to park the buggy down the road from Bontragers' farm where the auction took place. A massive green-and-white-striped tent stood where an empty field used to be, and the auctioneer busily chanted prices for farm implements and sewing machines. There looked to be two or three hundred people milling around, bidding on items and buying food from the tent that housed bakery. Englisch and Amish alike mingled in the yard.

Moses carried Anna's colorful pot holders to the roomy toolshed where handicrafts and household items were being sold. Lia deposited her pies on the long table under the tent where at least thirty other pies stood waiting to be cut and sold by the slice. Her two measly offerings seemed insignificant next to the sheer volume of food. Next time she would make more pies.

But every little bit helped. Auctions such as these helped raise money for medical bills and home repairs in the community. People came from all over Wisconsin to experience an Amish auction.

Four coolers marked "Zimmerman Cheese Factory" were full of baby swiss cheese. Some customers bought an entire wax-covered wheel while other wheels were sliced for sandwiches also being sold.

Felty came up behind Lia. "I know it ain't proper to be proud, but I do love seeing Moses's name on that cheese. He works mighty hard and gives a passel of money to the Amish Aid Fund." Felty leaned closer and cupped his hand over his mouth. "That is a great secret, and there's not nobody knows that I know."

Lia curled up the corners of her mouth. "I won't tell a soul."

Moses and Anna joined them in the kitchen tent. Moses put an arm around each of his grandparents. "So, what would you like to buy today?"

Felty looked around at the tents and people and items on the lawn up for sale. "I'm not aiming to buy anything. I come to be with Anna. Anna is the spender in the family."

"Now, Felty," Anna said. She pointed to a smaller tent. "I want to see what kitchen utensils are for sale."

Felty shook his head. "Oh, Annie girl, we don't need no more utensils. We got plenty of gadgets to home."

"I want to buy some cheese," Lia announced.

Moses stifled a smile and pretended he didn't know what cheese she was talking about. "I want a piece of pie."

Felty offered Anna his arm. "Come on, Banannie, I'll take you to see the gadgets. But we are only going for a visit."

Anna gave Lia a pointed look and raised her eyebrows. "You two enjoy some time alone together."

Lia and Moses studied each other before bursting into laughter at Anna's reminder that they were supposed to be falling in love. "I'm not looking for a wife," Moses said.

"I won't have you," Lia replied, her heart bouncing around like a rubber ball.

Lia pulled some money from her pocket, but Moses

shook his head. "I'll buy. That way if you don't like it, you won't feel like you wasted your money."

"Nae, nae," said Lia. "I can pay." She held out her money to one of the girls helping customers at the front table. "I would like a wheel of Zimmerman cheese."

Moses gently nudged Lia with his shoulder until he stood directly in front of the girl. "Don't take her money."

The girl, about eighteen years old, batted her eyes and smiled at Moses. Lia wasn't surprised. Moses's good looks could have melted snow in the dead of winter.

Moses leaned toward the girl. "I'm paying for the cheese and two pies."

"Do you want two slices or two whole pies?"

"I want to buy the pies that this girl baked."

"Okay, which pies are they?"

Moses motioned to the table laden with pastries. Lia's pies were nowhere to be seen. Lia watched as another Amish girl dunked her pie tins into a washtub overflowing with soapy water. She pointed them out to Moses. "I guess they sold already."

Moses groaned and slumped his shoulders. "What kind were they?"

"Butterscotch."

Moses groaned louder and bowed his head. "My favorite."

"Do you want a different kind?" said the girl.

"Nae, just the cheese." He nudged Lia farther away from the girl at the counter. "Which I am paying for."

The girl retrieved a wheel of cheese from one of the coolers. Moses handed it to Lia, who examined the label. White with blue and red letters that read "Zimmerman Cheese Factory."

The girl gave Moses his change without taking her eyes from him. "You're both so tall."

Lia offered no reply. She'd heard it too many times already.

Moses flashed those white teeth. "Thank you." And he meant it. He had been telling Lia the truth. When someone mentioned his height, he took it as a compliment.

Moses produced a pocketknife and handed it to Lia. "Don't eat the wax."

Lia laughed and took his knife while Moses turned his gaze to the ground. Lia understood the look. Humility warred against the longing inside him. It was the same for Lia when somebody ate one of her pies. She wanted people to like her baking but didn't want their praise to make her prideful.

She peeled back the wax, cut herself a thick slice, and took a bite. Moses glued his eyes to her face.

Milder than regular swiss, the cheese blanketed her taste buds with a distinctive tang and a buttery flavor Lia found irresistible. "Oh, Moses! This is delicious. I've never eaten cheese that seems to melt in my mouth."

Moses stuffed his hands in his pockets and moved some dirt around with his foot. "It took me two years to get it right." He glanced at her. "But I give all the glory to God. I know where my blessings come from."

"Of course you do. It is natural to feel pleased that your cheese brings people so much happiness."

Moses relaxed his shoulders. "I'm glad you like it. I am sorry I did not get to taste your pie."

"I will make you another one."

"I've been wishing for one of your pies ever since Mammi told me they taste like a slice of heaven."

"She only says that in hopes you'll be interested enough to marry me."

"I don't need a wife for that. I can hire a cook," Moses said.

"You will need to. I don't know what woman would have you. You're too tall."

"Girls like tall boys."

Two older women with chocolate brown skin marched up to Moses and Lia. The woman with ample curves wore a pair of tight blue jeans, a red sweater, and an impressive collection of chunky bracelets on both arms. The other, thinner, with an irresistible smile, wore a bright purple sundress with matching sweater and a straw hat tied with a yellow ribbon. They were definitely not local.

The first woman got right to the point. "Y'all are the cutest Amish couple I've ever seen."

She spoke with a Southern drawl that Lia found charming. *Definitely not from around here.*

Moses's lips twitched in annoyance. "We're not a couple."

The woman in purple put a hand on Lia's elbow. "Honey, if you weren't Amish, you could definitely have a career in modeling. You're so tall and beautiful, those magazine people would eat you up."

Brightening considerably, Moses wagged his finger at Lia. "I told you so."

Lia grabbed his hand and pushed it away and then turned her attention to the visitors. "Thank you."

"It's too bad you don't allow folks to take pictures. I'd love one of you."

"No, we don't allow it," Moses said, "but I understand why you want a picture of Lia."

Lia's heart started doing flips again. Why did she let him get to her like that?

The woman in purple stuck out her hand. "My name's Miss Ernestina and this is Miss Gloria. We're from Mississippi."

Moses was naturally friendly, but it amazed Lia at

how easily he conversed with two complete strangers. "People from Mississippi don't usually make their way up this far north."

"Gloria's son lives in Green Bay. He works for the Packers. We drove all the way up here for a visit. When we got here he said, 'Auntie Ernestina, you gotta see the Amish.' So we come out this way to see what all the fuss is about."

"I hope you like the auction," Moses said.

"You should try the baby swiss cheese," Lia said. "It is the best thing you ever tasted."

Ernestina's smile revealed a gold-capped tooth. "We will, thank you very kindly."

"Wait," Moses said. "Did you drive all the way from Mississippi?"

"Sure enough," said Miss Gloria.

"In your car?"

"Sure enough, again."

"Does it have a Mississippi license plate?"

"Yes, sir."

Moses was halfway to the gadget tent when he spoke. "Can you wait here while I get my grandpa? He would love to see it."

Moses pulled Felty away from his shopping long enough for him to walk to Gloria and Ernestina's car and log the Mississippi license plate in his notebook. Heading back to the tent, he walked with an extra spring to his step while twirling his pencil around his fingers. Lia had never seen him more excited.

In gratitude, Moses bought the two Southern ladies a block of cheese before they drove away in their cream-colored Cadillac.

Once again, Moses and Lia found themselves by the food tent. Moses grew temporarily solemn. "I'm sorry what they said about us being a couple. I don't want you to expect something from me. I'm just trying to be nice."

The sinking feeling in the pit of Lia's stomach took her by surprise. He'd already told her several times how he felt. Why did it feel as if he had rejected her for the first time?

To show that his declaration hadn't affected her in the least, she rolled her eyes and folded her arms. "You're not going to propose again, are you?"

"I want to make sure—"

"Don't bother, Moses. I'll not have you. Why do you think every girl wants to marry you?"

Moses's eyes twinkled with amusement. "My grandparents think I am a gute match."

"Jah, they tell me several times a day."

Moses thumbed his suspenders. "Oh, bless them. How can you help but fall in love with me when Anna and Felty Helmuth are on my side?"

Lia did her best to summon more cheer than she felt. "I'll do my best to resist."

Moses chuckled as he pulled a digital timepiece from his pocket. "It is exactly one o'clock. There is someone I want you to meet."

"Me?"

Moses scanned the crowd of people coming in and out of the large tent. "And there she is, right on time."

To her surprise, Moses grabbed Lia's scarred hand, in public, and pulled her in the direction of the tent. He didn't seem to care that the bumpy scars made her skin so rough.

She knew she should ask him to let go, but her hand felt nice tucked in his. Instead of pulling away in protest, she savored the warmth of his calloused skin.

He released her as they approached a sturdy woman with strands of gray streaking her dark brown hair.

"Well, Moses Zimmerman," the woman said, "here I am. One o'clock sharp. I'll have you know I'm missing a chance to bid on a fine goat." The corners of her mouth turned downward, but she had a good-natured gleam in her eye that immediately drew Lia to her. And she was tall. Only an inch or two shorter than Lia. The woman took a look at Lia and lifted her eyebrows. "Is this the girl you told me about?"

Moses cupped his hand around Lia's elbow. "Jah, this is Lia Shetler. Lia, this is my cousin, Sarah Beachy."

"Uh, hello. Nice to meet you," Lia said.

Sarah had a firm handshake. "He didn't tell me you were tall. Tall girls are better. They command more authority, more confidence."

Lia tried to mask her puzzlement. "Better for what?"

"Moses tells me you are interested in becoming a midwife."

Lia's confusion grew. "Jah, I am." She turned to Moses. "But how did you know?"

"Mammi told me," Moses said. "She wanted to be sure that I wouldn't mind marrying a midwife. She knows it might take you from home quite a bit."

Lia felt her face get hot. What would Moses's cousin think of such talk?

Sarah didn't seem to notice. "Stuff and nonsense. If a man can't endure his wife away from home now and then, he ain't been trained well. My Aaron can whip up fried chicken and greens for seven children without so much as a how-do-you-do. Come over here." Sarah directed them to a row of church benches set up outside the tent. She maneuvered herself to sit between Lia and Moses and proceeded to ignore Moses altogether. "Why do you want to be a midwife? Because it ain't for everybody."

Lia clasped her hands together and spoke haltingly. "I saw my nephew's birth last summer. Birth is a miracle. I suppose I want to be part of that miracle."

Sarah propped her forearms on her thighs. "Don't suppose anything. Helping babies into the world is hard work. You miss out on many a good night's sleep and there's some problems you can't fix. Babies die, and that's the worst part of all."

"It wonders me why you are a midwife if it's so hard," Moses said.

Sarah scolded him with her bright eyes. "I'm giving her the facts, Moses. If she can't take the bad, then it's no use talking about the good. I'm a midwife because it brings me closer to God. Plain and simple. There ain't nothing to compare to bringing in a new baby just come from heaven."

Moses folded his arms as a look of concern appeared on his face. "So, what do you think?"

Lia wasn't sure if he talked to her or Sarah.

"I can usually take the measure of a person right quick," Sarah said. "Moses likes you, and that counts for something. He hasn't given his approval to any girl in three years."

Moses pressed his lips into an inflexible line and turned his face away. Was he offended or uncomfortable?

"It can't hurt to try you out," Sarah added.

Lia looked from Moses to Sarah as her spirits soared. "I'm not sure what we are talking about. Are you offering to teach me to be a midwife?"

"That's what Moses said you wanted." Sarah pinned Moses with a look that could have peeled the paint off that new buggy of his. "You didn't tell Lia about these plans?"

Moses scooted away from his cousin. "I wanted her to be surprised."

"Next time, bring her some flowers. Having someone plan your life is not a nice surprise."

"Oh, I'm not angry," Lia said, pulling Sarah's attention from her hopeless cousin. "It's more than I ever thought would happen. It's been a dream for a very long time, but my dat didn't see how I would be able to train to be a midwife and still keep house."

Moses looked genuinely remorseful. "I'm sorry I didn't tell you, Lia. I didn't want you to be disappointed if Sarah couldn't take you on."

"Don't apologize. I've never seen a more thoughtful gesture."

Sarah patted Moses firmly on the knee. "You're off the hook, Moses. Now, Lia, there's a book I want you to read. I sent one of my boys to the buggy for it, but I ain't seen him for twenty minutes. That boy is sure enough a dawdler." She stood up and looked over the sea of people. "Menno," she called, waving her hand, "bring it over here."

A boy of eight or nine years appeared toting a thick pink book with a picture of two women on the cover. Sarah took the book from her son and handed it to Lia. "This is volume one. Read it and make notes to yourself. I'll send volume two with Moses when you are ready. Then the next time there's a birth, I'll send word so you can come watch."

Lia didn't know what to say or how to thank Moses or Sarah. The short conversation had opened up a new world of possibilities for her. "I'm so grateful. I don't know how to thank you."

"Don't thank me yet. You might decide midwifery doesn't suit you, or I might decide you don't suit me."

Moses slapped his hands on his knees. "You see why I like her, Lia? She's as blunt as you are."

Lia laughed but couldn't help noticing that, in a roundabout sort of way, he had just told her he liked her. This thought did nothing to calm her pounding heart.

I'll never marry. I'm too tall.

And Moses is not looking.

All three of them stood, and Moses took the book to his buggy. Lia couldn't resist giving Sarah a hasty hug. "Thank you again. I am thrilled."

Sarah waved off Lia's gratitude. "I like that you're tall. It will make new mothers feel more secure. But don't marry Moses. Your children would be giants."

"I don't suppose I'll ever marry," Lia said. "That's why being a midwife would be so satisfying."

The lines around Sarah's mouth deepened. "Of course you'll marry. As pretty as you are, it's a wonder some boy hasn't snatched you up already."

"Boys think I'm too tall."

"Stuff and nonsense. I am three inches taller than Aaron. He doesn't mind one single bit."

"Aaron must be an uncommon man."

"He is my treasure." Sarah tucked her sweater tightly around her neck. "I must go see about a goat."

Moses returned from the buggy with bright cheeks and dancing eyes. "Rudy Ebersole has rabbits for sale. Do you want to see them?"

"Denki for thinking of me for Sarah," Lia said.

"I really didn't do that much."

Lia wanted to be certain he knew how important this was to her and how much she appreciated it. She laid her hand on his arm. "It means the world to me."

He shrugged his shoulders, but his mouth curled upward. "I like people to be happy. Do you want to see the rabbits?"

Moses and Lia spent the next hour petting bunnies and goats and playing with the puppies that a local Englischer was giving away for free. Moses thought Anna and Felty would love a new puppy, but Lia put her foot down. Sparky would not take kindly to an uninvited guest.

The shadows lengthened and the drone of the auctioneer finally subsided. Moses and Lia found Felty and Anna making the last of their purchases in one of the tents. Anna carried two full shopping bags and Felty had his fingers tightly around another one while he paid the girl at the adding machine.

"Mammi, what did you buy?" Moses asked.

Her plastic bags ruffled as she lifted her arm and pointed to Felty. "I didn't buy anything."

Felty took his bag, and they walked out of the tent together. "I found exactly what I was looking for." They followed him to sit on a bench where they set the bags down, and Felty began shuffling through them. He pulled out a shiny metal hammer that came apart in two halves. Each piece looked like a bulldozer scooper. "This is an ice cube crusher," he said. "You put a piece of ice in here, and it will come out in pieces."

Anna sighed, but didn't speak.

"Very nice," said Moses.

"It looks heavy," said Lia.

Felty picked it up by the handle and flexed his arm. "Sturdy. This is fifty years old and will probably last another fifty." He took the next thing out of his bag, a two-piece glass jar with a lid. "This is a nut chopper. I've looked for one of these for years. Anna has been saying how bad she needs a nut chopper to make some of those recipes in her new book."

"I have not, Felty."

He unscrewed the lid. "You put the nuts in here and turn the crank and the nuts go through these metal gears and come out the bottom, chopped." Felty held it in his palm and turned it slowly so they could see. Back in the bag it went.

He pulled out a dull metal box about the size of a small book. "This is an ice shaver to go along with our ice cube crusher. It has a sharp blade and you run your ice block along the side here. It swings open so you can get your ice out."

"Now, Felty," Anna said, but she didn't elaborate.

Moses helped Felty put the shaver back in the bag and one by one pulled out all the things Felty had purchased. He had bought a fan for the egg incubator he wanted to build, a doughnut cutter, and a mount-on-the-counter meat grinder.

"We already have two of those," Anna said.

Felty reached his hand into the bag one last time. "And look at this. I never saw one of these before. It's a garlic press."

"Why do we need a garlic press?" Anna said.

"For all those new recipes. Lydia Mae says it makes garlic without having to peel it."

"Do you think it will really work?" Moses asked.

"We'll find out," Felty said. "If it doesn't, we can sell it back at the next auction."

Moses and Lia helped them gather up their bags. "Come on," Moses said. "I'll take you home."

Felty and Anna were slower in their steps going than they had been coming.

Lia thought about the book waiting for her in the buggy. She thought of how happy she was to be with the Helmuths on Huckleberry Hill. She thought of Moses's handsome face and the dimple that appeared when he smiled. She remembered his uncommon kindness. And even though he would never be her beau, he was her friend. "Denki for letting me come," she said. "I loved being with all of you."

Felty put his arm around Anna. "It's been a wonderful-gute day. All of Annie's pot holders sold, I found a nut chopper, and I saw Mississippi."

What more could anyone want from life?

Chapter Six

Moses snapped his head up when he heard the low hum of the mail truck's engine. While he cut the curds, he watched from the window as the mailman stuffed envelopes into the mailbox that stood in front of the cheese factory. Furrowing his brow, Moses puzzled silently over his memory lapse. How could he have forgotten about the mail?

Every Friday, without fail, a letter in a sunny yellow envelope came from Minneapolis. Moses could always depend on Barbara. He waited by the mailbox on Fridays so he could read Barbara's letter the moment it arrived. Friday nights were spent writing her back. His reply letter went into the mailbox early Saturday morning and reached Barbara by Tuesday.

Today, he hadn't even remembered. He'd been thinking about Lia, wondering if she liked her book, hoping she didn't just pretend to like his cheese. Even knowing as little about her as he did, he knew she wouldn't pretend. He liked that she didn't make a fuss about him like most unmarried girls.

Moses called for Adam, who took over Moses's job while Moses sprinted outside for the mail. Sure enough, the yellow envelope peeked out from under a seed catalog. He snatched it from the pile and carefully slid his finger underneath the flap to rip open the top. "Sorry, Barbara," he said, repenting of his momentary forgetfulness. No one should ever replace Barbara in his thoughts.

> *Dear Moses,*
>   *How is the new buggy? I hope I get to see it soon. I am thinking of coming for a visit sometime in August. I am not sure.*

Moses's heart beat a little faster. Would she really come? She hadn't set foot in Bonduel for more than three years. His hopes soared. It could happen.

Like always, Barbara filled her letter with accounts of her exciting life in Minneapolis where she worked at a clothing store and went to something she called beauty school. Could someone actually go to school to learn how to be beautiful? Moses found the idea both confusing and ridiculous. Either girls were beautiful or they weren't.

Like Lia Shetler. She didn't need beauty school. Her dark, intelligent eyes and flawless skin, framed by the wisps of curly hair that escaped from her kapp, were irresistibly attractive. And so much was hidden in her smile, as if she knew a thousand things she didn't tell.

Moses found his mind wandering from his precious letter and snapped himself back to attention. Barbara was pretty too.

> *I am learning and growing so much away from the community, but I am still thinking about coming back. I am not sure yet. Thank you for being patient*

with me. I feel better knowing there is someone
waiting for me.

She always ended her letters like that. *I am thinking*
of returning to the community. I depend on you, Moses. I
need you to stay faithful.

Sometimes he felt as if Barbara were dangling from
a cliff, and he, with his hand extended, was the only
one who could save her. He felt stretched mighty thin.
She had broken his heart when she decided to leave,
but he had told himself that if he truly loved her, he
would wait for her. For as long as it took. How strong
would his love prove if he stopped caring about Barbara
simply because she was away?

As penance for letting thoughts of Lia distract him,
Moses read the letter three times. Tonight he would
make his reply extra long so Barbara would be assured
of his loyalty.

He considered Lia Shetler a friend, nothing more.
And he would keep thoughts of her at bay, no matter
how tempted he was to indulge them.

With her hands caked in flour, Lia slowly pushed
the rolling pin across the dough as she watched out
the window. She fixed her eyes on the tree-lined lane
that crawled up Huckleberry Hill and ended at the
Helmuths' front yard.

"He'll be here soon," Anna said, stirring an orange-
red concoction on the cooktop.

Lia blushed and tore her gaze from the window as
she wiped the sweat from her face with her sleeve.
Surely Anna didn't think she expected anyone in particular, or even looked forward to his arrival. It just
happened to be the day of the week that Moses came

up the hill to help his grandparents. She wasn't watching for him particularly.

He did not want a wife. Especially one so plain as Lia Shetler.

"You know," Anna said, "this garlic press is a right handy tool. I did six whole cloves as easy as you please."

Lia's dough flattened nicely as she rolled it into an almost perfect circle. Pies were her specialty. Dat always asked her to make pies for his birthday. Every time he ate one, he decided Lia should teach her sister Rachel how to cook. He said that a pretty girl who could cook would attract every unmarried young man in the state. So two or three times a year, when Dat insisted, Lia would try to teach Rachel the basics of pie making. Lia dreaded the cooking lessons. Rachel didn't have the patience to roll out a smooth crust, and fractions like half a teaspoon sent her into a panic.

Cooking lessons would end when Rachel burst into tears and fled the hated kitchen. Lia would trudge up the stairs to comfort her sister with the assurance that she would always make the pies for the family, and Rachel could eat them.

Lia wrapped the finished crust around her rolling pin and laid it into the pie tin. She took the saucepan full of raisins mixed with butter and brown sugar and poured it into the crust. Raisin pie was a gute treat in early summer before other fruits were in season. Later she would make blueberry, apple, and even huckleberry pie. After topping the raisins with another crust, she opened the cookstove and looked at the temperature gauge.

"Do you mind if I close the damper a bit?" she asked Anna.

Anna dipped a wooden spoon in her mixture and stirred it around. "Jah, go ahead. I will bake my meatballs after the pie. Moses loves pie."

"I have never made meatballs."

"Neither have I, but my daughter, Abigail, gave me a new cookbook for Christmas and I am determined to try a new recipe every week. I've fed Felty the same meals for sixty years." She tapped her forehead and puckered her lips. "My doctor says trying new things keeps the mind sharp. Does your mamm ever try a new recipe?"

"Not often. We have our favorites we like to make."

"And your sister Rachel? Does she like to cook?"

"Nae. She's the pretty one. She can get a gute husband without knowing how to cook well."

"If my opinion counted for anything, I'd say you're the pretty one."

When she heard the buggy rumble up the lane, Lia kept her eyes glued to the pie as her heart skipped a beat or two. She might as well admit that she liked him. He was a nice young man who made her laugh and liked that she was tall. Anna and Felty were delightful and so welcoming, but she shouldn't feel guilty for now and then looking forward to conversing with someone closer to her age.

Of course, she had nothing more in mind when she thought of his coming. He had made his intentions very clear. Lia had to check a laugh before it escaped her lips. They had been blunt with each other. No guessing games needed between them. They could forget any pretense and be friends.

Just friends.

Besides, it was pure nonsense to even hope that such a man would take an interest in her, and any hopes she foolishly harbored would be dashed as sure as rain fell in Wisconsin in the spring.

Moses burst in the door like the sun poking through the gloomy clouds. Even in the uncomfortable heat, he wore the fire engine red scarf that Anna had knitted for him and a smile that took over his whole face. Lia couldn't get enough of that dimple. Bending over, he planted a kiss on the top of his mammi's head. "How is the prettiest girl on Huckleberry Hill?"

Anna reached up and cupped his chin in her hand. "She's standing right over there. Why don't you ask her yourself?"

Moses glanced at Lia and quickly looked away. "I told Dawdi I'd turn over the dirt in the garden today. Crist will bring compost next week."

"Supper is at five o'clock sharp."

Moses winked at his mammi. "I wouldn't be one minute tardy for your cooking."

He blew out the door as suddenly as he had come, and Lia spent the rest of the afternoon keeping her gaze away from the window.

An hour later, Lia pulled her golden brown pie from the cookstove as Anna slid her cookie sheet of nicely formed meatballs inside.

Anna's pot of red sauce still bubbled on the stove. Lia had never seen anything like it, but the meatballs looked delicious and the sauce smelled faintly of grapes. Anna's first recipe experiment looked to be a success.

Nearing suppertime, Lia brought a bottle of peaches from the basement and heated up some frozen corn. The Helmuths had a modern refrigerator powered by a generator but still used a cookstove powered by wood.

Felty, with Moses close behind, marched through the back door singing the song Lia had heard him sing every day before suppertime. He had a beautiful, deep voice that seemed to vibrate the floorboards.

"Life is like a mountain railroad, with a canyon deep and

wide, we must make the run successful, so we'll be by Jesus's side."

Even though it seemed to be his favorite song, he never sang the same lyrics twice. If he forgot them, he simply made them up. In the three weeks she'd been on Huckleberry Hill, Lia had heard a dozen different versions of "Life's Railway to Heaven." It was entirely endearing.

Both Moses and Felty hung up their hats, and Felty kissed his wife right on the lips without even a glance in Lia's direction.

Anna kissed him back and then nudged him away. "Felty, you stink like a wet raccoon."

"Oh, Annie-bell, you smell like a thick piece of strawberry rhubarb pie."

"Wash up so's you and Moses don't have to take supper on the back porch."

Lia refused to let Moses's boyish grin set her heart aflutter.

Moses and Felty obediently trudged to the bathroom to wash. Anna spread the table with one of her knit coverings. She had seven "tablecloths," all knitted with a different color yarn, to put on her round table. Although they proved a bit thick, Anna proudly pointed out that they never needed to use a trivet or pot holder to protect the table from hot dishes.

Lia laid out the corn, the peaches, and a pitcher of milk. By this time, Anna had ladled the meatballs into the red sauce and placed them on the table with a white dish of noodles.

"The book said to serve with egg noodles," she said, looking doubtfully from her bowl of meatballs to Lia's face.

"It will be wonderful gute. What is in the sauce?"

"Grape jelly and oriental chili sauce. I had to go to

three different stores for the sauce and even then I wasn't sure I got the right thing. The woman at the store in Green Bay didn't speak English. Or *Deitsch*."

Felty came back from the bathroom and peered curiously into the pot of meatballs. "Oh, Annie, this looks delicious. I always said you was the best cook in the world. It wonders me that I haven't got fat in the sixty years we been married."

Felty pulled the chair out for Anna to sit, and Moses did the same for Lia. She felt a little silly about that small gesture.

After silent grace, Anna scooped some noodles onto Felty's plate and then her own. She handed the dish to Lia. "Eat up. There's plenty."

Lia put more noodles on her plate than she really wanted to eat, but the healthy serving made Anna's smile grow wider. She handed the noodles to Moses, who piled his plate high. The saucy meatballs looked mighty tasty poured over the golden, buttery noodles.

"It looks just like the picture in the book," Anna said, her eyes bright.

Felty dished himself some corn. "The president of the United States doesn't eat this well."

Lia cut a meatball in half, skewered it, and rolled a noodle around it with her fork. As soon as she popped it into her mouth, her tongue burst into flames. Then the entire inside of her mouth felt as if it were breaking out into blisters. She chewed the meatball quickly, doing her best to avoid touching it with her tongue, and swallowed it. She might as well have poured scalding hot water down her throat.

Without a word, Moses reached over and poured her some milk as she began to cough violently. Grabbing her glass as if it held the answers to all her deepest questions, she took a gulp and let the milk sit on her tongue. The inside of her mouth cooled slightly, but her lips still felt like they were on fire—or numb. At the moment, she couldn't really tell the difference.

"Are you all right, Lia?" Anna asked.

Lia nodded and shoved a closed-mouth smile onto her face.

Lia looked at Moses. His eyes watered, and the color crept up his neck like a strange sunburn. He smiled reassuringly at Lia, then drank half his glass of milk.

The wrinkles around Anna's mouth deepened as she took a small bite. "I don't think I did it right. What do you think, Felty?"

Showing no signs of distress, Felty popped another meatball into his mouth. It wondered Lia that he could do it without choking. "Delicious. You have outdone yourself."

Anna's lips turned down, and she shook her head. It surprised Lia to see the light fade from her eyes. "It's too spicy. I ruined it. And I wanted to make such a nice dinner for Moses and Lia."

Felty scooped another meatball into his mouth with a generous forkful of noodles. Reaching over, he patted Anna's hand with his gnarled fingers. "Now, Annie Banannie, no need to fuss. This is delicious."

"Jah, Mammi. I love spicy food."

Lia marveled that Moses could speak. She felt as if her lips had melted together.

Felty waved his fork at Moses in agreement. "It'll grow hair on your chest."

"And clear out your sinuses," Moses added.

Lia took another gulp of milk. "And the noodles are so buttery," she said weakly, not wanting to lie but hoping to encourage Anna all the same.

Anna's expression relaxed. "They're a bit fiery for

my taste, but I feel better knowing all of you like them."

In addition to the tears provoked by the hot sauce, Lia's eyes stung with tears of distress. She wouldn't hurt Anna's feelings for the world, but it would be impossible to eat another bite of those meatballs. Taking a taste of corn, she tried to think of an excuse for not finishing her supper. She'd never been so uncomfortable in her life.

Anna rose from the table to fetch the butter—she said the noodles needed more—and while her back was turned, Moses reached his fork over to Lia's plate, skewered two meatballs, and stuffed them into his mouth. While he chewed, Lia was certain she saw smoke coming out of his ears.

She stared at him, first in sheer disbelief and then in pure gratitude. She shook her head slightly in his direction as if to say, "You don't need to do that," but he merely curled his lips, swiped a tear from his face, and turned to Felty. "I saw Delaware yesterday."

Felty's face lit up. "Delaware! That is rare. I only seen one Delaware last year."

There were only two and a half meatballs left on Lia's plate, plus all those noodles slathered in hot sauce. Would she be able to manage another bite? She took a swallow of milk to give her courage and reached out her fork. But Moses gently nudged her hand aside and stole another of her meatballs. With less enthusiasm than the first time, he stuffed it into his mouth, chewed painfully, and chased it down with another half glass of milk.

By this time, his entire face shone beet red, and sweat dripped from his forehead. Lia imagined that his skin color would match perfectly with his scarf. Her profound relief together with Moses's unmatched kindness rendered her almost giddy. The pained yet good-natured expression on his face, combined with the discomfort they both felt, struck Lia's funny bone. A giggle escaped before she could stifle it.

Moses glanced at her out of the corner of his eye and then coughed and chuckled at the same time.

Lia put her hand over her mouth, but as was usually the case when she tried to stop the laughter from overflowing, she succeeded in making it worse. She snickered and hissed and finally gave up and laughed out loud. Moses joined her.

Anna looked at both of them with wide eyes. "Whatever is the matter?"

Lia could think of nothing to say in her defense. And even if she had, she couldn't talk for the laughing.

But Moses, more quick-witted than she, said, "There is a joke about Delaware that I remembered."

Lia hoped Moses knew what he was doing, because if Anna asked her to repeat a joke about Delaware, she wouldn't be able to come up with one single thing.

Anna smiled her motherly smile. "Well, tell us. We don't want to be left out."

Moses pressed his lips together and furrowed his brow, but Lia didn't know if it was because he couldn't come up with a joke or because his stomach most likely burned with a raging fire. He sat silently for a few seconds and then a light turned on behind his eyes. "What do you call an Amish person in Delaware?"

Anna looked truly puzzled. "What?"

"A visitor."

Amazed and impressed that Moses could come up with something, anything, for Anna, Lia again burst into stomach-splitting laughter.

Anna watched both of them as if they had sprouted rabbit ears and horse tails right there at the supper table. When their mirth finally died down, Anna, ever the loving grandmother, said, "Oh, you two. A pair of peas in a pod. If that joke makes you happy, it makes me happy."

In the midst of more laughter, Moses reached over and took Lia's last one and a half meatballs. Lia ate around the edges of her noodles without getting too much of the sauce while Moses scooped up bite after bite when Anna looked away. Their efforts were enough to make Anna believe Lia had cleared her plate and to start Lia into worrying about Moses's health.

Felty's face glowed with sweat, and he repeatedly dabbed his nose with his handkerchief, but otherwise he gave no indication that his throat might be on fire. Anna had eaten only two bites of her own recipe. Compared to Moses's ruddy complexion, she looked fit as a fiddle. She hopped from her chair and gathered the empty plates. "Who wants pie?"

Lia nudged Moses's foot with hers. When he looked at her, she shook her head. "Don't eat one bite of my pie," she whispered. "You'll be sick."

He took another drink of milk and raised an eyebrow. "The pie is that bad?"

"You have done enough for me already."

Moses turned to Anna and flashed those nice teeth. "I'd love a piece, Mammi."

Lia lifted her eyes to heaven and shook her head in exasperation. Moses, still bright red in the face, blessed her with a boyish grin. "Remember, Mammi wants to convince me to marry you."

"I'll not have you."

"I'm not looking to marry—unless your pie is extra tasty."

Lia rose from the table and helped Anna cut pie. She tried to slip Moses an extra-small piece, knowing how terribly he must be suffering already, but Anna would have none of it.

"Moses will want the biggest piece." She peered at him over her glasses as if to determine what size of piece he would need to fall in love.

When they were all seated again, Moses stuffed a bite of pie in his mouth with more enthusiasm than Lia would have thought possible.

But she didn't really care if he liked it.

It was just a pie.

It took her a moment to notice that she gripped her fork and her knuckles had turned white.

Moses savored his bite and then nodded in approval. "Delicious. Puts every other raisin pie to shame."

Lia took a deep breath and relaxed her hand before she lost circulation.

"This is wonderful gute," Felty said with his mouth full.

Anna fluffed her fork along the top of her piece. "Your crust is so flaky. I was never able to master a flaky piecrust."

"Nonsense," Felty said. "Your piecrust is my favorite."

Lia took a bite. To her relief, the pie tasted delicious. The sticky-sweet raisins had cooked to the perfect consistency and texture. The crust held up nicely, soft and moist on the bottom, flaky and golden on the top.

Not that it mattered. It was just a pie.

Once Moses cleaned his plate, he stood slowly, as if he were toting a full jug of water on his head. "Denki, Mammi, for the wonderful meal."

"Will we see you next Tuesday?" Anna asked.

Moses made his way around the table and planted a kiss on his mammi's forehead. "Jah, of course. But I will come on Thursday to help Lia stack the limbs from the peach trees. I pruned in March and still haven't cleared them away."

Anna smiled as if she thought Moses's coming an extra day this week was a very good idea. Lia guessed that Anna saw the certainty of a happy wedding in the near future. Lia saw it as another demonstration of Moses's kindness. Stacking limbs was a muscle-numbing, back-aching chore. She would be glad for his help.

"Lia, walk out with Moses," Anna said. "The sunset over the hill will be beautiful tonight."

Moses cocked an eyebrow. "The sun won't set for another three hours yet."

Anna merely patted his arm as if he were a small child who needed guidance. "Better than being an hour late for it. Dawdi and I will do the dishes, never you mind about that."

Amused and pretending not to be suspicious of Anna's motives, Lia nodded cheerfully and stood.

Moses put a hand on his stomach as if protecting it from getting bumped while he opened the door and motioned for Lia to go first. They walked toward the barn as Moses looked faithfully to the west.

"Nope, no sunset." He chuckled. "I hope you're not offended, but I got milk to weigh and cheese to test. I won't have time to wait for the beautiful sunset."

"I've got chickens to feed and tomato plants to look after. I will be annoyed if you stay to look."

He threw his head back and laughed. "Have you ever considered that you might hurt my feelings with your plain-spokenness?"

"Are your feelings hurt?" she asked, with a tease in her voice.

"Not yet, but you never know when something you say will put me in my place right quick."

Lia folded her arms around her waist and gave him a teasing smile. "I'll keep trying to do just that."

He suddenly stopped walking and turned to study her face. He looked at her for several seconds without speaking. She stared right back, a mixture of discomfort and pleasure stirring around inside her. What was he looking for?

"The color of your dress makes your eyes pop out of your head," he said quietly.

"Sounds painful." Why did she have to choose this moment to make a joke?

He slid his hands into his pockets and shifted his gaze to the ground.

Lia took a step closer. "Denki for what you did for me at supper. You don't know how grateful—"

"Nae, thank you, for sparing Mammi's feelings. She only wants to make people happy, and food is one of the ways she shows love. She frets about her cooking like she frets over her grandchildren."

"Of course. I understand. To a woman, a good meal is an offering of love. She puts part of herself into the recipe."

"I have a request," Moses said. "Will you make another pie on Thursday?"

Lia felt herself blush although she wasn't sure why. "Jah, I can."

"It's just that, well, I think your pie was gute. What I mean is, from what I could tell . . ." He kicked the dirt at his feet. "I'll bet it was an extra-tasty pie, but I couldn't be sure because those meatballs seared my tongue, and I think all my taste buds are dead."

Lia sighed through her laughter. "Oh! I am so sorry. Very sorry. It could have been me."

"Better me than you, is that what you are saying?"

"Only so you understand that I am very, very grateful."

She felt his gaze intensify as they stood staring at each other. Without warning, he leaned forward, planted a swift kiss on her lips, and disappeared into the barn before Lia even realized what had happened.

Her head seemed to be doing cartwheels as she brushed her fingers lightly over her mouth. What in the world had he done?

Stunned into silence and paralyzed by the impact of Moses's touch, she watched him as, without another word, he led his horse from the barn, quickly hitched up his buggy, and drove it down the lane.

Her lips tingled pleasantly, but whether from the meatball sauce or the kiss, she couldn't tell.

Surely they would tingle for days.

Chapter Seven

Absentmindedly stirring a pot of stew, Lia gazed at the rain pouring off the eaves of her house. The cloudburst came so fast, outside the window looked like a waterfall. The shadows in the kitchen deepened as the sky grew dark with heavy rainclouds. Lia had been back in Wautoma for only five days, but she already missed Huckleberry Hill as if it were her true home.

The night following Moses's unexpected, uncalled for, and unnecessary kiss, Lia got word that Treva Bontrager had passed away and that Lia was wanted at home to help with food for the funeral. She caught a ride to Wautoma the very next day with a van full of mourners from Bonduel.

Treva's death was neither sudden nor unexpected. She passed at ninety-two years old and had been living with her granddaughter for over a decade. For the better part of two days, Mamm and Lia baked bread and pies and made three salads to serve at the dinner after services.

The funeral service took place Saturday, and even though Lia's time with her family had been short, she was ready to return to Bonduel. To see Anna and Felty. Oh, how she missed them.

Yes, Anna and Felty.

The van would stop by the house tomorrow morning to take her back to Huckleberry Hill. She had already packed.

Lia's nephew, Thomas, tugged on her apron. "Aunt Lia?" She hadn't even heard him come into the room. This dazed and distracted state of hers would have to stop.

"Aunt Lia, Mammi wants to know when supper will be ready."

Lia tousled Thomas's golden hair. "Tell Mammi the corn bread has ten more minutes, then we will be ready. Will you set the table?"

"Jah. I will tell Mammi first."

The chubby four-year-old raced out of the room to deliver his message. Lia grinned. She never tired of the nieces and nephews. Her four older brothers, Toby, Monroe, Luke, and Perry, were all married. Toby and Monroe had four children each. Luke had two sons, and Perry's wife was expecting their first.

Perry, twenty-five and newly married, was Lia's closest brother. He stood six foot five—as tall as Moses—and watched out for her like a shepherd would his favorite lamb.

Monroe's four children were sleeping over this week while Monroe and his wife were in Ohio visiting relatives.

Thomas, Monroe's youngest, bustled back into the room as if he couldn't wait to set the table for Aunt Lia. "How many are eating?"

"Hold up your fingers and count while I say the names. Mammi, Dawdi, Aunt Rachel, me, you, Susie Lynn, Mary, and Linda Rose."

Thomas clapped his hands in delight. "Nine."

"Eight. I will pull the bowls off the shelf for you."

The timer rang, and Lia pulled the pan of corn bread out of the cookstove and replaced it with a raisin pie. Moses liked her raisin pie. Or at least he thought he would once he got a chance to really taste it. Lia pressed her fingers to her lips. Six days since he had kissed her. She could still feel his feather-soft touch.

"Aunt Lia, why are you smiling?"

"Never you mind. Here are the napkins."

It meant nothing—the kiss. He'd offered it almost casually, like a handshake. What in the world did he mean by giving her a peck and then running away like his pants were on fire? Never mind that she had never been kissed in her life and that boys and girls weren't supposed to kiss until they were courting or engaged or maybe even married. Moses Zimmerman probably kissed girls with regularity just to brag about it to his friends.

Thomas finished with the table. "Gute job, Thomas. Now go find Mammi and the others and tell them time for supper."

Moses had made it plain that he didn't want a wife. He should have told her that he was still willing to kiss a few girls.

Rachel appeared in the kitchen with Monroe's three daughters, Susie Lynn, Mary, and Linda Rose. The nieces loved Rachel. She would sit with them in her bedroom, and they would brush each other's hair and giggle and tell stories about boys.

The four girls flopped down in their seats, followed closely behind by Mamm, who had been folding laundry. "What a blessing I had those clothes off the line before the rain started. It looks to make down heavy all night."

Dat appeared from outside and hung his dripping slicker on the hook in the washroom. He didn't waste time once he sat down. As soon as Lia slid into her seat, Dat bowed his head and the family joined him for prayer.

After silent grace, Mamm took the ladle and began serving up stew. "We must thank Lia for this delicious meal. I've missed your special corn bread."

"Denki, Lia," said Thomas.

Lia put her forehead against Thomas's. "You are welcome."

Lia cut the pan of corn bread into squares while Rachel poured milk. "You will never guess what happened to me on Saturday after the funeral," Rachel said, addressing the whole family. "The fun-er-al." She annunciated each syllable as if the very word would horrify the children.

"What?" Susie Lynn and Linda Rose asked at the same time.

Rachel paused for dramatic effect. "Clemens Schrock asked me to marry him. On the day of the fun-er-al. Can you believe that? Wouldn't a boy with any sense know not to propose marriage on the day someone dies?"

"It wasn't actually the day Aunt Treva died," Mamm said.

"I refused him. It was ridiculous that he would propose to me."

Lia knew better than to ask. She did anyway. "Why was it ridiculous? You are a pretty girl. Of course the boys want to marry you."

"Clemens works at the mill. At-the-mill." Those long, drawn-out syllables again. "He's short and has a pudgy face and pockmarks on his cheeks from all that acne he used to have. He doesn't even own his own farm or house or anything. If I married him, I would end up living in that tiny dawdi house with only a wall between me and his parents." Rachel sighed and stared into space as if she were trying to see her future. "I'll not marry a man who isn't handsome. He has to be handsome or I won't be able to stomach him. And tall."

Susie Lynn, eight years old, nodded. "Me too. I want to marry Floyd Weaver."

Lia knew better than to argue. She did anyway. "Clemens is a nice young man. The mill is a gute job, and he takes care of his dat's farm all by himself. And when the Bennetts lost half their shingles in the windstorm, he spent a week fixing their roof."

Rachel turned up her nose. "If you like him so well, why don't you marry him?"

"I didn't say I think you should marry him, only that he is a nice young man."

Mamm clicked the handle of the ladle on the edge of the pot and glanced at Lia. "Now, children. Don't argue. Rachel can marry whomever she pleases." That was Mamm's mild way of scolding Lia. Ever since they'd almost lost her as a little girl, both parents did their best to make sure Rachel was never displeased.

"Jah," Dat said. "Rachel is pretty enough to have her pick. We just need to find someone gute enough."

As soon as Rachel had turned eighteen last year, talk at the dinner table centered around finding a suitable husband for her, as if it were some impossible task. But to Lia, it didn't seem hard at all to find Rachel a boy. She was so beautiful and petite that the boys flocked to Shetlers' door like sparrows on the telephone wire. But Rachel and Dat were finicky. It had to be a handsome boy with an attractive income and a pious family, preferably with a gute piece of land of his own. No Wautoma boys measured up.

After Rachel had turned down her third marriage

proposal and despaired of ever finding the perfect husband, they joked that maybe Lia would be the first Shetler girl to marry after all. She and Rachel had a good laugh about that.

"Lia, would you get the cheese from the shelf?" Dat said.

Thomas swung his feet back and forth. "Can I have cheese?"

Lia found a small wheel of white cheese and sliced away the wax before she studied the label and caught her breath. "Where did you get this cheese?"

Mamm glanced in her direction. "I gave it to your dat for his birthday. It came in a gift basket."

"This is Moses's cheese!"

"Who is Moses?" Dat asked.

"The Helmuths' grandson, Moses Zimmerman. He runs a cheese factory in Bonduel."

"Do you know him?"

"Jah, he comes to Huckleberry Hill to help with chores. He bought me some of his baby swiss at auction. It is delicious."

Dat held out his hand. "Let's have a try."

Lia quickly cut seven slices and passed them out to her family.

"This is yummy," Mamm said. "I hoped it would be gute. I bought it at the T&M market."

"Very gute, very gute," Dat said. "We'll have to keep an eye out for more from Zimmerman Cheese. It is a gute thing to buy from other Amish."

Lia almost burst with pride for Moses. She put more slices on a plate and brought them to the table. "He bought the cheese factory from an Englischer five years ago when he was only twenty-one. He has worked hard. A man in Green Bay will buy all the cheese Moses can make, and for a gute price too."

Mamm took another piece and broke it into her stew. "Have you met his wife and children?"

"Oh, he's not married. Though, heaven knows, such a fine young man could be."

Rachel served herself another piece of corn bread. "He is probably homely."

Linda Rose and Susie Lynn giggled behind their hands.

Lia teasingly scolded Rachel with her eyes. "Nae. He is pleasant to look at." She grinned and poked Susie Lynn lightly in the ribs. "He is handsomer than Floyd Weaver."

Susie's laughter sounded like water tripping over the rocks. "He is not."

Dat laid down his spoon and propped an elbow on the table. "Is he a gute man of the Church?"

"As gute as they come, to be sure."

Leaning back in his chair, Dat folded his arms across his chest and cocked his head to the side in deep thought. "Just the thing for our Rachel."

"What do you mean, Dat?" Rachel said.

"We've gone through all the boys in Wautoma. Maybe your husband has been waiting in Bonduel all this time."

Rachel knit her brows together. "You mean the one who makes cheese?"

"Jah. I'm sure of it. If he is everything Lia says, he would make a fine husband for you."

Lia's heart sank to her toes, but she managed a weak smile. "Too bad he lives in Bonduel."

Dat's eyes sparkled with enthusiasm, and he leaned forward. "Bonduel is only an hour by car. You could take Rachel with you for a visit."

"That is a fine idea," Mamm chimed in. "He will be thrilled to meet our Rachel."

Rachel seemed mildly curious. "I might want to see for myself if he is so handsome."

Lia felt as if a buggy full of church benches had parked itself on her chest. She didn't want Rachel to come to Bonduel. Huckleberry Hill and the Helmuths belonged to Lia. Even if it was a silly notion, they felt like her own private family. She didn't want to share them with Rachel. And she knew what would happen. Once they met Rachel, Lia would cease to be important to them.

"He doesn't want to get married," Lia said.

Dat frowned. "He told you this?"

"Jah. He said he is not looking for a wife."

Dat laced his fingers together. "Of course he would tell you that, Lia. He does not want to marry you. But he has not met our Rachel. He'll change his mind when he lays eyes on her."

Mamm nodded her agreement. Dat and Rachel smiled triumphantly at each other.

Lia felt her power sink further. Whatever objections to marriage Moses had, they would vanish when he saw Rachel.

"Why don't you take Rachel to Bonduel with you tomorrow?" Mamm said. "Roy is bound to have room for one more in his van."

Dat slapped the table as a wonderful-gute idea came to him. "Better yet, why don't Rachel take Lia's place?"

Rachel's eyes opened wide. "You want me to go by myself?"

"Once Rachel goes, Lia will not be wanted there. She would only get in the way of their courtship."

Lia's voice rose with her distress. "Nae, Dat. The Helmuths hired me for the summer, not Rachel. It would not be proper to—"

"They need a girl to help them keep house and garden," Dat said. "Rachel will do as well as you. Why should they care who it is as long as she does the job? Besides, they will soon realize why Rachel has been sent and be happy for a wonderful-gute girl for their grandson."

Lia fought hard to keep the tears from her eyes. "Rachel might not like him," she said feebly. But once Dat set his mind to it, she knew he wouldn't be dissuaded.

"If I don't like him I won't have to stay there," Rachel said. "I can come home, and you can go back. I'd rather not work that hard on someone else's farm with nothing to show for it."

Every glimmer of hope died. Lia had no doubt that Rachel would like Moses. Not only was he tall and handsome, the two qualities highest on Rachel's list, but he had an easy laugh and a ready cheerfulness that put people instantly at ease. And he treated everyone so kindly. Who wouldn't like that?

Dat popped another piece of cheese into his mouth. "It's settled, then. Rachel will go in Lia's place, and Lord willing, we will have a wedding in November."

This was how it had always been with Lia and Rachel. Their parents catered to Rachel's every need and expected Lia to acquiesce cheerfully. After all, it had been Lia's fault that Rachel nearly died fourteen years ago.

Lia had been only nine years old, but she already loved to cook. She wanted to surprise Mamm with fresh greens and pork chops for supper, so she had sneaked out of the house to gather wild asparagus along the stream bank. Even as a five-year-old, Rachel liked getting her own way, and she stomped her feet and threatened to ruin Lia's surprise if Lia didn't let her tag along. Rachel had played by the shallow stream while Lia collected asparagus spears in her apron. More than once she had scolded Rachel for splashing her, but Rachel paid no heed until she got carried away and fell face-first into the water. The icy, early spring runoff soaked Rachel clear through.

By the time they got home, Rachel was shivering violently, and within hours, she had developed the gravelly cough that could only mean croup. Lia would never forget how pale Rachel looked as they loaded her into the ambulance. Lia had never seen her parents so terrified.

Why didn't you keep better watch over her? Dat had accused just before he climbed into the ambulance. Rachel spent the next four days in the hospital, and Lia had spent the next four days praying for Rachel's recovery and pleading for forgiveness for her carelessness. If Rachel died, it would have been her fault.

For the next month, Lia and Mamm had nursed Rachel back to health. Dat instructed Lia to keep Rachel happy at all costs. If Rachel got upset, she would cry and then scream, and her weak lungs couldn't take the strain. When she didn't get her way, she bawled until her lips turned blue, and Mamm agreed to anything Rachel wanted to keep her from making herself sicker.

Lia became the forgotten one, the girl whose mistake had almost cost the Shetlers their youngest child.

Mamm and Rachel chattered merrily about winter weddings while Lia silently cleared the dishes from the table. Rachel had stopped throwing tantrums years ago, but everything in the Shetler household still revolved around her.

Lia held her breath as unjustifiable sadness tore at her heart. Moses wasn't interested in her and never would be, so why would she grieve if she lost him to Rachel? He had never been hers to lose. She had only really been acquainted with him for four weeks. Still, she didn't know if she could bear his falling in love with her sister. And he would fall in love with Rachel. Beautiful, delicate Rachel was the perfect combination of coy and charming that attracted boys like honey. Moses's reluctance could not withstand Rachel's beauty.

Lia's cheeks were dry of tears but she sensed the slightest tingle on her lips where Moses Zimmerman had kissed her good-bye.

Moses found Mammi and Dawdi in the barn tending to the batch of newly hatched chicks in their incubator. The fuzzy yellow balls peeped and shivered like a pan of popcorn popping on the stove. Mammi had her fist wrapped around a tiny chick, petting its head with her index finger. Dawdi fiddled with his new fan while humming "I Need No Mansions."

"Can I help?" Moses said.

Mammi's face lit up like a summer morning. "Moses, you are here mighty early yet."

"Can you see what's clogging up my fan?" Dawdi asked.

Moses could see Mammi watching him out of the corner of her eye. "Come to see Lia?" she asked. "The van driver told us he'd be back this way about this time today."

Dawdi wiped off his greasy hands. "You told him three times already, Annie girl. He knows when Lia gets back."

"That's why he came early, isn't it, Moses?"

Moses knelt on one knee to have a look at Dawdi's fan. "I came early because the hair on the back of my neck twitched this morning, and I had a feeling Dawdi would need help with the fan. We don't want the chicks to freeze to death."

Mammi placed her chick into the sea of other chicks and propped her hands on her hips, looking very pleased with herself. "Oh, Moses, you are such a tease."

Moses picked up a screwdriver from Dawdi's box. He had promised Lia he'd help her stack those limbs, and he didn't want her to think he'd forgotten, even over the long six days she'd been gone. If Mammi thought there was any other reason for him to show up at exactly the time they expected Lia, well, she could go on believing what she wanted.

It had been a week since Moses had momentarily lost his reason and kissed Lia right on the mouth. His brain ached for trying to figure out why he'd done such a thing. He'd never even kissed Barbara before.

The best he could come up with was that curiosity got the better of him. Her lips looked like full, blushing pink rose petals, and he had wanted to see how soft they were. But that he would lose his mind in a blaze of curiosity made absolutely no sense. She had looked so pretty that day, with unruly chestnut curls peeking out from under her kapp and the aftereffects of hot sauce tinting her cheeks. It had seemed so natural, so easy, and he had wanted to kiss her in the worst way. So he did.

Either that or his overdose of hot sauce made him woozy. Could he really be held responsible for his actions?

Moses wondered if Lia had already forgotten it happened or if he should apologize for his behavior. She didn't seem embarrassed or angry. She'd probably laughed herself to sleep that night.

One thing was certain. He wouldn't do that again. Hot sauce or no hot sauce, he would keep his head. Lia didn't deserve false hope, and Moses had resolved to stay loyal to Barbara.

All three of them heard the van as it rattled up the lane. It needed a new muffler.

Mammi pointed out the door. "Lead the way, Moses. I want you to be the first to see her."

Moses merely grinned and shook his head. "And you think I am the tease?"

They walked out of the barn together, Moses with his arm wrapped protectively around Mammi's shoulders.

Roy Polter hopped out of his van and gave Felty a curt wave of his hand. Moses's mamm would call Roy portly. He'd confessed to Moses that he had a weakness for cheese fries and donuts, and sitting in a van all day didn't help his waistline. At age sixty-five, Roy had retired from his day job and now he drove Amish folks to weddings, funerals, and auctions all over Wisconsin. Roy sometimes delivered cheese to La Crosse for Moses when it was on his way.

"I brought her safe and sound," Roy said as he slid the door open.

A short blonde hopped out of the van. She looked at Moses and put her hand to the nape of her neck to smooth an imaginary strand of hair. "Hi," she said, studying him from top to bottom. Her eyes lit up, and she fluttered her long eyelashes. "Hel-lo," she said, drawing the word out so long she had to take a deep breath afterward.

Why did the girls have to look at him like he was the next thing up for bid on the auction block? Moses stuck his head inside the van. Mattie and Noah Schrock and their daughter, Nan, sat in the backseat.

"*Gute maiya*, Moses," Nan said. "How are you?"

"Fine," Moses replied. He looked at the short girl standing next to him. "Where's Lia?"

The girl sidled too close. "She's not coming."

By this time, Mammi and Dawdi had made their way around the side of the van. "Not coming?" Mammi said, the wrinkles around her mouth deepening to a frown.

The girl beamed from ear to ear. "I'm here instead," she said, as if this were the best news they could have heard all day.

Moses stared at her in puzzlement. "Who are you?"

"I'm Rachel, Lia's sister."

"Where's Lia?" Mammi asked.

"Dat thought it would be better if I came to Bonduel in Lia's place."

Mammi pasted a sweet, mildly concerned expression on her face, but Moses wasn't fooled. Mammi was hopping mad. A vein in her temple pulsed wildly, she wrung her hands, and her voice cracked in about five different places when she spoke. "Your dat thought it would be better?"

Rachel leaned close to Mammi's ear and lowered her voice, but Moses still heard every word. "He thinks I would be a more fitting choice," she inclined her head toward Moses, "for a certain person. How could you have known that when you asked Lia to stay with you over the summer instead of me? Dat says we've got to make hay, and all that."

Moses couldn't conceal his astonishment. He stared at Rachel as his jaw fell to the ground. Mammi's harmless scheming was nothing compared to Lia's dat's rudeness. Had he actually switched daughters because he thought Lia was an unlikely match and her sister a sure thing? The sheer audacity of such a suggestion left Moses breathless.

It seemed her dat moved his daughters around like pieces on a chessboard. Lia was the expendable one, and Rachel played the queen.

Well, Moses refused to be the pawn.

Mammi looked at Moses, and even with that sugary-sweet smile still hanging on her lips, her eyes flickered with fire. "What does Lia think about making hay?"

Rachel waved her hand around as if swatting a fly. "Oh, I don't know, but she was in one of her moods when I left. She wouldn't even come out to see me off. She can be so petty sometimes."

Roy handed Rachel her bag from the back of the van. Moses promptly took it from her. He might not be happy about her being here, but he remembered his manners. Rachel gave him an approving look. "I must say, I had my doubts, but you are just as Lia described."

Moses couldn't say the same about Rachel. Lia had told him that her sister was pretty, that she had broken dozens of hearts over the years. She possessed stunningly beautiful features with round blue eyes and rosebud lips, and her silky golden hair surely attracted many suitors. But she was a puny thing who carried a self-satisfied air about her that Moses found unappealing. Any girl who took pleasure in hurting boys' feelings was not worth his time.

"You're even taller than Lia. I bet she liked that. She usually towers over everybody, like a sycamore."

Roy said his good-byes to Mammi and Dawdi and drove away with his three remaining passengers.

Rachel watched the van disappear down the hill, breathed in the moist summer air, and clasped her hands together. "Will you show me to my room? I'll sleep wherever Lia did. I don't mind if it's terribly small. My room at home ain't much bigger than the washroom."

Mammi still had that smile painted on her face. If she kept it in place much longer, it would dry like that, and she might never be able to wipe it off. "Rebecca—"

"Rachel."

"Rachel, would you mind very much waiting for us in the house?" When Rachel paused, no doubt trying to guess what they were up to, Mammi motioned toward the front porch as if Rachel might not know the way.

"Um, I don't mind. If Moses could carry my bag and show me to my room—"

Mammi yanked the bag from Moses's fingers faster than he could say "ouch" and handed it to Rachel, who cradled it with both arms as if it weighed a hundred pounds. "I would appreciate it if you would take it in yourself."

Rachel pursed her lips and batted her baby blue eyes. "Which room?"

"Wait for us in the kitchen," Mammi said. Moses admired the way Mammi could pepper her sweet tone with the hint of a scolding.

Rachel lifted her nose slightly in the air, gifted them with a momentary smile, and shuffled to the house, dragging her bag behind her.

Mammi took Dawdi's arm. "Let's walk behind the barn where no one will hear me howl in frustration."

Dawdi and Mammi led the way. When they got out of sight of the house, Mammi didn't waste her breath. "If Owen Shetler thinks he can pull that with me, he's got another thing coming."

"As sure as rain, I'm going to miss that girl," Dawdi said. "A sweeter thing never come up our hill."

Mammi turned on Dawdi as if he had let his dentures fall down the well. "Felty, how can you say that? As if we'll never see Lia again! I refuse to give her up that easy."

Moses had to admire how fast Dawdi could change his tune. He squared his shoulders and wrapped an arm around Mammi. "Of course we're going to do something about it. How could Lia's dat send us a daughter we didn't ask for? What do you think, Moses?"

Secure that Dawdi was on her side, Mammi quit pacing and sat on the bench near the garden plot. "If I didn't care about sparing that girl's feelings, I'd send her packing back to Wautoma in two shakes of a lamb's tail. I mean for Moses to marry Lia, not her sister."

This would not be a good time to object to Mammi's interfering in his life. Moses wanted Lia back too, and not because he enjoyed her company. He simply felt better knowing that Mammi and Dawdi weren't on Huckleberry Hill all by themselves. Besides, Sarah planned on Lia's help delivering babies.

"They've convinced the poor girl that she is unworthy of any young man's love," Mammi said.

"What do you think, Moses?" Dawdi said. "Lia don't seem unhappy."

"Not our Lia," Mammi said. "She's been blessed with a sunshiny disposition. Happiness springs from her like water from a brook. But we can't let Lia believe for one moment that we don't want her back or that we don't care who we get. She's our girl. She needs to know where she stands with us."

Moses suddenly comprehended the full weight of what Mammi said. She was more perceptive than he gave her credit for. If Mammi and Dawdi let Rachel stay, Lia would feel the sting of it forever. He wouldn't want to see her hurt like that.

"What do you think, Moses?" Dawdi said.

Mammi waved her hand dismissively. "Oh, what young man knows his own heart?"

Felty thumbed his suspenders. "Annie, I'm asking Moses. Lia is his bride, not yours."

Moses coughed. He had to put a stop to this. "Lia is not my bride. I barely know her."

Mammi nodded. "We brought her here so you could become acquainted."

Moses affectionately placed his palm on Mammi's cheek. "I'm not looking to marry. I don't fit into your neatly arranged rows, Mammi. You can't plan my future as if you were knitting a sweater."

Mammi raised her eyebrows and looked shocked at the very thought. "Of course I can."

Moses was forced to chuckle at Mammi's determination. He took off his hat and ran his fingers through his hair. Giving in, he sank to the bench next to Mammi. "If we shame Rachel by sending her back, her dat might take offense and refuse to let Lia return."

Mammi stood and paced again. "Sometimes I wish I'd never given up cussing."

"I never heard you cuss ever," Felty said.

"On days like today, I wish I did."

Moses rubbed his chin. "What if we asked for Lia back and let Rachel stay? It wouldn't hurt to have two girls helping here."

Mammi perked up and clapped her hands. "Moses, you are so smart. When Rachel sees that your heart is set on Lia, maybe she will get bored and go back to Wautoma without being asked."

Moses groaned inwardly while his lips twitched a fraction of an inch southward. "We can only hope."

* * *

Rachel had already helped herself to the food. She sat at the kitchen table eating a slice of Mammi's bread slathered in strawberry jam. When Moses and his grandparents entered the room, she stuffed the last bite into her mouth and shot from her seat. She smiled at Moses and tilted her head just so. He marveled that she could manage to flirt with him with her mouth full. She chewed and swallowed quickly. "Moses can show me to my room now."

The minute Mammi walked into the kitchen, her sweet façade reappeared, and she showed nothing but delight at Rachel's presence. "Rachel, we have been talking, and we have grown quite fond of Lia. Do you think she would come back and join you for the summer?"

Rachel cocked an eyebrow and gazed pointedly at Moses. "I don't see that you'd need both of us."

"Lia knows how I like my dishes washed, and she scrubs the stove till it shines. And the toilets. The toilets have got to be swabbed at least once a day. All that work doesn't leave much time for anything else, like gatherings and buggy rides." Mammi looked at Moses as if he were the topic of conversation.

He *was* the topic of conversation, but neither Rachel nor Mammi would come right out and say it. They must have forgotten he had ears.

A small line appeared between Rachel's brows. She regarded Mammi, then Moses before a smile played at her lips. "Lia was always better with the chores. She's sturdy, while Dat says I'm delicate."

"Can your mamm spare both of you for the summer?" Mammi asked.

Rachel's excitement seemed to grow the more she considered Mammi's proposal. "Oh, Mamm and Dat won't mind a bit once they understand the circumstances. I can always count on Lia to help me out."

Mammi nodded in satisfaction. "Gute. Moses can show you where your room is, and I will write to your dat without delay." She winked at Moses.

Rachel saw the gesture, and her face practically exploded into a smile.

Moses winked back at Mammi as they shared a private laugh. Moses could only imagine what his mammi would write in her letter.

Chapter Eight

Lia fed the wet clothes through the wringer, being careful not to pinch her fingers in the process. She could get going so fast that if she wasn't careful, she'd end up with smashed fingers and blackish-blue fingernails. It had happened enough times to make her cautious. She worked with extra care today because she was trying to read her book and feed clothes at the same time.

The midwife book Sarah had given her sat open on the narrow counter with two cans of French-cut green beans holding the pages down so Lia could read. She wasn't being very efficient with either the reading or the laundry, but she had to steal time to read when she could. She had already finished Sarah's book twice and marked it thoroughly with penciled notes and questions in the margins.

Not that it mattered. Sarah Beachy and Moses Zimmerman lived in Bonduel, and Lia would probably be stuck in Wautoma for the rest of her life. Dat thought the book was a waste of time. Wautoma didn't need a midwife, he said. There was one only twenty minutes away in Coloma.

Rachel had been gone four days. Were the Helmuths glad to have a petite, delicate girl for their grandson instead of a ridiculously tall girl of twenty-three? Had Moses fallen in love with Rachel yet? Lia didn't expect to hear from Rachel for the rest of the summer unless she and Moses got engaged.

Ouch! She snatched back her hand before the wringer pulled her index finger in and flattened it like a pancake.

Lia didn't much like the thought of Moses as her brother-in-law. But one advantage of being stuck in Wautoma was she wouldn't have to see Rachel and Moses often. Bonduel wasn't far, but it was far enough that Lia could avoid seeing her sister most of the year. Lia's relationship with the Helmuths was lost too. Moses would be at their house too often for Lia's liking.

Finding it impossible to concentrate, Lia lifted the cans holding her pages and closed the book. She was usually such a cheerful person. Why did she stew over this?

Dat strolled into the washroom holding a torn envelope and a piece of stationery. "I have news from Bonduel."

Lia's heart fluttered irrationally. An engagement already?

She willed herself to remain calm.

Of course not. Not even Rachel could make a man lose his senses in less than a week—at least not a sensible man like Moses.

"It seems the Helmuths want you to go back to Bonduel."

Lia felt as if she could bounce around the house like a ball. She didn't even try to contain her smile. "They do?"

Dat's eyes scanned the letter. "Anna says, 'Lia is a

wonderful-gute worker and cook. She can help with the chores to give Moses and Rachel more time for courting.'"

Lia's bouncy ball crashed to the floor like a mushy potato. "Oh, I see."

Dat stroked his beard. "I suppose they still need the help, even with Rachel there."

From the beginning, Lia had known that Rachel would be of no real service to the Helmuths. Her value was measured in what she could do for their grandson. Lia wanted to know if they were scheming with or without Moses's approval.

It stung that the Helmuths had abandoned their plans for Lia and Moses and were encouraging Rachel instead. Lia couldn't blame them for their choice. Dat always said, "Youth is beauty."

Did she even want to go back?

The first time she went to Huckleberry Hill, Lia had expected to work hard, and she had never dreamed of meeting any interested boys. This time would be no different. She would work hard and not expect attention from any boy. If Sarah was obliging, Lia could still learn to be a midwife too, Lord willing.

Of course she wanted to go back.

She and Anna and Felty could take care of each other. The three of them could play Scrabble and Life on the Farm and knit pot holders while Moses and Rachel rode around Bonduel in Moses's new buggy visiting auctions and stealing kisses at sunset.

Dat folded the letter and stuffed it back in the envelope. "I can see the wisdom in sending you back. You have always been more levelheaded than your sister. Make sure that Moses sees all her best qualities, not only that she is pretty, but that she loves children and is a gute cook. And see to it that she is wise and doesn't make any marriage plans before consulting with your mother and me."

Lia nodded. Like Mamm and Dat, Rachel depended on her, but this time, Lia didn't think she could do what Dat asked. Moses was perfectly capable of falling in love with Rachel without Lia's interference. "I'll do my best, Dat."

Dat did not waste any time. The Helmuths' letter came on Saturday, and by Monday morning Lia caught her first glimpse of Huckleberry Hill in over a week. The trees were full to brimming with luxurious green leaves, and monarch butterflies floated lazily in the air everywhere she looked. Even the sky had the clear blue look of summer to it.

The gravel crunched under the tires of the car as it crept up the hill.

"Huckleberry Hill is a nice spot," said Judy, her driver. "My aunt used to live not ten miles from here."

Even though she knew they didn't want her, Lia practically leaped out of the car with her bag tucked under her arm. "Thank you for the ride, Mrs. Pendleton. Here is the money for the trip."

"Call me anytime. I come up every week to see my granny in Green Bay," Judy said.

Lia watched as she turned the car around and headed down the hill.

Rachel came bounding down the porch steps like a child skipping home from school. "I had no idea you would be here this sudden."

"Is Anna inside?" Lia asked.

"Jah, inspecting the toilets. I scrub them every day, but she is so fussy. You'll help me with those, won't you? The cleanser dries out my hands."

Lia marched into the house with Rachel close behind. Sparky waddled to the door on her stubby legs and wagged her tail. She barked a greeting and stood earnestly while Lia fondled her ears and rubbed her head. When Lia stood and Sparky realized she wouldn't get any more love, she pitter-pattered to the rug and plopped herself on her favorite corner.

After examining the floors, Lia deposited her bag on the table, hung her black bonnet on the hook, and rolled up her sleeves. "Have you mopped today?"

"Nae, not since I got here last week. The cleaner makes my fingernails peel. Anna said she could manage."

Lia pursed her lips. Anna should not mop. The motion hurt her elbows, and she could easily slip on the wet floor and break a hip. Mopping the kitchen floor was no small task. Whoever had built Helmuths' house had been generous with the room in the kitchen. The cookstove shared a wall with a long counter space while the fridge and sink and more counters stood against the adjacent wall. The round table that sat six could be expanded to fit twelve comfortably. An area rug spread over the wood floor at the other end of the room where sat Felty's overstuffed chair, Anna's rocker, and a plump blue davenport. A perfect room for playing with many grandchildren.

Lia popped the plug in the sink and turned on the water. "Sweep, would you, Rachel, and I'll mop."

She heard Anna before she saw her. "Oh, bless my soul, our Lia is back."

Lia turned to see Anna with her arms thrown wide. Lia accepted the invitation and walked into Anna's embrace. "I am so glad to see you," Anna said. She pulled Lia's shoulders downward so she could whisper in Lia's ear. "We were afraid your dat would not let you come back."

Lia's heart thawed to above freezing. Anna seemed sincerely glad to have Lia back. Even if Anna didn't think Lia was good enough for her grandson, at least she saw Lia's value as a hard worker.

"I thought I would mop first thing," Lia said. "Rachel says it hasn't been done yet."

Anna smiled in satisfaction. "I will sweep for you right quick."

Rachel failed to mention that Lia had asked her to do the job already.

Moses told Lia she was blunt. Rachel called her bossy. Lia poured some wood soap in the sink. "No need, Anna. Rachel will sweep."

Anna sprouted a crooked smile. "Rachel says she has a headache. Why don't you take your bag to your room while I sweep, and Rachel can show you the scarf I knitted for her."

Lia turned off the water and glanced at Rachel. "Jah, okay."

She picked up her bag and marched down the hall with Rachel following close behind. Her room was situated on the south side of the house with a big window looking out onto the lane that came up the hill. Lia loved the sunny room with its lemon yellow and forest green quilt. The walls were bare except for a cross-stitch hanging above the bed that read, "Sing unto the Lord a new song. Sing unto the Lord, all the earth."

Rachel's mouth dropped open in indignation. "This is your room?"

"You don't mind if we share? The bed is big enough."

Rachel narrowed her eyes. "Share? They gave me the one at the back of the house as small as a broom closet." She sank to the bed. "They hate me."

"Of course they don't hate you. They barely know you."

Rachel's eyes glistened with tears. Lia always admired how quickly Rachel could turn on the water. "Anna keeps asking me to do things like I am her maid."

Lia lifted her brows. "You are her maid."

"But does she want me to work myself to death? That dog hates me too. Why do I have to give her a bath? And I only saw Moses for a few minutes on the day I arrived, and he hasn't shown his face since."

"What did he say?"

"Not much. At first he looked very annoyed like I had done something to offend him."

"He is often annoyed. You'll get used to it."

"I think he warmed up to me because he offered to carry my bag, but Anna wouldn't let him. How can Anna expect us to court if she never invites him to come over?"

Lia pretended her bag urgently needed to be unpacked. "Do you want him to court you?"

"Oh, yes. You were right, Lia. He is so-good-look-ing. And tall. When I stand next to him I feel safe, like he is protecting me just by being so tall. We are so natu-rally suited for each other."

Lia hadn't expected anything different, but a cavern opened up in the pit of her stomach. "Show me what Anna knitted for you."

"It's an ugly old gray scarf. And I can't wear it now. It's too warm outside for a scarf." Rachel leaned back, spread herself on Lia's bed, and sighed in obvious com-fort. "Anna says Moses will come tomorrow for supper. I hope he does. I am so bored. They haven't taken me to one singeon or gathering or anything. All we do is scrub toilets and weed the garden and polish lamps."

Lia slid the empty overnight bag under her bed

and tried to sound as indifferent as possible. "Maybe you would be happier back in Wautoma."

"Nae, I am patient. Once Moses comes for dinner tomorrow, things will move fast. I wouldn't be surprised if we were engaged by the end of July."

"Three weeks?"

"Well, I'm not going to wait forever." Rachel rolled onto her stomach. "I feel like I'm sleeping on a board in that little room at the back of the house. My back is so sensitive. You don't mind trading bedrooms, do you? I'll work so much better if my spine isn't going into spasms all day long."

Lia gave Rachel a half smile and shook her head. "I'll share my bed with you."

"It won't do any good to share. I've got to be able to spread out. You know how I am."

Jah, Lia knew how Rachel was.

Dat had said to take care of Rachel. Lia would be selfish not to give up her bed.

Rachel is the pretty one. She deserves the best.

Chapter Nine

Lia ran into her new bedroom, glad for once that there was only a tiny window that faced the back of the house. She didn't know if she wanted to jump up and down with excitement or burst into despondent tears. The minute she saw Moses's buggy rolling up the lane, she had abandoned her bread dough and disappeared into her room to gather her wits.

To her dismay, she found she had missed Moses more than she wanted to. When he came into a room, it was as if someone turned on a bright electric light that banished the shadows to another county. He didn't mind her height or her scolding, and she felt like she didn't have to behave herself around him. She was overjoyed to see him.

But she knew she could not let her excitement gallop away from her. Moses was meant for Rachel. Dat, Mamm, even Anna and Felty wanted them to be together, and the sooner Lia got that notion into her head, the less the actual engagement would sting.

Lia felt a twinge of jealousy, but quickly smothered it. She should not bear ill will for Rachel. It was not Rachel's fault that everyone preferred her. Lia had reconciled herself to the fact that Rachel would always be the favored one. Lia wanted the best for her sister. How could she let her feelings for a man she barely knew come between her and Rachel?

She smoothed her apron and secured the pins in her kapp before squaring her shoulders and going back into the kitchen. By this time, Moses had un-hitched his buggy and already worked out back with Felty. She told her heart to resume its normal pace. She wouldn't see Moses until suppertime.

Anna sat in her rocker examining her cookbook.

Rachel emerged from her room, her lips shiny with Vaseline. "I'm going out to help in the garden," she said, checking the hair tucked into her kapp. She glided out the door as if Moses would be watching for her the moment she stepped outside.

Holding on to her precious cookbook, Anna stood and came to Lia. "Sure as you're born, she'll get a sun-burn on those lips."

"The dough is ready to rise," Lia said, without crack-ing a smile. "What next?"

"The book says we let it rise for an hour, then roll it out and spread the sausage and cheese over the top."

"Sounds delicious."

"Another special meal for Moses. Are you going to make a pie?"

Lia kept her eyes on the dough as she formed it into a ball. "Do you want me to?"

"Only if you do, my dear."

"I can't find any happiness in it today."

Anna reached up and took Lia's face in her hands. "You've been extra quiet since you came back from Wautoma. You are usually full of pep. Is all well at home?"

"Oh, jah, certainly. My dat bought a new cow."

"I hope he got a good milker."

"It's a Jersey."

"And how is the expectant mother?"

"My sister-in-law is doing well. Two months to go and no swelling yet."

Anna studied Lia's face as if expecting her to say more, but Lia simply turned away to rinse her hands in the sink. Anna would be unhappy if she knew Lia had read the contents of the letter meant for Dat.

Lia took a plastic spatula from the drawer and scraped the globs of sticky dough off the counter. "Has Felty found any new states?"

A movement out the window caught her eye. Lia looked up to see Moses hurrying toward the house with Rachel in his arms. Rachel's hands were locked securely around his neck, and she rested her head against his chest. They looked quite the romantic pair.

"Anna, look." Lia dropped her spatula and raced to open the door.

Moses maneuvered through the doorway, strode across the kitchen, and deposited Rachel on the cushy sofa. Lia's rebellious heart galloped away from her, and she couldn't help remembering the feel of his lips on hers.

"What happened?" said Anna.

Rachel fell back into the sofa, wrinkled her nose, and grimaced in pain. "I was weeding cucumbers. My grip slipped, and I banged my toe with the hoe."

She sounded excessively breathless, considering Moses had done all the work getting her to the house.

"Take off my shoe, Lia. I'm certain I'll lose a nail. I don't know how I would have made it back to the house if Moses hadn't been there. He saved me."

Lia glanced at Moses to see how he would soak up such generous praise. She had to stifle a laugh when she saw that familiar look of annoyance on his face. It seemed the Shetler girls were destined to irritate Moses Zimmerman instead of charm him. Though she wasn't sure why, that thought gave Lia a great deal of comfort. Perhaps Moses didn't think any worse of her than he did of Rachel.

Moses caught her staring and twitched his mouth downward before turning his attention to Rachel. "You're in good hands. I'll get back to weeding tomatoes."

As he shut the front door, Lia noticed his hat where he must have deposited it on the kitchen table. She picked it up and followed him outside. "You forgot your hat."

Still behaving as if he had a burr under his saddle, he reached out and practically snatched it from her hand. "Denki."

In spite of the fact that his presence made her legs feel all shaky, she wouldn't let him get away with such behavior. "You are annoyed again, Moses Zimmerman."

Halting mid-stride, he raised an eyebrow and quit frowning. "Do you always say what you think?"

"What I think about you? Hardly ever."

He tapped his hat against his thigh. "You haven't asked for an apology yet, but I should probably give you one. I am very sorry for kissing you."

Lia ignored the thump that was her heart dropping to her toes. "You are?"

"Did I embarrass you?"

"Nae."

"I'm sure it took you by surprise. I surprised myself. Whatever the reason, it was inappropriate. I don't want to give either you or your sister the wrong impression about my feelings."

"You don't want Rachel to think you are interested in me."

"Jah."

"Because you would rather kiss Rachel."

He looked up at the sky and pressed his lips into a hard line. "Oh, jah, that is the reason," he said, clearly irritated beyond endurance.

He turned away, leaving Lia to puzzle over his reaction. He couldn't be teasing her. His irritation was plain enough. Was he irritated that she would ask what was obvious to everyone else? Or annoyed that she pried into his private business?

Was he poking fun at her? Maybe he didn't want to kiss either one of them. Nae, if he felt that way, he would have told her. They were unfailingly blunt with one another.

Lia's head began to throb. She was tempted to tell Anna she didn't feel well and go lie down on her bed. But then Anna would have to tend to Rachel all by herself. Lia hadn't the time to nurse a trifling headache. Or a heavy heart.

Rachel reclined on the davenport with her gray scarf wrapped around her foot. Though she insisted her entire foot would be black-and-blue by tomorrow morning, Lia hadn't been able to see so much as a pink mark or a swollen toe. Anna had wrapped Rachel's foot in a bandage and then they had padded the injured foot with Rachel's scarf.

When Moses and Felty tromped in for supper, Rachel sank deeper into the sofa and gave a little sigh of pain.

Poor Rachel never had a high tolerance for discomfort.

Lia smiled to herself as Felty sang his pre-supper

melody. *"On the mountain is a railroad, the conductor is our friend, He will make the run successful, till our train reaches the end."*

Rachel pushed herself up to a sitting position. "Felty, I've told you every day for four days. That's the wrong words. I already sang the right words to you twice."

Felty's eyes twinkled, and he disregarded Rachel's criticism with a wave of his arm. Moses, on the other hand, furrowed his brow and stared at Rachel for several seconds. He didn't seem very happy with the girl he wanted to kiss.

Lia set a pitcher of milk on the table. "Felty is a poet. I can't believe how many new rhymes he comes up with."

Anna pulled her golden brown creation out of the cookstove. Melty, gooey cheese crackled and bubbled from the seams of the bread as Anna held it out for her husband to inspect.

Felty bent over the baking sheet and took a whiff. "Annie, that smells delicious. There ain't no better cook. I don't think even Lia can match you."

Lia grinned. "Never. Anna is a wonderful cook."

Anna blushed like a schoolgirl. "Now, Felty."

Lia took the baking sheet from Anna and cut the sausage-cheese bread into slices. She arranged the savory pinwheels on a platter and put the platter on the table. Moses plopped himself in a chair and smiled as if he'd never told her he didn't like kissing her. She didn't want it to, but her heart did its usual flip-flops. She could almost pretend she'd never been away—except now she knew what they really thought of her.

In her distracted state, Lia forgot Rachel sat by herself on the sofa.

"Would you like me to bring you a plate of food?" Anna asked.

Rachel sat up eagerly. "Oh, I would much rather eat at the table if Moses wouldn't mind carrying me over there. I don't think I can manage to walk anywhere just yet."

Moses seemed unimpressed. He probably didn't want to appear too eager in case Rachel rejected him in the end. "Jah, of course."

He went to the sofa and bent over so Rachel could get her arms all the way around his neck and then lifted her with ease and carried her to the table.

Rachel pointed to the chair next to Moses where Lia sat. "Can I take that chair, Lia? It is closer to the cookstove and I am feeling a slight chill."

In July?

Lia jumped up and ignored the pile of stones pressing down on her chest. If Moses would rather sit next to Rachel, Lia had been selfish to sit there in the first place.

"No need to move. My seat is closer to the stove," Anna said, with an affected sweetness that surprised Lia. Why was Anna bent out of shape?

Moses stood with Rachel in his arms as if it were no trouble to hold her there for another three hours.

"Your seat is too close to the stove. I will be too hot," Rachel said.

Moses stared at Lia before shrugging his shoulders and depositing Rachel in Lia's place.

Lia rubbed a spot on her forehead above her eyebrow. If she couldn't snap out of her dull mood, she might as well go back to Wautoma. She stopped massaging her forehead, shook her head, and decided to laugh at herself for being so touchy and at Rachel for the way she could maneuver any situation to her advantage. "Perhaps we should make a seating chart next time," Lia said.

Moses chuckled. "Jah, it's like rearranging furniture. Let's decide where to put everybody so I don't have to keep moving Rachel."

Rachel spread her napkin on her lap. "I don't mind."

After silent grace, Anna served everyone a piece of her sausage bread.

"This is a clever meal," said Felty. "The bread and meat and cheese rolled into one."

Lia's first bite was the perfect blend of crusty bread, sausage, and swiss cheese. And not spicy, thank goodness. This meal she would be able to eat without Moses's assistance. But her second bite molded to her teeth like putty, and she found herself chewing a mouthful of nearly raw bread dough. The crust of the loaf was a beautiful wheat-brown, but the bread on the inside hadn't baked properly.

She poured herself a glass of apple juice and forced the thick dough down her throat. She glanced at Moses, who concentrated very hard on chewing and swallowing. Felty, as usual, ate as if this meal were the finest of his life.

Lia caught Moses's eye, and he flashed that boyish grin. "Has anyone heard any more jokes about Delaware?"

Lia stifled a laugh by covering her mouth with her hand.

Moses noticed the gesture and said, "I think Lia knows a funny joke."

Before Lia could come up with a reply, Rachel grimaced. "Is anybody else's bread doughy?" She put down her fork and huffed to indicate that she was put out. "I can't eat it. It's raw in the center."

Lia's mirth evaporated. She glanced at Anna in

concern. All her worst fears were realized. The distress was evident on Anna's face, and her voice shook when she spoke. "Oh dear. I must have read the recipe wrong. I wanted it to be so special."

Moses stopped eating and stared pointedly at Rachel, as if willing her to repair the damage she had done. Lia's mind raced for something to smooth things over with Anna.

Felty patted Anna's hand. "Nae, Annie Banannie, it is delicious. I never tasted better."

Lia tried to find Rachel a way out of the corner she'd painted herself into. "Rachel, I think you've mistaken the melted cheese for bread dough. They both have the same consistency."

"No, I haven't. This bread is raw."

"Well, don't eat it," Anna said, blinking rapidly to keep the tears from pooling in her eyes. She stood and picked up the platter of pinwheels. "Don't anybody eat it. I will whip up a batch of pancakes." She smiled weakly. "That's why we try new recipes, to see which ones are good and which ones aren't."

Moses cleared his throat, took the platter from Mammi, and laid it back on the table. "There is no reason to make pancakes when this food is so tasty, Mammi. Lia and Dawdi and I love it. But remember what Lia told us about Rachel? She is delicate." Moses reached over and brushed the back of his index finger along Rachel's cheek.

Lia tried not to flinch as Rachel seemed to melt like butter. She half closed her eyes and leaned a few inches closer to Moses.

Moses pulled his hand away from her face. "Some people are extra sensitive to food textures. Rachel probably has very ticklish taste buds."

Rachel gazed at Moses as if he were the only person

in the room. "I do. When I was little I would gag if Mamm made me eat broccoli."

Anna nodded doubtfully at Moses and sat down. She scooted in her chair and picked up her napkin. "I am glad to know that most of you like it. Lia worked hard rolling out the dough."

The exchange between Moses and Rachel struck Lia mute. In another week, they'd be professing their undying love for one another.

She ate the rest of her mushy bread in silence while Felty and Moses talked about Moses's newfangled buggy and disagreed about getting a telephone shack installed at the top of the lane.

Felty was adamant that he didn't need one. "What would I do with a telephone? Listen to it ring all day long and try to talk salesmen out of selling me things?"

"I worry about you two up here all by yourselves," Moses said. "The bishop would approve a phone for emergencies. What if one of you fell? You'd have to crawl all the way to a hospital."

Anna patted Lia's hand. "We have Lia. She takes good care of us. Don't you, Lia?"

Lia still couldn't speak. She glanced at Moses and nodded.

Anna studied Lia's face and furrowed her brow. "We can't get along without our Lia."

Moses sprouted a crooked grin. "Maybe we'll have to convince Lia to stay year-round to take the place of a telephone."

"Jah," Anna said. "We want Lia to stay forever."

Rachel bit her bottom lip and looked up coyly at Moses. "What about me?"

"Friends of Lia's are always welcome here," Felty said.

Lia chastised herself for being so irritable. She gave

Anna a good imitation of a cheerful expression and rose to clear the plates.

Moses gathered forks and knives and cups and joined her at the sink. "What? No pie tonight?"

"I got busy doctoring Rachel's foot."

"You did a gute job. Did you knit that wrapping around her foot while she sat there? It seems to fit perfectly."

Lia cracked a smile. "I'm not as fast as Anna."

Moses put the plug in the sink and turned on the water. "Who is?"

Lia buried her hands in the water, but Moses nudged her aside. "My turn to wash."

"I can wash."

"Why should you get all the fun? My skin gets all wrinkly like old-man hands."

A laugh tripped from Lia's lips. She found it difficult to be gloomy when Moses was near.

Rachel remained on her perch at the table while Felty, Anna, Lia, and Moses did up the dishes. Felty dried while leading them in a chorus of "In the Sweet By-and-By." It seemed the only times Felty didn't sing were when he slept and when he ate. And as he had a fondness for making up his own words, Lia, Anna, and Moses followed along as best they could.

Lia forgot all her unhappiness when Moses tried to harmonize with Felty. He sang perfectly awful off-key notes at the top of his lungs. Sparky howled along and kept time with her tail.

Rachel kindly lifted her feet when Lia swept under her chair, and Moses held the dustpan for her dirt.

"I'm trying to improve my sweeping skills," she said as she swept up the last of the crumbs. "I have discovered there are men who don't want to marry me because I am not a gute sweeper."

"That's silly," Rachel said. "Nobody cares how you sweep. It's because you're too tall."

A cloud passed over Moses's face before he grinned mischievously and said, "You think I'm too tall?" He clutched his chest. "I'm crushed."

Rachel giggled at Moses's dramatics. "I'm talking about Lia, not you."

"Lia thinks I'm too tall?" Moses put his hand to his throat and made a choking sound. "I'm devastated."

Rachel knew he was teasing, but she must have wanted to make herself perfectly clear. "No, Moses. Lia is too tall for the boys."

Moses draped an arm around Lia's shoulder. A thrill traveled up Lia's spine even as she tried to think of him as a brother—or more likely—a brother-in-law. "I love tall girls. Two women at the auction told Lia she should be a model for a magazine."

Lia tried hard not to let his praise wheedle its way into her emotions. He didn't mean anything by it.

Rachel acted bored with the conversation. "Who cares what the Englisch like? I'm glad I'm not tall." She pushed her chair out from under the table with her good foot. "Moses, will you carry me back to the sofa?"

"Jah, I will." Moses handed the full dustpan to Lia, picked up Rachel, and hastily deposited her on the sofa. "I must go, Mammi."

Mammi finished wiping the table. "So soon? Don't you have time for a game of Scrabble?"

"Nae, but I will return Thursday. Lia and I still need to stack those limbs. We could have a bonfire."

Rachel fluffed the pillow on the sofa. "If my toe is better, we can roast marshmallows."

Moses grinned sideways at Lia. "Are you planning on holding your stick with your foot?"

Lia rewarded his teasing with a smile.

"Oh, I almost forgot," Moses said. "I have something for you in my buggy."

Rachel beamed. "For me?"

"For Lia."

Rachel's face fell to the cellar.

Lia felt a twinge of guilt for not having more sympathy for her sister. "I'll walk out with you to fetch it."

Moses kissed his mammi and hugged Felty and retrieved his hat from the hook. "I'll hitch up the buggy," he said before nodding to Lia and closing the door behind him.

Rachel frowned. "Help me up, Lia. If you let me lean on you, I can walk out too."

Lia hung the broom in the closet. "I'll just be a minute."

"I've been sitting on this sofa all afternoon. I want to say good-bye to Moses and get some fresh air. We'll make it out there in plenty of time before he has the buggy hitched."

Reluctantly, Lia helped Rachel from the sofa and put her arm around Rachel's waist. Rachel hooked her hand around Lia's shoulder and leaned on her for support.

Rachel winced as she put weight on her injured foot. "Lia, you've got to hold me up better than that."

"Why don't you stay put?" Lia said. "I'll be out and back before you even get comfortable on the couch."

Rachel took a tentative step with her good leg. "I want to go out."

They stumbled a few steps together before Rachel scowled and let go of Lia completely. "We're wasting time." She glanced out the window, sighed in annoyance, and hopped deftly across the kitchen. After opening the door, she turned to Lia and pursed her lips. "Well, come on. I need your help across the yard."

Lia wanted to point out that Rachel seemed to be doing a much better job of getting around on her own. Instead, she wrapped her arm around Rachel's waist, and they shambled to the porch together.

Moses caught sight of them while guiding the horse between the buggy shafts, and Lia wasn't surprised by the look of irritation that flashed across his face. Determined that they would not delay him further, Lia released Rachel and jogged to Moses's buggy.

"Lia, stop. Come back and help me."

Lia tried to ignore the protests behind her. If Rachel wanted to be near Moses, she would have to find a way to him all by herself.

As Lia got close, Moses's annoyance seemed to evaporate, and he reached into the buggy and pulled out a thick purple book. "Sarah wanted me to bring this to you."

Midwifery, volume two. Lia's heart swelled with gratitude. Sarah had not forgotten her. "Oh, denki, Moses. I have finished the first one. I'll get it so you can take it back to Sarah."

Cradling the heavy book in her arms like a baby, Lia ran past Rachel and ignored the sour look her sister gave her. The first book sat on her bed, available for easy reference at any hour of the day. Lia thumbed through its pages, doing her best to hold a picture of each lesson in her memory. She didn't want to forget a bit of the precious information. The margins were filled with plentiful notes, and several makeshift bookmarks made from scraps of newspaper poked out of the top of the book. Those held places with especially important information. Should she pull them out? No. Perhaps Sarah would let her borrow it back sometime.

She came into the kitchen and saw Anna and Felty gazing out the window. Felty wore a crooked grin and Anna's puckered lips hinted at a smile. Lia scooted next to them to see why they were so amused.

Rachel hopped daintily toward Moses, all the while calling out to him and trying to engage him in conversation. Lia couldn't hear what Rachel said, but she kept up a steady stream of words as she hopped ever closer. Moses didn't seem to notice her or rather was too busy fiddling with a strap and buckle to pay her any mind.

When Rachel got close enough, Moses turned slowly to look at her. The shadow hovering over his face gave way to a kindly smile.

"She's determined," Felty said.

Anna turned from the window and patted Felty on the arm. "Now, Felty."

Should she give Moses and Rachel some time alone together before racing outside with her book? The stones piled on her chest again, and she recognized that unreasonable sadness she felt every time she thought of Moses.

Lia pressed her lips together and stepped outside. If Moses wanted time with Rachel, he would have to finagle a way to get it. Lia would not be his faithful assistant, even if Dat wanted her to.

"Here's Sarah's book," Lia said, striding across the yard. "Thank her for me."

"Why do you need a book like that?" Rachel asked.

Moses eyed Lia and turned the book over in his hand. "You've read this a few times."

"Should I buy Sarah a new one? She told me to make notes."

"I think Sarah will be impressed that you studied so hard."

Rachel reached out and held on to Lia's arm to steady herself. "I'd die of boredom if I had to read a book that long."

Moses kept his eyes on Lia and laid the book on the seat of his buggy. "Lia is smart. I don't think learning something new would ever bore her."

Lia's heart jumped about for a few seconds while Moses checked the straps one more time. "I will see you on Thursday."

Rachel put a small amount of weight on her injured foot. "Before you go, will you carry me back to the house? Lia isn't strong enough."

Moses climbed into his buggy. "You seem to be able to get around on your own quite well." Without another word, he slid his door shut and coaxed the horse forward.

Lia knew she shouldn't, but she wanted to laugh at Rachel's dumbfounded expression. No man had ever withstood Rachel's charms before.

Lia couldn't fathom why Moses would pass up an opportunity to be close to Rachel. Maybe he thought his resistance would make him more desirable, but Moses didn't seem the type to play such games. Lia didn't take her eyes off Moses until his buggy disappeared down the hill. What went on in that man's head was a mystery.

"Cum, Rachel. I will help you back."

Rachel rolled her eyes and huffed out a big breath of air. "Don't bother, Lia. You are no help at all."

She bent over, unrolled the scarf wrapped around her foot, and tossed it at Lia. After pausing to cautiously wiggle her toes, she marched back to the house with a barely discernible limp.

Chapter Ten

Moses groaned inwardly. Rachel must have seen him coming. She swung the door open with such force it fanned up a breeze. Stepping forward, she gifted him with a coy smile that must send the boys in Wautoma over the moon. It only served to irritate Moses. He didn't like it when girls thought they could manipulate him.

"Moses, we didn't expect you until tomorrow. You just can't stay away, can you?"

"Actually, I've come for Lia," he said.

Rachel pressed her rosebud lips into a rigid line and glanced over Moses's shoulder as if hoping someone more accommodating waited for her in line behind him.

Moses tried not to take satisfaction in her reaction. He didn't want to be spiteful, but one afternoon spent in Rachel's company was quite enough. He had forced himself to be nice because it wasn't in his nature to be rude and because Rachel was Lia's sister. He would never want to injure Lia by doing anything to embarrass Rachel. When Rachel had insulted Mammi's cooking, he remembered his manners and tried to find a way to spare Mammi's feelings without embarrassing Rachel. For Lia's sake.

How did Lia put up with such a sister?

Folding her arms, Rachel stood in the doorway silently conveying the message that if Moses wanted someone else in the house besides her, he'd have to do his own work.

Luckily, Mammi saved him from Rachel's withering stare. Mammi came into the kitchen and saw Moses standing on the porch. "Moses. What a nice surprise. Come in, come in."

She took his hand and pulled him past Rachel. "Would you like a piece of pie? Lia made it for supper, but I sometimes eat pie right after breakfast. It looks delicious. We still have apples in the cellar."

"I came to fetch Lia," Moses said. "Is she here?"

Mammi's eyes twinkled like sunlight on the water. "Jah, scrubbing the toilet. I will go see about her." She tripped lightly down the hall with Sparky following close behind.

Moses glanced at Rachel, who still regarded him with an air of displeasure. "I see your foot has made a speedy recovery."

She slightly shifted her weight off yesterday's injured foot. "It hurts something terrible, but Anna really needs my help, so I am enduring through the pain."

"Denki for helping my mammi. She is slowing down a bit."

Rachel softened her posture and tilted her head to one side. "Anything for Anna. She is a dear. You are blessed to have such a wonderful grandmother."

With Mammi following, Lia appeared wearing bright yellow plastic gloves and holding a spray bottle of window cleaner. Her face was flushed, and her eyes briefly darted from Rachel to Moses. "I thought we were stacking limbs tomorrow."

Must he be in a constant state of annoyance whenever he came within ten feet of one of the Shetler girls? He was annoyed with Rachel because he didn't like her and she wanted him for a husband. He was annoyed with Lia because she was too beautiful and the perfect height and she spoke her mind. And the most annoying thing was that he enjoyed the sensation of his heart flopping around in his chest whenever he saw her. If he had more self-control, he wouldn't be so irritated.

"Sarah is delivering a baby. She called my factory and asked me to bring you over. If you want to."

Lia's face bloomed into a dazzling smile—the one that always took Moses's breath from him. "Oh, yes. Thank you so much." She lifted her spray bottle. "Do you think I have time to finish the bathroom?"

"Now, Lia," Mammi said in her kindly, scolding tone, "Rachel will manage fine."

Rachel regained her good humor. "I think I will go too. I have never seen a baby be born."

It took everything in Moses's power to be nice. "I'm sure Lia would enjoy having you there, but Sarah is very particular. No one is allowed but who she allows. They'll make out better if you stay to home."

Rachel stuck out her bottom lip. She must have believed that this somehow made her irresistible. "They need lots of help when a baby comes into the world. Sarah will be happy for an extra pair of hands."

Moses felt his face get hot. For Lia's sake, he didn't want to hurt Rachel's feelings, but her coming was out of the question.

Lia snapped the gloves off her hands. Her soft, indulgent tone surprised Moses. "You were not invited,

Rachel. You will only be in the way and what you see could make you very upset." Lia rubbed her hand up and down Rachel's arm. "I'm sorry. You can't come."

Tears pooled in Rachel's eyes. "And what am I supposed to do, clean toilets all day? How can you feel good about leaving me to do all the work?"

One corner of Mammi's mouth curled upward. "I think it would be wonderful gute to let Rachel tag along. You can all get to know each other better."

Rachel squealed in elation and threw her arms around Mammi. "You see? Anna wants me to go."

Moses fully expected Lia to protest. Instead, her creamy cheeks lost all their color, and she stared at Mammi with an undecipherable look in her eyes. "I'll finish the bathroom tonight if I don't get home too late." She turned and plodded down the hall as if her best friend had abandoned her.

Moses shook his head. "Mammi, I don't think—"

"Now, Moses, take her with you." Mammi didn't seem concerned at all. "It will be a very educational trip."

Rachel had not stopped talking since she climbed daintily into Moses's buggy. "And I told him plain-as-day, I won't marry you, John Petersheim. Just because I let him drive me home from gatherings did not mean I wanted to mar-ry-him. Dat said I could do better. Much better."

Moses didn't even make an effort to listen to the steady stream of words coming from Rachel's mouth. He hadn't wanted her along in the first place. He shouldn't have to pay her any attention.

Lia sat like a statue in the backseat of the buggy clutching Sarah's book to her chest like a security blanket. Moses glanced at her periodically, but she kept her posture stiff and fixed her eyes on the road ahead as if she were trying to be invisible.

"The boys who ask me to marry them do such a shoddy job of it. Clemens asked me on the day of my aunt's fun-er-al. Paul got down on one knee and sang me a song he wrote himself. He didn't have the voice for it."

Moses jiggled the reins to pick up the horse's pace. He couldn't stand much more of this chatter. Right now, he wished he were Paul or Clemens, whoever they were, blessedly living their lives free of Rachel Shetler.

The directions Sarah had given Moses took them four miles out of Bonduel where they turned onto a dirt road marked by a red piece of yarn tied to a weathered fence post. The road skirted an orchard that turned into a forest of pines on a seldom-traveled path to a cabin made of rough-hewn logs with a tin roof.

Moses secured the reins and turned to look at Lia. For the first time since she got into the buggy, Moses saw an honest emotion, as excitement intermingled with anxiety on her face. She gazed at the book in her hands as if seeing it for the first time. "I shouldn't have brought this. Can I leave it here?"

Moses nodded and offered his hand to help her from the buggy. She waved it away. "You'll want to help Rachel, no doubt."

He would? Lia was always so mindful of her sister, but Moses couldn't muster that level of consideration.

As Moses expected, Rachel sat in her seat as if frozen in place until Moses came around to her side and gave her his hand.

"Oh, thank you. My foot still aches something awful."

Filtered light peeked from between the trees and

danced along the walls of the cabin. A rusty plow grown over with weeds rested against the rough-hewn log walls, and an unruly bush with tiny yellow flowers grew next to the door with branches stretching several feet in every direction along the ground. A hundred feet behind the cabin stood an outhouse with deep green ivy spreading its tentacles up one side.

Lia trudged to the cabin, hesitated while Moses and Rachel caught up to her, and knocked softly.

A loud creak greeted them as Sarah opened the door. She looked Lia up and down as if deciding if she were healthy enough to enter. "Good, you're here. Moses, you can come back to fetch her at noon."

Rachel stepped forward. Lia's face turned pale, and she lowered her eyes. Moses wondered if she might be sick.

"I'm here to help," Rachel said.

Sarah knitted her brows together and glanced at Moses. "Who are you?"

"I'm Lia's sister Rachel. I want to help deliver the baby too."

"Do you know anything about birthing babies?"

"Jah, a bit."

Moses could have sworn Lia held her breath.

Sarah narrowed her eyes and frowned unapologetically. "Why did you bring this girl, Moses?"

"Mammi wanted her to come."

Sarah's hard expression gave way to puzzlement before her frown deepened, and she shook her head vigorously. "I don't know you and Mattie don't know you, and you are not setting foot in this house."

Moses smiled to himself. Rachel wouldn't be able to walk all over Sarah like she had Mammi.

Rachel pursed her lips and batted her lashes. "Anna said I should—"

"I will speak with my mammi another day, but you are absolutely not allowed in here." Sarah took Lia by the shoulders and guided her into the cabin.

Moses heard Lia breathe a pent-up sigh as she relaxed and went eagerly in.

Rachel balled her hands into fists and stomped her foot. "Lia is my sister. I should be able to come in if I want."

Sarah propped her hand on her hip and eyed Rachel. "I'm sorry you came all the way out here." She shut the door more quickly than Moses could say "oy anyhow."

Rachel stomped her foot again and crushed one of the dainty yellow flowers at her feet. Growling, she turned on her heels and marched to the buggy, showing no signs of her critical injury of the day before. She deftly pounced into the buggy and sat with her arms folded tightly across her chest glaring at the front door of the cabin.

Moses chuckled quietly. He adored his cousin Sarah.

He hauled himself into the buggy, took up the reins, and prodded the horse forward. The trip back to Huckleberry Hill would be more pleasant, only because he would be getting rid of Rachel at the end of it.

Rachel still held her arms clamped around her waist as she turned up her pretty little nose. "Can you believe how she treated me? I can guess she sleeps through church services instead of learning how to do unto others as she would have done unto her."

Moses didn't feel a bit sorry for her. "Lia warned you."

"What does Lia know? She didn't want me to come, that's all. Did you see how smug she looked when Sarah slammed the door in my face? Dat is going to give Lia what for. She is supposed to watch out for me."

"She was watching out for you. She knew if you came that you'd be embarrassed when Sarah said no."

"Whose side are you on? Do I look like I'm embarrassed? I'm not embarrassed. I'm irritated."

Moses knew there was no point arguing with her, but if she made it out to her father to be worse than it was, he might not let Lia stay for the rest of the summer. Could he think of anything to say to appease her?

"I would have worried if you had stayed. You are so delicate, I'm afraid of how the experience might have frightened you." A more apt description for Rachel would be touchy or high-strung or downright cranky, but Moses wasn't going to say that.

Rachel studied Moses's face, and he could tell she was deciding how to react.

He smiled sympathetically.

She cracked a weak grin that soon bloomed into a full-fledged smile. "Thank you for caring about my well-being."

Moses hadn't forgotten that Rachel expected to marry him, and he hadn't had the chance to set her straight. But he could have that conversation with her another time. Right now, she must be placated so Lia wouldn't feel the brunt of her father's disapproval.

Rachel relaxed her back against the seat and seemed to notice her surroundings for the first time. "The woods are pretty. This would be a fine place for a picnic."

"Jah, and I saw a little stream flowing near the path where we came in."

Rachel took in her breath sharply. "I know why Anna wanted me to come with you. She didn't mean for me to help with the baby at all." Rachel smiled as if she knew a terrific secret.

Moses's heart sank. He knew precisely what she

thought the secret was, and he wouldn't spend a minute more with Rachel than he had to. Mammi made it plain that she wanted Moses to marry Lia, not Rachel. She wouldn't think of suggesting that Rachel come along so they could spend time together. Would she? Had Mammi changed her mind about which Shetler girl she wanted Moses to marry?

Well, if he married any Shetler girl, it would not be Rachel.

Any man would be a fool not to choose Lia, with her eyes as rich as melted chocolate and a certain curve of her lips that took his breath away. Moses rubbed his thumb and index finger together as he thought of caressing Lia's silky cheek.

He tightened his fingers around the reins and sat up straight.

Barbara, not Lia, was the girl he wanted.

"What should we do while we wait for Lia?" Rachel said.

"I'll take you back to Huckleberry Hill."

Rachel leaned toward Moses. "Oh, Anna doesn't expect either of us back for hours."

Moses ground his teeth together in an effort to keep from growling like a bear. He was taking her straight home, no debate. "I really need to get back to the factory."

"The factory? I would love to see your factory. Is it far from here?"

"Pretty far."

Rachel clapped her hands. "You must take me. I want to see how you make cheese."

Moses reluctantly considered her request. He and Adam had started a batch of cheese that morning. It would be about time to separate the curds. They could always use another pair of hands. Studying Rachel out of the corner of his eye, he had a feeling she'd be useless, but maybe she would decide cheese wasn't all that exciting and make up her mind that she didn't want to marry him after all.

"We could separate curds."

"Is it hard?"

"My ten-year-old cousin can do it."

Rachel playfully twirled an errant lock of hair with her finger. "I want to know everything about you, and if I can be of service to you by learning to make cheese, then I would be so happy."

They arrived just in time. Moses's cousin, Adam, met them at the back door. "Good thing you come when you did, Moses. Lonnie went home sick, and we only just transferred the curds to the curd sink."

Moses led Rachel to the small hand-washing station where they both scrubbed their hands thoroughly.

Adam, his wife Rose, and Moses's cousin, Alfy, stood at the curd sink up to their elbows in curds and whey. All three eyed Rachel curiously, and Alfy couldn't seem to take his eyes off her. Alfy, at eighteen, was the right age to be taken in by a pretty face.

They stirred and sifted the curds around and around, making certain that the fresh curds didn't form into clumps and breaking up the curds that wanted to stick together. It took a good deal of arm strength, and Moses always felt as if he'd run a mile or two by the time all the curds were pressed into molds.

"Am I supposed to stick my hands in?" Rachel asked. "Without gloves?"

Adam motioned to the shelf. "In that box, if you want."

Rachel went to the shelf and glanced doubtfully at Moses before pulling every glove out of the box on the top shelf.

"They're all the same size," Moses said.

"Smaller sizes on the next shelf down," Adam added.

"Oh, I didn't see those." Rachel stuffed the gloves back into the box as best she could. Three or four gloves fell onto the floor.

She took five minutes trying on three different sizes of gloves before finding the perfect fit. After being properly equipped, she sidled next to Moses and eyed him doubtfully. "Should I put my hands in now?"

"Jah, move the curds around like this so they don't clump."

Rachel stuck her hands in an inch from the top of her gloves.

Moses plunged his hands and arms into the mix to show her how to do it. "You have to go deeper or you won't get enough leverage to move the curds around."

Rachel disregarded his advice and basically smoothed over the top of the curds like she was frosting a cake. Moses didn't try to correct her again. He hadn't planned on her being much help anyway.

Adam watched Rachel's feeble attempts and raised an eyebrow to Moses before lowering his head and attending to his work.

After barely a minute, Rachel wiped her brow with her forearm. "My muscles feel like they are burning. How long does this take?"

"A few minutes. We have to mix in the salt and let the whey drain out before we put it into the hoops."

After what must have been three grueling minutes, Rachel began breathing heavily. She rested one hand on the edge of the sink while working the other hand more and more slowly through the curds. "No wonder you have such big muscles, Moses. This is heavy work."

Finally, with a sigh, she rested both elbows on the edge of the sink. "My arms are shaking. I can't move them far enough to do it anymore."

Moses pointed to a chair in the corner. "You can sit over there if you want."

She smiled weakly and snapped her gloves off with haste. "I'm sorry I can't help you finish, but you know how delicate I am." She ambled to the chair, limping slightly. Moses gritted his teeth. Yesterday's injury must be flaring up.

He forced his mind back to his work. It wasn't Christian to think harshly of Rachel. As Lia's sister, she deserved his kindness, not his judgment. But right or not, he sincerely dreaded having to drive her home.

Rachel perched expectantly on her chair looking out the window until the cheese sat in the molds and Moses felt comfortable leaving Adam and Alfy to press.

Moses rinsed his hands in the sink and got Rachel's attention. "Cum. I will take you back to Mammi's."

Rachel walked toward him, smoothing her hand along the stainless steel sink as she came. "Will you show me the rest of your factory? We haven't spent near enough time together."

Nope. He'd put up with enough for one day. "Another time. I have to get Lia at noon."

Wrong thing to say. "I'll go with you. I'll have to clean the toilet if I go back to Huckleberry Hill."

Moses knew he would have to put his foot down or Rachel might arrange things so he'd be stuck with her the rest of the day. She was clever that way.

"What a nice surprise for Lia if the toilet was clean when she came home. I know how kindhearted you are to your sister."

Rachel bit her bottom lip, and Moses could see the

wheels turning in her head. "Thank you for noticing. I would never sing my own praises."

What a blessing that Huckleberry Hill was only fifteen minutes from the cheese factory! By the time he turned the buggy up the hill, Moses swore he would never let Mammi talk him into such an outing again. Rachel loved to hear the sound of her own voice, and she seemed intent on listing every one of her good qualities in case they weren't evident to Moses. He didn't want to hear it anymore.

When the buggy finally crested the hill and the house came in sight, Moses didn't unhitch the horse. Jumping out of the buggy, he motioned for Rachel to slide out. Her hands lingered on his arms as he helped her down. They walked to the porch with Rachel nearly glued to his side.

Moses stood on the welcome mat that Mammi had knitted out of double-thickness yarn. "Rachel, I must tell you something."

Rachel's eyes sparkled in anticipation as she stepped close enough to be kissed. She lifted her face to his and smiled shyly.

He took a giant step backward and found himself up against the door. "I've already told Lia. I am not looking to marry."

To his surprise, Rachel widened her smile and took a step closer. He was trapped between her and the front door. Luckily, she wouldn't be able to kiss him unless he bent over. He squared his shoulders so he stood taller.

"I know what you told Lia," Rachel said. "We can let her go on believing whatever you want her to believe, but there is no point sparing her feelings. She's already accepted the fact that she won't marry."

Moses tried not to let his eyes pop out of his head

in surprise. "You misunderstand me. I am not ready to get married—"

"I'll be patient." She clasped her hands together behind her back. "But remember, I'll only be here until September, and there is plenty of competition back home. You will want to make your intentions known sooner than later. And Lia won't mind at all. Dat gave her specific instructions about her responsibilities while we are here on Huckleberry Hill."

Moses slid to his left, scooted away from the door, and put some space between them. He didn't want to be rude, or he would have come right out and told her that the thought of marrying her sent him into a full panic. "Rachel, I do not want to marry you."

Surprise flashed in her eyes only to be replaced by amusement. "You can keep me guessing if you want. I do that with boys all the time." She got on her tiptoes as if trying to be as close as possible to him. "But don't make me wait too long, or I might get bored and refuse to have you."

"I don't want to marry you."

Rachel grinned, raised her eyebrows, and slipped into the house before Moses could say another word. He stood looking stupidly at the door. And Lia thought *he* was arrogant?

Lia followed Sarah into the small cabin. The knobbly wooden floor creaked under her feet. To her right, a water pump stuck right up through the floor and drained into a white plastic basin that served as a sink. Shelves against the wall were lined with cans and bottles of every kind of food. A cookstove stood in the corner with a pot of water bubbling on top.

A double bed covered with a gray blanket stood at

the other end of the room. The girl in the bed, with her lips pressed together in pain, looked younger than Rachel. Another woman, probably the girl's mother, pressed her fists into the girl's back as the girl panted feverishly.

Sarah held Lia's gaze for a second before grabbing her arm and pulling her forward. "This is Lia. She has come to help with the baby."

Expressionless, the mother eyed Lia while keeping up her pressure on the girl's back.

Sarah gave Lia another pointed look. Lia knew without having to be told that she must appear completely comfortable and confident in front of these women. Any hesitation or uncertainty she showed would make both mother and daughter uneasy.

The girl's face slowly relaxed and her mother stopped massaging her back. "They are closer together now," the mother said.

Sarah pointed to the girl in the bed. The girl wore a fleecy cream nightgown that seemed to swallow her up in its folds. "This is Mary, and this is her mamm, Eva."

Mary, still panting from the last contraction, managed a smile. "Denki for coming, Lia."

An assortment of towels and blankets was draped over a chair, and another empty chair at the foot of the bed waited for Sarah.

Sarah stood at the side of the bed opposite Eva and rubbed her hand up and down Mary's arm. "The baby is posterior," she told Lia.

Lia nodded. She had read that section at least three times.

"So, we put her on her side to see if the baby won't turn before delivery," Sarah said.

"Will he be okay?" Mary asked.

"Jah, do not worry yourself one bit. They come out

a might bit easier when they are facedown, so I like to see if they will turn. But he'll come out fine either way."

Mary began panting furiously. "Another one is coming."

Her mother dug her fists into Mary's back as Mary groaned.

"Remember your breathing," Sarah said. "Think of it as the path through the contraction. Follow that path until the pain fades."

Mary immediately relaxed her shoulders and slowed down her breathing. Sarah pulled the covers up to the bottom of Mary's abdomen and gently lifted her nightgown. She put the stethoscope that hung around her neck to her ears and touched the listening end on Mary's stomach. "The heartbeat is strong. You're doing well."

Sarah directed Lia to warm up two receiving blankets by putting them into a specially shaped pan with tiny holes in the bottom on the cookstove over another pan that contained boiling water. The blankets were steamy warm in less than half an hour.

Even though it was warm inside the cabin, Lia kept the fire in the stove burning with the blanket warmer and two additional pans of boiling water on the surface. She opened the windows in the cabin to keep the fresh air circulating and took turns rubbing Mary's back.

After an hour, Sarah checked Mary's progress. "The head is an inch away. You might have this baby by dinnertime, Lord willing."

"Is it turned?" Mary asked.

"Still faceup. Even if he turns, the baby will have a cone-shaped head from being squeezed into the birth canal that long. But don't be alarmed. The baby's head will turn out nice and round in a day or two."

Lia loved Sarah's no-nonsense way of reporting the facts without causing Mary anxiety or concern. Sarah's talent of making things sound routine and matter-of-fact surely comforted worried mothers. Mary knew exactly what to expect without thinking anything was dire or out of the ordinary. Could Lia ever develop that sort of calm in serious situations?

After another hour of endless waiting and helping Mary get through her contractions, everything seemed to happen at once.

"I've got to push!" Mary moaned.

Sarah slid her quickly into position to the foot of the bed. "Lia, hold her leg like this."

Lia saw a little crown of dark hair as Mary pushed with all her might. Seven agonizing contractions, seven gut-splitting pushes, and the baby seemed to leap from his mother's womb.

"It's a boy!" Sarah announced as Mary sighed in blessed relief.

The baby screamed as if his feelings had been hurt beyond repair. His dark hair was matted with moisture and he did indeed appear with a cone head, but he also had a chubby round face and perfectly formed fingers. Tears sprang to Lia's eyes. There was nothing sweeter than a newborn *buplie*.

She took a towel from the back of the chair and quickly rubbed the moisture from the wailing baby as Sarah tied a piece of twine around the cord and cut it. Lia retrieved one of the warm blankets from the cookstove, took the baby from Sarah, and laid him on his mother's chest. As soon as she covered his little body with the warm blanket, he cuddled up against his mother and fell asleep.

"Oh, look at him," Lia cooed. "He is the most beautiful thing in the whole world."

Mary moved her arms around his tiny body. "Is he all right? He's not crying. Is he okay?"

Lia tried to copy Sarah's calm reassurances. "He is wonderful gute. He's had a long trip, and he is just happy to fall asleep in his mama's arms."

Mary rubbed her finger up and down the baby's cheek. "Luke Matthew," she said.

"Only a little tearing," Sarah said as she opened a sterile plastic bag and took out a special needle and thread.

Mary and Eva fussed over the baby while Lia helped Sarah clean up. Sarah periodically checked Mary and the baby while Lia gathered laundry and wiped down the floor.

"I will give the baby a sponge bath," Sarah said, "while Lia changes the sheets. Once we're all cleaned up, the new papa can come see his baby."

Mary moved to a chair while Lia changed her bed-clothes and then helped her change into a clean nightgown. Mary returned to bed, and Sarah placed baby Luke, swaddled tightly, in his mother's arms. Lia's heart swelled to fill the cabin.

Although Mary had dark circles under her eyes and looked too exhausted to raise her head, she didn't stop smiling as she tucked her finger into Luke's tiny fist. "Could we fetch Matthew now?"

"I'll go," said Eva. "He's been outside all morning, like as not hoeing the garden to pieces so's there ain't one clod of dirt."

Eva soon returned with a fresh-faced young man who didn't look any older than Mary. He had a husky build with a good attempt at a beard growing from his chin. He took one look at his wife and rushed to her side. "Mary, I was praying the whole time."

Sarah nudged Lia's elbow and led her outside.

"Always gute to let them have some time alone, if you can." She pulled a small round watch from her pocket and studied it. "Just the time I expected. You did well today. I could tell you was nervous, but you kept your head. That's the most important thing. The mothers mustn't be frightened more than they already are."

"Sarah, you are a wonderful-gute midwife. No mother would fear anything with you there."

Sarah waved off the compliment. "I don't get ruffled hardly. My kids'll tell you that much. When Joe cut his finger clean off last fall, I packed his whole hand in ice and put his finger in a cooler and took him to the hospital. No use to panic. Panic only causes mistakes. And Joe would have been a whole sight more afraid if I was afraid. They sewed his finger back on, no harm done."

Sarah pulled out her watch again as they saw Moses's buggy bounce up the dirt road. "Ten minutes late." She folded her arms. "Arlene Bontrager might deliver in two weeks. I'll send for you."

Lia felt as if she could float with the clouds. "Thank you, Sarah. I would be so thrilled."

"Read the rest of that book. You still have much to learn." She waved and moved toward the cabin. "I'll let you cut the cord next time and listen to the heartbeat."

"Do you want me to help you finish cleaning up?"

"Nae, not much left and you don't want to keep Moses waiting. He's spent enough of his day driving you places." Sarah furrowed her brow. "Ask Mammi if I can come by on Saturday at dinnertime. Twelve thirty. I'll bring sandwiches. And make sure that girl is away so we can talk about her."

"That girl? You mean my sister?"

"Jah, that one. Can you arrange it?"

Lia stifled a smile at Sarah's plain-spokenness. "I will do my best."

Sarah pinned Lia with a stern eye. "It's no use me coming all the way out there if that girl is to home. Make sure she ain't."

"I will."

The cabin door gave an ear-piercing groan as Sarah opened it. "And tell Moses he owes me a visit. The boys have been asking for him."

Lia stood at the front of the cabin waiting for Moses. His pounding heart rushed way out ahead of the buggy. After the morning spent with Rachel, he was astonished at how eager he felt to see Lia.

Her smile could have melted the ice on White Clay Lake in the dead of winter. Her cheeks glowed, and her brown eyes seemed to possess their own fire. Moses's chest ached with the desire to see her this happy every day. She deserved to be happy.

He motioned for her to come, and she darted around the horse and hopped into the buggy. "Do you need to water the horse?" she said.

"Nae. We stopped a mile back. I thought I might be early. How did it go?"

Lia put her palm to her cheek. "Am I flushed? I feel flushed."

Moses tore his gaze away from her to turn the horse. "You are glowing."

She picked up her book that sat on the seat between them and clutched it to her chest. "It was a miracle, Moses. I felt confident enough to be a help to Sarah. And she said I was."

Her excitement only succeeded in lending heightened color to her cheeks and brightness to her eyes. Moses couldn't look away. "Well, Sarah doesn't sugarcoat her praise, you can be sure of that."

"Are we taking a different way home?"

Moses snapped his head around. In his distraction he'd barely noticed the reins, and the horse had taken it upon himself to trot down a side path that led deeper into the woods. "Oops, I wasn't paying attention." The woods grew thicker the farther they went. "I don't see a place to turn around."

"There is bound to be a wide spot sooner or later."

Moses scanned the muddy lane ahead. "Either that or we will end up in Canada."

"I hear Canada is lovely this time of year."

"Okay, we will keep going while you tell me about your morning."

Lia blushed and looked away. "You don't have to hear my stories."

"You're my prisoner until you decide to get out of this buggy and walk. You might as well talk."

She grinned, and Moses caught a glimpse of those white teeth. "Mary was very brave. My book says some mothers scream and holler and call the midwife all sorts of names."

"It must be unbearable pain."

"After seeing it, I can imagine it would be."

"I don't know them," Moses said. "Are they Swartzentruber?"

"Jah."

The Swartzentruber sect had broken off from the Old Order Amish almost a hundred years ago. Their lifestyle was primitive with no indoor plumbing, more conservative dress, and stricter rules for traveling. Most Swartzentrubers kept to themselves, but some made no bones about their contempt for less conservative

Amish. Because of the strictness of their church, their youth tended to be extremely wild during rum-schpringe. Or at least that was Moses's observation. He didn't know many Swartzentruber.

"The cabin was cozy, but they live so far from anyone," Lia said. "I would miss not having neighbors."

Moses trained his eyes out the front window. "We seem to be curving west. I don't know that this path leads anywhere. It probably goes for another three miles and ends at a tall, thick pine in the middle of the road. I might have to get out and walk Sammy backward."

Moses stopped the buggy where a stream crossed the overgrown path. "I think this is the stream I saw from the road coming in. I'll have a look around while Sammy gets a sip of water."

He jumped out of the buggy and Lia followed. Trees grew thick on either side of the narrow path. Birds and crickets and a thousand other creatures filled the woods with sound, a hum of life that Moses found comforting.

Moses hiked farther down the path to see if it promised to lead them home. No sign of a better road or even a place to turn around. He turned back.

Lia had taken the blanket out of his buggy and spread it on the ground next to the stream. She held out a brown paper sack. "I forgot that I brought my dinner and left it in your buggy. Do you want to share? It's a nice spot for a picnic."

"What did you bring?"

"Peanut butter and honey sandwich, apple, Anna's ginger snaps."

"Milk?" Moses asked. Couldn't eat Mammi's ginger snaps without soaking them first.

"No milk."

Moses couldn't suppress a smile. Lia looked so pretty standing there in the filtered sunlight of midday. "We might have to save the sandwich to leave a trail of bread crumbs in case we are lost for weeks in the wilderness."

Lia laughed and sat down on the blanket. "I have a gute sense of direction. We won't get lost."

Sharing a meal with Lia without being pestered by her little sister was too tempting an offer to pass up. Lia didn't expect a proposal. She didn't even want a proposal.

Moses felt a catch in his breath. That thought didn't make him happy today.

She gazed at him and cocked an eyebrow. "Annoyed?"

Moses wiped the frown from his face. He would have to stop betraying that particular emotion.

"Annoyed that I can't find a way out of the woods."

He sat next to her, and she handed him half the sandwich. "You'll think better on a full stomach."

"I feel bad eating half your lunch. It could be days before we eat again."

Lia giggled. "If this is my last meal, I'm going to enjoy it." She took a big bite of her sandwich.

"Delicious," Moses said. "You are a very gute cook."

Lia leaned back on her hand. "Even though we're lost, I'm so happy. I have you to thank for a wonderful-gute day."

"Don't look at me. Sarah wouldn't have agreed to it if she didn't like you. I knew she would." Moses couldn't imagine anyone not liking Lia at first meeting.

Her piercing gaze made his heart do a little jig beneath his rib cage. "Do you have a pocketknife?" she said. "I will slice this apple."

Moses handed her his knife. Warmth spread up his

arm when her skin touched his. He squeezed his fingers into a fist. What a childish, teenage reaction!

Lia cut a wedge out of the apple and handed it to him. "Did you take Rachel back to Huckleberry Hill?"

Moses cringed. He didn't want to talk about Rachel. He might say something he regretted right in front of her sister.

Lia studied his face. "Would you rather I not ask how things are going with Rachel?"

"Things are not going with Rachel."

She lowered her eyes and concentrated on slicing the apple. "If you want a chance with her, make her believe she is chasing you. She likes that."

Her words stung more than Moses cared to admit. "Are you saying you want me to court her?"

Lia would not meet his eyes. "Dat said it is my responsibility."

"To marry me off to Rachel?"

"Anna and Felty want you to marry her."

Moses wanted to protest, but after Mammi had insisted that Rachel come along today, he wasn't so sure. He took the apple from Lia's hand and laid it on the blanket. Then he placed both hands on Lia's arms. She opened wide her eyes and pressed her lips together. He had her attention. "Lia, you have always been honest with me. Do you want me to marry Rachel?"

"If you want to marry Rachel, I won't interfere."

"That's not what I asked. Do you want me to marry Rachel?"

She picked up one of Mammi's ginger snaps and rolled it in her open hand like a pebble. "It doesn't matter what I want."

"Apparently it doesn't matter what I want either. And why won't you answer my question?"

"Before I do, you must be honest with me. Do you want to marry Rachel?"

Moses took off his hat and shoved his fingers through his hair. "I don't want to hurt your feelings, but I have no interest in your sister."

Lia sighed as if she had been holding her breath for an hour. "Really?"

"I told her so this morning."

"What did she say?"

Moses growled under his breath. "She didn't believe me."

Lia's face exploded into a grin and she laughed—deep, throaty laughs that soon produced tears.

In puzzled amusement, Moses watched her until she calmed down enough to speak. "Rachel has never been rejected in her life. She thought you were teasing."

"Are you angry that I don't want to marry her?"

Lia wiped her eyes and let out a leftover giggle. "No. Of course not."

Moses thought that he had never heard better news in his life.

She knit her brows together. "But I am surprised. Rachel is pretty. I was certain you would be interested."

Moses shook his head. "Jah, she is pretty. But do you think I am that foolish, to want a pretty wife and nothing else? The Lord doesn't see as man sees. He looks on the heart."

"Dat quotes that scripture often. It is his way of reminding me that since I am plain, I had better be nice."

Moses felt the indignation rise up in him like a boiling saucepan of jelly. "You're not plain."

"Rachel is the pretty one."

This time Moses took her hand and squeezed it so she would understand how wrong she was. He ignored the sensation of warmth pulsing through his veins. She lowered her eyes and stared at his fingers intertwined with hers. "Lia, you are like one of the angels of heaven the way you take care of my grandparents. I am very grateful. But don't believe for one minute that you are not pretty."

She started to protest, but he cut her off. "Prettier than Rachel."

"You are just being silly now."

"Nae," Moses protested. "I've been places with you. I see how boys stare at you, wishing they were taller or wishing they knew who you were. You are lovely, and I won't let go of your hand until you admit it."

He shouldn't have made such a threat. The sensation of her hand in his traveled up his arm and tingled at his lips. He couldn't muster any rational thought as the desire to kiss her ambushed him and made his head spin.

Her irresistible lips curled slightly. "You'll never make me believe it, even if you hold my hand until it falls off."

He couldn't stop staring at her mouth even as she pulled away from him. Moses quickly released her hand and began massaging the whiskers on his chin in hopes of rubbing away any thought of planting his lips on hers.

Lia turned her face away and fiddled with the hem of her apron. "Don't tell Rachel what I said. She and Dat would never forgive me. Besides, you could still fall in love with her."

Moses stood and brushed off his trousers and reached out his hand to pull Lia to her feet. "I am not looking to marry." Clearing his throat, he walked to the buggy and mentally measured its width. "If I guide Sammy between those two trees, then go backward, the buggy will make it around those bushes. I'll need to go forward and back about ten times, but I think we can get turned around by Christmas yet."

"That is a very gute plan."

Moses discovered that he couldn't turn his gaze away. Good he was so loyal to Barbara or he would be in serious danger.

Chapter Eleven

"Why do I have to go? I hate smelly feed stores, and that wagon is torture to ride in."

Ever since her excursion to Moses's cheese factory on Wednesday, Rachel had resolved to stay close to Huckleberry Hill in case Moses decided to drop by and ask to take her for a ride. She was sure every minute of every day that Moses would come up the lane in a courting buggy and whisk her away from her dull and unnecessary chores. She spent hours sitting by the big window hoping for the first glimpse of the man destined to be her husband.

Unruffled by Rachel's tantrum, Anna kneaded her bread dough and smiled her innocent smile. "I suppose Lia could go with Felty."

"Yes, let Lia go. I can't lift those feed bags."

"You will need to scrub the toilet and bathtub while she's gone."

"I'm not good at toilets. The cleanser makes my hands chappy."

Anna didn't even look up as she handed Lia the loaf pans to be greased. "I've known Moses to visit the feed store on a Saturday morning. Lia, you should take a plate of cookies in case you run into him."

Lia felt that familiar prick of rejection that Anna wanted Moses to marry Rachel instead of her, but today they really did need Rachel gone, so any method Anna wanted to use was acceptable.

Rachel tore her attention from the window. "Oh, Anna. Why didn't you say so? Of course I'll go. I haven't seen Moses for three days. I'm surprised he doesn't spend more time here."

Anna deftly formed her dough into three loaves. "He's very busy. Hardly has time to breathe."

They heard Felty singing before he came into the house. *"Keep your hand upon the throttle and your eyes upon the rail."* He stamped his boots on the rug inside the door. "Wagon's hitched. You ready, Rachel?"

Rachel leaped from her perch by the window and retrieved a paper plate from the cupboard. She quickly loaded the plate with more than half the cookies Lia had baked that morning. "Moses will love these. I'll see that he puts some meat on those bones yet." She quickly covered them with plastic wrap. "Don't have too much fun here without me," she said as she followed Felty out the door.

Peering out the window, Anna sighed as she watched Rachel hop into Felty's wagon as if she were going to a picnic. "Next time we will go to Sarah's house. I had to do seventeen somersaults to get Rachel out of here."

Lia twitched her lips downward. "At least maybe she will get to see Moses."

Anna waved her hands in the air as if swatting a fly. "Oh, fiddle. Moses never goes to the feed store."

"You told a fib?"

"Jah, a fib. It couldn't be helped, and I can repent later."

Lia couldn't keep the smile from her face. "Anna, you are a wonder."

"When I get to the other side, I'll say, 'Lord, I was too old to know any better.'"

They heard a sound outside, and Lia moved to the window. "Sarah's here." She drove an open-air buggy with room for two people—sometimes used as a courting buggy.

Anna glanced at her clock on the wall. "Right on time. Sarah is prompt as the sunrise."

With the speed born of constant practice, Sarah unhitched the horse and led him to the small corral to the side of the barn. Lia stood at the door waiting for her when she made her way to the house.

Sarah placed a paper grocery sack on the table and gave Anna an enormous hug. "Mammi, you look very well."

"Lia is taking good care of us," Anna said.

"It is gute to have a youngster here looking after you." Sarah motioned toward the window. "I passed that girl going down the hill with Dawdi. How long will they be gone?"

"At least an hour," Anna said. "Probably longer. Felty's been given strict instructions to dawdle."

"Gute." Sarah picked up her sack. "I thought I would make cucumber mayonnaise sandwiches."

"My favorite," Anna said.

Lia wondered if defective taste buds ran in the Helmuth family. Cucumber and mayonnaise sandwiches? It was a very good thing Rachel was not here.

Sarah refused to let Lia help her as she peeled and chopped cucumbers, sliced the bread, and spread mayonnaise. She put one sandwich on each of three plates plus a handful of potato chips and clusters of grapes from her grocery bag.

They sat at the table and said silent grace. Then Anna and Sarah both dug in to their sandwiches. Lia wasn't so sure, so she popped a grape in her mouth to prepare herself.

Anna dabbed her lips with a napkin. "Lia, did you know that Sarah is my oldest grandchild? Born three years before my youngest daughter, Ruth Anne."

"How many grandchildren do you have?"

"Sixty-four and ninety-six great-grandchildren. By the end of the year we will have ninety-nine greats."

"And one great-great," said Sarah. "My daughter Beth is expecting."

Lia took a bite of cucumber sandwich. It tasted surprisingly refreshing and delicious. "That is a wonderful posterity."

Sarah finished half of her sandwich and wiped her hands on her napkin. "Now, Mammi, I come today to set you straight."

Anna flashed a wide smile. "I'm happy that you came at all."

"Moses said you sent that girl to help me with Yoder's baby."

Anna's smile did not fade. "I suppose I did."

Sarah folded her arms across her chest. "You know how touchy I am about who I let sit in. I allow Lia to help because she's got the temperament for it, and she's done her reading. I won't let that girl barge in and think she can interfere."

Anna patted Sarah's hand. "I had my reasons."

When Anna didn't elaborate, Sarah said, "Well, what are they?"

"I guessed you wouldn't let Rachel go in. I wanted Moses to have some time to get to know her."

Hearing the truth from Anna's own mouth proved more painful than Lia could have imagined. She almost choked out her next words. "She wants Moses to marry my sister."

Anna snapped her head around as her eyes grew big as saucers. "What are you saying, dear?"

Lia felt her face get warm. "I saw the letter you wrote Dat. You wanted me to come back to Huckleberry Hill so Moses and Rachel would have more time for courting."

Alarm leaped into Anna's eyes. "Oh, my dear. No wonder you have been moping about since you returned. I never meant for you to see that letter."

"Don't be troubled about it. I am glad I can help you and Felty even if you don't think I am good enough for your grandson."

Anna reached over and wrapped her hand around Lia's wrist. "You are quite mistaken. I have never for one minute changed my mind about who I want Moses to marry. I knew your fater would not agree to send you back unless I gave him a gute reason. Rachel told me what his plans were, and I knew what I needed to write in my letter to convince him."

Warmth spread through Lia's entire body. "You told my dat a fib?"

Anna waved her arms in the air. "I'll tell the Lord that my handwriting's bad. How could Owen tell for sure what I wrote in that note?"

"But why did you insist Rachel come with us on Wednesday?"

Anna lowered her voice even though there were only the three of them within a mile. "I can't find it in my heart to like your sister very much. Don't be angry."

"I am not angry."

"I am putting pressure on that grandson of mine. I knew if he spent the day with Rachel, he would see how different she is from you—that he would realize what a wonderful-gute girl you are and ask you to marry him."

Lia couldn't smile wide enough. They'd never wanted Moses to marry Rachel. They still valued her even though she wasn't as petite or as pretty as Rachel. Her spirit soared.

Anna pressed her lips together. "But he is fighting it harder than I thought he would."

Lia scooted her chair closer and put her arm around Anna. "I do not expect him to like me. He told me on the day we met that he does not want to marry."

"He only thinks he doesn't want to marry," Anna said.

Sarah crinkled her napkin in her fist. "When a man's heart gets broke that bad, he ain't likely to snap out of it fast."

"It's been three years," said Anna, "and Lia is so much better than that one."

In shock, Lia looked at Sarah. "What happened?"

"Moses and Barbara Gingerich were published. Published even. But she kept dabbling in the world and finally decided to leave the church. Moses tried to persuade her to stay. He even told her she could keep getting her magazines after they were married. But in the end, she didn't love him enough to stay. That's what stung the worst, I expect."

"And Moses ain't one to spend his love lightly," Anna said. "If he commits to someone, they've got his whole heart, nothing held back. He doesn't hand it over easy, and he's more loyal than a bird dog. I expect he still feels beholden to Barbara after three years."

Lia's mouth went dry. Moses loved someone else?

"He used to get a letter from her every week," Sarah said.

"She wanted to keep him hoping even though we all knew she would never come back. Adam hasn't said anything about the letters for months. I think she finally quit writing."

Sarah shook her head. "Mammi, I know you mean well for Moses, but what if Lia doesn't want him? Are you setting him up to have his heart broken all over again?"

"Moses doesn't want to marry me," Lia said, her heart sinking even as she voiced it.

Annoyance flashed in Sarah's eyes. "Stuff and non-sense. Your problem is that you sell yourself short at every turn. If you can't make him change his mind, nobody will."

"It's all right," Lia said. "Don't worry about my feelings. I don't think I will ever marry. I'm too tall."

Sarah snorted. "Too tall for Moses? What are you thinking?"

The room got hot. "I told him I wouldn't have him," she whispered.

Anna and Sarah stared at her as words seemed to fail them.

Lia shifted uncomfortably in her chair. "He told me he's not looking to marry, and I told him I wouldn't have someone so arrogant to assume I wanted to marry him."

"What did he say?"

"He was relieved."

Anna seemed to consider this good news. The laugh lines around her mouth deepened as she turned to Sarah. "They've talked about marriage."

Sarah leaned her elbows on the table. "Now, Mammi.

Matchmaking is dangerous. What if Moses decides to marry that blond girl?"

"I think I wouldn't allow him on my property again."

"And what if Lia decides to marry one of your other grandsons? I count five of marriageable age."

"Lia is meant for Moses."

"I am here on Huckleberry Hill to help Anna and Felty, not find a husband. I never expected to."

Sarah wrinkled her forehead. "Moses might break Lia's heart. Or Lia will break his."

Lia felt a little silly talking about something that couldn't possibly happen. "I promise to never break Moses's heart."

Sarah pointed a finger at her. "I hold you to that promise."

Lia stopped scrubbing and lifted her head. There was that strange tapping noise again. She looked around the bathroom. Was it coming from the sink? The drain sometimes gurgled when Anna turned on the water in the kitchen.

She poured more cleanser on her scrub brush and swished it back and forth until a louder tapping startled her and the scrub brush thudded to the bottom of the tub. She scanned the room again and saw a movement at the small window above the toilet. In puzzlement, she gingerly stood on the toilet seat, pushed open the hinged window, and stuck her head out.

Below the bathroom window, the foundation rose halfway aboveground. Moses stood in a thicket of alder shrubs and huckleberry bushes with his hand reaching to the sky.

Lia couldn't help but smile every time she saw him.

"Moses, what are you doing down there? Come through the front door like normal folks."

He put his finger to his lips. "Shh. Sarah wants me to take you to Bontragers. Arlene is having her baby."

Lia did her best to contain her laughter as Moses shushed her. "Is it a big secret?"

"Nae, but if Rachel finds out, she'll want to come with us, and Mammi will make me take her. Can you sneak out of the house? My buggy is halfway down the lane."

Maybe it wasn't right, but Lia felt so giddy she could have giggled for three days. "I'll be there before you are."

She fastened the catch on the window and jumped down from the toilet. After quickly rinsing the cleanser from the tub, she stowed the cleaning supplies underneath the sink. Lia slipped into her room and packed a few things in her bag before scurrying down the hall. Rachel lay on her bed picking lint from a pair of her black stockings. "Who were you talking to?"

Lia didn't have the time or the inclination to fabricate an explanation. "The clothes should be brought down from the line."

"I will get to it. It's too warm to go out right now."

She found Anna in the kitchen studying her new recipe book. "Anna," she whispered, "Sarah is asking for me, and Moses is here with his buggy. I'll be back as soon as I can."

Anna's eyes lit up. She bustled to the closet and pulled out a tiny pair of knitted white booties. "For the new baby."

Lia took them and laid them carefully in her bag. "Denki, Anna. The baby's first gift."

Both Anna and Lia jumped when they heard Rachel calling from her room. "You better be off," said Anna.

"I don't have a strong enough grip to stop her if she gets it in her head to go."

Lia slipped out the door so quietly she didn't even hear herself. She ran until the bushes blocked the sight of her from the house. Then she skipped down the lane to where Moses stood patiently waiting for her.

His smile was like a bonfire on a frosty evening.

Chapter Twelve

"Well, he's here—come to set you straight, Lia. I hope you're satisfied."

Rachel sat at her usual place at the window while Lia put the finishing touches on the peach pie for dessert tonight. Lia didn't even bat an eye. Why would Moses want to set her straight?

Rachel jumped from her seat and opened the door. A feather could have knocked Lia over as her dat walked into the kitchen. Rachel squealed and threw her arms around him. He patted her on the back and then took off his hat when she let go of him.

"Dat," Lia said. "Rachel didn't mention you were coming for a visit."

Dat took a few steps into the kitchen and gazed around the room. "I came to check up on you, to see if you two were treating each other well. Where are Anna and Felty?"

Rachel sauntered to the sofa and sat down. "They're out in the garden. Come sit down, Dat."

Lia covered her pie with plastic wrap and put it in the fridge. "Who brought you up here?"

"David Groen. He'll be back at six to pick me up. I

told Rachel I would be staying for supper. I'm sorry she didn't tell you I was coming."

"I wanted everyone to be surprised," Rachel said, looking like a guilty child with an unpleasant secret. "Moses will be here too."

Dat sat down next to Rachel. "Gute. I made a special effort to come today because you said he's always here on Thursdays."

Lia felt indignation bubble up inside her that Dat and Rachel were scheming against poor Moses. She hated to see how uncomfortable it made Moses to always be dodging Rachel's advances.

Taking a deep breath, Lia let the anger pass through her like water through a sieve. They couldn't help themselves. Who wouldn't want to scheme for Moses Zimmerman? Besides, Moses could take care of himself. If Rachel succeeded in drawing him in, then he deserved what he got.

Dat leaned back on the sofa and draped his arm over the back of it. "Tell me all about Bonduel. What is the gmay like? Is the district small?"

"Thirteen families," said Rachel, "but there are probably fifteen widows on top of that. Mostly old people."

"No suitable boys?"

Lia dried her hands and hesitantly sat in Anna's rocker. She knew she should be sociable, especially for Dat's first visit to Huckleberry Hill, but if Rachel and Dat wanted to talk about boys, Lia had no interest. And she still needed to put together a meatloaf.

"Besides Moses, there isn't much. Four or five boys of the right age, but one is fat and the others aren't at all good-looking. Moses is really the only one, but he is the right one, so it doesn't matter about the rest."

Dat and Rachel shared a meaningful look that Lia was not up to interpreting. Then Dat patted Rachel on the leg, leaned forward, and propped his elbows on his knees. He pinned his gaze on Lia and frowned.

"Lia, I came because Rachel tells me you've been inconsiderate of her feelings." He shook a finger at her. "This selfishness must stop."

His accusations struck Lia quite mute. Inconsiderate? Selfish? Was she not doing enough of Rachel's chores?

Dat kept wagging his finger as if Lia wouldn't pay attention otherwise. "I sent you up here to make sure Moses falls in love with Rachel, and you've been sneaking off with Moses and leaving Rachel to do all the work. I won't stand for it, Lia. If you can't find some love in your heart for your sister, then you can come back home."

Rachel settled back into the sofa and got that smug look on her face she had whenever Dat took her side of a disagreement—which was every time.

Lia's mouth went dry. Moses had come knocking at the bathroom window almost two weeks ago. Lia had been gone most of the day, and she had never seen Rachel so livid as when she returned home. Rachel had stomped her feet and gnashed her teeth and screamed at the injustice of it all. It took Lia a full hour to calm her down and even then Lia knew this outburst would not be the last she heard about it. She had no inkling that Rachel would summon their dat. But it shouldn't have surprised her. Dat came to Rachel's rescue all the time at home, as if she were that five-year-old who had nearly died. Of course he would take the day off to set things right for his favorite child.

Would it do any good to defend herself? "It was not an outing. I helped the midwife deliver a baby. Rachel would not have wanted to help with the baby."

Rachel folded her arms in stubborn denial. "Yes, I

would have. I tried once, but that woman wouldn't even let me in the house."

"Sarah is very particular about who she lets help her. I am sorry, but she did not want you to come."

Dat glared at Lia. "And you think you are better than your sister because the midwife lets you help?"

"Nae, not at all. I have read the books. I know a little of what to do."

"And you think Rachel is not smart enough?"

Lia heaved a great sigh. "Rachel does not know how to be a midwife."

"Neither do you," Rachel snapped. "Just because you've read the books doesn't mean you know anything."

Lia felt the sweat trickle down the back of her neck. She was foolish to think Rachel would ever see reason. "If you are so set on being a midwife, why don't you talk to Sarah and ask her to help you?"

Rachel stared at Lia as if she had said the stupidest thing in the world. "I don't want to be a midwife. I want to be with Moses. Even Anna sees the sense in it. While you are delivering slimy babies, I should be with Moses. The first time you were away, he took me to his cheese factory. I helped him make cheese." Rachel turned to Dat. "He told me I am delicate."

Lia wanted to throw up her hands in surrender. There was no making sense of Rachel's reasoning. "So you don't want to come with me to deliver babies?"

"Yes, I want to come. Moses will be more than happy to drop you off so he can be alone with me. He told me so."

He told her so?

"But, Dat," Lia said. "Moses is doing me a favor when he comes to pick me up. How can I impose on his kindness like this? He might refuse to drive me if it becomes a burden."

Dat knitted his brow. "A burden? Driving you all over the county might be a burden, but I don't imagine he sees spending time with Rachel as a burden."

"I don't feel good about asking him. He is busy with his factory."

Dat stood up and glared at Lia. "You will take Rachel with you whenever you leave this house or you will come back to Wautoma and forget about being a midwife. Do you understand? If I hear you're leaving Rachel out or treating her unkindly, I will bring you back home so fast you won't even remember how you got there."

Lia felt as if she'd been shoved to the ground with the heel of Dat's boot. "Dat, you are not listening. Moses is not at my beck and call and—"

He pointed an accusing finger in Lia's direction. "You will not argue with me."

Lia bowed her head and squeezed her eyes shut. She would be absolutely mortified to ask Moses if she could bring Rachel along. He had made it clear last time that he did not want to take her. But Lia couldn't bear the thought of giving up on midwifing. What was she to do? "Yes, Dat."

"And it wouldn't hurt you to quit thinking of yourself and help Rachel make pies and goodies for Moses. Men like women who can cook."

As if nothing were amiss between them, Rachel's expression brightened considerably. "Oh, Lia. Wouldn't it be fun to plan a picnic? If you helped me make the food, I could take Moses to the top of Huckleberry Hill and we could watch the sunset."

That's how it was between Rachel and Lia. Since

Rachel's illness fourteen years ago, Lia felt too guilty or too worn down to put up a fuss, and Rachel was accustomed to being everybody's favorite. Once she got her way, all was right with the world.

"We are at the top," Lia said. Huckleberry Hill wasn't all that tall. Sunsets were viewed through the trees and only on cloudless evenings. Rachel liked the idea of a picnic at sunset, but Moses seemed too busy to wait around for a sunset.

Dat turned his attention to Rachel. "That is a gute idea. You could make something using cheese from his factory."

They all turned when they heard the horse clomping up the lane.

Rachel ran to the window and began to breathe rapidly. "It's him, Dat. It's Moses. I knew he would come."

Lia's heart raced even as she scraped it off the floor. She didn't even glance out the window as she went to the sink and turned on the water. Let Dat and Rachel make a fuss over Moses while she washed dishes and made a meatloaf for supper.

"Lia didn't exaggerate," Dat said. "He is tall as a tree. And very good-looking. He will do very well, I think."

Rachel tapped rapidly on the window. "Yoo-hoo, Moses. Look over here."

Her tapping must not have achieved the desired results, because she pounded louder and raised her voice in hopes of catching his attention. "Moses, come here! Moses." She stopped tapping and looked at Dat. "I guess he's going straight out back. He told Anna he'd help her in the garden."

Dat wasted no time in putting on his hat. "Let's go meet him, then."

He and Rachel hurried out the door and left Lia in what should have been welcome silence, but the solitude only succeeded in making her feel utterly lonely.

No matter how she scolded herself or reminded herself of his indifference, Lia could not chase Moses from her head. Why, when she tried so studiously to be realistic, did Moses fill her thoughts every hour of every day? Why did a pang of jealousy squeeze her lungs every time Rachel talked about Moses? How could she be so foolish as to dream about him when he pined for a fiancée who was probably ten times more beautiful than Rachel and a hundred times less blunt than Lia?

It didn't matter. Rachel would drive Moses away with her persistence, and he would spend less and less time on Huckleberry Hill. Lord willing, he would not be too annoyed to drive her to do midwifing.

With her hands submerged in dishwater, Lia prayed that Moses would take pity on her and keep coming back to pick her up. It was the most she could hope for.

"Mammi, I can do that for you. You'll hurt your knees." Moses tromped out of the barn with an armload of rebar and was greeted with the sight of Mammi kneeling on the ground pulling tiny weeds from around the tomatoes.

"I love playing in the dirt," Mammi said.

"And how will you get back on your feet once you're done?"

"That's what I have a grandson for."

Dawdi sprinkled fertilizer around the raspberry bushes. "I told her to use a hoe, but she won't have any of it."

"I slice up more tomatoes than weeds that way, even when I wear my glasses."

Moses dropped the rebar, and it landed with a thud next to the neat row of sagging tomato plants. They should have been staked weeks ago—another reminder of how much help Mammi and Dawdi needed here. If he secured the rebar in the ground today, they still had time to salvage the tomatoes.

"Where is Lia?" Moses asked.

"She offered to make supper. And pie."

Moses's mouth began to water. He still hadn't really tasted one of Lia's pies. The anticipation tortured him.

Hoping he might catch a glimpse of Lia at the kitchen window, Moses looked to the house and saw Rachel shuffling quickly toward him followed by an older man who could only be her father. His hair and eyes were the same color as Lia's, and he stood well over six feet tall. Moses knew it was Rachel's father because they both wore that same self-satisfied smirk that always put Moses's teeth on edge.

Mammi glanced up from the weeding. "Remember," she whispered loudly, "we've all got to do our best to make sure Owen has no reason to take our Lia away from us."

Moses nodded. Rachel staying at Huckleberry Hill without Lia was out of the question. She couldn't be trusted with chores, and she'd probably burn down the house or ruin every meal with her sour disposition.

Rachel, in bare feet, tiptoed over the dirt clods and stood in the sifted soil where Anna had planted cucumbers. "Moses, this is my dat, Owen Shetler."

Mammi winked at Moses with a twinkle in her eye and then twisted her body to get a quick look at Owen. "Good to see you again, Owen."

Owen reached out to shake Moses's hand. "Good

to see you, Anna, Felty. And I'm glad to meet you, Moses."

"I invited Dat to stay for supper," Rachel said. "His driver won't be by till six. Lia is making meatloaf."

"Using Rachel's recipe," said Owen. "Rachel makes a meatloaf like nothing you've ever tasted."

Mammi smoothed the dirt around one of her precious plants. "Is that so? I hope you will cook for us sometime, dear."

Her father pressed his lips into a rigid line, and Rachel smiled sheepishly at him. "I get so busy with all the chores, and Lia insists on preparing the meals."

Owen rubbed his hands together. "Well, she will have to be less selfish in the kitchen so you have a chance to show Moses how you can cook."

Moses groaned inwardly. They both looked at him like a hungry wolf looks at a helpless little lamb with nowhere to run. He guessed their plan without even thinking hard. Owen would sing Rachel's praises until the driver carted him away at six o'clock tonight, and Rachel would simper and blush and try to show Moses how delicate and charming she could be.

"Rachel told me she helped at your cheese factory," Owen said.

Moses felt so hostile he didn't know how else to respond but with a bald-faced lie. "She was a big help with the curd."

"Have you your own house?"

"Jah, I bought it last year from my uncle plus three acres to go with it."

"That's a gute amount of land to manage without having the trouble of a big farm. Especially where you have the factory and all. Last year Rachel planted roses on the south side of our house and tended them until they bloomed to overflowing."

Rachel pushed the dirt with her toes. "Mamm says I have a green thumb."

"Two green thumbs," Owen insisted.

Mammi looked like she would burst into laughter any second. "Would you like to help with the weeding, then? These old bones are creaking like a rusty gate."

Rachel glanced at Moses and pasted on her best smile. "Jah, sure. Do you have a pair of gloves?"

"In the barn," Felty said. "Top shelf above the clay pots."

Rachel tiptoed gingerly to the barn and disappeared after a look behind her to make sure Moses watched.

"Staking the tomatoes?" Owen said.

"Would you like to help?"

"I used to lay roof for a living. I know how to drive a nail pretty gute."

Moses gave Owen his leather gloves and the hammer. "I'll hold while you drive it."

Owen donned the gloves and raised the hammer. Moses twisted a section of rebar into the ground a few inches from the first tomato plant. Owen aimed true, and it only took him three hits to firmly drive the stake.

Rachel appeared at the door of the barn holding a bright green pair of gloves. "Do you have smaller ones?"

"Look in the brown bin," Felty yelled.

Owen chuckled. "That girl sure is petite. We have to buy child-size garden gloves for her at home. Not like Lia. There ain't nothing small about Lia. She's tall enough for birds to perch on her head like a telephone pole."

Owen's voice grated like fingernails on a chalkboard. Moses interrupted him just so he would quit talking. "I think Lia has beautiful long fingers. And graceful, like a swan in flight."

Owen looked mildly surprised. "I suppose she does. She's not favored like Rachel, but Lia has her own good qualities. Rachel is a beauty, ain't not?" He leaned closer to Moses and lowered his voice. "I'll tell you one thing about Rachel. She likes to go riding. Don't matter where you take her, she just likes to be off somewhere with the wind in her face."

"I don't have an open-air buggy," Moses said.

"That don't matter. Take her riding anywhere." He lowered his voice further. "And if Lia is any sort of a bother, you send the word and I'll bring her back home."

There was the bottom line. As long as Rachel was satisfied with Moses's attentions, Lia could stay. But if Lia inconvenienced her sister in any way, Lia's dat would ship her home.

Had Lia's fater always treated her this way? She must have the patience of Job. Moses wanted to growl in indignation for Lia. Instead, he turned his back on Owen and trudged toward the house. "I need a Band-Aid," he said. "I'll be back."

He flung open the door more violently than he meant to. Owen Shetler had really gotten to him. Lia stood at the counter with her hands submerged in a bowl of ground beef. She smiled weakly at him, but she looked weary, like all the sunshine had seeped out of her.

Moses felt that he should say something to make her feel better, but he'd really come in so she would make him feel better. She always did.

"I came for a drink of water," he said lamely, momentarily distracted by her deep chocolate eyes.

"Are you staking tomatoes?"

"Slowly. Your dat is helping, and Rachel is scouring the entire barn for a suitable pair of gloves."

One corner of her mouth twitched upward. "It's one of her tricks to avoid work."

"Jah, I figured."

Lia's eyes glistened with instant tears. "I am sorry. I should not have said anything against my sister."

Moses hadn't expected tears. He'd never seen Lia cry before. "Don't cry about it," he said, frozen in place where he stood. "I promise I won't tell a soul."

Lia sniffled softly and blinked back the moisture before anything trickled down her face. "Must be the onions."

Moses snatched a tissue from the box with the knitted cover and held it ready for any leakage. "The strategy is to make sure there is a pair of extra-small gloves for Rachel ready for every occasion. We'll need latex, gardening, and rubber. Did I forget anything?"

There was a smile. Weak, but better than the unhappiness that overspread her features a few moments ago. "Oven mitts."

"Smaller oven mitts. Maybe Mammi could knit a pair."

Lia pressed her hamburger mixture into a pan. "You're annoyed."

"You always think I'm annoyed."

"You always are."

Moses ran his fingers through his hair. "Not always. Just today. I wish people would quit trying to marry me off to people I don't want to marry."

Lia's face clouded over. "Then I have news that will annoy you more than ever."

"Sounds like very bad news."

"My dat says I have to take Rachel midwifing with me, or he will make me come home."

"But Sarah doesn't want her to come," Moses said.

"Oh, she's not planning on accompanying me. She's planning on being with you."

Moses had no reply for that. He clenched his teeth until he thought they might crack.

"I would never ask you to do that for me," Lia said. "Is there another way to get me to the homes without you having to fetch me? One of Sarah's sons might be able to pick me up, or I could borrow Felty's horse and go myself."

Moses couldn't go along with that plan. He liked being with Lia, maybe more than he would admit to anybody. Why should he let Rachel take that from him? "That will never do. I take all the credit for introducing you to Sarah. I should have the privilege of driving you places."

She blushed and looked away. "It is more appropriate to say 'the burden.'"

"You deserve to learn with Sarah. You've studied hard." Moses searched for the words to reassure Lia. There was no way he would let her sister ruin things for her in Bonduel. "Don't fret. I don't mind spending time with Rachel."

Lia's countenance fell further. "Oh, you don't?"

"She is really a very pleasant girl. And helpful. She can help me make cheese on the days we are together. I will buy a supply of small gloves."

He meant for her to laugh. Instead, Lia acted as if he had said something very hurtful. He didn't like her reaction.

"You're annoyed again," she said.

"Because I hate trying to guess what you are thinking."

"I am thinking that you and Rachel would make a striking couple."

Moses grunted. "And you must keep learning from

Sarah. I won't allow you to quit or let your dat ruin things for you."

Lia sighed deeply. "I can never repay all you've done for me."

"A piece of pie will be all the thanks I need."

Mammi came huffing into the house with Isaac Weaver close behind. Isaac and his wife, Lindy, were Mammi and Dawdi's closest neighbors. They had six small children and twenty head of cattle. Moses bought all Isaac's milk for the cheese factory.

"Isaac," said Moses, "Gute to see you."

"Gute maiya, Moses."

"Lindy is feeling poorly," Mammi said, rummaging through her kitchen cupboards.

Isaac stood just inside the door. "I came for some raspberry leaf. I know Anna always keeps some about."

"Are the kinner feeling okay?" Lia asked.

"Jah, all well, but it's a burden when their mother is so sick."

Lia reached into the fridge and pulled out a delectable-looking pie. She showed it to Anna. "Is it all right?"

Anna nodded.

Lia glanced apologetically at Moses and handed the pie to Isaac. "Take this for your family. Pie is such a comfort when things are out of sorts."

Isaac smiled. "Denki, Lia. They will really enjoy it."

Mammi handed Isaac a plastic bag full of raspberry leaves plus a pink dishrag from her knitting closet. "Here. These will make her feel better."

Isaac smiled and took his treasures. Moses watched out the window as his pie disappeared down the hill. He slumped his shoulders and groaned as if his heart would break.

"Sorry, Moses," said Lia. "I will bake you a pie next week."

Moses flashed Lia a mischievous grin. "That is a piecrust promise. Easily made, easily broken."

Lia propped her hands on her hips. "I'll have you know, piecrusts are not easily made."

"All I know is that Lia Shetler's pies are as rare as hen's teeth."

Owen Shetler ate two big pieces of meatloaf and three helpings of corn all the while praising Rachel for the meal she might have cooked if Lia had only given her a turn. He cleaned his plate and held his fork at the ready. "I'm ready for pie."

Moses didn't mourn for the pie quite so badly when he saw Owen Shetler's disappointment that there would be none. Lia's dad would be going to bed without dessert.

It was precisely what he deserved.

Dat's driver pulled up the lane promptly at six. Dat laid his napkin over his plate and scooted from the table. "That was delicious." He shook his finger at Rachel. "Next time I come, I want to see you do the cooking."

Rachel tilted her head playfully. "Of course."

Moses, his grandparents, and the Shetlers stood in unison, and Lia and Moses began clearing the dishes from the table.

"Come again, Owen," said Felty, shaking Dat's hand. "And bring Eliza next time. Tell her your girls are getting along right as rain."

"I will." Dat motioned to the door. "Moses, can you come out and point my driver in the direction of your cheese factory? I'd like to go by and see the place before heading home."

Moses laid a stack of dirty silverware on the counter and flashed an apologetic look at Lia before following Dat out the door. Butterflies fluttered around Lia's insides when Moses flashed his teeth at her. He had a way of making her feel more important than she was.

Dat closed the door behind them, and Anna gave Rachel's arm a motherly pat. "Well, dear, I'm sure your dat was satisfied with what he saw."

Rachel stared out the window. "I guess so. He probably wants to make things clear to Moses. One more time. Maybe." Her voice trailed off as she watched Moses and Dat, no doubt wishing she could hear the conversation.

Felty winked in Lia's direction. "It's good Lia is here to make things easier for you."

"Uh-huh."

Anna carried a stack of cups to the counter. "Rachel, would you go down to the cellar and fetch a bottle of peaches? They would taste so gute for dessert."

Rachel turned from the window. "Lia, you go. I want to wave to Dat one more time."

Lia pressed her lips together and dried her hands. It was easier to do it herself than to talk Rachel into anything. She tromped down the thick wooden steps to the long shelf full of colorful bottles of fruits and vegetables. She studied the labels and picked a bottle of peaches that had been canned last year. Best use the oldest fruit first.

She didn't realize the small cellar window stood open until she heard heavy footsteps on the porch above her. The window sat below and to the side of the porch, and when it was open, Lia could hear everything that went on up there. Moses was probably coming back into the house.

The clomping stopped on the porch, and Lia heard the voices of both Moses and her dat.

"It's no trouble for me to come back," she heard Dat say. "The phone shack is but a ten-minute walk from the house. Here's the number. I check messages almost every day. Make no bones about calling me if Lia gets in the way."

"I think it's better if Lia stays here and does the choring so Rachel will have more free time to be with me."

Lia held her breath and moved away from the window. Had Moses changed his mind about Rachel? Maybe Dat's praise of Rachel at supper had been more convincing than Lia had believed. Two hours ago, Moses had positively assured Lia that he wasn't interested.

No. He had said, *I don't mind spending time with Rachel. She is really a very pleasant girl.*

Lia cradled two bottles of peaches in her arms and made her way up the steps.

Moses's comment probably didn't mean anything but a way to placate Dat.

It probably didn't mean anything at all.

"Rachel, wake up," Lia whispered.

The only thing that moved on the lump under the covers was Rachel's mouth. "What time is it?"

"Two thirty. Moses is waiting outside. Diane Nelson's baby is on the way."

Rachel groaned and rolled onto her back. "Go without me."

"Dat said I can't leave the house without you."

"He didn't mean in the middle of the night."

"It doesn't matter what you think he meant. Get up. Moses is waiting."

Rachel sat up slowly and then sank back into her pillow. "What am I to do with Moses at two in the morning? I'm not going."

Lia felt guilty about her swelling sense of satisfaction. Rachel really was delicate and really did need her sleep, but being yanked out of bed at two in the morning was her just desserts. Lia grasped Rachel's arm and pulled hard. "You're going. This is what you said you wanted, and I won't go against Dat."

Rachel tried to swat Lia away. Lia doubled her efforts, and Rachel would have ended up in a heap on the floor if she had not caught herself and stood up. "You're only making me go because you're mad I told Dat."

"He won't fault me for strictly obeying his directions."

"Jah, he will. You'll see."

Lia pulled Rachel's nightgown up over Rachel's head and quickly helped her into her dress. She didn't bother with the bertha. Rachel smoothed her hands over her hair. "I look a mess. I'm not going. What will Moses think?"

"I don't care what Moses thinks."

"Is he in his buggy?"

"Jah," said Lia, "and it will take us almost an hour to get there."

Rachel glared at Lia. "Your hair is nicely in place. I bet you spent twenty minutes getting ready before you woke me."

Lia handed Rachel a scarf to cover her head. No time

to spare for a kapp. Even by the dim kerosene lantern, Lia could see the darts Rachel shot with her eyes.

"Put on your shoes and stockings. I will wait for you outside."

Lia retrieved her bag from her bedroom and walked out into the pleasant summer night. The chirp of crickets amplified the stillness. Moses fed Sammy a few oats from the palm of his hand.

"Is she coming?" he said, taking Lia's bag.

"Any minute."

"I don't think this is her idea of a fun outing."

Lia tried not to grin.

Clutching her scarf just below her chin, Rachel stumbled out of the house as if her feet weighed a hundred pounds each.

Moses was especially chipper and ignored her resistance. "It's so gute to see you, Rachel. I'm glad your dat insisted you come."

Lia tried to suppress the nagging feeling that Moses actually meant what he said. Surely he just wanted to humor Rachel.

Rachel perked up a bit when she saw him. "I wanted to come."

Moses slid the buggy door open. "Rachel, you'll want the backseat so you can sleep."

Rachel looked as if she would protest. The front seat next to Moses was a prime spot. Instead, she opened her mouth wide for a tremendous yawn and nodded. "I need my sleep. I told Lia I need my sleep. She wouldn't listen."

Moses actually winked at Lia. She thought her heart would leap out of her chest. "You have a delicate constitution. This must be hard for you."

"I try not to complain."

Rachel curled up in the backseat as Moses helped

Lia into the front. He squeezed her hand. "This will be fun."

"Denki for giving up your sleep for me."

"Don't mention it. I want you to have the experience."

They descended the lane and pulled out onto the main road. Not a car in sight. Moses prompted the horse into a trot. "I don't want you to miss the whole thing."

"What time did Sarah call you?"

"About thirty minutes ago. This time we are going halfway to Marion. I am glad for my new buggy. The lights make it safer on the dark roads." Moses pointed to the floor at Lia's feet. "I brought something for you."

Lia leaned over and felt around the floor until her fingers encountered a thick book with lots of papers sticking out the top. She lifted it onto her lap. "The midwife book. Does Sarah want me to read it again?"

Moses glanced at Lia and curled his lips. "Nae. I saw how reluctant you were to part with that book. I bought Sarah a new copy, and she says you can keep this one."

"Oh, Moses, you shouldn't have." Lia sighed, hugging the book to her like an old friend. A cheery fire glowed inside her even as she knew she couldn't keep the book. "I can't accept this. I wanted to order my own until I found out how much it cost, and I refuse to let you put out your hard-earned money just so I can have my own book."

"I like it when you're happy. You must keep that book or I will be in the depths of despair."

"You'll get over it. Take the book back and bring me a tub of shortening, and that will be gift enough."

Moses chuckled. "You're the easiest girl to please I've ever met. Barbara used to . . ." He stopped laughing and twisted his lips into a slight frown, but the momentary chill didn't last long. "Shortening is not on my list of good gifts."

"Good enough for me."

"Keep the book. It's too much trouble to lug back to the bookstore."

"You will manage."

Moses's feathers didn't seem to be ruffled at all. "Why are we talking about this in the middle of the night when you are clearly not thinking straight? We'll discuss it in the morning when I have more energy to persuade you of my point of view."

Lia pursed her lips and gave him the look she would have given a naughty schoolboy. "You won't persuade me. I'm stubborn when I want to be."

He raised an eyebrow. "Only when you want to be? That trait seems pretty consistent to me."

Lia flashed a sickly-sweet smile, nibbled on a finger-nail, and batted her eyes at Moses. The gesture only made him laugh. With that, the debate was decidedly over, but Lia couldn't figure out who had won.

The road stretched on before them, and Lia didn't resist the rhythmic *clip-clop* of Sammy's hooves against the blacktop. The sound lulled her into a sleepy daze where dreams and reality jumbled together in her head.

The buggy lurched to a halt, and Lia awoke with her cheek resting quite comfortably into Moses's shoulder. She snapped her head up as Moses secured the reins. He looked into her eyes with a guarded expression. Was he annoyed or simply tired?

Clearing his throat, he appeared very interested in the knobs on his dashboard. "We're here."

Lia smoothed an imaginary piece of hair from her face and scooted a few inches away from his warmth. Why hadn't he nudged her away earlier?

She studied his face in the dim light. Had she made him feel uncomfortable sleeping so peacefully like that? He was definitely uncomfortable about something.

"What shall we do with Rachel?"

"She'll have to go in with you," Moses said, "even if Sarah resists. I'm going to unhitch Sammy and sleep out here in the buggy."

Lia reached back and shook Rachel's shoulder. "Rachel, wake up. We're here."

Rachel sat up with a start. "What time is it?"

"Cum. Let's go."

Lia climbed out of the buggy and helped a groggy Rachel to the ground. Moses carried the bag to the front porch of the two-story red-brick house where a light burned in an upstairs window. Lia knocked softly as Rachel trudged up the steps behind her. No answer. She cracked the door open. If everyone in the house was busy bringing the baby into the world, there would be no one available to answer the door.

Rachel turned to Moses and mustered a little enthusiasm. "What shall we do while Lia's in there?"

Moses took off his hat. "You should get some rest. I am going to catch some sleep in the buggy."

"Lia shouldn't have woke me up."

Moses smiled at Rachel as if she were a toddler who had just taken her first step. "I'm glad Lia woke you so you could be with us."

Moses was certainly being considerate of Rachel's mood. Lia pursed her lips and ignored the prick in her heart. It was too early in the morning to make any sense of what Moses did or did not mean by his kindness. He always treated others kindly. Why should Lia feel threatened by that?

Lia took Rachel's arm. "Come in the house. We will find you a place to lie down."

"Wake me if you need anything," Moses said.

Lia peeked inside the house. All quiet downstairs. The front door opened to a spacious family room with two sofas facing each other. The rhythmic ticking of a grandfather clock punctuated the silence.

Lia pointed to one of the sofas. "You can sleep here while I am upstairs." Lord willing, Sarah would not discover Rachel until it was time to leave.

"I need a blanket."

Lia felt around in the shadows until she found an afghan sitting in a basket next to the end table. Rachel made herself comfortable on the sofa, and Lia spread the afghan over her. "Sleep well."

"I won't be able to sleep a wink."

Lia followed the faint light up the stairs and down a long hallway. She passed three closed doors where the family most likely slept. Light seeped from under the fourth door. Lia tapped lightly and cracked the door open. A propane floor lantern hissed as it cast its white light around the room. Sarah bent over the expectant mother, who sat in a straight-backed chair next to the bed.

Two open windows met at one corner of the room and a cool breeze teased the curtains back and forth.

Sarah wiped her hands on a towel and nodded to Lia. "Gute. You are here. Close the door. The time is almost come. Did Moses have trouble finding the place?"

Lia shook her head and felt her face get warm. She wasn't entirely sure how they got there. She had slept very comfortably on Moses's shoulder most of the trip.

Sarah pointed to the soon-to-be mother, who must have been between contractions. She breathed heavily but looked relatively comfortable. "This is Diane."

"Sarah says you have skill at getting women through their pain," Diane said.

Lia smiled. "I'm glad I can help. I am sorry I couldn't be here sooner."

"This is Diane's sixth," Sarah said.

"You sit up for labor?" Lia asked.

"Jah. Let gravity do the work."

Sarah rubbed her hand up and down Diane's arm. "I've been here two hours yet, and she's almost ready to push."

"I try not to make too much noise," Diane said, panting as new pain seized her. "The kinner are fast asleep, and Elijah is in the barn getting a head start on his chores."

"You're in transition," Sarah said. "Now the hard work begins."

An hour later, Diane held a bouncing baby boy in her arms while Sarah and Lia cleaned up the linens. Sarah, who could guess any baby's weight within an ounce, declared him to be a nine pounder, a healthy baby, with a full head of curly brown hair and a double chin.

Lia felt completely drained of energy but couldn't have been more satisfied. Sarah had let her catch the baby this time. "Don't drop it," she had whispered before the head popped out. New babies were slippery.

The sun peeked over the horizon as Lia and Sarah finished tidying the room. Sarah slipped a tiny knitted hat onto the baby's head. "I'll go fetch Elijah."

Diane smiled as only a relieved mother after delivery can smile. "Denki. That one wasn't as hard as the last."

"You did a wonderful-gute job. It comes natural to

some." Sarah gathered up the soiled sheets. "Would you like me to stay until your sister comes?"

"Nae, she will be here soon. Both of you go home and get some sleep. You did good work."

"Nae, you did good work," Sarah said.

Lia took up her bag and trudged down the stairs. Sarah followed close behind with her armload of laundry. She caught sight of Rachel snoring softly on the sofa and pursed her lips.

"It's a long story," Lia said.

"Write me a letter. I'm too weary for explanations." Sarah turned down the hallway to the washroom. "I will get Elijah. Tell Moses he is to come to dinner on Wednesday. We will have pot roast."

Lia nudged Rachel several times without a response. She resorted to poking her sister in the ribs. Rachel finally stirred and opened her eyes. "Where's Moses?"

"Come on, before the whole house wakes up."

Rachel sat up and cradled her head in her hands. "Oy anyhow, what a headache."

Lia and Rachel walked outside where Moses's horse was already hitched to the buggy and waiting patiently for them. Rachel peered in the buggy window. "I don't see Moses."

As if conjured by Rachel's voice, Moses appeared around the side of the house with a sack of flour slung over his back. Lia could see the straining muscles of his shoulders and arms. That bag couldn't weigh less than a hundred pounds.

His countenance put the sunrise to shame. "Sarah says you're ready to go."

Rachel sighed and massaged her neck. "Ach, please take us home. I hurt all over from sleeping on that lumpy sofa."

Moses stood there as if the flour weighed nothing

and he had all the time in the world to chat. "How did it go?"

Lia loved the warmth that spread over her whenever she saw Moses. "I got to catch the baby and cut the cord. Sarah said I did well."

"I'm sure you did. She probably wonders how she got along without you."

Rachel stomped her foot weakly. "Can we go?"

Moses patted the bag of flour. "Let me dump this in the bin, and I'll be right out."

He strode into the house with his flour sack, and Lia and Rachel climbed into the buggy.

"I'm sitting in the front this time," Rachel said. "It's a long ride home, and I want to be close to Moses."

Lia dutifully climbed in the back. She could sleep while Rachel flirted with Moses.

"I've been thinking," Rachel said as she settled into her seat of honor. "Moses will never be able to speak freely if you are always with us."

"But you can be alone when he drops me off for midwifing."

Rachel batted her eyelashes as if she had something very irritating in her eye. "Well, we saw how well that worked out today, didn't we? I want to have a picnic. With just Moses and me. Will you help me make fried chicken? Men love fried chicken, and I don't make it because I don't want to get burned when the oil pops out of the pan."

"I can show you how to avoid that."

"And a pie. Moses loves pie. He told me so himself. Will you make a pie for our picnic?"

Lia couldn't think of anything less appealing than putting together a picnic lunch for Moses and Rachel. If Rachel wanted Moses, she should make her own hay. But Lia already knew that she would help her sister.

Dat would demand it, and Rachel truly was helpless in the kitchen. Lia would rather Rachel didn't burn down the Helmuths' house.

It wasn't as if Moses would fall in love with Rachel simply because of the delicious food. Lia wasn't that good a cook.

Moses jogged out of the house like a man who had a good eight hours of sleep. He leaped into the buggy, paused for a moment when he saw that Rachel sat in the front seat, and took up the reins. "Elijah's got his work cut out for him. Six little ones, cattle to feed, crops to tend to. They pulled up roots from Lancaster four years ago. Land is less expensive here."

"Did you sleep okay?" Lia asked.

Rachel propped her elbow against the window. "I didn't sleep one minute."

Moses joggled the reins and got Sammy moving forward. "I slept like a baby. I can sleep anywhere, but I can't sleep past the light."

"So you got up and helped Elijah with his chores," Lia said.

"He's got a nice little place here, but he still has to work at the packing plant to support his family." Moses pulled a small watch from his pocket. "If we hurry, we'll have time to get back to Huckleberry Hill to help Mammi and Dawdi get ready for gmay."

Rachel pinched her face into a frown. "I forgot church is at Anna's today. I can't go. I'm exhausted."

Moses took her resistance as a joke. "It would be strange for you to be sleeping while people are worshipping outside your door."

"And they'll need your room for mothers tending to babies," Lia said.

Rachel snapped her head around and pinned Lia

with a glare. "This is your doing, Lia. You insisted on waking me up."

Moses's face clouded over, and he riveted his gaze to the road ahead. "I hope you do not blame Lia." He coughed. "I wanted to spend the time with you."

Rachel's expression melted into a glowing smile. "Oh, I didn't mean that in a bad way, to accuse Lia. I am glad we can be together."

Lia wanted to shrink into a little ball and make herself invisible in case they declared their undying love.

Rachel inched closer to him, but he had stacked a jacket and some work boots between them, so she couldn't get close enough to touch. "Moses, what are you doing next Friday?"

"Same as I always do. Making cheese."

"How would you like to go on a picnic with me?"

"Okay," Moses said. "We could hike to the place where the huckleberry bushes are the thickest and find some shade. It's not a hard walk. Mammi and Dawdi could do it with our help, if Mammi will let me help her."

"This picnic would be for the two of us. Do you like fried chicken?"

Moses snapped the reins. The horse picked up its pace. "The more, the merrier on a picnic."

"I want to explore the hill. Anna and Felty can't walk that far, and Lia is always so busy." Rachel stuck her bottom lip out in that way that always seemed to charm boys. "Please, Moses. I want to take you exploring."

Moses glanced back at Lia, and his frown seemed to sink deeper into his face. He either didn't know how to tell Rachel no, or didn't want to say yes with Lia looking over his shoulder. It was what he'd told Dat he wanted.

"Okay," Moses said, irritation still etched into his features. "I will come Friday at dinnertime."

Rachel giggled. "We are going to have so much fun."

When they arrived at Huckleberry Hill, men from the district were already setting up benches in Anna and Felty's great room. Moses helped move the sofa to the side before Rachel collapsed onto it and didn't move until people filed in for services.

Before they had finished the Lob Song, Rachel laid her head on Lia's shoulder and fell asleep. She woke herself up with a rafter-rattling snort during the preacher's sermon. The kind people of the district pretended not to notice, but Lia heard a few chuckles from Moses's side of the room.

Chapter Thirteen

"Is it too hot to wag your tail for me, Sparky?" Moses called as he jumped off his horse and led him to the barn with less enthusiasm than he'd ever had in his life. Sparky, lounging lazily under the shade of the porch, looked more excited than Moses felt.

Why had Moses ever agreed to a picnic with Rachel? Some people considered her pretty, but Moses was convinced that those lovesick boys in Wautoma were either blind or foolish. Couldn't they recognize a spoiled princess within ten minutes of knowing her?

Did Rachel always lie in wait for him just inside the house? She threw open the front door and squealed. "Moses! I was afraid you wouldn't come."

Moses lifted his hand in an unenthusiastic wave and kept walking to the barn. Rachel held Lia's fate in her hands. If Rachel complained about how things were going between her and Moses, Lia would be commanded home without a second thought. Moses could not let that happen. Lia needed to stay here where she could learn from Sarah and where Moses could see her often.

There, he'd admitted it. He liked being with Lia.

The happiest days he spent were with her, telling her dumb jokes, making her laugh, hearing her wisdom about everything. But the price of Lia's company became increasingly steep. Not only was he forced to coddle Rachel, but Rachel might get her heart broken by his reluctant attentions. He didn't care for Rachel, but he didn't want to raise her hopes only to dash them. He wasn't that cruel.

He would have to tread carefully. That's why he'd said something encouraging to her fater about wanting to spend time with her. But when Rachel truly recognized his rejection, her anger would be swift, harsh, and unreasonable. And Lia would feel the brunt of Rachel's displeasure.

And then he thought of Barbara. He had actually forgotten to send her his letter last week. He'd written it, but it had been buried under some papers on his desk. He had remembered it this morning when Barbara's letter came in the mail. She was more constant than he.

Moses could tell by the tone of her letter how upset Barbara had been not to receive his. *Have you forgotten me like everybody else in Bonduel? I depend on your steadiness, Moses. You are the only person who still believes in me.*

He felt so ashamed that he wrote a seven-pager to Barbara this morning and rode to the post office to make sure it got in the mail. He swam in guilt. Barbara depended on his faithfulness, but she dominated his thoughts less and less these days. Lia had a way of shoving memories of Barbara completely out of his mind. And worse, he didn't want to stop thinking about Lia, no matter how disloyal he felt to Barbara. Lia made him so happy.

Leaving his riding horse, Red, in the barn, Moses emerged to find Rachel standing on the front porch with a basket tucked into the crook of her elbow. Moses felt like a teenager on the first day of school as he walked up the steps and took the heavy basket from Rachel's arm. Was she planning on being gone for a few days?

Rachel wore a robin's-egg blue dress that made her eyes shine extra bright. Her skin looked smooth and freshly scrubbed. "Which way to the top of the hill?" she asked.

Out of the corner of his eye, Moses saw a movement at the window and glanced in time to see Lia pull away from his view. He wished she were coming with them. He could stare at her all day. "Um, this is the top of the hill, where the house stands."

"Oh. Lia didn't tell me that."

"We could hike to the north where most of the huckleberry bushes grow. It's only a couple of miles."

Rachel bit her lip and raised her eyebrows. "How long will it take? I don't want to be worn out before we get there."

Gute. If she didn't want to venture too far from the house, they wouldn't have to spend more than an hour together. Closer was definitely better. He pointed to the east. "There is a nice little clearing not a hundred yards from here."

"Okay. I packed a blanket to spread on the ground so we'll be comfy."

She took his arm. He hadn't offered it. He pulled away and made a point to walk three steps ahead of her. It was easy to keep his distance. She had come barefoot—to a picnic in the woods.

Moses shook his head. Those boys in Wautoma? Blind and foolish.

"Here we are," announced Moses when he reached the clearing. By this time, Rachel lagged ten steps behind him. He reached into the basket and pulled out the blanket. It was a puny thing, no more than baby size. Rachel wasn't dense. She wanted to sit close and had brought the perfect size blanket to do just that.

No matter. Moses would simply sit in the dirt. He hadn't dressed up or anything.

He spread the blanket on a flat piece of ground and laid the basket on it. Rachel finally caught up. "Nae, Moses," she scolded. "It is the woman's job to lay out the food."

Reluctant to sit until Rachel had chosen her spot, Moses stood idly by as Rachel pulled her treasures out of the basket. She placed two paper plates on the blanket and then produced a brown paper grocery bag saturated with grease. She rolled down the sides of the bag to reveal four generous pieces of cold fried chicken. The smell made Moses's mouth water. Maybe Rachel did have talent with the skillet.

Another paper bag contained golden brown rolls, still warm from the oven. They smelled heavenly. Two small plastic containers held creamy butter and red raspberry jam. Moses knelt down to get a closer look.

Rachel saw his expression. Smiling in satisfaction, she produced a small bowl of coleslaw plus forks and napkins from the basket.

No matter how delicious it looked, none of the food could compare to the pie. It might have come straight out of a magazine, with stiff peaks of whipped cream sprinkled with flakes of chocolate. His taste buds did a dance of anticipation. Maybe the hour wouldn't be completely wasted after all.

Rachel served him the biggest piece of chicken with three spoonfuls of coleslaw and a flaky roll. He made sure to keep with the basket conveniently between them as he sat down on the ground just off the edge of Rachel's blanket. He spread a liberal dollop of jam on his roll and let Rachel talk while he ate. The bread melted in his mouth and the crispy fried chicken had just the right blend of spices to make his eyes water and his tongue crave more.

"Do you like the chicken?" Rachel asked.

Moses barely paid enough attention to catch her question. "Very good. It has a kick to it."

"Lia doesn't like spicy food, but I talked her into it. It's our mother's recipe."

Of course. Lia had made the chicken and probably the rolls and the coleslaw and the pie too. Anything to humor Rachel and placate her father. Hadn't Rachel said that Lia had been given certain responsibilities from her dat—like helping Rachel trap Moses into marriage? If she didn't fulfill those duties well, she would be shipped home.

"Dat had high hopes for Lia because she is such a gute cook, but then she got tall and lost her bloom. She's a big help to Mamm at home, though, which is good because that's probably where she'll be all her life. But Lia's happy with what God has given her. She doesn't pine for anything better."

Moses didn't know what to say. Would it make any difference to anybody if he defended Lia? Rachel thought Lia had lost her bloom? How absurd. Lia was the most beautiful girl Moses had ever met.

The guilt crashed into him like a barn door swinging shut. Did he really consider Lia more beautiful than Barbara? Barbara possessed perfect skin with a beauty mark at the corner of her lip that Moses had always found fascinating. Her eyes were the color of a frozen Wisconsin lake.

Lia's eyes were the color of chocolate cream sauce.

"Did Lia do the cooking?"

Rachel batted her eyelashes in irritation and swatted the thought of Lia away with a wave of her hand. "She helped. I'm not as good at pies as her. I get along fine in my life without knowing how to roll out crust."

Moses sank his teeth into his chicken as his indignation grew. Lia's family had convinced her that her talents and qualities were of little importance compared to Rachel's. And Lia, with her good heart, would never stand up for herself. In truth, she didn't believe she was worthy of any consideration.

Once Moses had cleaned his plate, Rachel casually moved the picnic basket off the blanket and sidled closer to him. He responded by standing up and running his hand over the bark of a maple close by. "We tapped this tree for syrup last winter."

Rachel didn't seem to notice his resistance. "Did you like the rolls?"

Moses hated giving Rachel compliments that were meant for Lia. He knit his brows together. "They were delicious. The best I've ever tasted."

Rachel blushed with pleasure. "Thank you. We had to get up extra early to make the dough so it would have a chance to rise. Lia woke me before sunrise. I think she takes satisfaction in robbing me of my sleep."

"Tell Lia I am very grateful."

Annoyance flitted across her face as she retrieved a knife and spatula from the basket. "Are you ready for some pie? It's chocolate cream."

Moses wanted a piece of that pie so badly he was tempted to scoop it from the blanket and run deeper into the woods where he could enjoy it in solitude. But if he took a piece of pie offered by Rachel, it would be like accepting a stolen gift. Lia had made the pie, but Rachel would take all the credit for it.

Moses couldn't stomach the thought. He wanted to be sitting next to Lia, not Rachel, when he took his first taste of Lia's pie. He wanted her to take pleasure in the look on his face. Lia should be the first to hear his praise. Rachel didn't deserve it.

He patted his stomach. "Couldn't eat another bite."

Rachel turned down the corners of her mouth. "Lia said you'd like chocolate."

"I love chocolate, but I really am stuffed."

Rachel held the pie out to him, most likely hoping the mere sight of it would convince him to change his mind. It almost did. There was nothing Moses liked better than pie.

When he didn't take the bait, her frown deepened, and she shoved the pie into its special plastic container as if she were angry at it. Back into the basket it went. "I told Lia we should have done cherry."

Did she have to be vexed with Lia every time she didn't get her way? In hopes of diverting Rachel's wrath, Moses surrendered and sat next to her on the blanket. "Cherries give me a rash."

Rachel's expression softened immediately. She giggled demurely and fingered the ties of her kapp, all the while keeping her sparkling eyes glued to his face. "I don't like cherry all that much myself."

Rachel stretched her legs out in front of her, crossed her ankles, and leaned back on her hands. "I could sit in the sun all day." She tilted her head back, closed her eyes, and let her face soak up the filtered sunlight. Her tactics were impressive. She knew how to show off her good looks. With her eyes closed, a boy would feel free to gaze at her lovely face and dream about kissing those full lips.

Little did she know that Moses was immune to her charms. "Pretty is as pretty does," Dawdi would say.

With her eyes still shut, Rachel sighed and puckered her lips slightly. Oh, she had a strategy, all right.

Moses wasn't in a mood to humor her for very long. "Rachel?" he said softly so as not to startle her.

She fluttered her eyelids, turned her face to him, and smiled in anticipation. Oh, sis yuscht, she expected a kiss!

He'd let this go on long enough. Practically leaping to his feet, he put several feet between them. "I've got to make one more batch of cheese today."

Rachel didn't even attempt to hide her surprise or her displeasure. She raised an eyebrow and glared at him with those stormy blue eyes. "Right now?"

"Jah. I don't want to be up all night pressing."

She quickly composed herself and smoothed her hands down the front of her dress. "But it's such a nice day."

"We will have to do this again sometime." Had he really opened the door to that possibility just to soothe Rachel's wrath? Yep. He was a coward. But he couldn't figure out how to deflate Rachel's hopes without losing Lia.

Rachel pursed her lips and took her time putting things back in the picnic basket. Once she had everything loaded, she looked up at him and smiled warmly. Gute. She had decided to be sweet instead of vindictive. She reached out her hand, and Moses helped her to her feet. Her hand lingered in his, and her eyes danced playfully. Moses pulled from her grasp and picked up the blanket. He stuffed it into the basket and started walking.

This time his conscience nagged him to wait for

Rachel. He shouldn't leave her behind to limp around in the woods, even if they were only a few hundred feet from the house. He slowed his pace until she caught up to him. She smiled weakly as she tiptoed over the rough ground. Why hadn't she worn her shoes?

"What is your house like?" she said, breaking the silence that had prevailed since they left the clearing.

"Do you remember seeing it? It is right next to the cheese factory."

Suddenly, Rachel halted, grabbed her shin, and howled in pain.

"What happened?"

"My foot. I think I stepped on something." Grasping her ankle, she limped awkwardly to a fallen log and sat down. She propped her right ankle on her left knee and examined the bottom of her foot.

Moses sat next to her. "Did it feel sharp?"

"It felt like a snake bite or something," Rachel said, panting as if she had lost a toe.

Studying her foot closely, Moses gently pressed his thumb around her heel and up to her toes. He didn't feel or see anything, but he tried to be sympathetic. Rachel really had convinced herself that she was delicate.

She hissed through her teeth when he felt around the pad of her foot. "There. That's where it hurts."

"It didn't break the skin."

"Do you think it was a snake?"

"Nae. Probably a sticker."

A single tear trickled down Rachel's cheek. "I don't think I can make it back."

Still lugging the picnic basket, Moses stood up and cupped Rachel's elbow in his hand. "Here. I will put my arm around you if you can manage to limp the rest of the way. It's only another hundred steps or so."

The corner of Rachel's mouth twitched upward. "I will try."

Moses wrapped his arm securely around her waist, and she in turn put her arm around him. When he took a step, she gasped and nearly fell over. "Hold on," he said, tightening his grip and pulling her closer.

She tilted her head back and flashed a delighted smile at him. Oh, jah, surely the pain was excruciating.

When they hobbled into the clearing where the house stood, Rachel stopped limping altogether.

Moses relaxed his hold. "Does it feel better?"

"A little, but don't let go. I don't think I can make it by myself." She slipped her hand into his, which made balancing the basket a bit tricky.

Grinding his teeth together, Moses walked Rachel up the porch steps and to the front door. "I will help you into the house." It gave him a good excuse to see Lia, to try to explain to her about the pie.

Rachel suddenly regained all her energy. "No need. I am feeling much better now. Denki for a wonderful day."

"Tell Lia I will help her pick tomatoes on Tuesday."

"You can help me pick tomatoes. I am faster than Lia. Her hands are too big."

Moses didn't mean to sigh out loud. "I will see you on Tuesday, then."

She blew him a kiss as she slid into the house. A kiss.

Moses trudged away wishing Owen Shetler and his daughter Rachel had never set foot on Huckleberry Hill.

Lia didn't watch for them. She wasn't so pathetic as to stand at the kitchen window all afternoon and hope to catch a glimpse of Rachel and Moses picnicking in the woods.

But she happened to be washing dishes when her sister came stumbling out of the trees with her arm around Moses and his arm securely around her. Rachel looked quite satisfied with herself and Moses did not look particularly annoyed. The air in the kitchen suddenly became unbreathable. Lia let her rag sink into the dishwater as she hastily dried her hands and ran down the hall and into her bedroom. She didn't want to hear about the picnic, and Rachel would surely want to tell. Better to be unavailable when Rachel came skipping into the house.

She should have known better. She heard the front door close and Rachel's light footsteps tripping down the hall.

Rachel pounded on her door. "Lia, I'm back." Rachel opened the door without waiting for Lia to let her in. She sprawled on Lia's bed and let her feet hang over the side.

Lia stood in the middle of her tiny room as if she were a propane lamp waiting for the darkness. She didn't speak but she tried to smile. She should rejoice in Rachel's happiness.

Rachel sighed as if to expel every bit of air from her lungs. "What a glorious, glorious day. I told you we needed time alone together. Moses couldn't have been nicer."

"You weren't gone very long."

"I didn't want to walk far in my bare feet."

Lia clicked her tongue. "You should have worn shoes."

Rachel sat up, straightened her legs, and studied her feet. "Men think bare feet are sexy."

"Sexy? What a word!"

"The magazine at the grocery store said so."

"Did he like the chicken?"

"He ate two pieces. And the rolls. He loved the rolls. He finished off every last bite of jam, and you didn't think I should bring it."

"I always have good fortune with that roll recipe."

"But he didn't eat one bite of pie."

Moses had to know she made the pie. "He didn't?" A sudden headache pounded behind Lia's eyes.

Rachel leaned back on her hands and pinned Lia with a critical eye. "I'm not stupid. You like him."

"Of course I like him. He was my friend before you even knew him."

"You're going to get your feelings hurt, and I don't want you to get your feelings hurt."

Lia decided she didn't like her bedroom so much when Rachel sat in it. "I'm going to finish the dishes."

"Moses is interested in me, not you. He held my hand, Lia. Held-my-hand. And he put his arm around me."

Anna might marvel at Moses's change of heart, but not Lia. Rachel knew how to make herself irresistible. "Then you have nothing to fear from me."

Rachel stood and put her arms around Lia in a sisterly hug. "I'm saying this for your own good. I'd hate to see you make a fool of yourself. Moses cares about your feelings too."

Lia wanted to melt in a puddle of tears and run into the woods where she could be alone. Instead, she surrendered and pulled Rachel close for an embrace.

She hadn't planned on caring so much about Moses. He'd warned her the very first day they met. Why hadn't she heeded him? Taking a deep breath, Lia pulled herself from Rachel's grasp and pasted on a convincing smile. "I am only here to help Anna and Felty. I am very happy for you and Moses."

Rachel let go of Lia and did a little twirl around the room. "He is so handsome. And strong." She gave Lia's hand a squeeze. "Thank you for making the food. You must make a dozen pies for our wedding. Moses loves pie."

Chapter Fourteen

Moses stood on the porch and leaned a hand on the door frame. Why did he have to be so handsome? Lia would be able to forget him more easily if acne scars pocked his cheeks or his eyebrows grew as thick as juniper bushes. And why did that dimple on his cheek enchant her so? "Sarah said to fetch you right quick," Moses said. "She's just two miles down the road at Millers'."

Lia's hand flew to her mouth. "Saloma's early."

"Sarah said she might have to send her to the hospital."

Lia glanced at her half-kneaded bread dough on the counter. It would have to wait. "I'll fetch my bag. Will you get Rachel? She's hanging the wash."

Lia got her bag and took it to the buggy. She automatically climbed in back. Moses would want to sit next to Rachel. Clasping her hands together, Lia tried to mentally review what she knew about pre-term babies. At the moment, she couldn't remember one blasted thing.

What was taking Rachel and Moses so long?

They finally appeared around the corner of the

house, Rachel chatting merrily while Moses strode with purpose. At least one of them felt a sense of urgency.

Rachel jumped in the buggy and giggled. "I thought I would be stuck doing chores all day. What a wonderful-gute surprise."

Moses seemed in good humor as well. "As soon as we drop Lia off, we're coming back here. I told Dawdi I'd mend the barn roof."

Rachel stuck out her bottom lip so far that a bird could have perched on it. "Can't you do that another time? We have the whole day to ourselves."

Moses smiled brightly and shook his head. "That roof won't last another storm."

Vernon Miller's place was small and bursting with children. Saloma, forty-three years old, expected her seventh child. And perhaps eighth. She was convinced she was pregnant with twins. Sarah had tried to talk her into seeing a doctor and delivering at a hospital, but Saloma would have none of it. "I've had plenty of babies and got along fine without a doctor."

Two mighty oaks stood watch in the Millers' front yard where three barefoot children chased each other around the lawn. A shock of purple petunias grew up against the house next to an unruly rosebush laden with fat, pink blooms. Sarah's buggy already sat on the gravel lane that led to the barn.

Moses got out and took Lia's hand to help her down. She willed her heart to slow. How would she ever get used to him as a brother-in-law?

He took Lia's bag and the three of them walked to the house. Why Rachel even bothered getting out of the buggy was anybody's guess. She probably felt as if she were missing something very important if she was more than ten feet from Moses's side.

Sarah opened the door before they could knock.

Her eyes held a look of controlled desperation, and her face glowed ghostly pale. Lia's heart began to gallop.

Sarah glanced at Rachel with a look of distaste before grabbing Moses's arm. "Get the horse from the barn," she said in panicked whisper. "Ride to the Englisch neighbors as fast as you can. They are but five minutes west."

"The Van deGraffs?" Moses said.

Sarah nodded. "Use their phone and call an ambulance. We've got to get Saloma to the hospital now."

Moses didn't waste time asking questions. He sprinted to the barn and disappeared inside.

Sarah took both Lia and Rachel by the elbows and led them a few feet from the door. "There's six children and a husband who need reassuring, so don't neither of you make a fuss."

Lia nodded. Rachel looked as if she would be sick.

"Is the baby too early?" Lia asked.

"He's early, but that's not the worst of it. Saloma has started bleeding."

Rachel whimpered. Lia squeezed her hand hard until she stopped.

"It looks like placenta previa."

Lia felt dizzy. She'd read about placenta previa in her midwife book. Both the baby and the mother could die.

Sarah locked her fingers around Lia's arm. "We must get her to the hospital immediately, or she will bleed to death."

"What do you want me to do?" Lia said.

Rachel breathed in and out until Lia thought she might hyperventilate. "I can't do it," Rachel panted. "I can't go in there. The sight of blood makes me ill."

Still holding her hand, Lia dragged Rachel to the

base of one of the trees in the front yard and pushed her to sit. "Stay here and don't make a fuss. And don't let the kinner see there is anything amiss." Lia knelt down and sternly shook her finger at Rachel, who couldn't seem to catch her breath. "You must stay calm or I will make you walk home by yourself. Do you understand?"

Rachel's complexion turned red and splotchy. "It's too far."

"Do you understand?"

Rachel nodded.

Lia pulled a small washcloth from her bag and opened the bottle of water she always kept there. She poured some water onto the cloth. "Here, put this on the back of your neck. It will make you feel better."

Without waiting to see if Rachel could manage, Lia jogged back to Sarah, who had her hands propped impatiently on her hips. "Gute," Sarah said. "Let's go."

They strode into the house and straight to Saloma's room. She lay on her bed, deathly white, while her husband stroked her hand and her oldest daughter, Hannah, sponged her forehead with a damp rag. Two teenage sons stood in the corner of the room, unsure of what to do but not wanting to leave their mother's side.

All signs of Sarah's anxiety disappeared when she walked into the room. She looked at the two boys. "Peter, do you have more towels and blankets?"

"Jah. Plenty of both."

"The two of you go and get all the clean towels and blankets you can find and bring them to me."

Both boys raced out of the room.

Sarah pulled Lia next to the bed. "Saloma, I think the placenta has formed over your cervix. That is why there is so much bleeding. We must get you to a hospital."

Sweat beaded on Vernon's forehead. "Our neighbors have a car."

Sarah patted Vernon's arm reassuringly. "I've sent Moses to call an ambulance. In the meantime, we must slow the bleeding and arrest labor. Saloma, Lia is going to help you lie flat on your back and we are going to elevate your legs and hips. You must hold as still as you can."

"Should I get her something to drink?" Vernon said.

"No, nothing to drink. How long has it been since you've eaten or drunk anything, Saloma?"

"An hour or so."

Lia and Hannah helped Saloma scoot flat on her back. Then Lia propped pillows underneath her hips to elevate her bottom half. She glanced at Sarah, who gave her a slight nod to tell her she'd done it right.

Peter and his brother came in with the towels and blankets. Sarah took a thick towel and carefully slid it underneath Saloma while pulling the soiled one away from her. The gray cast to Saloma's face alarmed Lia. She feared Saloma might pass out.

Lia had never seen Sarah so rigid, almost as if she were made of stone. She pressed her lips into a hard line, and her face shone with sweat. The sight of Sarah so unyielding terrified Lia more than anything else.

The distant moan of a siren was the most welcome sound Lia had ever heard. She ran outside but ceased breathing when the sheriff's car pulled into the lane. Sarah followed right behind Lia.

The sheriff jumped out of his car. "What's the problem?"

"Where is the ambulance?" Sarah asked.

"It will be here in fifteen minutes."

Sarah hurried around the front of the car and stood face-to-face with the sheriff. "We don't have fifteen minutes to wait. She's in danger of bleeding to death. We need to take her in your car."

The sheriff fingered the radio hooked to his shirt pocket. "Are you sure? I'm not equipped to handle an emergency like this. The paramedics can give her an IV."

Moses jogged from the barn out of breath and with sweat trickling down his neck. It was a blistering-hot day. "What's happening?" he whispered. Lia merely inclined her head toward Sarah.

Sarah kept her attention on the sheriff. She glanced toward the house and lowered her voice. "By the time the ambulance gets here, it could be too late. And it's twenty minutes to the hospital."

The sheriff nodded gravely. "I can make it in fifteen."

This was all Sarah needed to hear. "Lia, Moses, cum. Moses, you must carry Saloma to the car. Vernon is in no condition."

Moses nodded curtly.

The three of them hurried into the house, and Sarah directed Moses on how she wanted him to lift Saloma. Saloma feebly wrapped her hands around Moses's neck, and he picked her up as if she weighed no more than an empty cardboard box. The muscles of his arms bulged, and Lia felt comforted by his strength.

Taking care to handle her gently, Moses whisked Saloma outside while she moaned quietly. Hannah spread two blankets in the backseat of the sheriff's car while the sheriff radioed ahead to the hospital. Moses set Saloma onto the seat, and Sarah reached in from the other side of the car and pulled Saloma so she could lie with her feet braced against the side door. Moses closed the door and stepped away, trying to give Saloma some privacy, even if she didn't notice.

Sarah firmly took Lia's arms and pulled her close.

"Get the family to the hospital as soon as you can, in case they must say good-bye to their mother."

A pang of dread traveled up Lia's spine. How could they abide so much sorrow?

Lia didn't know how she managed it with such long legs, but Sarah folded herself onto the floor of the backseat and began sponging Saloma's brow. "Vernon, get in the front."

"You both should have a seat belt back there," said the sheriff.

"If we crash, I ain't going to budge," Sarah said. "And Saloma's got to lie down. Don't get in an accident."

The sheriff responded with a half smile and a helpless shake of his head. "I am flouting about seven regulations. I'd be grateful if you kept this to yourself."

Lia closed one door, and Moses shut the other. As soon as Vernon climbed into the front, the sheriff turned on his lights, and his tires kicked up gravel as he sped out of the driveway.

The blaring siren soon obscured the roar of the engine. Both noises faded into the distance as Lia, Moses, and the children watched after them. Hannah had two of her little sisters gathered close, and the two teenage brothers each held one of the smallest girl's hands. The little one cried softly while the rest of the children stared at Lia as if she had the answers to all of life's questions.

Rachel, still red in the face, stood and went to Moses. "Take me home. I don't want to be here anymore. What if she dies?"

The two girls clinging to Hannah began to wail in dismay. Hannah knelt down and hugged them to her breast. "Hush, hush," she said. "It will be all right."

Pressing his lips together, Moses cupped his hand

around Rachel's elbow and led her away from the children. "Wait for me in the buggy."

Rachel looked at him doubtfully, but she shuffled to the buggy and climbed in.

Lia didn't want to impose on his kindness, but she wasn't sure she could handle things by herself. Every muscle stretched as tight as a wire, her legs felt shaky, and she feared she might collapse under the weight of her anxiety. "Moses, I know you want to see Rachel home but—"

Moses turned his back on the buggy. "I'm not going anywhere. Let her sit in the buggy where she won't cause trouble." He reached out and took Lia's hand. Her legs quit shaking. "What do you want me to do?"

"These children need to get to the hospital. Can you go back to Van deGraffs' and call a driver?"

"I knew they would want to be with their mother, so I called Roy once the ambulance was on its way. He should be here soon."

Lia sighed in relief and turned to Hannah, who looked almost as pale as her mother had. "A driver is coming to take you to the hospital. You might want to pack a bag for her and bring some snacks for your brothers and sisters. I don't know how long you will be there."

Hannah nodded and hurried into the house. Her two sisters cried louder when she left them.

Moses bent over and scooped both girls into his arms. They cried out in surprise, but he held them securely and bounced up and down. The girls, about ten and eight years old, stopped crying and stared at Moses with a mixture of puzzlement and fascination. He kept bouncing.

Peter pressed his palm against one eye and swiped

away whatever tear was thinking of forming there. "Will Mamm die?"

Moses, still bouncing, hardened his expression. "It is very serious. She has lost a lot of blood. But Lord willing, they will get her to the hospital on time. By the grace of God, Sarah knew what to do. He sent a wonderful-gute person to help your mother."

"That's right," said Lia. "Sarah is smart. She knows what to do for your mother."

Peter's brother bowed his head and squeezed the bridge of his nose as he began to weep. This prompted all three little girls to start bawling again. Peter lifted the littlest sister off the ground and cuddled her in his arms.

Lia felt utterly helpless. She dug her fingers into her palms and blinked back her own tears. No good for them to see her crying. She was supposed to be the one with everything under control.

"We need to pray." Moses placed the two weeping girls on the ground and took their hands. "Everybody hold hands."

The girls swallowed their sobs and sniffled softly when they formed a circle chain. Lia tucked herself between Peter and one of the girls.

Moses bowed his head. Everyone else followed suit. "Heavenly Father, we give thee thanks for thy bounties. Wilt thou save a mother for her children and give us thy peace and comfort in this time of trial and help the sheriff to drive fast and safe. Thy will be done. Amen."

They stood in silence holding hands until they heard Rachel tapping on the buggy window. No one could hear what she said, so she slid the door open. "Are you coming?"

Moses sighed as if all the weariness in the world had

caught up to him. He let go of the girls' hands and trudged to the buggy where Rachel waited impatiently. Lia didn't hear what they said to each other, but she saw Moses cup his hand under Rachel's chin. Rachel's expression softened, and she scooted farther into the buggy as Moses slid the door shut.

Hannah came from the house with two bulging canvas bags as Roy pulled into the driveway in his clunky white van.

"Cum," said Lia. "Get in."

She herded the children to the van while Moses gave Roy instructions. Peter lifted all three of his little sisters into the backseat, and Lia helped them buckle their seat belts and handed each of them a tissue from her bag. She saw Moses give Roy two twenty-dollar bills. Hiring a driver wasn't cheap.

The two boys climbed into the middle seat and buckled their seat belts. Hannah chose the front seat. Moses came around the front of the van and motioned for Hannah to roll down her window. He glanced at Lia and then held out his hand to Hannah. Lia caught a glimpse of green that could only be more cash. "Call my cheese factory if you need anything."

Hannah nodded but didn't speak.

Moses signaled Roy. "Let me know if more is needed."

Roy put his van into gear and backed out of the driveway. Hannah kept her eyes glued to Moses's face until Roy drove away.

Moses gazed into Lia's eyes with concern lining his face as he wrapped his fingers around her upper arms. "What now?"

"Take Rachel home. I'm going to strip the bed and wash everything," Lia said numbly. "They must not be burdened when they come back."

"I'll help."

"You should get Rachel home."

"I'm not going anywhere."

Lia all but burst with gratitude. What would she do without Moses?

They took a few steps toward the house when another knock from the buggy pulled them up short.

Again, Rachel slid the door open. "Are you coming?"

"I need to help Lia with the laundry. You don't have to wait. Walk home, if you want."

"I can't hike up that hill," Rachel whined.

Moses smiled sweetly. "Then wait for me."

Rachel slipped out of the buggy. "I'm coming in."

"There's a lot of blood," Moses said, his words dripping with sympathy for Rachel's delicateness.

Rachel halted as if she'd run into a brick wall. "Why do you have to help Lia? She is plenty able to do laundry by herself."

"It wouldn't take too long to walk home."

Rachel's mouth twisted in annoyance. "I will wait, but don't be long. You said you had to fix Anna and Felty's roof."

Rachel slammed the buggy door, and behind the glass, Lia could see her clasp her arms tightly around her waist and turn her face away from them. Rachel would be fit to be tied when she finally made it home, and Lia would never hear the end of how badly she had been treated. Dat would hear of it before week's end and probably summon Lia home in a matter of days.

Lia felt too emotionally spent to concern herself with Dat's displeasure. Who could worry about Dat when Saloma's life hung in the balance?

In Saloma's bedroom, blood stained the bedsheets and towels—a vivid reminder that six children might lose their mother today and that Lia wouldn't have known what to do if she had been called upon to care for Saloma by herself. Saloma would have died for certain under Lia's care. The thought frightened her.

A sob escaped her lips, and before she could control herself, the floodgates opened and she dissolved into tears. Moses immediately wrapped his strong arms around her and laid a tender kiss on her forehead. She soaked his shoulder with salt water, but he didn't seem to mind. His arms held her securely with no hint that he would ever let her go.

"It will be all right," he whispered. "You are safe. Everything will be all right."

"I can't do this," she said, weeping harder, touched that he wanted to comfort her. "I'm so weak."

"You stayed calm, especially after Sarah left. The children were afraid, and you soothed them."

"Nae, you did that."

"I did no such thing. How much could I have helped if you had been running around the house screaming or pulling your hair out with fear? I distracted them. You gave them assurance."

With her breath still coming in spasms, Lia stopped crying and savored the sound of Moses's heartbeat against her ear and the warmth of his arms wrapped tightly around her. She could stand like this forever. For the moment, he was not her future brother-in-law or simply a good friend. He was a handsome, wonderful man with whom she wouldn't mind spending the rest of her life.

She tilted her chin to look at his face. His brows were knit in confusion as if two conflicting emotions were feuding in his brain.

He cleared his throat and pulled his arms from around her as the corners of his mouth turned down. "Sorry."

Why did he feel the need to apologize for something

so pleasant? Did he feel disloyal to Rachel by giving Lia his shoulder?

Lia felt no such obligation to apologize to him. She would cherish his touch forever.

With his lips pressed in a hard line and his expression guarded, Moses pulled a handkerchief from his back pocket and handed it to Lia.

She took it and mopped up the moisture from her face. "Denki. I am not usually a crier." She must look a sight. Her nose had probably turned bright red.

"It has been a difficult morning." He didn't take his piercing gaze from her face. "Your eyes are even prettier after you cry."

Lia didn't know how to respond to that, so she sniffled into his handkerchief until she regained her composure.

With heightened color in his face, he finally broke eye contact and took two steps away from her. "I will go find a bucket."

Suddenly too flustered to utter a word, Lia busied herself stripping the bed. She gathered the sheets and mattress pad and took them to the washroom where Moses filled a bucket with a soapy solution. "I'll do the floor," he said.

Lia soaped and scrubbed and agitated the sheets until they probably looked whiter than the day they were purchased. Once she rinsed, she ran everything through the wringer twice so it would dry extra fast on the line. The wet sheets went into a basket for hanging.

She went down the hall to check on Moses's progress. The bucket of filthy water stood in the hall outside Saloma's room, and Moses was on his hands and knees buffing the floor with a dry towel. The refreshing scent of lemon and pine hung in the air.

Moses stood up, a satisfied smile playing at his lips. "Does it look okay?"

"I wouldn't dare walk on it. How did you get the wood so shiny?"

"My mamm is very particular about her floors. She trained me well."

Moses was the finest man Lia knew. His mamm had trained him well indeed.

He picked up his bucket. "How is the bedding coming?"

"Ready to be hung. The sun will give them an extra whitening."

"I will help you." Moses dumped his dirty water down the sink in the washroom and picked up the basket of wet sheets. "Let's go out the back door. If I give Rachel one more excuse, she'll probably want to throw very large rocks at me."

Lia couldn't help but smile. Moses knew Rachel too well. Lia didn't try to understand why he liked her.

Lia grabbed a small plastic box of clothespins and they marched, somewhat stealthily, out to the clothesline on the side of the house opposite where Moses had parked his buggy.

They each held up a corner of the first sheet and pinned it to the line. Moses's fingers weren't deft with the clothespins, but he managed to fasten the sheet securely. Lia handed him another pin as they worked their way fixing the long folds of fabric to the line and raising the sheet higher in the air with the pulley.

Moses held out his hand for another pin. "Did I ever tell you I like tall girls? Your height comes in very handy when hanging clothes."

"A short girl can hang laundry just fine."

"But it gives her sore shoulders and a crick in the neck."

Lia raised an eyebrow and grinned. Moses had been talking to Rachel.

His eyes twinkled mischievously, and he showed his dimple. "Will Rachel start throwing things at me if we stop at the Van deGraffs before I take you both home? I need to apologize to them and beg them not to have me arrested."

Lia laughed out loud. "What are you talking about?"

His face clouded over before he smiled reassuringly. "I broke into their house."

"You did?"

"They weren't home, so I bent a screen and crawled in through a basement window. I made two calls, left some money and a note."

Lia tried not to think about what might have happened if Moses hadn't been determined to get into the Van deGraffs' house. "Do you think they'll be mad?"

Moses shrugged his shoulders. "Maybe not. I left a lot of money."

With a teasing note to her voice, she said, "You must be very wealthy. How much money do you usually carry on outings with me?"

"Not enough. That screen is going to cost more than the fifty dollars I left."

"I will help you pay for it. I got my wages from Anna yesterday."

"That's a ridiculous thought. You weren't within a mile of Van deGraffs' when that screen broke."

"But I am partly responsible."

Moses pulled the clothesline toward him, propelling the fitted sheet higher into the air. "No, you are so graceful and slender, you would have been able to fit through their doggie door, and the screen need never have been damaged."

Lia smiled and tossed him another clothespin. "The sheets should not take too long to dry. After we go to Van deGraffs, you can drop me off here, and I will make up the bed before the Millers return. Then I can walk home."

"I would not think of letting you make up the bed by yourself."

"Do you know how to make a hospital corner?"

Lia's heartbeat set some sort of speed record when Moses winked at her. "My mamm is very particular about her beds."

"Moses!"

Both Lia and Moses snapped their heads in the direction of Rachel's voice. She stood at the back door, hands on hips, glaring in their direction.

Moses lost his smile but his eyes shone with amusement as he glanced at Lia and turned to face the attack. "I think it is best we take Rachel home before going to the Van deGraffs'," he said out of the corner of his mouth.

"Uh-huh," Lia agreed without moving her lips or changing her expression.

Rachel's high-pitched voice sounded like fingernails against a chalkboard. "I ran through the entire house screaming for you. I've been waiting for hours, and neither of you had the decency to tell me you would be in the backyard."

Moses flashed that winning smile that always turned Lia's knees into jelly. "I'm just about ready."

Rachel let the screen door slam and stormed toward them with her hands held stiffly at her sides and clenched into fists. Not paying attention, she passed under a tree, and a low-hanging branch ripped the kapp off her head, along with some strands of hair that came with the pins. She squeaked in annoyance and pain as her hands flew to her head in an effort to smooth her hair. It didn't help. Unruly tufts of golden locks stuck out from her bun in all directions.

Moses sprouted a sheepish smile. "I guess you could have driven the buggy home an hour ago. I don't mind walking."

Rachel growled like a guard dog, and Lia was grateful there were no rocks nearby. Rachel would have been hurling them at Moses for sure.

Rachel had a very gute arm.

Chapter Fifteen

Hoping to catch a glimpse of Lia, Moses didn't take his eyes from the window as he walked his horse up the lane. It had been three whole days since the scare at Saloma's, and only the demands of running a cheese factory had kept Moses from Huckleberry Hill.

Lia was nowhere to be seen, and not even Rachel sat at her usual perch. Disappointed, he trained his eyes on the ground and kept walking. He didn't know Lia's whereabouts, but at least Rachel would not attack him the minute he set foot on the porch. Always the trade-off—if he wanted to see Lia, he had to endure Rachel.

He shook his head a couple of times. No matter how many curds and whey he separated or how many molds he pressed or how many days he stayed away from Huckleberry Hill, Moses could not get Lia off his mind. Thoughts of her played in his head like a graceful melody floating through the fragrant summer air. She smelled of roses and pine trees, apple spice and lilacs.

Nor could he banish the feel of Lia in his arms as she'd soaked his shirt with her tears on Tuesday at the

Millers'. The desire to protect and care for her had almost overwhelmed him, and it took all the willpower he could muster to kiss her forehead instead of those soft, inviting lips that surely tasted of vanilla and sugar.

As he led Red into the barn, Moses took off his hat and ran his fingers through his hair. Had it been this way with Barbara? He loved her, but he remembered the heartache as she pulled further and further away from the church and him. She hadn't loved him enough to stay.

Jah, he remembered the heartache.

In her stall, Dawdi's horse bobbed her head up and down and whinnied softly as she restlessly stomped her feet with no place to go. Moses led Red to the stall opposite Dawdi's horse, but Red didn't seem to want to cooperate. He threw his head back and grunted rebelliously, and Moses had to tighten his grip so the reins wouldn't be ripped from his hand.

"Whoa there, calm down, boy."

Red reared on his hind legs and this time Moses couldn't keep hold of the reins. He took a few steps back to avoid getting kicked, then circled to see if he could reach the reins dangling around Red's neck. Red perked up his ears and snorted in panic. Something had him spooked all right.

Moses held up his hands and spoke soothing words to his horse as Red shuffled his feet in one direction and then another. "Whoa, it's okay. It's okay."

Red turned a complete circle as Moses tried to dance around him. Without warning, Red swished his tail into the air and kicked up his back legs. He forcefully smashed into Moses's leg with his metal-shod hoof. Moses felt a sickening snap, and he screamed in agony as his leg gave out from under him.

Red shook his head, whinnied, and trotted to the

far end of the barn where he stood with his snout nudging the wall.

Moses gasped. It felt like Red had kicked him in the gut as well as the leg. He lay on his back, trying desperately to catch his breath, and focused squarely on the pain that radiated from his leg and filled every space in his body. He resolved not to pass out even though the pain made him unbearably light-headed and the warm sensation of blood trickled into his boots. The blow must have broken the skin as well as the bone.

Taking deep, deliberate breaths in an attempt to calm his racing heart, Moses moaned as he slowly pulled himself to a sitting position to take a look at his injury. The bottom half of his left pant leg was saturated with blood. He carefully pulled the fabric back to examine the wound and nearly collapsed in shock. The sight of blood usually didn't bother him, but the sight of his bone sticking straight out of his skin made him a bit dizzy. He clamped his eyes shut and pulled the pant leg back over the wound. He should probably get to a hospital right quick.

But how would he get there?

He regretted being glad earlier that Rachel had not been watching for him at the window. No one would even know that he was on Huckleberry Hill. Leaning back on his hands, he yelled at the top of his lungs. "Help! Lia? Anybody, help!"

He strained his ears for any sound from outside, but all he heard were the two horses in the barn still fussing about something. He yelled again. No response.

Could he hop to the house?

Impossible. He couldn't even stand up.

Maybe if he pushed backward with his good leg, he could drag himself outside where Lia would find him. Or Rachel. Maybe Rachel, with her incessant eagerness, would come to his rescue.

Bracing himself for the pain, he scooted himself two inches backward and almost lost consciousness. An agonizing jolt of electricity shot up his leg. He groaned involuntarily as he held his head in his hands to stop the spinning.

He wouldn't be stuck here forever. Dawdi would be in to milk in another four hours. Moses pretended this was a happy thought. Only four more hours to go.

Light flooded the barn as someone behind him opened the door. He strained to see who had come in, but he couldn't rotate his head that far, and turning his body around was out of the question. "Help me," was all he could say.

He had never been so happy to see Rachel. Ever.

She walked slowly into his peripheral vision. "Rachel, I've hurt my leg. Go get Lia."

Rachel inched closer to him and her eyes grew round as saucers as she caught sight of the blood. She clapped her hands over her mouth. This muffled her screaming but did not stop it. For a few seconds, she squealed hysterically behind her hands and then let them drop to her sides so she could scream louder. Her neck seemed to bloom with hives that traveled up her cheeks and overspread her face.

"Rachel, it's okay. I'm okay. Get Lia. Please."

The screaming deteriorated to incoherent sentences and babylike whimpers. "I don't . . . I what . . . you shouldn't," Rachel whined as she disappeared from Moses's line of sight. He was pretty sure she ran out of the barn because the blubbering grew softer, but he couldn't be certain she would deliver the message. She might have run into the woods to hide from the horror of Moses's injury.

Well, Dawdi would be here in four hours to milk the cows. Only four hours to go.

To his relief, Moses heard footsteps approaching not three minutes later, and Lia stood mercifully at his side. Dawdi and Mammi followed close behind, but Rachel did not return. It was turning out to be a gute day after all.

"Moses, dear, are you hurt?" Mammi said, nudging Lia forward and taking Dawdi's hand.

"I see blood," said Dawdi.

Distress darkened Lia's expression as she knelt beside Moses and pressed a soft, cool hand to his cheek. "What happened?"

Moses's relief at seeing her was as palpable as the pain. "Red got spooked and kicked me hard. My leg is broken."

"Are you sure?" she said, in the calm voice that she probably used with her most hopeless patients.

"Jah, I'm sure."

Lia gently pushed his pant leg up past his knee. Not wanting to see the horrible sight again, Moses kept his gaze glued to Lia's face. She blanched and held her breath.

"Pretty bad?" Moses said, wanting Lia's reassurance.

She flashed a weak half smile. "I've seen worse."

Despite his pain, he gave her a quirky grin. "Really? When?"

She began unlacing his boot. "During the great Bonduel earthquake of two thousand eleven."

He hissed as she cautiously pulled his boot from his foot. "Hey! There was no Bonduel earthquake of two thousand eleven."

"We must stop the bleeding." Lia sounded like the determined physician now, the professional who never revealed how bad a patient really was. She looked at Mammi. "Will you bring the milking stool? Felty, can you bend well enough to help me?"

"Jah, sure," said Dawdi. "I'm as chipper as a seventy-year-old."

"Okay, come over here." Lia pointed to where she wanted Dawdi to stand and then stroked Moses's hand with her silky fingers. "This is going to hurt something wonderful, but it will help slow the bleeding."

Moses swallowed hard and nodded. He wouldn't complain. Lia would see he could be at least as tough as any mother in labor, even if it killed him.

"Anna, we are going to lift Moses's leg. You need to slip the stool under it as soon as we get it high enough. If we elevate the leg, it might stop the bleeding. If not . . ."

"If not?" prompted Moses.

Lia gave him a reassuring nod. "We will cross that bridge when we come to it."

Dawdi, on the other side of Moses's leg from Lia, patted Moses's hand. "Don't worry. We won't let her amputate."

We won't let her amputate? That was Dawdi's attempt at reassuring him? Moses was definitely going to pass out.

Lia glanced at Moses. "It's okay. You will be fine. Felty, put one hand under his ankle and the other under his knee."

The simple act of both of them sliding their flat hands under his leg was excruciating. Moses panted for control.

Mammi stood at his feet with the stool in hand.

"Ready, Anna?"

"Ready."

Lia locked eyes with Dawdi. "We lift on three. One, two, three."

All thoughts of impressing Lia with his bravery vanished. Moses cried out in agony as they lifted his leg a mere foot and a half off the ground. Mammi must have deftly placed the stool because in less than ten seconds the ordeal was over. His leg rested uncomfortably on the stool as Lia tied his ankle loosely to it with some yarn from Mammi's pocket. He could tell by her trembling fingers that Lia was trying to maintain her composure.

"This yarn should keep your leg on the stool in case it jerks suddenly."

"I'm not moving an inch."

"How is the pain?" she asked.

He didn't want to upset her, but he might as well be honest. "Bad."

"Oh, Moses, I am so sorry, but we had to do it. I think the bleeding is slowing."

He tried to smile. He managed a wince. "I am glad you are here."

"We need to get you to the hospital."

"I can't move," Moses said.

"We'll have to call an ambulance."

The pain made him dizzy again. "This is why you need a phone, Dawdi."

"You said I needed a phone if I had an emergency. Not if *you* had one."

"Where is the nearest phone?" Lia asked.

Moses covered his eyes with his hand and tried to breathe normally. The pain would not let up. "Van deGraffs'. You know, where I broke their screen."

Lia looked at Mammi and then Dawdi. "I'll saddle the horse and ride down there."

Mammi shook her head. "Have Rachel go. You must look after Moses."

"Rachel's hysterical," Lia said. "She's curled up in a ball

on the sofa and can't even form a complete sentence. I'll go."

"The horses are acting funny," Moses said. "It's too dangerous to take one of them."

Lia gazed out the open barn door, considering her options. "Then I'll run," she said, taking another look at his leg.

"It's pretty far," Moses said.

Her eyes twinkled despite the worry on her face. "But you're always reminding me what long legs I have."

"Then go," Dawdi said. "We'll take care of Moses. I'll sing to him."

"Anna, if you got a bag of ice and laid it below his knee, I think that would help the bleeding." Lia reached down and laid a light hand on Moses's arm. "The bleeding has slowed quite a bit. I'll hurry. Nothing to eat or drink while I'm gone."

He didn't want her to go. Even though the pain made him queasy, he'd have to be dead not to be touched by her beauty. She made him feel better just being there.

The pain intensified when she left the barn. "Be careful," he called after her, too late for her to hear.

Mammi bent over as far as she could but she couldn't reach Moses. She settled for kissing her index finger and pointing it at his cheek. "I'll go fetch a pillow and a blanket. And some ice."

Moses held perfectly still. It was the only way to avoid aggravating the pain. "And a cold lemonade?"

Mammi walked out of his view, but Moses could still hear her voice floating with the dust motes in the air. "Lia said no."

Dawdi shuffled toward Red. The crazy horse stood

innocently at the far wall of the barn. "I should get your horse in the stall so he doesn't step on you."

"No, Dawdi. He's spooked."

Dawdi knitted his brows and thumbed his suspenders. "I better have a look around, then." He sniffed the air and studied his own horse, still restless in the stall. "Maybe a tornado's coming."

Moses lay with his arm spread over his eyes and tried to concentrate on Dawdi instead of his leg throbbing torturously.

Dawdi casually stepped over Moses as he went to the door and looked to the sky. "Not a cloud." He shuffled to Moses, looked down, and shrugged in puzzlement.

Just a normal conversation about the weather, except Moses could barely lift his head and his leg was bent at an awkward angle.

Dawdi didn't seem to notice. He walked to the stall that kept his horse, again stepping over Moses's prostrate body. Moses held his breath and braced for Dawdi to come tumbling over onto him. Dawdi was not so sure on his feet as Mammi.

"Animals can sense an earthquake," Dawdi said, patting his horse on the nose.

"In Wisconsin?"

Dawdi nodded, seemingly unconcerned that his grandson lay on the ground racked with pain. "Nineteen seventy-two an earthquake in Illinois cracked plaster in Kewaskum. My uncle Joe was there."

Dawdi fiddled with his beard before retrieving a rake hanging from the sturdy hook on the wall. He walked into the empty stall, and from the rustle of hay, he must have been stirring it around.

The barn brightened as Mammi marched in with

her arms full of supplies. "Now, Felty, this is not the time to be mucking out. Moses is in very serious condition." She helped Moses raise his head and slipped a fluffy pillow underneath him. Much better than the cement floor. Then she unfolded a thick blanket knitted from lime green yarn. "Green is a healing color," she said as she laid it over the top of him. The blanket felt stifling in the heat of August, but Moses didn't complain. Mammi was doing all she could to make him comfortable. She carefully laid a small bag of ice below his knee near the wound. The cold burned his skin, but he didn't argue. Lia was concerned about the bleeding.

"Oh!" Dawdi yelled, and it sounded as if he were doing a wild dance in the stall. Mammi jumped out of her skin, and Moses sat straight up only to groan and sink back to his pillow as the pain shot up his leg.

To Moses's great relief, Mammi stepped around instead of over him to get to the stall where Dawdi made such a fuss. "Felty, what in the world are you doing?"

"Step back, Annie. Stay back." The stall door swung open slowly, and Dawdi stepped out with a chocolate brown and white snake dangling from his rake. A big chocolate brown and white snake. Had to be at least three feet long. And it was alive. Its tail made a sickening hiss.

Mammi plastered herself against the door of the opposite stall where Dawdi's horse squealed out a warning. Red stayed put but shuffled his feet and whinnied nervously.

"Kill it, Felty," Mammi said.

To Moses's great distress, Dawdi slowly walked toward him, keeping his eye firmly on the snake entangled in his rake. Moses held his breath and prayed desperately that the snake would not escape and use him to soften its landing.

Without looking down, Dawdi tiptoed carefully over Moses, who thought he would die of a heart attack, and plodded cautiously to the door.

"Dawdi, what are you doing?" Moses said through clenched teeth. It was a miracle he could speak at all.

"I ain't never seen a massasauga this far north. They're endangered."

"Now, Felty," Mammi said. "What do you think you are going to do with it?"

"Open the door for me, Banannie."

"I'm not coming near that thing."

Without taking his gaze from the hissing head of the frightening snake, Dawdi reached out slowly and opened the door. "I'm going to hike over to the rocky side and release him."

"Dawdi, this is reckless. You could get bitten."

Dawdi shook his head slightly. "I know how to handle a snake."

"That's a two-mile walk, Felty," Mammi scolded, propping her hands on her hips. "What am I to do if you fall over, break a hip, and get bitten by a snake?"

"I won't be long."

"What about Moses?"

"Take care, Moses. We'll come see you in the hospital."

Dawdi didn't shut the door as he concentrated on his balancing act and disappeared from Moses's sight.

Moses furrowed his brow. "Maybe you should send Rachel to follow him."

Mammi waved away his concerns. "Oh, Felty will be all right. I can't imagine he'd do better with Rachel chasing after him." She grunted and with some effort, knelt down next to Moses. "How is the pain?"

"Pretty bad."

"Don't you worry. Lia is bound to be back before your horse tramples you or you bleed to death."

Moses forced a smile and squeezed Mammi's hand. Dear Mammi.

He felt worse already.

Lia ran down the lane as fast as her feet would take her without losing control and falling on her face. She'd never seen anything as gruesome as Moses's leg before. She had to go faster. Moses might lose too much blood or go into shock before an ambulance could reach him.

A steep shortcut through the trees and bushes would get her there faster. She hopped off the lane and dodged low branches and fallen logs as she made a beeline for the main road. As she plowed through the underbrush, she felt like a clumsy cow trampling wild-flowers and ripping leaves off bushes.

A thick root protruding from the ground proved to be her downfall. She caught her toe and went tumbling like a sack of flour. Her right forearm took the brunt of the fall as it slid into a very sharp rock. She yelled out, more in frustration than pain, although the pain was real enough. She did not have time to fall. Moses needed her.

Only after she stood and brushed the dried leaves off her dress did she take a second to examine her stinging forearm. A nasty gash, three inches long, traveled up the back of her arm. Blood already soaked her sleeve. Lia groaned. She'd seen enough blood that week to last a lifetime. The cut was deep but not unmanageable, and she would probably need a tetanus shot.

Cradling her arm in her other hand, she continued her trek through the trees to the road, saying a silent prayer for haste. She ignored the pain, didn't have time to give it any attention. She had to get to a phone.

Once she reached the paved country road, she ran in the direction of the Van deGraffs' with all her might. It was still a four-mile journey. She wished she could have brought a horse. Soon every muscle ached and her lungs burned painfully, not to mention how badly her arm throbbed.

She heard the rumble of a car behind her. A car! Surely the driver would have a cell phone. It would save her at least three miles and several minutes. She turned and frantically waved her injured arm at a gigantic white motor home lumbering up the road. The driver slowed his vehicle and finally stopped a hundred feet past her.

A woman with disorderly gray curls and round glasses much like Anna's stuck her head out the window and beamed at Lia. "Look, David, a real Amish person. She's hurt."

Lia tried to catch her breath.

A thin man with a full head of salt-and-pepper gray hair joined the woman at the window. "Come on, honey. We've got a first aid kit in the back."

"Do you have a cell phone?" Lia panted. "Someone up the hill is hurt worse, and I need to call an ambulance."

"Oh my," said the woman, gesturing to the man. "Yes, we have one."

The man disappeared, Lia hoped, so he could retrieve a cell phone.

"You poor girl. Come in and we'll get you fixed up."

"After we call an ambulance," Lia said.

The woman looked over her right shoulder to

check on the man's progress. "Our son gave us the phone to use on the trip in case we had trouble, but I don't know the phone number for the police in this area. I'm Colleen, by the way. And that is my husband, David."

"I'm Lia."

Lia heard the side door close, and David hobbled around the back of the motor home supported by a cane, the sturdy kind with four little legs each covered with a rubber tip. The rumble of the engine died, and Colleen soon followed David onto the road.

David held a thin, black phone in his fist. "Here it is. We couldn't get any bars a few miles back."

"Thank you. Thank you so very much." Lia tried to decipher how to use the phone, a newfangled contraption, Felty would say. Rachel had a cell phone two years ago before she got baptized, but this one was completely foreign to Lia. It had no buttons to push. "Do you know how to dial?"

David took the phone and squinted at the screen. "I can usually figure it out. My son calls this a smartphone, but it seems pretty dumb to me."

Colleen put her hands on her hips and leaned in to get a better look at the phone. "I don't need any of the fancy gadgets, I just want to be able to call my kids once in a while."

David touched the screen a few times and it lit up like a television set. "Do I dial nine-one-one?"

"Jah, that's right."

He dialed slowly, even though it was only three numbers, and Lia tried not to lose her patience. These nice people had saved her a good thirty minutes of running.

Lia heard a faint voice on the other end of the line, and David's face lit up. "Hello, yes, this is David Tolley.

I am calling from northern Wisconsin. Can you connect me to northern Wisconsin? Oh, I am already there?" He covered the receiver with his palm. "They already know where I am. This *is* a smartphone." He listened to the voice on the other end. "Hello. This is David Tolley. We are out here near—" He put his hand over the receiver end of the phone. "Where are we?"

"West of Bonduel," Lia said.

"Tell them we just left Shawano," Colleen added in a hushed whisper.

"We are west of Bonduel and someone is seriously injured." He nodded at Lia to get confirmation that whatever the injury, it was serious. "Yes, I'm not sure how serious. Uh . . . yes . . . we are on a road with lots of trees."

"Outside of Shawano," Colleen prompted.

"We left Shawano about ten, fifteen minutes ago."

With concern for Moses increasing every second, Lia tapped David's elbow. "Would you like me to tell them how to get here?"

David pulled the phone from his ear. "What . . . oh, you want to give them directions?" He went back to the phone. "Okay, this young lady is going to give you directions."

He handed the phone to Lia, who quickly described Moses's injuries and relayed directions to the dispatcher. Unsure of how to hang up, she gave the phone back to David. "They're coming," she said, considerably reassured, but still worried for Moses. He must certainly be in agony. At least Felty and Anna were looking after him.

David slipped the phone into his pocket and gave Lia a fatherly smile. "Now, why don't you come in our motor home, and we'll clean up that cut?"

Lia refused to waste a minute of time on herself. "Thank you kindly, but I must get back up the hill to see how Moses is doing."

"Moses? Is he the one who's injured?" Colleen asked.

"He broke his leg, and the bone is sticking through the skin."

David winced. "Ouch. Is he up there?" He pointed to the Helmuths' house, which could be seen on the hill through the trees.

"Yes, I ran down to call an ambulance. Thank you again. I would still be running if you had not stopped, but I must go back now and tend to him."

"That's a long walk."

Colleen jangled her keys. "At least let us drive you up the hill. Is there a road?"

"Yes, it's fairly wide. But I do not want to impose."

"Are you kidding?" Colleen said. "We came all the way out here to see Amish people. It's a thrill to be talking to one."

Lia couldn't resist such enthusiasm. She cracked a smile.

"We'll take that as a yes," David said. "Climb in."

David took Colleen's hand, and Lia ambled behind, matching their slow pace. Perhaps it would have been faster to run back up the hill.

Lia had never been inside a motor home before. It was as cozy as a real house with a kitchen table and cupboards and even a fridge.

"This pulls out into a bed," David said, motioning to different parts of his house on wheels. "And the bathroom is at the back."

"The bathroom? You can carry your bathroom right along with you?"

"Yep. The lap of luxury."

Colleen slid into the driver's seat and revved up the engine. David sat on the bench across from Lia at the table. Lia's heart pounded as she looked out the window—as big as the one in Anna's kitchen. The motor home leaned and creaked as Colleen stepped on the gas. It almost felt like being on the lake in a wobbly canoe.

Lia had thought that Moses had a hard time turning his buggy around that day when they got stuck on the trail into the thick woods, but his difficulty paled in comparison to what Colleen had to go through to turn her motor home and maneuver it up the lane. Turning the huge vehicle completely around took backing up and pulling forward seven times and then Colleen had to slow to one mile an hour to pass over the dip where the pavement ended and the lane up Huckleberry Hill began.

They were finally bouncing up the hill with Lia holding her breath the whole way. She was terrified the huge vehicle would tip over any minute with all the pitching back and forth it did on the uneven lane. She almost asked Colleen to stop and let her get out so she wouldn't die, but David and Colleen seemed unconcerned about the rough ride, so she laced her fingers tightly together, clenched her teeth, and pretended to enjoy the trip.

Lia saw the chickens scatter and heard Sparky bark as the rolling house pulled to the top of the hill. Would Colleen be able to turn this thing around to get back down? They might be stuck up there for a long time.

David pointed toward the house. "Park off to the side so the ambulance has room."

"David's a dentist," Colleen said as she brought the vehicle to a stop. "He might be able to help."

Lia jumped from the bench as soon as the motor home jerked to a stop. "Jah, come, if you like. I appreciate the ride so much." She popped open the door and was running as soon as she met the ground.

The barn door stood open, and someone had managed to get Red into the stall. Pasty and sweating, Moses lay with his eyes closed and a grimace on his lips. Even with pain etched across his features, he was still as handsome as ever. Lia sighed inwardly and concentrated on his injury. His leg looked ghastly but the bleeding had stopped. A bright green afghan rested over him, and Anna had found him a pillow. Oh, dear. The pillow off Rachel's bed. She would be extremely annoyed that it had spent the afternoon on the floor of the barn. Anna sat on the ground next to Moses—an amazing feat for someone her age—holding his hand.

"How is he?" Lia whispered, in case he was asleep.

Moses quirked the corners of his lips upward and spoke without opening his eyes. "I've been better."

Anna tried to get to her feet by rocking side to side and propping her hands on the floor. She finally gave up and reached out to Lia. Lia clasped her hands tightly and pulled Anna to her feet. "I'm too old to sit on the floor. It used to be my favorite spot when my children were little. But I was a lot younger then." She brushed the errant pieces of straw from her dress. "You are back long before I thought you would be."

David and Colleen shuffled tentatively into the barn, letting their eyes adjust to the dimness.

"These people let me use their cell phone. The ambulance is on its way."

Moses turned his head as best he could to see the Tolleys. He gave them a weak smile of acknowledgment.

Still stiff from sitting on the floor, Anna hobbled

to David and Colleen. "We are so grateful for your kindness."

Colleen beamed as if she were meeting a celebrity. "We should be thanking you. I am fascinated with the Amish. I never thought I'd get to meet you this close."

"Then you had better stay for dinner."

It might as well have been the best day of Colleen's life. She clapped her hands and threw her arms around Anna. "We would be delighted."

David stepped closer to Moses and took a look at his leg.

"Can you do anything else for him that I haven't thought of?" Lia said.

David studied the injury for a few seconds. "No, but he has nice teeth."

"Are you a doctor?" Moses asked breathlessly.

Lia bit her bottom lip. Moses must be suffering terribly. She found his pain unbearable.

"Only about ten more minutes," Lia said, readjusting the half-melted bag of ice sitting below Moses's knee.

Moses lifted his head and gasped in pain before sinking back to the pillow. "What happened to your arm?"

Lia shoved her injured arm behind her back. Moses didn't need one more thing to burden him. "It's nothing."

"She needs stitches," David said.

Moses frowned and furrowed his brow. "Did you fall?"

"You know how clumsy I am."

"You are not clumsy."

David nodded in agreement. "Tall girls are so graceful. And you have those beautiful, long fingers. One of my sons has long fingers like that. He plays the piano."

Moses grinned at Lia until she averted her eyes.

Why, lying flat on his back, could he make her feel so giddy and shy?

"I keep telling her that, but she won't believe me," Moses said. He held out his hand, gesturing for her to come closer. She extended her wounded arm and let Moses take her hand. His fingers were ice cold, but warmth traveled up her arm at his touch. He turned her hand over in his palm so he could see her cut and pulled her closer so she had to kneel down next to him. "This looks almost as sore as my leg."

"I've had worse."

He turned her hand over again. The ugly, mottled scar covered the entire back of her hand. "I can see you have."

Yes, I know how ugly my hand is. It is one of the reasons boys shrink from me. Believe me, Moses, I am fully aware of my many flaws.

Feeling as if someone had stolen her breath, she pulled away from his grasp, stood, and turned her back on him under the pretense of talking to Anna. She didn't want him to see the hurt in her eyes. He hadn't meant to humiliate her.

"Anna," Lia said, unable to keep her voice from cracking, "where is Felty?"

Anna flicked a piece of hay from her sleeve. "Oh, he's off trying to save the rattlesnake population of Wisconsin. Only through the good Lord's intervention will he come back unharmed."

Lia could not make heads or tails of this comment. Felty's location was a mystery.

They heard the police car coming from the main road with its siren blaring. The noise got louder as it came up the lane.

"I think he can turn his siren off now," Moses mumbled.

Lia ran out to meet the policeman, who turned out to be the sheriff who'd taken Saloma Miller to the hospital on Tuesday. He parked next to the formidable motor home and popped out of his car. "This isn't another baby emergency, is it?"

Lia pointed inside the barn. "Moses has broken his leg. The bone is sticking through the skin. I am afraid he has lost a lot of blood."

"Nasty," said the sheriff. "You've seen a lot of blood this week."

"Too much."

"The ambulance should be right behind me. Let's have a look." He let Lia lead him to the barn. "How did things turn out with the pregnant lady? She could barely lift her head when we got her to the hospital, but she was alive. I heard she made it okay, but I didn't know about the baby."

"He is small, probably another three weeks in the hospital, but they are both well enough, thanks to you."

The sheriff turned a dark shade of pink and hooked his thumbs into his belt. "Thanks to that midwife. She was very insistent. But I did get them there fast. Twelve minutes. A new record."

The ambulance announced its approach before the sheriff had a chance to look at Moses. The bright white truck came into sight, spitting up dust and gravel as it raced up the hill.

Anna, Colleen, and David emerged from the barn, leaving Moses to fend for himself. Even Rachel made an appearance on the porch. She didn't venture any closer to the gruesome sight in the barn, but she did telegraph her concern by blowing her nose loudly into her handkerchief.

Lia hurried into the barn and knelt beside Moses. "They're here. Hopefully they can give you something for the pain."

"At the moment, I'm sort of numb."

Two paramedics rushed into the barn. Lia got out of their way. One carried a bulky plastic box and the other carried a black plastic board with Velcro straps. Probably a device to stabilize Moses's leg before they moved him. One man opened the box, which held an impressive array of medical supplies, and each man snapped on a pair of rubber gloves. One paramedic asked Moses questions while shining a penlight into his eyes while the other recorded Moses's pulse and took his blood pressure.

Anxious for Moses, Lia watched the beehive of activity. The paramedics spoke over their radio in some sort of code that Lia could not begin to understand. With the sheriff's assistance, they had an IV in Moses's arm, his leg covered with gauze and strapped to the board, and Moses on a stretcher in a matter of minutes.

Lia felt helpless to comfort Moses as his face grew paler with each tug or bump he endured. For a moment she thought he had lost consciousness until he opened his eyes and stopped them from wheeling him out to the ambulance. "Lia must come with us. She needs stitches in her arm."

The short paramedic hesitated and turned to Lia. Reluctantly, she lifted her arm so he could see the gash. "Okay. You can ride with us." His bright eyes shone with compassion. "Two for the price of one."

Once they wheeled him out of the barn, Moses winced as the stretcher bounced along the dirt to the waiting ambulance. Lia caught up to him and grabbed his hand.

"I'm a big baby," he said, panting and grimacing all the way.

Lia raised her eyebrows. "You should be bawling your eyes out. I saw the leg."

"Oh, Moses!" Rachel called from the porch, before bursting into tears and ducking into the house.

Moses actually laughed. "Rachel can do my bawling for me. I am grateful she found me. If not for her, I'd still be lying in the barn yelling my lungs out."

Lia didn't welcome the pang of jealousy that attacked her. Of course Moses thought of Rachel at a time like this.

As Lia waited with Anna and the Tolleys, Felty, without a hat, trudged out of the woods using a rake as a walking stick and singing at the top of his lungs. *"Life is like a mountain railroad, and the snakes are crawling 'round."* He waved at Anna and watched as the paramedics lifted Moses into the ambulance.

The corners of Anna's mouth curled upward. "Well, he made it back alive." Felty spread his arms wide, and Anna stepped into his embrace. "I sure hope that snake appreciates what you done for it."

"It would have been a shame to kill such a handsome creature."

"Where's your hat?"

Felty arched his eyebrows in surprise and touched the top of his head. "Of all the crazy things, I lost my hat." He shrugged his shoulders. "How's Moses?"

"He should be all right, Lord willing. Lia is going with him to the hospital."

David stepped forward and stuck out his hand. "I'm David Tolley, and this is my wife, Colleen."

"Is this your contraption?" Felty asked, pointing to the motor home looming over his front yard.

"Yeah, we've driven this clear across the country."

Anna patted Lia on the cheek. "Take care of Moses, and take care of yourself. I don't want to see infection in that cut."

Lia nodded and let one of the paramedics help her into the back of the ambulance. She watched Felty as he chatted with David Tolley. It appeared he would not worry himself to death over Moses.

Before they swung the ambulance doors closed, Lia saw Felty's gaze roam over the motor home, and he smiled as if Anna had just given him a big kiss. "Utah! I don't have a Utah." The doors closed as he pulled his small notebook out of his pocket and cheerfully jotted his new discovery on the page.

Lia sat facing Moses as the ambulance backed up, found a place to turn around, and headed down the hill. She could tell that Moses fought to keep his eyes open. They must have given him something for the pain that made him drowsy.

With slow, deliberate movements, Moses found her hand and pressed it gently in his. Even though she didn't pull away, she wished he wouldn't do that. He was only looking for comfort, but to Lia, the touch of his hand meant much more. She savored his warmth even as she chastised herself for letting the feel of his hand upset her so.

He gave her a groggy smile and stroked his thumb across the lumpy back of her hand. "How did you get this burn?" She tried to pull away, but this time Moses held tight and wouldn't let her. "I've sensed you're self-conscious about it and I don't want to embarrass you, but I've been wanting to ask about it for a long time. It looks like it must have been very traumatic."

"Oh, yes, you don't have to remind me how hideous it is."

He opened his eyes wide enough to appear fully awake. "Hideous? I don't think it looks hideous. It makes you look tough, like you've been through something really hard and come out unscathed."

Lia laughed mirthlessly. "Unscathed."

"I'm sorry you got burned like that. It must have been very painful."

Lia looked down at her hand in his. "I was ten. My brother, Perry, and I were horsing around near the water heater. I fell against the kettle." Lia flinched as she remembered the searing agony. "They gave me a skin graft. And then I had to wear this funny glove for a year to help the skin grow back smooth. But it didn't. Then I started growing. By the time I reached fourteen, I was as tall as I am now." That was about the time Dat shifted all his attention to Rachel because he'd almost lost her. Rachel wanted for nothing, while Lia's charge was to watch out for her delicate younger sister. If Rachel didn't know how to roll out a piecrust, it was Lia's fault for neglecting to teach her. If Rachel felt unhappy, Dat blamed Rachel's discontent on Lia.

"I like tall girls," he said, letting his eyes close, as if he were unable to keep them open for one more second.

He might like tall girls, but he wouldn't marry one.

Lia held her breath as a wave of pain washed over her. She loved Moses Zimmerman. She loved his kindness and his cheerful spirit, and yes, even though appearance shouldn't matter, his handsome face and tall, strong figure. She couldn't imagine ever wanting anyone but Moses. No one else would measure up—literally.

It didn't matter that he didn't want to marry her or that he favored her sister or even that Lia was too plain to dream of such a match. She loved him. Her heart broke even as she realized how completely it belonged to him.

She clenched her teeth and took a deep breath, but it was no use. The tears escaped from her eyes like a wall of water from a broken dam, impossible to hold back. In hopes that Moses would be too wrapped up in his own pain to notice, she smeared the tears off her face with her free hand.

He squeezed her fingers and spoke with slurred consonants. "I'm so sorry. Is the pain very bad?"

The empty space in her chest ached with longing. "What?"

"Does your arm hurt? It looks really sore."

He'd just given her an excuse for the crying. "Jah, it is really starting to hurt now."

He lifted her hand so he could see the cut. "We should have sent Rachel."

Jah. Rachel wouldn't have tripped over her short legs running recklessly down the hill. Graceful Rachel would have been able to stay on her feet. The tears came full force, and Lia clapped her free hand over her mouth to keep a sob from escaping her lips.

Moses inclined his head to the paramedic sitting behind Lia. "Can you give her something for the pain?"

"It's better to wait till we get there. Only ten minutes."

Moses frowned, his gaze riveted to Lia's face, and looked as if he were about to argue. Lia sniffled and dabbed her handkerchief over her face. "I'm all right."

Moses looked into her face until he must have been satisfied, then closed his eyes and let sleep overtake him.

I'm all right.

But she wasn't all right. Being near Moses would be pure torture, watching him fall further in love with her sister, knowing what she had lost.

Squaring her shoulders, Lia closed her eyes to block out the sight of Moses Zimmerman and set to building an iron box around her heart.

Chapter Sixteen

The haze of the painkillers wore off, and Moses's leg throbbed enough to wake him up. Through his closed eyelids, he could sense the bright light of midday streaming through the big window. How long had he been asleep? Twelve hours? Three days?

Moses opened his eyes and almost jumped out of his skin when he saw Rachel standing over him, her face close to his. Was she checking to see if he was dead?

She smiled weakly and took a step back. "I was afraid you'd sleep forever. It's almost ten o'clock."

The unwelcome sight of Rachel in his—well, her—room made his leg ache intensely. He had a feeling recovery under Rachel's care would be slow going. Even though he knew it was selfish, he found himself wishing for Lia. But he should be thoughtful enough to let her be for a few hours.

Moses sat up and stifled the moan that wanted to escape his lips. They had really done a job on his leg. It felt as if someone had tried to flatten it with a sledgehammer. He covered his eyes and hoped he wouldn't be stuck with Rachel for the rest of the day. "Do you think you could bring me a painkiller?"

Rachel sidled backward until she reached the door. "I'll be back."

He watched her go, doubt playing inside his head like a fly buzzing in the corner of the room. Would Rachel know to bring water as well?

He slowly slipped the blanket off his injured leg. They had given him a pair of flimsy cotton pants at the hospital that easily fit over his thickly bandaged leg. His foot was slightly swollen and about six shades of purple, but he felt fortunate that he could feel his toes.

Gritting his teeth, he slid the pant leg past his knee and examined his wrappings. The doctor had bandaged the leg up good and tight and given Moses strict instructions to stay off it. In a few days, the doctor would take the stitches out and put Moses in a sturdy cast. It wasn't ideal, but at least then Moses would be able to get around on his own.

He hoped Lia had been allowed to sleep in. She had spent a day and a half with him at the hospital, waiting with him until he went to surgery, staying glued to his side after they wheeled him to recovery, and consulting with the doctors about the care of his leg. He didn't know when she got any sleep. Would Barbara have taken such good care of him? He'd never know. Barbara wasn't here.

Lia had communicated with Mammi and Dawdi and Moses's parents by calling David Tolley's phone. The Tolleys ended up camping out on Huckleberry Hill and spending the day with his grandparents.

They decided that Moses would recuperate at Mammi and Dawdi's house. His own parents lived more than an hour away, and he really wanted to be close to his cheese factory even if he couldn't set foot inside the place for a couple of weeks.

Roy Polter had driven Moses and Lia to Huckleberry Hill last night where Anna and Lia helped him into Rachel's bed, gave him a painkiller, and made him comfortable before he fell hard into sleep.

Rachel strolled back into the room empty-handed. Moses sighed inwardly. She was as useless as he had anticipated. Would he have to crawl to the kitchen himself and find his own medicine?

But his prayers were answered when Lia followed close behind with a tall glass of water and two baby-blue pills in her hand. She smiled at him, but her smile didn't reach her eyes. She must have been bone-tired. He glanced at the bandage covering her forearm and remembered he wasn't the only one who'd been injured.

"How is your arm?" he asked.

"Who cares about my arm when your toes look like you've been tiptoeing through the huckleberries?"

Again the halfhearted smile. Moses didn't like it one bit.

"How is the pain?" she said.

"I am very grateful for the painkillers."

"How many stitches did you get?" Rachel asked as she sat uncomfortably on the edge of her bed, her eyes glued to the thick bandages cocooning Moses's leg.

Moses took the pills and the water and gave Lia a grateful smile, but she seemed very interested in looking at a spot on the wall about two feet above his head.

"Thirty-seven stitches," Moses said, taking Lia's hand under the pretense of looking at her bandages. "How many did you get, Lia?"

Lia glanced from Moses to Rachel and gently pulled her hand from his grasp. "Four. Not near so impressive."

Moses kept the frustration off his face and let his hand drop to the bed.

"What did the doctor say?" Rachel asked, leaning toward him even as Lia stepped away.

"He told me not to smoke," Moses said.

Lia let a wisp of a grin play at her lips. When had her smile become his favorite sight?

"And I'll be in a cast for seven or eight weeks."

Rachel looked truly sympathetic. "Don't you worry. I am going to take good care of you."

Out of the corner of his eye, Moses saw Lia turn her face away.

He attempted to keep his attention on Rachel. "Once the cast is on, I shouldn't need any help." He raised his hands. "I'm blessed to have two good hands so I can still make cheese."

To his annoyance, Rachel grabbed his hand and gave it a squeeze. Lia was already out the door. "I'll get your breakfast," she called over her shoulder.

Rachel frowned and spoke loudly to make sure Lia could hear her all the way to the kitchen. "Remember, we agreed I would bring Moses his food."

Moses pulled his hand from Rachel's grasp.

Rachel studied his face, smiled, and nodded as if she knew all his thoughts. He found the gesture annoying.

Pulling the blanket back over his leg, she said, "When I saw you lying there in the barn in a pool of blood, I almost fainted with fright." She sighed in a long drawn-out breath that reminded Moses of the wind hissing through the slats of the barn. "I feel things so deeply where you are concerned, and I panicked you might die. Lia doesn't care about you like I do, so she could abide the sight of your leg where I could not. She's always been cold like that."

Moses decided he'd had enough of such talk. "If it weren't for Lia, I'd probably be dead."

"I don't think you'd be dead."

"There would be few problems in this world if more people were as brave as Lia." He pinned Rachel with a stern eye, hoping his look would inspire her to think better of criticizing her sister.

Rachel pursed her lips and looked away in confusion, probably formulating another strategy for winning his favor. Why wouldn't she give up?

Dawdi ambled into the room to take a look at Moses. "You look no worse for the wear," he declared, thumbing his suspenders. He pulled back the blanket Rachel had spread over Moses and examined his foot. "Mighty fine bruises."

Beaming from ear to ear, Mammi bustled in with a beautiful bouquet of red roses in a tall vase. "These are from the Tolleys. Seventy-five dollars."

Moses winced when he scooted his back against his pillow. "Are they here?"

"Jah, but they don't want to disturb you. We're going to Green Bay with them today. We hope you don't mind. Lia will be here to care for you."

Rachel blinked rapidly as if trying to remove some irritating dust from her eyes. "I'll be here too. Lia isn't the only one who knows how to care for the sick. I nursed my mamm for a whole week with the flu."

Anna smiled patiently at Rachel. "Of course, dear."

"Lia said you went to the auction with the Tolleys yesterday," Moses said.

"They are such lovely people. They drove us all the way to Marion." Mammi leaned toward Moses and her eyes danced. "In their motor home."

"That's a mighty fine contraption," said Dawdi.

Mammi grinned as if sharing a big secret. "He used the bathroom in it twice."

Moses couldn't help laughing. "Did he?"

Dawdi nodded and slipped his hands into his pockets. "Fanciest thing I ever saw. And I got Nevada and South Carolina. It was a very gute day."

Mammi set the vase on the windowsill and retrieved something from her apron pocket. She held up two furry, baby-blue knitted things. "I made you some slippers. So your feet will stay toasty."

Moses looked out the window at the sunny August morning. The sun beating down through the trees made him feel sweaty already. "Denki, Mammi. I don't want my toes to freeze."

Mammi smiled in satisfaction and slid the slipper onto his good foot. He held his breath as she carefully eased the other slipper over his purple toes. The movement didn't make the pain worse, but he felt like he had suddenly grown fluffy bunny feet. He didn't fault Mammi. It might have been impossible to make a pair of slippers look manly.

Mammi pointed to the crutches propped against the wall. "You can walk around in the slippers if you need to."

"The doctor says to stay off my feet except to go to the bathroom."

Mammi smoothed his blanket over his legs.

He took her hand and squeezed it. "Thank you for letting me recuperate here for a few days."

"I don't mind sharing a room with Lia," Rachel piped in. "I want you to be as comfortable as possible. We'll manage fine for as long as you want to stay."

Moses had seen that tiny room with the thin twin bed. He suspected that Rachel managed by insisting Lia sleep on the floor.

Mammi curled her lips and winked at Moses behind Rachel's back. "The girls will take gute care of you. We'll probably be back before supper."

Dawdi patted his shirt pocket. "I've got my notebook ready. I plan on seeing a lot of new states today."

Mammi laid a kiss on Moses's forehead before walking out the door, hand in hand with Dawdi.

Rachel went to the door and watched them walk down the hall. When she turned to Moses, she looked like a cat with a mouthful of mouse. She sat back on the bed. "We're going to have so much fun today being together."

Was it too late to scream for his grandparents to come back?

Don't leave me alone with her!

Lia appeared at the threshold of his room with a steaming tray of food. Rachel leaped up with enthusiasm and took the tray from Lia. "Look what we made for breakfast," Rachel said as Lia turned on her heels and disappeared from view. Moses should have called her back to tell her he knew who made the food, that he knew who worked her fingers to the bone, even as Rachel took the credit.

I'm not like your father, Lia. I know how to value a gute woman.

Rachel, with the smug look of someone who expected to be thanked, set the tray on his lap, and the heavenly aromas of blueberry pancakes and bacon made his mouth water.

"The pancakes are my recipe," said Rachel.

Lia marched back into the room with a bottle of syrup and a tall glass of orange juice that she set on the small nightstand next to the bed.

What could he say to make her linger? The overwhelming desire to have her near him took him by surprise. When had she become this important to him? Or was it merely his wish to avoid Rachel that made him long for Lia's company?

"Thank you for the breakfast, Lia. Don't tell my mamm, but you are even a better cook than she is."

His comment seemed to strike Lia as an unhappy thought. "It was Rachel's idea to make pancakes." Without another word, she glided out of the room, leaving Moses with a plate full of delectable food and at the mercy of Rachel Shetler, a girl who would never tire of talking about herself.

It was going to be a very long day.

Flustered at the sight of Moses hobbling down the hall, Lia pulled her soapy hands from the dishwater, propped her wet fists on her hips, and tried to look stern. "Moses, what are you doing out of bed? The doctor said—"

"The doctor said I should use the crutches in emergencies, and since I can't get you to set foot near my bedside, I must come to you."

Lia pulled a chair from under the table and commanded Moses to sit. "If you break your leg all over again, don't come crying to me."

Moses sat, panted with exertion, and rested the crutches against his shoulder. "I wouldn't dare. Two weeks cooped up in that room, and I'm ready to pull my hair out."

Lia wiped her hands dry and didn't bother to correct Moses on his timing. It had been less than two weeks. Ten days, near time for the stitches to come out. Ten full days with Moses in the house only served to make Lia more miserable than ever. Rachel seldom left his side, unless he slept, and that was fine. Lia was more efficient with chores anyway.

Except when she administered medicine or checked his bandages, Lia studiously avoided Moses's room. Her breathing stopped and her heart shattered every time she looked into those blue eyes, and she didn't want the hourly torment. She had been perfectly content to bury her sorrows in the kitchen and let Rachel serve him his meals. For the first three days, Rachel disappeared into Moses's room at mealtime with two plates of food, leaving Lia and Anna and Felty to enjoy eating in peace in the kitchen. Anna and Felty truly loved her, and Lia could pretend that there was no such person as Moses Zimmerman who didn't care one whit about her private heartbreak.

But after three days, Moses hobbled to the kitchen on his crutches for meals, swearing he would go stir-crazy lying in that room.

Anna had insisted on making supper every night after that, using ideas from her new recipe book. They had eaten slimy kale soup that Moses had chosen to gulp down instead of chew, fried tofu patties that weren't too bad smothered in soy sauce, and something called aspic that made Lia shudder as it slid down her throat. It puzzled her how Felty seemed to enjoy every dish set before him as if he were eating off the king's table.

Rachel came tripping down the hall from Lia's room and looked at Moses. "Shame on you," she said, shaking a finger at him. "How are you ever going to heal if you keep disobeying the doctor's orders?"

Moses pressed his lips together and let out a sigh. "I needed to talk to Lia."

Rachel turned all her displeasure on Lia. "He shouldn't have to come out here to talk to you. It wonders me that you are too busy to walk twenty feet down the hall."

Moses shook his head and rubbed the left side of his face. "Rachel, let Lia be. She's done nothing wrong." Lia recognized a hint of crossness in his voice.

Maybe Rachel was starting to wear on him a bit. Whatever the reason, Lia felt grateful he had come to her defense. She couldn't help it if the emptiness in her chest threatened to consume her every time she laid eyes on Moses.

Rachel rolled her eyes, plopped herself on the sofa, and pretended to read the newspaper.

Moses ignored her. "I get my stitches out tomorrow and a cast. Will you come with me?"

Rachel snapped her head up. "I want to come."

Lia brushed her hand across the table in an imaginary search for crumbs. Moses wasn't aware of how she felt about him and therefore couldn't know the turmoil his request threw her into. He wanted her along because she kept her wits about her in a crisis, but the more time she spent with him, the greater the risk of disintegrating into a puddle of tears.

"I don't mind if you take Rachel."

Rachel scowled and slapped the paper down on the sofa. "I don't need your permission. Who has taken care of Moses day and night since he got hurt?"

Moses's gaze intensified until Lia had to look away. "Lia came with me to the hospital. She will know all the medication I have taken."

Rachel waved her hand dismissively. "She can write all that down. I'm sick of sitting around this house without anything to do. I'm coming."

Moses inclined his head to Rachel without looking at her. "Rachel can come if she wants, but I would appreciate it if you came too." He must have seen that his pleas were going nowhere because he flashed that mischievous grin that Lia found charmingly irresistible.

But Lia's heart was too heavy to be lifted by a set of perfectly straight teeth. If Rachel was going to be Moses's wife, Moses must learn to put up with her fits of panic and anger. Rachel's beauty came at a price.

Rachel stood and grabbed Moses's crutches. "We don't need Lia to come."

Lia turned her back on them both. "Nae, you don't need me."

She deliberately kept her face away from them as she heard Rachel say, "Now take these crutches and get right back to bed, young man. I'm in charge of your care, and I won't stand for such disobedience."

Lia refused to watch Moses limp down the hall as she busied herself with nothing in the kitchen. Only when the sound of the rubber-tipped crutches faded did she turn and quickly finish the dishes.

Rachel had left the door to her room open—it wasn't exactly proper to shut it—and the sound of her laughter skipping down the hall proved more than Lia could bear.

With slow, deliberate movements, she wiped up the water from the counter, slid Felty's Bible from the side table, and sauntered out the front door. Once she shut it behind her, she lifted her skirts and raced into the woods without looking back.

The tears cascaded unimpeded down her face as she ran as far away from Moses as possible. Being careful not to repeat her embarrassing fall, she dodged bushes and branches and protruding roots, stumbling once but not falling. Her heaving lungs and burning legs did not slow her as she passed under ancient, majestic maples into a clearing on the north face of

Huckleberry Hill. She quit running when she found herself in a purple sea of huckleberries.

Lia caught her breath at the sight. Huckleberry bushes grew all over Huckleberry Hill in small clumps like splashes from a spilled can of green paint, but here the ripe berries glowed in over two acres of concentrated, dazzling color. A ray of sunlight peeked through the blanket of summer clouds and seemed to illuminate the field of berries and nothing else. No wonder they had named it Huckleberry Hill. It was a sight Lia would never forget.

Moses had brought her here in late June, before Rachel had interfered with her perfect summer.

Thinking of Moses called forth fresh tears. Why had she come to Huckleberry Hill? She had been content enough in Wautoma, working alongside her father in the fields and helping Mamm in the kitchen. She had met Moses only to realize that she couldn't have him. A soft moan came from deep in her throat. It would have been much better not to know.

"Do you always take your Bible with you on walks?"

Startled, Lia whirled around to see Felty wearing a new straw hat, carrying a small galvanized metal bucket, and grinning from ear to ear. He studied the book in her hand, which she had almost forgotten about. "Or is that my Bible?"

Lia brushed the tears from her face and tried to return his smile. It couldn't be done. "I needed some comfort from the good word. I was in a hurry and took your scriptures instead of mine. I'm sorry."

"No need to be sorry. The good book doesn't do any good unless somebody's reading it." Felty stepped close and put a grandfatherly arm around her shoulder. Lia could tell he used to be taller, but now they were the same height, and he looked straight into her eyes. "Would you rather be alone? I can come back another time."

"Nae." No need to tell him that she would be fine as long as she was away from Moses and Rachel. "It's silly that I let myself cry."

"Nothing wrong with that. Everyone should indulge in a few tears now and then. It washes out the dust in your soul."

"Did you come to pick berries? They are beautiful."

"You should see the bushes come autumn. The leaves are so red, they look like they're on fire." He let his eyes drink in the sight. "I came to check if the berries are ripe. Then we can have a berry-picking frolic. I usually pick a few dozen and take them to Annie to taste, but you can do the tasting right here for me."

"Don't you like to taste them yourself?"

Felty put down his bucket, took off his hat, and wiped his forehead with a red bandanna from his pocket. "Oh, I can't taste anything. My taste buds was seared, the doctor said."

"What happened?"

"I don't really remember. I think I was but three years old. I got into some kerosene and the fumes burned my nose and tongue. My lungs almost gave out, but I pulled through with a lot of prayer."

"But you can't taste anything?"

"Or smell much. I can smell real strong smells like a fresh pile of manure or a good, smoky fire. But I can't tell when a huckleberry is ripe."

A memory brought a smile to Lia's face. In her mind's eye, she saw Felty popping scorching hot meatballs into his mouth without a hint of discomfort. *The president of the United States doesn't eat this well.* An adventurous cook like Anna couldn't have asked for a more fitting husband.

Felty flashed her a puzzled grin. "I wish I saw that smile more often. You smiled all the time when you first came here, then Rachel showed up and you smiled less and less."

Lia wrapped her arms around Felty's Bible and hugged it to her chest. "I guess I don't feel very happy."

"When I'm troubled, I like to do my reading in Job. Helps me remember I don't have many problems."

Lia slumped her shoulders. "Job makes me feel guilty for ever feeling sorry for myself."

Felty took her by the wrist and led her to a fallen tree at the edge of the berry patch. They sat, and he took his Bible from her hands. After leafing through the pages, he found what he looked for. "'I have learned, in whatsoever state I am, therewith to be content.'"

"Paul was one of the greatest men to ever live. I don't measure up."

Felty knit his brows together and began thumbing through pages again. Lia cast her gaze to the ground. Felty wouldn't ever be able to find a scripture to solve her problems.

"Here's a good one. 'In every thing give thanks: for this is the will of God in Christ Jesus concerning you.'"

"I give thanks in my prayers every day," Lia said.

Felty reached out his gnarled fingers and took Lia's hand. She liked the feel of his hand—calloused and big, a farmer's hands, hands of a man who hadn't wasted one day of his life in idleness. "What are you grateful for?"

"I'm grateful for you and Anna, for inviting me here and being kind to me. I'm grateful for my family and my health. I'm grateful to Jesus for saving my soul. Many, many things."

"Does thinking of that make you feel better?"

Lia breathed in the moist air. "Jah, of course."

"That's the easy part. Can you thank your Heavenly Father for the things you aren't particularly grateful for?"

"I can't think that deep."

Felty opened his Bible again. "Don't feel guilty, but I'm pulling out Job. 'The Lord gave, and the Lord hath taken away; blessed be the name of the Lord.'"

"I don't think Job was very happy."

"He knew where all things came from. He knew that he lived and breathed by the Lord's good pleasure." Felty grew solemn and got a faraway look in his eye. "When the Lord took three of my little ones, a prayer of gratitude in my heart every minute was the only thing that saw me through."

His revelation stunned her. "You lost three children?"

Felty rubbed the side of his face and seemed to snap out of his sadness as he patted Lia's hand. "My little Andrew drowned in a puddle of water no bigger than a bathtub. Martha Sue and Barty got hit by a car on the way to school."

"How terrible! You must have been heartbroken."

"It was like God ripped my heart right out of my chest. I thought of Job every minute of every day, and then Anna found that scripture about giving thanks. So I started thanking Father in Heaven for everything— for my three angels already in heaven and my ten angels still with us. I thanked Him for my sorrow because it brought me closer to Him and the memory of His Son on the cross. I got to thinking that He didn't have to lend those children to me at all. I got two years with Andy and lots more than that with Martha Sue and Barty, and I am grateful for the time we had. I thank the Lord every day for His promises." He turned the pages of his Bible once again. "'And God shall wipe away all tears from their eyes; and there shall be no more death, neither sorrow, nor crying, neither shall there be any more pain.' That's what I'm waiting for. To see my little ones again."

"I'm so sorry."

Felty lifted his eyes to heaven as if to catch a glimpse of his children. "God gave me a new heart. From then on, I decided to praise the Lord and to be happy. I choose to be happy."

Lia took deliberate breaths to hold back her tears. "I feel like I have always been a cheerful person, but I can't summon it now."

"I had this very conversation with Moses when that girl left him three years ago. She put him down so low his chin scraped on the ground when he walked."

"Well, he's over it now." Her voice cracked and she couldn't finish. Felty glued his gaze to her face as she chastised herself for being so transparent.

Felty leaned back and almost fell off the fallen tree in an attempt to find a place to rest his hand. He slapped his knee energetically as if he'd solved the world's greatest riddle. "This is where the rubber meets the road. All Annie Banannie's scheming worked."

"Please don't tell anyone. If Rachel knew, things would get very unpleasant. Especially when Moses is my brother-in-law."

Felty's mouth fell open. "You think Moses is going to marry your sister?"

Lia's words came out more like a sob than a reply. "Can you see why I'm so unhappy?"

Felty lifted his eyebrow and acted like he had a mouth full of news he wasn't telling. "Moses is juggling so many balls that he doesn't even know which way is up. He's so concerned about Barbara and Rachel and your dat that he hasn't noticed the nose on his face. The good news is that Moses's mamm is my daughter, and she didn't raise Moses to be a fool, even if he's a little slow to see things clearly."

Lia wished she could decipher what Felty tried to say. "So you won't tell anybody?"

Felty made a show of zipping his lips, locking them, and throwing away the imaginary key. "Only, promise me you won't cast Moses off like moldy bread yet."

Lia lowered her eyes and nodded. "I will try."

"You can choose to be happy. Try thanking the Lord for things you're not grateful for."

Lia hesitated, reluctant to reveal her uncharitable thoughts. "I don't know. . . ."

"Try it."

"Thank you, Lord, that Rachel is here on Huckleberry Hill with me."

Felty smirked and nodded.

"I am grateful that Rachel is here because she is teaching me patience."

"Gute. What else?"

"I am grateful I am tall. I never have to strain my neck to see the preacher at gmay." Lia didn't want to feel better, but the invisible burden of gloom lifted somewhat. "I am grateful that Moses broke his leg so we can take care of him." Even though his eyes, twinkling with amusement, broke her heart every day.

Felty snapped the Bible shut and stood up without even a nudge from Lia. "Now, daylight's a-wasting. Let's test these huckleberries."

He hobbled to the nearest bush and plucked three plump berries from a leafy branch. He handed them to Lia, and she popped them into her mouth. She puckered her lips when the juice met her tongue. "They're tart."

"How tart? Do they taste green or will a spoon of sugar do the trick?"

"I think they're ready."

"Gute. We can send the word out to the children and tell them we'll have a berry frolic tomorrow. We make huckleberry jam and maple syrup for the market."

"That will be wonderful gute."

Felty stuffed a few berries in his mouth. "Mark my words. All you need to do to push Moses over the edge is to make him a wild huckleberry pie."

Push him over the edge of what? A cliff? It didn't matter. Rachel would take credit for whatever Lia baked for Moses. Lia clenched her fists and clamped her eyes shut.

I am grateful that Rachel gets so much benefit from my cooking.

Won't Moses be surprised when they are married and Rachel actually does cook something for him?

I choose to be happy.

Felty dropped a handful of huckleberries into his bucket and winked at Lia. "Anna will be disappointed if I don't bring at least a few for her to taste."

"If we pick a bucketful now, I can make some pies for the frolic tomorrow."

"Make sure Moses gets the biggest piece. That ought to do the trick."

One wheel of Moses's scooter met a giant-sized pebble in the lane, and he nearly had a spectacular crash. Instead, he caught his breath, gripped his handlebars tighter, and hopped on his good leg until he regained his balance. It would take a while to get used to this new gadget, and the crutches might be more practical outdoors.

"Oh, oh, be careful," Rachel encouraged as she tiptoed to catch up and tried to slip her arm into the crook of his elbow.

Honestly? Did she think he should help her to the door?

He subtly dodged her grasp by turning his handlebars and maneuvering to the driver's side of the car, wishing Lia had gone to the doctor with him instead of Rachel.

Rachel had turned pale when the doctor started picking out Moses's stitches, and the assistant had led her to the waiting room to sit for the duration of the doctor visit.

Moses paid the driver and scooted himself to Mammi's front porch as efficiently as possible while avoiding Rachel's clingy hands. She must have realized she was useless, because she stayed two feet behind him as he studied the steps. The scooter wouldn't make it up to the porch. Grabbing the railing, Moses pulled the substantial scooter out from under him and hopped up the steps with the scooter dangling from his grasp. Up the stairs took more effort than he anticipated, and he paused at the top to catch his breath. He'd lounged in bed entirely too long. Positioning the scooter underneath his cast, he waited for Rachel to catch up and open the door for him. Much as he hated to admit it, he couldn't do everything for himself.

Instead, Mammi threw the door open, squealed with glee, and hugged him tight. "Look at you. You're getting around on your own."

"He's like a toddler learning how to walk all over again," Rachel insisted.

While Mammi hugged him, Moses caught sight of Lia kneading dough. His heart jumped around a bit. She granted him a brilliant smile, which made his heart jump higher. Even though sadness shone in her eyes, he sensed she was happy to see him. Happier than she had been for days.

Moses winked at her—anything to keep her smiling. "I didn't miss huckleberry picking, did I?"

"Nae, they are coming after dinner to pick," Lia said.

He rolled himself farther into the room. Rachel sauntered in behind Moses and hovered around him like a pesky fly.

Mammi patted the handlebars of his scooter. "And what in the world is this piece of machinery?"

"This is my knee scooter, so I don't have to use crutches all the time."

Lia rinsed her hands and came to see the new arrival. She spoke directly to the scooter as if it were a new baby. "You've got a cute little basket and everything. We should tie a ribbon around you."

Moses pretended to be offended. "I'll have you know, this basket is for carrying important things. It's very manly."

Lia laughed. Moses tried to remember how long it had been since she had been amused at something he said. Too long. If he could, he'd be funny every minute just to hear that musical laugh.

"What did the doctor say?" Lia asked.

Rachel grabbed Moses's arm possessively. "He took out the stitches, which made me sick, and I had to lie down in the waiting room."

Lia's crooked grin did not escape Moses. He smiled

to placate Rachel and slid his arm from her fingers. "He said I'd need to be in the cast for probably seven weeks. But he took an X-ray and said my leg is healing straight."

"Gute," Mammi said, knocking on Moses's cast. "I will have to knit a cover for this thing, or you'll be putting dents in all the walls."

Hopefully not. If he was unstable enough to be crashing into walls, he had worse problems than his broken leg.

Mammi wrapped her arm around Lia. "Lia has made something special for supper tonight. Your mamm and dat are coming and so are Uncle Titus and Aunt Abigail and their families."

He hadn't seen Mamm and Dat since the accident. Moses glanced at Lia. It shouldn't really matter, but he hoped she liked his parents. Of course, his parents would like Lia. Everybody liked Lia the minute they met her.

"We will bring you back plenty of huckleberries," Lia said. "There are so many, you could like as not swim in them."

"Do I have to come?" Rachel said.

Lia, Mammi, and Moses spoke in unison. "No."

"Gute, I'll stay and take care of Moses."

Moses shook his head and widened his eyes in mock displeasure. "I'm not letting them pick huckleberries without me. I've done it every year since I was a baby."

Lia opened her mouth to speak.

Moses interrupted. "And it's not easy holding a bucket crawling on your hands and knees."

Lia couldn't hide her smile even as she tried to be

firm. "You won't be able to scoot all the way to the north side."

"I'll ride the horse and then use my crutches. I've been stuck inside for two weeks. I'll get there even if I have to crawl. I've got real tough knees."

Again Mammi put her arm around Lia. "Did I mention Lia has made something special for supper tonight?"

Chapter Seventeen

Moses stood at the top of the lane with his crutches tucked under his arms and a bucket in one hand. His parents rode up the hill in their buggy, and another buggy followed close behind. Mamm and Dat lived almost an hour and a half away from Huckleberry Hill and didn't get here often. They counted on Moses to look out for Mammi and Dawdi.

"We probably should have tried to make it sooner, but your dat's been sick and then we had to catch up with the mowing."

"Don't worry," Moses said. "They took good care of me."

Mamm jumped from the buggy and gave Moses a loud kiss on the cheek. Dat, who stood only six feet tall, put his arms around Moses and patted him hard on the back. "You don't look too bad."

"Neither do you," countered Moses, who couldn't stop smiling at the sight of his parents.

Mamm quit smiling and pulled a bright yellow envelope out of her pocket. "I stopped by your house and got your mail." She handed Moses the letter and stared into his eyes as if she were trying to see the back of his head.

Moses wrapped his fingers around the envelope with Barbara's handwriting on it. She'd drawn little hearts next to his name. Hearts? Hadn't seen that before. Surprised at his disinterest in the contents of the letter, he folded the envelope once and stuffed it into the pocket of his trousers.

Moses's mamm was the fourth of Mammi and Dawdi's children, and Moses was her youngest child. Aunt Abigail, the sister just older than Mamm, came with Uncle Titus and his wife, Sally Mae, in their extra-long buggy. Titus and Sally Mae's two unmarried sons, Ben and Titus Junior, hopped out of the buggy along with cousins Max and Amanda, twins from Ohio.

At twenty-two years old, Ben was a fine young man. He stood three inches shorter than Moses and looked as skinny as a broomstick. His brother, Titus Junior, always had a toothpick in his teeth. They both worked for their dat on his farm and also at the harness shop. They didn't have much time to come up to Huckleberry Hill.

Moses hadn't seen Max and Amanda since a year ago last Christmas. They lived in Ohio but had come to Wisconsin to visit Uncle Titus and his family. Cousin Amanda, still as petite and wiry as ever, gave Moses a cautious hug, careful not to upset his delicate balance on the crutches. "That cast is huge. You must have broken your leg something awful."

Max shook Moses's hand. "Some people will do anything to get out of harvest time."

Moses raised his bucket. "Do I look like I'm planning on taking a nap?"

Moses couldn't even remember how old Max and

Mandy were. Old enough to be looking for someone to marry. Neither of them would have much trouble with that. Mandy's dark brows succeeded in perfectly framing her greenish-blue eyes, and Max's full head of curly, thick hair must surely attract the girls like moths to a lantern.

Mammi, Dawdi, and Rachel came from the barn each carrying a bucket of their own. Mammi hugged all her relatives and marveled at how big Titus Junior was getting even though she had seen him just last week at the country store.

Ben, Titus Junior, and Max caught sight of Rachel and made no attempt to hide their interest. Ben nudged Titus and grinned, and Max followed Rachel's every move with his eyes. Gute. His cousins could flirt with Rachel while they picked berries, and Moses would be free of her for the afternoon.

Mammi introduced Rachel to all the relatives, and Rachel batted her eyes and giggled at all the appropriate moments. Max was handsome enough. Maybe Moses could convince him to take Rachel off his hands.

Nae, Moses wouldn't wish that fate on anyone, especially not his cousin.

Lia finally emerged from the barn leading the already-saddled horse. Mammi beckoned to Lia to meet the family. "This is Lia Shetler. She has made something very special for supper. I don't know what we would do without her."

Where Mamm had been polite and attentive to Rachel, she seemed intensely interested in making Lia's acquaintance. She stepped forward and gave Lia a hug. "I have heard so much about you, Lia. I am glad to finally meet you."

Mammi smiled like a cat with a mouthful of the pet

bird. Jah, Mammi must have told Mamm a great deal about her hopes for Moses and Lia. Moses found himself hoping that Mamm would approve.

Lia's smile never ceased to send warmth pulsating through his veins. "I am thrilled to meet you," she said. "Moses is such a fine man, I knew he must have very fine parents."

Moses's three cousins stood with their heads together like three wise old trees studying Lia as she spoke. Their looks of admiration did not escape his notice. It didn't surprise him that they found Lia pretty. He felt extremely annoyed. He silently willed them to return their attention to Rachel.

Moses knit his brows and narrowed his gaze. Each of his three cousins was taller than Lia. Her height would not scare them off. It would, unfortunately, draw them in, as it had Moses. Tall boys couldn't resist tall girls.

Uncle Titus pulled a stack of buckets from his buggy and handed them to the cousins. Mammi stuffed her hands into her apron pocket and retrieved brightly colored knitted things, each about the length of Sparky's tail. "These are handle covers for your buckets," she said, her eyes twinkling with delight. "They fit around your handle so you won't get blisters."

Rachel turned her head and rolled her eyes at Moses, who ignored her. Everyone else gratefully accepted Mammi's handmade creations. With every breath, she thought of how she could make other people's lives easier or more pleasant.

"Let's get moving," said Uncle Titus. "I've been craving huckleberries since November."

Lia took Moses's crutches while Max and Ben helped him onto the horse. He felt out of balance with the clunky cast on his leg. Someone would probably have to lead him to the field. But, all things considered, it was better than not getting there at all.

Aunt Abigail and Mandy led the way with Uncle Titus and Aunt Sally Mae following.

"Watch for bears," Mammi called.

"And snakes," Dawdi added. "I know for a fact there's one out there somewhere." He took Mammi's hand, and they shambled slowly into the woods, taking the lightly worn path to the north side of the hill. They'd all make enough noise to scare predators away.

Titus Junior took the toothpick out of his mouth and stuffed it in his pocket. It was obviously a special occasion. "I'll carry your bucket, Rachel."

Rachel glanced at Moses, probably calculating the risk of losing his affection if she strayed more than four feet from his side. She must have decided it was safe, because she gave Titus a half smile and handed him her bucket. They sauntered into the woods, Titus taking up the lead and Rachel keeping a safe distance between Titus and Moses's horse.

With crutches and bucket clutched in one hand, Lia scooped up the reins. Max quickly took them from her hand. "I'll lead the horse." He smiled a very nice smile filled with nicely straight teeth.

Lia smiled back, and a black raincloud parked right over Moses's head. His mind raced for something, anything to say that would make Lia smile at him. "I hope you're going to run all the way, Max. I want to get there before anyone else."

But Lia didn't even hear him because at that moment, Ben appeared at her left and offered to take her bucket and the crutches. She bestowed a smile on him and handed over her load.

Moses kept his focus glued to the back of Lia's head as she walked with Ben and Max on either side of her. They talked and laughed and ignored Moses altogether.

At the first opportunity, Moses would have to have a stern talk with both of his cousins. If they wanted to flirt, they should chase after Rachel. He would not allow them to flirt with Lia.

A gaping hole formed in the pit of his stomach as he realized he had no say in what Lia or his cousins did. She might just as soon decide to marry one of them. The pit in his stomach expanded to fill every space inside of him. He didn't like that at all.

Lia had said she wouldn't marry. Wait a minute. No, she had said she wouldn't marry Moses. And that was on the first day they met. Had she changed her opinion? And why did he care? He had Barbara.

Thoughts of Barbara gave him no comfort today. If anything, they made him feel worse. Had his loyalty waned?

Moses felt more like an invalid than ever when they arrived at the huckleberry patch and Lia watched while Ben and Max had to help him down from the horse. He took his crutches and insisted on clumsily leading Red to a nice patch of grass where he took off the bridle and let him graze.

Moses limped and dragged himself to the bush where Lia, Ben, and Max picked berries, deftly maneuvering himself between Ben and Lia. Lia smiled warmly at him, but her smile might have been inspired by the story Ben was telling her about his mishap with an ornery cow. Never before had Moses craved that smile so badly.

"Can you bend low enough to pick the berries?" Lia asked.

Moses winked. "I'll sit and scoot myself around."

Lia blushed. "Would you like to put your berries in my bucket? I'll hold it between us."

Moses nodded and flashed her a boyish smile. Any excuse to keep her close.

Rachel migrated to the popular bush as soon as she saw which one Moses sat by, and Titus followed close behind.

Lia moved aside cheerfully to make way as Rachel inserted herself between her sister and Moses. Did Lia honestly think he would rather stand by Rachel? Moses ground his teeth together. Everyone, it seemed, was expected to accommodate Rachel.

Rachel held out her bucket in Moses's direction. "You can put your berries in my bucket."

Not being able to reach Lia's bucket anymore, Moses reluctantly plopped his handful into Rachel's bucket.

Since Rachel insisted on taking up so much space, Lia moved farther from Moses to another thicket of huckleberry bushes.

"My cousin Sarah says you are learning to be a midwife," Ben said as he followed Lia to the next bush.

"Jah, Sarah is kind enough to teach me."

Max pointed to a clump of berries for Lia to pick as Ben offered his hand so she wouldn't trip over a rock in her path. Why couldn't they quit bothering her? Moses knew for a fact that she didn't like to be babied. The problem was, Lia didn't look annoyed by their pestering. At least Titus Junior's attention seemed to be riveted firmly to Rachel.

"I hear you saved Moses's life," Max added. "Mammi said he could have bled to death."

"Oh, I didn't do much at all. I ran to the road and

flagged down a motor home and used their cell phone. I was very frightened."

"I was more frightened than Lia," Rachel said. "I couldn't even bear to look at his leg. It's because I'm delicate."

Moses looked at his cousins to see how they took the news of Rachel's frail constitution. Ben merely nodded. Max wouldn't take his eyes off Lia, even to look for berries.

Only Titus was encouraging. "Mammi said it was disgusting."

Rachel drew back her hand as if she had been stung. "Look at my fingers. They're stained."

Almost in unison, Max, Ben, and Moses held up their hands to show Rachel the purple berry stains on their fingers.

"Part of the job," Ben said.

Rachel examined her fingernails. "Will it wash off?"

"Not to worry. It will disappear after a few days," Lia said, in that calm, appeasing tone of voice that she reserved for Rachel.

"A few days? Why didn't you tell me? I would have worn gloves."

Gloves. Rachel's little trick to get out of doing her share of the work. If only they'd told her she needed gloves, Rachel would still be back at the house looking for the perfect size. For all the irritation broiling inside him, the thought forced a laugh from Moses's lips. Lia didn't meet his gaze, but he saw a ghost of a smile playing at her lips.

Rachel shot fire at Moses with her glare. "What's so funny?"

Moses decided he'd rather not tell Rachel a fib. He

kept his mouth shut and made himself very busy picking berries.

Once she stripped her bush, Lia moved farther and farther from Moses with Ben and Max following her every step. Titus finally moved away and also gravitated toward Lia when he saw how much laughing Lia, Ben, and Max were doing.

Moses now wished he hadn't sat down. It would be difficult enough to stand and even more difficult to follow Lia through the woods under the pretense of picking berries.

Continuous laughter floated over the huckleberry patch and slammed into Moses's ears like a blaring horn. Lia and the three cousins were having a fine time. On the other side of the huckleberry patch, Mammi and Dawdi kept a lookout for ripe berries while the aunts and Mamm and Dat hunched over the bushes, picking feverishly. They looked as if they were having a very agreeable conversation. Uncle Titus and Mandy were off in different directions foraging for berries farther into the woods. Huckleberry bushes grew here and there all over the hill.

And Moses was stuck with Glove Girl.

Increasingly irritated that Lia was over there and he was over here, Moses picked every berry he could reach, took up his crutches, and groaned as he made it to his feet. Foot.

Rachel propped her hands behind her and arched her back. "Ach, my muscles are aching something wonderful."

At last. His chance to escape. "I would hate to see you overexert yourself. Why don't you sit over there on that log? Or you could walk back to the house and lie down." Dared he hope she'd take him up on that suggestion?

"I'm so tired. Will you take me back on your horse?"

"I'm afraid once they got over here and hefted me onto the horse, it would take more time than walking. And you wouldn't be able to get me off the horse once we got there."

Rachel tilted her head and massaged her neck. "I guess you're right. I'll sit for a minute until my back feels better."

Moses almost cheered out loud. With any luck, Rachel would tire of waiting, hike home by herself, and leave him alone. With her hand pressing against her lower back, she groaned softly, limped away, and eased her body to the log. If she weren't Amish, that girl would make a mighty fine actress.

Determined to follow Lia even if he developed blisters on his armpits, Moses picked up his empty bucket and hobbled feverishly in Lia's direction. He knew he couldn't possibly be subtle. There were several perfectly good bushes to pick between Lia and himself.

He walked so rapidly and clumsily, he sounded like a bear crashing through the underbrush. All three cousins and Lia looked up as he approached.

"Glad you could join us," said Ben, teasingly glancing at Lia as if they were already the best of friends.

Moses forced a casual smile. "It sounds like you're having more fun over here than I am over there."

Lia pointed to a few feet from where she picked. "Here are some taller branches so you don't have to bend over so far."

His drab mood lightened as he limped to the bush. Lia hadn't forgotten him completely.

"Lia said a snake spooked the horses," Max said. "That's how you broke your leg."

Moses put his bucket on the ground and started to fill it as best he could. "Jah. And Dawdi picked up the snake with a rake and waved it in the air like a flag. I thought for sure that thing would finish me off."

Max hooted with glee. "Dawdi never could hurt a living thing."

Moses chuckled. "He won't even let us kill the spiders. And Rachel screams until her face turns purple whenever she sees one."

Lia's face glowed with affection. Moses had never seen a more attractive look. "We have been given strict instructions to leave the spiders to Felty. He has a special little bottle he puts them in before he releases them into the wild."

"Lia really did save my life," Moses blurted out. "The doctor said I could have gone into shock or lost too much blood."

"I knew she was being modest," Ben said, showing that annoyingly handsome smile again.

"Nae, I ran down the hill, tripped and fell, and then borrowed someone's phone to call the ambulance."

"Lia kept her head and knew exactly what to do even though she got injured herself."

"And Mammi says she is a very gute cook," Titus added.

"The best." Even though his admiration would make his cousins even more interested than they already were, Moses wanted to make sure Lia realized he'd been watching. He knew how little notice she got at home. "Her rolls melt in your mouth."

Lia shook her head. "Don't exaggerate. You've never tasted my rolls."

"Oh, yes, I have. At the picnic with Rachel."

Lia fell silent and looked thoughtful for a minute as her lips curled ever so slightly. Did she really believe

Moses could be so blind as to think Rachel made those rolls?

"You are quite taken with Lia, aren't you, Moses?"

With Lia close, Moses felt more playful. "Of course. Look how pretty she is. And tall."

"There aren't enough tall girls to go around," Ben said, his eyes twinkling in amusement.

"But I'll have you know, she has refused to marry me."

The cousins gaped at Moses, unsure if he was teasing, and then they turned to Lia for confirmation.

Her laugh tripped past her lips like a brook tickling the pebbles. "He thought I wanted him for a husband, but he didn't like the way I swept the floor."

"That's not true," Moses said. "I love the way you sweep the floor."

Max folded his arms across his chest. "It doesn't matter. Moses is glued so tight to that girl in Minneapolis, a crowbar couldn't pry him loose."

The sunshine in Lia's face disappeared, and she lowered her eyes to the ground.

"She writes him every week," Ben said. "Going on three years yet."

Moses didn't like that look on Lia's face. He wanted to grab her by the shoulders and compel her to look in his eyes. He needed to set her straight. He wasn't glued to Barbara anymore.

Wasn't glued to Barbara?

When had this happened?

He slid his hand in his pocket and fingered the yellow envelope. He used to watch out the window for the mailman every Friday while he separated curd. But lately, Barbara's letters felt more like burdens than blessings. She was so far away.

Far away from Bonduel. Far away from the Amish way of life. Far away from Moses's heart.

Would his cousins believe him if he denied everything? Probably not today.

A movement through the trees caught their attention, and they watched as cousin Sarah Beachy's son, Gabe, rode toward them on a dappled gray mare. Gabe was fourteen years old and happy as a clam since he'd finished his last year of school in May and didn't have to return with his younger siblings next week.

Gabe caught sight of Moses first. "Is Lia with you?"

Lia stepped out from the shade. "Is another baby coming?"

"Mamm said there's plenty of time, but all I had was this horse to deliver the message. Do you want to come on my horse or can Moses take you in the buggy?"

Moses must have broken every berry branch in his way to put himself forward. "I will take her in Dawdi's buggy."

Ben had always been real sharp. "You can't hitch up the horse with that leg. I'll take Lia."

Absolutely not, Moses wanted to protest. Moses and Lia shared the midwifing jobs together, the two of them—except when Rachel came along, and she didn't count. It didn't seem right that anyone else should take his place. Moses looked to Lia. Surely she wouldn't agree to anything else.

Lia smiled the unhappy smile that Moses saw more and more often. "You should stay here with Rachel."

Moses wanted to shout in exasperation but decided it would be unseemly to pitch a fit. Why in the world would he want to stay here with Rachel?

Maybe Lia was tired of taking Rachel along and having to care for her sister as well as her patients. But more likely, Lia would much rather be with Ben or Max than Moses Zimmerman, the boy who wouldn't let go of the memory of a girl who had rejected him. Why wouldn't Lia want to be with a boy who found her fascinating instead of one who took her for granted?

Moses watched Ben put a light hand at the small of Lia's back to guide her to the path that would take them back to the house. Lia smiled, still unhappy, and let Ben lead her away. Moses couldn't catch his breath.

Moses had never seen any food so mouthwateringly tempting. Plump huckleberries peeked from under a golden, flaky lattice crust on top of the three pies Lia had made for dessert. She had a gift for making food look delicious.

After three hours, they had finally finished picking the berries, making sure to leave a sufficient amount for the bears as Dawdi wanted. Moses had picked like a madman. Maybe he thought if he finished soon enough, he could take a horse to Lia and be there when she walked out of the house, her face aglow with the exhaustion and satisfaction of hard work. He loved that face.

His daydreams were ridiculous. Moses didn't even know where they had gone. He'd have to ask Mammi the names of all the women in Bonduel expecting a baby this month and go to each of their houses. It was a wild-goose chase, and with this worthless leg of his, it would take him the better part of a week.

When he and his family walked into the warm kitchen, they were greeted with the sight of three huckleberry pies on the table and the aroma of potato soup in a Dutch oven on the cookstove.

A good-sized wedge had been carved out of one of the pies and a note lay on the table beside it.

*I begged Lia for a piece. She made me write this
apology note. I hope I left enough for the rest of you.*

Ben.

P.S. It is even better with ice cream.

Moses didn't think his heart could sink any lower.
Ben had eaten the first piece. Moses's piece. Ben had
probably smiled and told Lia how heavenly it was, and
Lia had soaked it up like a desert soaks up the rain.

Moses should have been the one to tell Lia how
good it tasted. He'd been waiting for three months for
this chance. Ben had innocently stolen it from him.

Dejectedly, Moses helped Rachel set the bowls and
spoons while Max and Titus Junior put two more
leaves in the table and brought up folding chairs from
the cellar. Moses studied his leg encased in a cast. He
couldn't help with the heavy lifting, and he couldn't
drive Lia places. He was truly worthless.

At supper, Moses ate his soup—the best potato soup
he'd ever tasted—in silence while the family chattered
merrily away. Rachel scooped up his slice of bread and
buttered it for him. He wanted to growl in frustration.
Rachel's hovering had become unbearable.

"Now that your leg is in a cast, how long do you
plan on staying here, Moses?" Mamm asked.

"We've enjoyed taking care of him," Mammi said.
Her eyes twinkled. "The girls especially have."

Mammi and Mamm shared a knowing look.

Rachel poured Moses another glass of milk and
smiled ever so sweetly. "All the hard work has been a
true pleasure."

Moses coughed to cover up the protest that broke
free from his throat. Had Rachel known a day of hard
work in her life? Ach, but she was very good at playing

the long-suffering nurse. An actress. She should have been an actress.

"I am going home tonight," he announced. "I still have two good hands to make cheese. Adam has been running the factory almost by himself since I've been gone."

"Adam is a gute boy," Mammi said.

"He takes after his dawdi," said Dawdi, waving his spoon for emphasis. "This soup is the best I've ever tasted. The queen of Mexico doesn't eat this well."

An overwhelming desire for solitude wrapped itself around Moses's chest. He would have liked nothing better than to hike to the rocky side of the hill and recline on a boulder while he tried to make sense of his jumbled emotions. But going anywhere proved to be a huge production with his casted leg as heavy and clunky as a motor home negotiating a narrow road and Rachel clinging to him like a cocklebur on his pant leg.

Mammi scooted her chair from the table. "And now for the best part."

Mandy stood to help Mammi as she pulled ice cream from the freezer and got ready to cut the pie.

Rachel leaped from her seat. "I'll serve the pie if you want to scoop ice cream, Mandy."

Mandy shrugged her shoulders and handed Rachel the spatula. "Okay, sure."

Rachel picked up one of the pies and tilted it so everyone at the table could see the lattice top crafted by skilled hands. "Lia and I made the pies."

Rachel had been with Moses at the doctor when Lia made the pies. He pressed his lips together so something impolite wouldn't accidentally come out of his mouth.

"They look delicious," Mamm said, not suspecting

that Rachel stretched the truth beyond recognition. "Do you use lard or shortening for the crust?"

Rachel looked confused for a fraction of a second, put the pie on the counter, and waved her hand dismissively. "Oh, Lia did the crust this time. I'm not sure which she used."

Moses couldn't stand it. He'd break his other leg before he took anything from Rachel's hand ever again. Even Lia's pie.

Grabbing the crutches that rested against the back of his chair, he said, "I'll go pack the rest of my things so Mamm and Dat can take me back to my house tonight."

Rachel held out a generous piece of pie, with luscious purple berries dripping from between the crusts. "Don't you want pie?"

"I'll eat a piece with Lia when she gets home. She ought to have a taste of her own pie."

"But that might not be for hours."

Without replying, Moses limped into Rachel's room to gather his things. He stopped short. A whole pie sat in the middle of Rachel's bed, complete with a fork tied with a ribbon and an envelope addressed to Moses. He eagerly ripped open the envelope and pulled out a card filled with Lia's handwriting.

Moses, You always seem to miss out on dessert. I wanted to make sure that you got a piece today, so I made a whole pie especially for you. I hope you enjoy it. Thank you for being such a good friend to me. You can share it with Rachel, if you like.

From Lia

Moses couldn't hold back the smile that sprouted on his face. She hadn't forgotten him. He read her note four times, delighted with the way she curled the tails of her *y*'s and *g*'s.

On the fifth time reading through her note, his eyes got stuck on "friend," and he sucked in his breath because it felt like a semi truck crashed through the house and ran over him.

He didn't want to be friends.

Staggering with the weight of this realization, Moses dropped his crutches and sank to the bed where he sat in stunned silence. He wanted so much more than friendship.

The feeling overtook him like a flash flood, crashing into him and tossing and turning him until he didn't know which way was up.

He loved Lia Shetler.

He loved Lia Shetler! He loved her laugh and her smile. He loved the way her graceful hands shaped bread into pans and plucked huckleberries from bushes. And he hated it when she smiled at one of his cousins.

Moses kneaded his forehead as if trying to pull out every confusing thought in his brain. Did he really love Lia more than Barbara? He couldn't decipher his deepest emotions.

But he did know that he loved Lia so much that he couldn't bear the thought of not being with her. He remembered their embrace at the Millers' house. He'd never felt so strong or secure, even with Barbara.

Especially not with Barbara.

Barbara had always kept one foot in the community and one foot in the world. When they got engaged, fear that he might lose her followed him like a cloud of black, choking smoke. He never felt sure of her love.

His world had shattered when she chose to leave the community, but then she dangled that carrot. *I need to see what it's like, but I will come back. You'll wait for me, won't you, Moses? If you truly love me, you'll wait.* So he had waited.

The guilt that had been sitting on Moses's shoulder since he met Lia slapped him in the face. Was he being untrue to Barbara by entertaining such feelings for Lia?

With his clenched fist, Moses pressed on the spot between his eyebrows. How true had Barbara been to him? She had crushed him when she left and then expected all the sacrifice on his part. She wrote every week, but she hadn't visited once in three years. She had told him she thought of coming back to the community no less than a dozen times yet had registered for school in Minneapolis and bought a car.

Moses took a deep breath.

Barbara wasn't coming back.

And he didn't want her anymore.

He'd been so young when he'd fallen in love with Barbara. She now seemed like a wisp of smoke compared to the raging fire that was his love for Lia. He had wasted so much time pining for Barbara that he failed to acknowledge the girl right in front of him— the tall beauty who was his perfect match.

His perfect match.

Moses's heart soared through the clouds as he felt the weight of Barbara's expectations fall from his shoulders. He loved Lia Shetler!

He thudded to earth when he thought of Lia's face that afternoon. She had been silent and withdrawn ever since his accident. Had she sensed his growing affection and didn't return it? She always pushed Rachel forward and drew herself back.

Moses slapped his forehead and growled in frustration. Did Lia believe he loved Rachel?

What a ridiculous notion!

But maybe not ridiculous to Lia. Why else would she have left him at the mercy of Rachel when he recovered from his accident? She insisted that Rachel accompany him to the doctor. In her note she told him he could share the pie with Rachel.

Lia was trying to get out of the way.

Moses felt ill as the pieces of the puzzle came together. He had told Lia plainly that he had no interest in her sister. But Lia was so accustomed to people showering Rachel with attention and taking no notice of her, she would have naturally concluded that Moses had changed his mind.

He clenched his fists until his knuckles turned white. Lia, no doubt, had seen Rachel and him emerging from the woods on the day of the picnic. As he recalled, he had put his arm around Rachel and held her hand in plain sight of the house. His efforts to mollify Rachel had convinced Lia of something that wasn't true.

But surely it wasn't too late to persuade Lia he loved her. She'd only known Ben for a few hours.

He yanked the reins of his racing heart. What if Lia wasn't interested? She had told him he was arrogant to think that she would want to marry him. What if she didn't even like him? Considering that possibility made him feel as if a large hand had shoved him to the ground.

He breathed in the aroma of warm huckleberries.

She had made a pie for him. His heart jumped around inside his chest. She liked him.

Could she love him?

Rachel burst into the room and slammed the door behind her. Her eyes grew wide. "What are you doing? Where did you get that?"

"Lia left it for me."

She raised her eyebrows in surprise and tried to snatch the pie from his hand. He pulled it from her reach. "Did you steal this from the kitchen?"

"Nae. Lia made it for me. She left a note."

Frowning, Rachel folded her arms and studied Moses's face. "Why would she do that?" she said, more to herself than Moses.

"She wanted to be sure I got a taste."

Rachel narrowed her eyes. "She wanted to take the credit and leave me out of it."

Moses's sigh came from deep within his chest. No matter the consequences, he had to have this talk with Rachel. Again. And he must have it now.

He stood up and hopped to the small nightstand next to the bed, where he placed his precious pie.

"I could have done that for you," Rachel said resentfully.

Moses eased himself back onto the bed and patted the space next to him for Rachel to sit. She relaxed her posture and tweaked the corner of her mouth upward as she sidled next to him.

"Remember when I told you I wasn't looking to marry?" he said.

Rachel's eyes popped wide open and her smile spread so far it almost flew off her face. She nodded in anticipation.

Wrong thing to say. Moses slumped his shoulders.

"Rachel, I told the truth. I do not want to marry you, and I never will."

Rachel stiffened beside him. "Lia is not a better cook than me, if that's what you're thinking."

Moses wanted to laugh. Oh, that choosing a wife were that easy. "It has nothing to do with the pie. I do not love you."

"And I told you, if you are worried about Lia getting her feelings hurt, my dat will make her go back home."

Could Rachel possibly perceive that a man might not be interested in her? He would have to be blunt. "No, Rachel. I am not going to marry you. Ever. Not in a million years. Never, ever. I-do-not-like-you." He lengthened his syllables for emphasis, as she always did.

His using her own tone of voice caught her attention, and she fluttered her eyelashes in indignation. "You don't even like me?"

Oops. He'd meant to say "love," but his choice of words was accurate. He did not even like her. "Not in the way you want me to like you." How could Lia not have recognized his dislike?

Rachel stood up with a huff and stared at Moses with fire in her eyes. "So, you love Lia?"

The pace of his heart quickened at the mention of her name, but Rachel would not be the first to hear his declaration of love. "This has nothing to do with Lia."

Rachel rolled her eyes and threw up her hands. "Ha! It has everything to do with Lia. She's been pushing herself on you all summer."

"Rachel, I don't want to marry you."

"A man who lets a stupid pie sway his affection is not worthy of me."

Moses gave up. "You're right. I am not worthy of you. You deserve better."

To his surprise, Rachel burst into tears. She put her hand to her cheek. "Is this the thanks I get for nursing you back to health? I stayed by your side even when I wanted to fall over with being so tired."

"I never asked you to—"

"You held my hand. I wrote my dat that you loved me. I'll be humiliated in front of my family."

Her tears only served to heighten Moses's agitation. "I'm sorry if I made you believe that." Was it useless to defend himself? "And you held my hand. I never wanted to hold yours."

"What a liar you are! You were teasing me because I'm so beautiful. You wanted all your cousins to see you with a pretty girl."

"Another reason that you should never want a husband like me."

She snapped her head up and glared at him. "Don't make fun of me."

She sniffled and cried while he sat in silence. He knew he couldn't say anything to make her feel better. Moses had assumed that Rachel had no proper feelings, but she seemed genuinely heartbroken, and a broken heart didn't heal overnight. He knew that from very personal experience.

"I'm sorry that I hurt your feelings."

Rachel sniffed and seemed to remember that he was in the room. "You didn't hurt my feelings. I'm crying because you're such a liar. Liars go to hell, you know."

All the fight drained out of him. He could never make Rachel see what she would not see.

Before he even registered what she did, Rachel

snatched the pie from the nightstand and flung it to the floor. Moses called out in surprise as the glass pie plate shattered. Rachel stomped indignantly until huckleberry pie filling covered her shoe, and the pie and plate were beyond recognition. With that, she turned on her heels and stomped out of the room, leaving a trail of purple footprints behind her.

In mourning, Moses slid off the bed and knelt beside his pie. So much for trying to spare Rachel's feelings.

Mammi came shuffling into the room, and her eyes grew big as buggy wheels. "I heard a noise and thought you had fallen."

Moses looked up at Mammi with a guilty curve of his lips. "We had an accident with the pie."

Mammi pushed her glasses up as her gaze fell on Rachel's purple trail out the door. "Rachel must not like huckleberries."

The quirky lift of her eyebrows and the pathetic mound of glass and pie tickled Moses's funny bone. He couldn't help it. Guttural laughter exploded from his lips and left him breathless. Mammi shut the door behind her, smiled, and let a giggle trip out of her mouth. Her whole body seemed to be laughing. She wrapped her arms around her stomach as she bobbed up and down.

After a few minutes of uncontrolled mirth, Mammi composed herself and wiped the tears from her eyes. "That girl is getting some valuable lessons. I hope she learns something from them."

"It wasn't really her fault—"

Mammi patted him on the shoulder. "Oh, Moses, I could write a book about all the things you think I don't know."

Bracing his arm on the bed, Moses stood up. "I'll go get the mop."

"You are helpless with that cast on. Rachel made the mess. She should clean it up."

"She's probably halfway to Wautoma by now."

Mammi opened the door and gazed down the hall. "No, she's left a trail to Lia's room. Although if I were her, I'd get that shoe into a bucket of soapy water before it stains purple." Mammi put her hand over her mouth to stifle a laugh. "I'll see Rachel cleans it up. You go in the kitchen and be with your parents."

"Okay," Moses said, searching the room for his crutches. "I'll have a piece of pie."

The corners of Mammi's mouth turned down. "Oh, dear. Lia told me she made a pie for you, so we finished the other three. Sorry. The pies are all."

Moses huffed the air out of his lungs. "I suppose I should have expected that."

"Max had three pieces."

Of course Max had three pieces.

And Moses had none.

It had been an eventful day. He had gotten a cast put on, offended Rachel, and decided he finally wanted to get married. He had picked huckleberries, watched Lia ride away with his cousin, and realized that he loved her more than anyone ever loved before.

And he had still never tasted a piece of Lia Shetler's pie.

The house was dark, except for the lantern hissing on the table in the hallway, and quiet, except for the sniffling coming from Moses's recently vacated room. Felty tapped softly on the door. "Could I come in?"

He heard soft footsteps, and then Rachel cracked her door open. She made no secret that she had been crying. The tears glistened on her cheeks and her nose was moist and red. "I'm cleaning my shoe."

"I can help," Felty said.

Peering at him from under hooded eyes, Rachel opened the door wider and stepped back. Felty walked into the room towing a chair behind him. He placed the chair facing the bed and sat on it, breathless from dragging the thing from the kitchen. He felt his eighty-plus years more every day.

Rachel stared at him in puzzlement, clutching her light brown leather shoe in one hand and a damp towel in the other. The towel was already smeared purple with berry stains, but the shoe didn't look any closer to being clean. Felty didn't want to discourage her, but that shoe would never be the same. It would probably be easier to dip the other one into a huckleberry pie of its own. At least then she'd have a matching pair.

"Is Lia back yet?" Rachel asked, although she didn't seem particularly interested in the answer.

"Nae. You know how long babies can take sometimes."

"Jah, I've slept on one too many sofas."

Felty held out his hand, and after some hesitation, Rachel gave him the shoe and the rag. He laid the shoe in his lap and began rubbing it vigorously. His efforts weren't going to make a bit of difference, but at least Rachel would see that he cared.

Rachel slumped her shoulders and plopped onto the bed. "If Lia hadn't been showing off with that ver-y spec-ial pie, this never would have happened. She's always trying to make me look deerich."

Felty dropped the shoe and rag into his lap,

reached over, and patted Rachel on the knee. He tried to make his expression kindly as he pinned Rachel with an intense gaze. "Rachel, you're a gute . . . a kind . . ." He cleared his throat. "You're a pretty little girl, and you and I are soon going to be related."

Rachel lifted her eyebrows and seemed to perk up a bit. "Related?"

"Can I give you some advice as if you was my own granddaughter?"

Rachel dabbed the tears from her face and exploded into a toothy grin. "I knew Moses must be teasing. Did he tell you he wants to marry me?"

Felty sighed and held up his hand to halt Rachel's overactive imagination. "Not you, Rachel. Moses is not going to marry you."

Suddenly cross, Rachel pursed her lips and folded her arms. "It won't be Lia, if that's what you're thinking."

Felty, not one to lose his temper, made his voice soft and comforting. "You're a wonderful-pretty girl, Rachel. Your hair's a pretty color and your eyes look as blue as the afternoon sky. It wonders me why someone as pretty as you wouldn't want to be pretty on the inside. The Lord doesn't see your outward appearance. The Lord looketh on the heart."

Rachel waved her hand in dismissal. "That's just a Bible verse to make ugly people feel better."

"But not you?"

"The good Lord made me pretty for a reason. Queen Esther was pretty, and she saved her people."

"You are no Queen Esther," Felty said.

Rachel studied Felty and nibbled her bottom lip. "I'm pretty on the outside. And on the inside."

"Pretty is as pretty does."

"I hardly left Moses's side for weeks. I served him

food and kept him company. I went with him to the doctor and helped him make cheese. I've been an angel. What do you expect from me?"

"But how have you treated Lia—your own flesh and blood? And what about those boys who asked for your hand in marriage?"

Rachel looked down at her hands. "They didn't deserve—"

"Everyone deserves to be treated with kindness. Did you tend to Moses out of the goodness of your heart or because you want a handsome husband? Or maybe you want to steal Moses because Lia likes him. A girl who is pretty on the inside would not do something so cruel to her sister."

"I'm not like that," Rachel protested. "I try to protect Lia from getting her feelings hurt, that's all. Some sisters wouldn't even care. I've always been good to Lia. Just ask her."

Felty stroked his beard and then leaned closer and took Rachel's hand. She resisted at first but then relaxed. Her expression softened, and she appeared at least willing to listen.

"I know you have it in you to be a gute, sweet girl—the kind of girl Moses would want. But you haven't shown it yet."

He could see the wheels turning in Rachel's head. Maybe he was getting through to her. "What . . . what kind of girl does Moses want?"

"A godly man wants a gute and generous woman who thinks more about others than she does about herself—someone who never speaks guile and treats others as Jesus would treat them."

Rachel pulled from his grasp. She balled her hands into fists and pressed down on the mattress. Tears pooled in her eyes and threatened to run down her cheeks. "What more can I do? I've tried everything to make Moses love me."

"My dear, you need to practice kindness before you even think about getting a husband. Follow Lia's example. She never thinks of herself."

Rachel burst into frustrated tears. Felty patted her leg comfortingly as she cried.

"All I hear is Lia this and Lia that. It was never like this at home. I'm the favorite."

Felty stifled a snort. He'd met Rachel's dat. Of course Rachel was the favorite.

"Despite what you think, Lia is not a better cook than me," Rachel said between sobs. "And I'm so much prettier. Why does Moses like her better?"

"Because she is pretty on the inside."

Rachel started to protest, but instead she leaned back on her hands and fell silent.

Gute. Maybe she was giving his advice a chance to sink in.

Rachel sat up straight, sniffed once, and blinked the tears from her eyes. "So I need to be more like Lia? Nicer?"

"Jah," Felty said. "More like Lia."

Felty could see a light go on as a wonderful idea struck Rachel. She glanced at Felty before closing her eyes and massaging the side of her face with her dainty fingers. "Would you take me to the market tomorrow to call my dat? I think I need to go home."

Felty nodded. "Just what the doctor ordered. We'll go first thing in the morning."

Rachel pulled a tissue from her pocket and mopped up her face. "You'll see. I'll be better than Lia. I know I can be the kind of wife Moses wants."

"That's a gute girl." Holding out Rachel's shoe, Felty stood and raised his eyebrows sympathetically. "I am afraid your shoe will never be clean. Huckleberries stain everything."

"It doesn't matter," Rachel said, taking her purple shoe from Felty. "At least I've learned a lesson."

Chapter Eighteen

Lia rolled on her back and stretched her legs, luxuriating in the feel of her soft bed. Two weeks of sleeping on the floor because Rachel needed the bed had taken a toll on Lia's lower back.

She lifted her head from the pillow and promptly lowered it. Sleeping during the day always left her feeling groggy. By the bright light streaming through her tiny window, Lia determined it must be after noon. Well past time to get up. Her chores wouldn't do themselves, and Rachel certainly wouldn't have done them.

Lia took a deep breath and shook her head. She would have to bury her jealousy and quit this nasty habit of thinking poorly of Rachel. It wasn't Rachel's fault that Moses liked her.

Lia had stayed up all night helping Sarah with the delivery. She and Ben had arrived at the Kings' house a little after five in the early evening. After a couple of hours, when it looked like the baby was in no hurry to arrive, Lia had sent Ben home, promising to contact him if she needed anything.

Ben Helmuth was almost as handsome and as tall

as his cousin Moses. Lia knew she would always prefer Moses, but it felt so nice to have someone pay her a little attention. Eventually she would have to learn to see Moses without thinking about how much she loved him, and if boys like Ben could help, then all the better.

The baby had finally come early this morning, and the new father paid a driver to take Lia home. Bone-tired, she had arrived at Huckleberry Hill in time to say good morning to Anna and Felty and stumble wearily down the hall for some sleep. It was a bitter-sweet surprise when she found her room empty. It meant Rachel slept in the big room again and Lia could have her bed back, but it also meant that Moses had gone home. She should have been ecstatic. It was less painful when he wasn't around.

A succession of loud raps at the door startled her, motivating her to sit up. Without waiting for an invitation, Rachel blew into the room with that smug smile that meant she was about to get her way. "I'm back."

Lia began unraveling her braid. "Where have you been?"

"It's one thirty. Don't you think you should get up, lazybones?"

With her waist-length hair free from its braid, Lia brushed it before rebraiding it and fashioning it into a bun at the back of her head. "Jah, I need to get supper started."

"Anna is making supper tonight from her new cook-book. I'm praying I'm not hungry because it will, like as not, taste terrible. They took me to the market this morning, and Anna bought stuff called couscous."

"It's a Mideastern food."

"She's going to mix it with turnips and cinnamon. Cin-na-mon. So I ate a big dinner." Rachel walked deliberately to the chest of drawers and ran her finger over the top as if checking for dust. "They have a phone at the market."

When Lia made no attempt to grasp the significance of this news, Rachel added, "I called Dat."

Rachel called Dat? She must really be upset about something. Well, it couldn't be Lia's latest midwifing trip. Lia had left Moses behind too. "What did he say?"

"He doesn't stand by the phone shack and wait for calls. I left a message."

Lia felt too tired to grill Rachel on the reason she had called Dat. A letter of chastisement would probably arrive in a couple of days, and then Lia would know what all the fuss was about. Today, she was too beaten down by Rachel's fits of temper to care very much. Rachel turned and looked at her with a knowing glint in her eye. Lia merely changed the subject.

"Moses must have gone home last night."

Rachel pursed her lips and glared at Lia. "You-have-got to get over this in-fat-u-ation with Moses."

"What . . . what are you talking about?"

"You're embarrassing yourself," Rachel snapped. "Can't you see how awkward it is for him? You make him pies and write him notes and simper whenever he's within ten feet. He doesn't know how to make you quit bothering him."

Lia felt her face get hot. She had tried to guard her emotions, but if self-centered Rachel suspected something, perhaps her feelings weren't as secret as she hoped.

The more Rachel talked, the more agitated she became. Her voice rose, and her syllables grew farther and farther apart. "Do you know what happened to that pie you made for him? It ended up on the floor. On-the-floor. The stain won't come out of the wood. It's got to stop, Lia."

Lia refused to let Rachel see her cry—pretty and petite Rachel, who had the love of the one man Lia would never get over. Rachel always got what she wanted, but she would not have the satisfaction of humiliating Lia today. She'd keep her self-respect if it was the last thing she did.

Lia held her breath and bit her tongue to keep from crying while she positioned her kapp and pinned it into her hair. She didn't look at Rachel and didn't risk saying anything until she could do it with composure. She forced her thoughts outdoors to the huckleberry patch where she and Moses had picked yesterday. No, best not go there. She thought of Sarah and the Millers' new baby, but Lia couldn't help but remember who first introduced her to Sarah. The day at the auction was one of the happiest of her life.

Lia cleared her mind and thought of fishing. She'd been fishing with her dat a time or two. Fishing was boring and had no strong emotions connected with it. Fishing. She thought of fishing.

Lia pinned her apron and then sat on the bed and donned her shoes and stockings.

Dat caught a very big fish once in Alpine Lake. It weighed ten pounds.

Rachel folded her arms across her chest and stared at Lia, obviously rejoicing in her conquest with Moses. Why didn't she go away? She had her own room. Why did she have to come take up space in Lia's?

Rachel didn't seem inclined to leave anytime soon, so Lia slid past her and made her way to the kitchen where she hoped she would see Anna's friendly face. At least Anna loved her.

Anna did not disappoint. She looked up from her cookbook and erupted into a smile as genuine as it was wide. "There you are. Did you get enough sleep? I'd hate to see you get all worn out."

Rachel followed Lia into the kitchen, probably hoping to see her burst into tears yet.

Lia finally felt calm enough to speak. "I came to see if I could help you with supper."

"Always so thoughtful. How did the delivery go last night?"

"Very gute. A baby girl for the Kings. Their second. Labor took all night, but Lila did not have too bad a time of it."

"Did Ben drive you back?"

"When I saw it would take most of the night, I sent him home. A driver brought me home this morning."

Anna clutched her cookbook to her chest. "Ben, he is such a gute boy, but he hasn't learned how things are done. Moses would have stayed the night to wait for you."

Jah, Moses would have waited.

Luckily, Lia had her back turned to Rachel. The tears escaped from her eyes, and she had no power to stop them.

Anna's expression didn't change as she looked past Lia to Rachel. "Rachel," she said, bustling around Lia. "I need to show you the special wood soap I want you to use on your floor."

"It's already clean," Rachel said.

Lia didn't look, but in her mind's eye she could imagine Anna taking Rachel firmly by the elbow. "It's not clean enough, especially in the hall. Cum, and I will show you."

Their footsteps faded down the hall. Lia snatched four tissues from the box by Felty's chair and mopped up her face thoroughly. Then she splashed cold water on her cheeks so not even a hint of crying would be visible.

Thank you, Anna!

Usually, standing at the kitchen sink she saw anyone who came to the door, but this time she must have been drying the water from her face. The forceful knock took her by surprise. Before Lia could even hang up the towel, Rachel sprinted from the hallway and swung the door open.

Dat.

Dat, with a seriously dismal frown on his face.

Rachel had only called him that morning. He must have rushed to Bonduel as soon as he got her message. Rachel probably sounded desperately urgent on the phone. Lia's heart sank. Dat's presence could only mean one thing.

He didn't even take the time to say hello. "You are coming home with me, Lia. Get your things."

Anna bustled into the kitchen and plastered on the fake smile she used when she was especially peeved. "I planned on her staying for at least six more weeks."

"I'm sorry, Anna, but Lia is needed at home."

Anna squared her shoulders and did one of the nicest things anyone had ever done for Lia. She took Rachel by the elbow and nudged her toward Dat. "Take Rachel instead. Lia has important midwife work to do."

Rachel's mouth fell open. "I have important work here too."

Dat shook his head. "We need Lia to help with the canning and cooking, and we must teach her obedience. She too often disregards her parents' wishes."

Lia's anger at the injustice of it all filled every space in her body, and for the first time in her life, she lashed out at her dat. "Why did you let me come to Bonduel in the first place if you need me so badly at home?"

"We thought it would be gute for you to go away for a few months, grow up a little."

Lia took deliberate breaths as she willed herself to calm down. Jesus said, "He who is angry with his brother is in danger of judgment." Knowing she would regret any words she spoke in anger, she said a quick prayer of repentance. Taking pity on the father who didn't have enough room in his heart to love his oldest daughter, she softened her tone. "You wanted to get me out of the way so boys could court Rachel without her older sister towering over them."

Thinking that she might have scared off potential boyfriends made Lia want to shake her head in disbelief. Why were boys so intimidated by a tall girl?

She loved being tall. She didn't use to, but now she did. And some boys didn't mind her height so much.

She shouldn't have thought of Moses. The memories made it harder to leave.

But, really, wouldn't it be better if she were gone? She wouldn't be forced to watch Moses and Rachel flaunt their love, and she would be away from everything that reminded her of him—the Scrabble game waiting on the table, Anna's knitted pot holders, Sarah Beachy's strong chin, Huckleberry Hill itself.

Whom was she kidding? She'd think about him every minute of the day no matter what.

Dat's face turned a shade redder. "We wanted Rachel to be free to go out with young men without her sister always with her. We didn't dream that the most fitting husband would be here in Bonduel." Dat fixed his eyes on Anna. "You saw that Moses and Rachel were coming along. When you wrote, you said that Rachel and Moses would have more time to court if Lia did the choring."

Anna was like a bubbling teapot on the verge of letting out steam. "Then let her stay."

"Rachel tells me that Lia is trying to steal Moses, when I gave her strict instructions to help bring Moses and Rachel together. I will not condone such selfishness."

Rachel thought she was trying to steal Moses? "What about the picnic?" she said, staring at Rachel in astonishment. "What about the times you rode with us for midwifing? I even made Moses take you with him to the doctor."

"You left me in the buggy for over an hour while you two hung sheets on the line. And what about the pie? Why did you make a special pie just-for-him? I'm not stupid. I saw the note you wrote."

"He showed you the note?"

"He wanted advice about how to let you down gently."

Any doubt that Moses loved Rachel vanished. He was now sharing secrets with her. Lia wanted to crawl under a rock and never come out. "And that's why he threw my pie on the floor?"

Rachel inclined her head noncommittally. Anna cleared her throat and shook her head ever so slightly at Lia as a ghost of a grin flitted across her face.

"If Moses loves you," Lia said, "then you don't need to worry that I'll steal him. He's very loyal."

Rachel gave Lia that condescending look she used when she wanted Lia to stop contradicting her. She came near and put a sisterly arm around Lia's waist. "He won't declare his love to me because he thinks he'll hurt your feelings. He's very mindful of other people's feelings."

What was left of her heart shattered like thin ice on a deep pond.

Dat stepped forward. "I won't let you ruin this for Rachel. You are coming home with me."

Lia stood completely still, staring at her father and seeing her dreams evaporate like mist on a blistering hot day.

The rumble of Felty's deep voice caught their attention. He came into the house carrying a bucket of plump tomatoes and singing, as usual. *"What though the way be lonely, and dark the shadows fall, I know wherever it leadeth, my Father planned it all."* He paused as he noticed Lia's dat, placed his bucket on the table, and continued singing as if he were giving a concert. *"I sing through the shade and the sunshine, I'll trust Him whatever befall, I sing for I cannot be silent, my Father planned it all."*

Felty walked to Anna with outstretched hands and gave her a kiss. "I picked some tomatoes for that gourmet coze-coze you are fixing us tonight, Annie Banannie."

Anna affectionately patted Felty on the cheek. "That's couscous, dear."

Felty winked and gave Rachel a cheerful nod of his head. "So, Rachel, you are leaving us. Have a gute trip and be sure to write."

Anna tugged on his arm. "Nae, Felty. Owen is taking Lia home."

To Lia's surprise, Felty cocked an eyebrow, turned

up the corners of his mouth, and shook his finger at Rachel. "You are a clever girl," he said.

With guilt written all over her face, Rachel's gaze darted between Felty and Anna.

Anna opened her eyes wide, as if she couldn't see clearly unless her eyelids were completely out of the way. "What are you saying, Felty?"

"I'm saying that I'm never going to stick my nose into anything ever again."

Anna obviously expected her husband to do more than surrender. "Now, Felty," she said, propping her hands on her hips and frowning at him.

Felty squeezed Anna's elbow and sauntered to the sink, singing softly. *"There may be sunshine tomorrow, shadows may break and flee, 'twill be the way He chooses, my Father's plan for me."*

And that was the final word on everything.

It will be the way He chooses, my Father's plan for me.

In that moment of humble clarity, Lia surrendered her will. All things would work together for her good if she loved God. If God had a plan for her life, maybe her going home was a part of that plan.

Anna gave up trying to get Felty involved and turned to Dat. "Owen, we can't spare Lia."

Dat shifted his feet. "Rachel will stay to help."

Felty, happily washing tomatoes at the sink, began to whistle. He and Anna exchanged a look that spoke volumes, but Lia couldn't interpret it. Two people married for over half a century could probably read each other's minds.

Anna's temper cooled to a simmer. "Very well, Owen. You have the final say over your children. Will you stay for supper?"

"Nae, the driver is waiting."

Anna sighed in resignation. "Lia, I will help you gather your things."

Once again, Rachel had gotten her way. Her combative demeanor transformed instantly. She glanced at Felty before she said, "Oh, Lia. I will miss you so much. Cum, I will help you pack too." Lia had never heard such sympathy flow from Rachel's mouth.

Anna held up her hand. "Stay," she said, as if she were addressing the dog.

Rachel's lips twisted in frustration, but she stayed put. Sometimes Anna used her voice in a way that left no room for argument.

Anna took Lia's hand and led her down the hall to the bedroom. She reached up and took Lia's face between her hands. "Never you worry. This snag in our plans will force Moses to quit lollygagging. Mark my words. He'll be down to fetch you back in no time."

Lia's heart felt like a lump of coal as she pursed her lips and shook her head. Anna was the only one who still believed that Moses and Lia were meant for each other. But Anna's hopes would die a welcome death once Rachel and Moses got engaged.

Lia pulled her small suitcase from under the bed. "I'll miss you something terrible."

Anna smiled knowingly and winked. "You'll be back so fast, you won't have time to miss me."

Lia stopped and took Anna's hand in hers. "Nae, Anna. Moses loves Rachel. They'll be very happy to have me gone."

The wrinkles between Anna's eyes deepened. "Please, don't be so upset. You'll see. Like I told Moses, I see a lot more than you think. Love is blind, and so it's my job to keep track of the goings-on. Grandmas notice everything, even if their grandchildren think they're not paying attention. That's why I know Moses will be in

Wautoma before you can even unpack." Anna bustled out of the room.

Lia didn't have the energy or the desire to argue with Anna. If it made her happy, let her believe what she wanted to believe.

As quickly as she had left, Anna came back carrying three pot holders and a pair of charcoal gray knitted slippers. "These are for your mamm. I hope she planted celery this year."

Lia didn't want to think about the fact that the bride's mamm planted celery in anticipation of a wedding. The celery crop was not for Lia. "My mamm has planted celery every summer since Rachel turned sixteen, just in case."

Anna threw up her hands as a sign that she was finished trying to convince Lia of anything. "I will fix you a sandwich for the ride home. You haven't had anything to eat since yesterday."

Lia watched Anna shuffle down the hall and wished Anna were her grandmother. Then she would be able to stay forever.

Even moving slowly, it didn't take Lia much time to pack. Her four dresses went into the suitcase with her stockings, Sunday shoes, aprons, and underwear. The midwifing book Moses had given her lay in the top drawer. She traced her finger along the spine and smoothed her hand over the cover. She leafed through the pages, reading highlighted passages and remembering her time spent with Sarah. Would she be able to pick up her studies in Wautoma? Lord willing, she would.

The front cover fell open, and Lia recognized Moses's handwriting. He'd written in her book? How had she not discovered it before?

*Dear Lia, I hope you understand the words in this
book, because it seems to be written in another
language. Have fun reading again. Moses*

How could Moses always manage to make her
smile, even today? After a quick glance to make sure
her dat wasn't looking in, she closed the door, sat
down on her bed, and indulged in a soul-cleansing,
gut-wrenching cry.

Chapter Nineteen

"Sir, sir. Come over here. I want to show you something." The man with a heavy foreign accent and thick blond hair beckoned as Moses, bewildered and agitated, rolled along the walkway on his knee scooter. "Only a dollar a ball," said the man, now standing uncomfortably close. "Knock down the pins and win a prize."

"Nae, no, thank you," Moses stuttered. He could hardly focus his attention on an eager salesman when noise and neon attacked all five of his senses and left him feeling queasy.

This surely had to be the biggest building in the world. The ceiling looked like a construction site with metal bars crisscrossing each other as if a million ladders were bolted into the sky. Delighted screams rent the air as a bright orange car filled with teenagers roared around a loopy track that made Moses dizzy just watching. Metal and lights and color exploded from the floor and loomed menacingly above his head. He didn't dare stay in one place for long in case it all came crashing down on him, burying him in a pile of rubble ten feet high.

But most overwhelming was the noise. The pounding music, the screams, the echoes that left him unable to hear his own thoughts. How could people bear to be here without clapping their hands over their ears for relief?

Moses stopped next to a large, yellow statue of . . . he couldn't tell what, and studied the brochure in his fist. He couldn't figure out his location. There was no picture of a smiling piece of swiss cheese with outstretched arms anywhere on the map. He knew where he wanted to go but not how to get there.

That salesman came back. He wore a bright red Hawaiian shirt and flip-flops. "Sir. Come over. You have a good arm. Only a dollar a ball."

Moses held out his map and pointed to Barbara's shop. "Can you tell me how to get here?"

The man's smile faded briefly before he shook his head and looked at the map. "I only work here three months. I come in door, work all day, and go out door. I think this on level three." He pointed to the left. "Go there, up the elevator."

"Thank you very much."

"You don't want to play? I have good prizes."

"No, but thank you for the directions."

"Okay, okay." With his outstretched hand, the man beckoned Moses to stay put even as he walked away. He retrieved something from behind his counter and handed it to Moses. "Take sticker. Put it on your broken leg. Good advertising." Probably not trusting Moses to actually do it, the salesman peeled the paper from the back of the bright pink sticker and slapped it on Moses's cast.

Why not? Now Moses had a cheap souvenir of his trip to Minneapolis.

"Thank you," he said before turning his handlebars and scooting in the direction of the elevator.

Level three. Moses took a deep breath. In a few minutes, he'd lay eyes on Barbara for the first time in three years. He stood waiting for the elevator while his mind reeled with a sudden jolt of self-condemnation.

Why in the world had he waited for three years?

Moses's pulse raced as he thought of Lia. Maybe all this time he was convinced he waited for Barbara, when the good Lord actually prepared his heart for Lia.

Lia! The gentlest, loveliest person to ever come into his life. Three years seemed like nothing to wait for a treasure like Lia. Praise the Lord that he had not married Barbara.

Rolling off the elevator, Moses felt giddy. He ached to see Lia again and finally declare his love.

He studied his map. What floor was he on? He rolled over one walkway and then another trying to figure out what direction he faced. He finally had to ask another shopper to point him to the right place.

As Moses approached Barbara's store, he couldn't tell if dread or anticipation was his strongest emotion. He knew that Barbara had no intention of coming back to the settlement, but if she didn't realize it herself, her feelings would be hurt. He didn't want to hurt anybody.

The ZOO-ZOO-ZOOSA sign blinked neon pink, orange, and green above the entrance to the clothing store where Barbara worked. A wall of sound attacked Moses's ears as he rolled into the store. The deep bass of the wild music rattled his bones and seemed to originate from inside his head. If he lingered in this place too long, he would surely come out with a pounding headache.

Bizarre mannequins with animal faces where their

real heads should be were draped in tattered clothing that looked like it belonged in the rag pile instead of a fancy store. The walls sparkled pink and yellow, and Moses could see his reflection in the polished black floor.

Barbara was not part of his world anymore. And he was not part of hers.

Slowly negotiating his scooter around racks laden with clothes, Moses swept the store with his gaze. At times like these, he remembered to thank the good Lord for his height. He could survey the entire scene without straining his neck.

He took a deep breath. There she stood, helping a customer at the cash register. Moses was amazed that he actually recognized her. She had cut her chestnut hair and colored it white-platinum. It hung above her shoulders perfectly straight with not a hair out of place. Her dangly hoop earrings were bigger than canning lids, and she wore chunky beaded bracelets on both wrists. A coworker standing next to her wore a tank top that didn't even make it past her belly button, while Barbara's short-sleeved pink turtleneck covered everything. She looked fancy, but still modest.

Moses's breathing grew shallow and his heartbeat quickened as Barbara smiled at the customer and handed her the bag filled with her purchases. Of course he was nervous. It had been three years, after all.

Barbara caught sight of him staring and did a double take. A look of confusion flitted across her features before she flashed a dazzling smile. "Moses!" she squealed as she ran from behind the counter with her arms outspread.

Moses scooted back a few feet but couldn't go far without bumping into a rack of clothes behind him.

If she recognized his resistance, she didn't show it as she catapulted herself into his arms. He lifted his hands to catch her so she wouldn't crash to the floor, but quickly nudged her away as soon as she regained her balance.

Barbara grinned and rolled her eyes. "Oh, Moses. We're not in Bonduel. It's okay to give me a hug."

Moses smiled but didn't reply. He hadn't expected to be glad to see her. Their courtship had been a very happy time in his life, even if it had ended painfully.

Barbara shoved her hands into the back pockets of her jeans and looked Moses up and down. "I almost forgot how tall you are. And what happened to your leg?"

"I got kicked by a horse. Probably seven weeks in a cast."

Barbara sighed in sympathy. "I bet that hurt. But the scooter is pretty cool."

"Mammi is knitting handlebar covers for me. Bright blue."

Her eyes twinkled. "I love your mammi. I still have the throw she made for me. It's sitting at the foot of my bed in my apartment. How is your mammi? And your family? I need the update on everybody."

Moses did his best to be heard above the incessant music. "Mamm and Dat are still working the farm, like I said in my letter. Adam and Lonnie help me full-time at the cheese factory now. Lonnie is looking to marry this winter."

"I thought Lonnie would die a bachelor. He's so shy, I could never get more than three words out of him at a time. When we first met, his dat made him recite a poem to me just so I would hear his voice."

Moses scratched the whiskers on his chin. "The girl

he's sweet on doesn't stop talking, so they should do fine together."

Barbara seemed to almost burst with delight. "There's a match for everybody, I guess. How are your grandparents?"

"Mammi and Dawdi are as spry as ever. Dawdi's raising maran hens this year."

"Does he still sing everywhere he goes, at the top of his lungs?"

"Of course. And he's still making up words to songs."

Barbara flashed an affectionate smile and giggled. "And the license plate game?"

"Plays it every year. Last year, he got all fifty states."

"Oh, he must have been happy as a clam."

They shared a laugh, which only made Moses feel worse. This would be harder than he thought. What if Barbara burst into tears when he told her? What if she got mad and accused him of being unfaithful?

Barbara tapped him on the arm as if to get his attention. "Guess what. My mamm started writing me about three months ago."

Moses raised an eyebrow and nodded. "I know. You told me in one of your letters."

"I guess she figured three years of the ban was enough."

"She was very sad when you left. We all were."

Barbara's lips twitched downward, and silence, accompanied by blaring music, prevailed between them.

"Hey," Barbara said, perking up and dragging Moses forward, "come meet Summer and Brook."

The other two store clerks stood together folding T-shirts. They looked up in unison. Amusement and surprise registered on both their faces. The reaction didn't bother Moses. He didn't go anywhere among the Englisch without being an object of curiosity. The Apostle Paul had said that Christians were a peculiar people.

To her credit, Barbara seemed proud to introduce Moses to the others. At least she wasn't ashamed of where she came from. "Hey, guys, this is Moses. He's from Bonduel, where I grew up."

Brook contained her amusement and shook Moses's hand firmly. "Nice to meet you. Barbie talks about you all the time. I can see why. You're hot for an Amish guy." Moses puzzled that Brook found him an oddity when she wore black lipstick, black fingernail polish, and three sparkling studs in her left nostril.

Moses smiled. "I'm glad to meet you."

Summer giggled. "I love your accent. Barbie has lost most of hers."

"Denki, I like yours too," Moses said in Deitsch.

Summer giggled harder. "What did he say, Barbie? Was it something mean?"

Barbara winked at Moses and snaked her arms around his elbow. "Do you mind if I take my break early? I want to show Moses around."

"Take him on the roller coaster," Brook said.

They ambled toward the exit and once again, Moses extracted himself from Barbara's grasp. "Is there somewhere quiet we can go to talk?"

Barbara stopped walking and studied Moses's face. Her smile faded, and she seemed to wilt before his eyes. "Oh. I see." She dragged her feet all the way out of the store. The pounding of one song faded behind them, but more music blared from unseen loudspeakers somewhere above Moses's head. The racket from the amusement park bounced down the walkway. The voices and screams and electronic beeps combined so that noise seemed thicker than the air. Moses feared that if they wanted to talk in peace, they'd have to hike back to Bonduel.

Barbara seemed to have lost all enthusiasm for their conversation. She gazed down the hall in one direction and then turned to look the other way. "The mall's pretty noisy. I guess we could go sit in my car, but that would be super hot." Barbara slipped her hands into her back pockets again and looked at Moses, as if challenging him to come up with a solution.

He pressed his lips into a hard line. He'd rather not break up with his ex-fiancée sitting in a food court.

Barbara nibbled on her bottom lip. "I have an idea."

She headed back into the store without checking to see if Moses followed her. He broke a scooter speed record trying to keep up. Sheepishly, he waved at Brook and Summer as he passed. Barbara waited for him at the entrance to the fitting rooms at the back of the store. "In here. We've got a pretty big handicap stall."

An invisible curtain of blessed silence met Moses's ears as soon as he crossed the threshold. He didn't know if it was proper being in a women's fitting room, but the stillness beckoned to him. He would never take quietness for granted again.

Barbara opened the wide door to the compartment at the end of the hall and Moses obediently wheeled himself in. For a fitting room, there was a lot of space. He could probably stable his horse quite comfortably in here. A long bench stood against one wall and an oversized mirror covered the wall opposite. Rachel would like this room. She could sit on the bench and gaze at herself.

Thinking of Rachel steered Moses's mind to Lia, and a thrill of emotion bubbled up inside him. As soon as he settled things with Barbara, he would rush home to her. Lord willing, she would return his affection and make him happier than he ever thought possible.

With some effort, Moses slid his casted leg from the scooter and sat down.

Frowning, Barbara closed the stall door and sat next to him. "I know why you're here," she said, lightly laying a hand on Moses's arm. Her fingernails were bright orange-red—exactly the color of maple leaves in autumn. "But I'm not ready to come home, Moses. Give me a few more months."

She thought he wanted to talk her into coming home?

"I'm done with school in December," she said, as if this solved all their problems.

Moses cleared his throat and swallowed hard as everything he had planned to say completely left his head. He had loved Barbara once. How could he break the news to her? "Barbara," he cleared his throat again, "I know you expect me to hang on forever, but I am not going to wait for you anymore."

Barbara cocked her perfectly plucked eyebrows. "Is this an ultimatum?"

That sounded tricky. "What's an ultimatum?"

"You're saying either I come back to Bonduel now, or you're going to dump me."

Was that what she thought he said?

No wonder it had taken Moses two months to convince Rachel that he didn't want to marry her. Apparently, he couldn't explain himself in a way that girls could understand. Even Lia had misinterpreted his feelings.

Moses sighed in frustration. He was making a complete mess of things. Barbara would probably end up in tears. Either that or she would change her mind altogether and start planning their Amish wedding. The way things were going, he'd miss his bus back to Bonduel and have to spend the night huddled beneath the roller coaster with cotton stuffed in his ears.

Moses huffed out a breath and shook his head. "This is not one of those ultimatums. I don't want to marry you."

Barbara was the second girl he'd said those words to in less than forty-eight hours. Could things get any more absurd? "Even if you came back to Bonduel tonight, I wouldn't marry you. I don't love you anymore."

Eyeing him in disbelief, Barbara stood up and paced the length of the small room. "I thought you were different, Moses. The boy I fell in love with wouldn't break a promise, no matter how hard it got. The boy I fell in love with was faithful to a fault." She stopped moving and stared at him with anger flashing in her eyes. "What happened to that boy?"

"The girl I fell in love with asked me to give her some time. Six months, you said."

"I said a few months. I never thought you, of all people, would give up on me. I thought I could trust you."

Moses patted the bench. "Barbara, come sit down—"

She gazed at him intently and sank to the seat next to him. "You told me you'd wait. I finish school in four months."

Moses leaned away from her and folded his arms in resignation. "And after that, you're planning on coming home?"

She shrugged her shoulders. "I have to pay off my car."

Moses pinned her with a knowing look. "And after that?"

Barbara's frown deepened, and she massaged a spot directly above her eyebrow. "I might want to start my own business."

"How long were you planning on keeping me guessing? Four more months? Three more years?"

"I'll know better what I want when school is over. I really like it here, but maybe by December I'll decide I'd rather go home."

Moses stroked her cheek with his thumb. "Barbara. You're not coming back."

Slowly exhaling, Barbara turned her face away. She remained silent for a few moments and mulled things over. "You could move out here with me," she said softly.

"I won't do that, and you know it."

"But I still love you," she said weakly, as if knowing it didn't make any difference.

"You did once," Moses said, a slight smile curling his lips, "but now you love the world more. Your job, your car. Those fingernails."

A giggle mingled with a sigh burst from Barbara's lips.

Moses chuckled, and their eyes met. Studying her face, he could pinpoint the moment she resigned herself to the fact that she'd lost him.

He wanted to explain, maybe to justify himself for finally letting go. He had prized loyalty above all else. "I kept telling myself that you'd be back because I couldn't live with the alternative. But I've been living with persistent unhappiness. I can't live like that anymore, and it's unfair of you to ask me to wait, to waste the best years of my life on a false hope."

Barbara laced her fingers through his. "I never

meant for it to be hard on you. My folks wouldn't have anything to do with me, and knowing you would always be waiting gave me the courage to come out here. You were my backup plan in case things got too hard. I guess I was being pretty selfish."

"I'm not going to be your backup plan anymore, Barb. I have my own life to live, and I'm not going to spend it waiting."

Tears glistened in Barbara's eyes. "Is there somebody else?"

Moses's heart did a flip. "Jah."

"A good Amish girl?"

"The most wonderful Amish girl ever."

"I hope she deserves you."

"I hope I deserve her."

"Then I have to let you go." Barbara leaned over and pulled Moses into an embrace. This time he didn't pull back. "I love you, Moses."

"But not enough. And that's okay."

"Then it's time for me to truly find my wings."

"Time for both of us."

The stall door flew open and a young teenage girl with an armload of clothes squeaked and turned bright red when she saw them.

They quickly pulled apart and slid away from each other on the bench.

"Sorry," the girl said. "I didn't know anybody was in here."

She backed out of the stall and shut the door as softly as she could, as if Moses and Barbara would forget she had even been there. They could still see her feet under the door as they heard her yell, "Hey, there are two people making out in here!"

In surprise, Moses and Barbara locked gazes, and it took three full minutes before they stopped laughing.

Chapter Twenty

Six A.M., too early for a social call, but Moses couldn't wait one more minute to proclaim his love. He would have come over last night, but he hadn't returned until twelve from Minneapolis—too late for even Moses's impatient heart. Neither Lia nor his grandparents would have taken kindly to a midnight caller. He had arisen two hours earlier to clumsily do his early-morning chores and hitch up the buggy. Everything took twice as long on crutches, but he wanted to be bright and early to Huckleberry Hill.

The dim light of morning cast a golden glow over Mammi and Dawdi's tiny farm as the gravel crunched beneath the buggy wheels. Moses pulled back on the reins and set the brake. He decided to unhitch the horse. Even though it would take extra time doing it with crutches, he wanted to spend the whole day with Lia. Sammy would need to be stalled.

A slight breeze whispered through the trees overhead, and a black rooster, perched on a fence post, fluttered its wings and studied Moses indifferently. A chickadee whistled his two-note song into the air as Moses fed Sammy a handful of oats. After his experience yesterday, Moses briefly closed his eyes and savored the peace.

But there wasn't much time to spare. His eagerness to see Lia would not let him linger.

With any luck, Rachel would still be abed, and he and Lia could slip out of the house unnoticed. He could ask her to marry him in the privacy of the barn.

Moses knitted his brows together. The barn, with dust motes floating in the air like snowflakes and unsavory odors attacking the nostrils, wasn't a very romantic spot. They could ride horses to the east side of the hill and watch the sun make its morning trip across the sky, except that they would waste a lot of time saddling the horses when they could be kissing.

Moses shook his head a few times to bridle his galloping daydreams. One kiss would be plenty. Two at most. He thought of those soft, inviting lips. Would Lia think it improper if he kissed her three times? Three kisses. He would limit himself to three. He could control himself, even though his love for Lia threatened to explode from his chest. He wouldn't even have to bend in half to reach her lips.

The memory of their first kiss came unbidden to his mind. Even with his mouth on fire, he could tell her lips were silky soft.

Four kisses. No more.

But what if Lia didn't want to kiss him?

Pulling the scooter out of his buggy, he did his best to bury that thought so it would never resurface. If Lia didn't return his love, he might just dry up and blow away. The very possibility made him ill as he slowly unhitched his horse and hopped to the barn with the lead firmly in his fist.

Once he settled Sammy, Moses retrieved his scooter,

rolled to the front porch, hopped up the steps, and opened the door.

Mammi, Dawdi, and Rachel were at the table eating breakfast. Mammi sat with her back ramrod straight, sipping a cup of coffee. Rachel picked at her food as if she were trying to separate worms and crickets on the plate.

"Hello!" Moses shouted, leaning his bad leg on the scooter and throwing his arms out wide. The door banged against the wall behind it. His enthusiasm probably put a dent in the plaster.

Mammi and Rachel acted as if there were a contest to see who could stand up the fastest. They leaped to their feet and attacked Moses from either side.

Rachel smiled so wide, Moses had a good view of her twelve-year molars.

Mammi, on the other hand, clicked her tongue and looked like she was about to scold her seven-year-old grandson. "Where have you been, young man? We haven't seen hide nor hair of you for two days."

He took a step back so he wouldn't lose his balance with two women hovering over him. "I went out of town."

Mammi wagged her finger at him. "Out of town? You could at least tell your mammi these things." She shook her head and motioned at the table. "Cum, sit and have some breakfast. I made quiche. We have important things to discuss."

Moses glanced at the table. Some sort of soupy egg mixture floated in a pie tin. One of Mammi's new creations, no doubt.

Rachel batted her eyelashes and flashed a fake smile. "If you stay for supper, I'll make those rolls you like so much."

Moses's heart sank. Rachel's voice dripped with sugary sweetness. Maple-syrup-mixed-with-honey sweetness. Either she had decided to forgive him for not wanting to marry her, or she was redoubling her efforts. And she didn't seem the forgiving kind.

"Where's Lia?"

Rachel's smile grew wider and more fake. "She's gone."

"Where is she? I'll go fetch her."

After glancing at Dawdi, Rachel began lightly stroking Moses's arm. "Poor, sweet girl. Dat came by two days ago to take her home."

A puff of wind could have knocked Moses over. "Home? Why would . . ." His voice trailed off as the obvious reason caught up to him. Disbelief left him barely able to speak. "Rachel," he whispered, "what have you done?"

Rachel stroked Moses's arm double-time until he pulled away from her. "My dear dat wanted her home, and that dear, sweet girl wanted to go." Rachel caught Dawdi's eye and nodded.

A ghost of a smirk crossed Dawdi's lips before he looked away and took another bite of whatever that was on his plate.

"Of all the nonsense," Mammi said as she sat down at the table and picked up her coffee cup.

The anger boiled so hot inside Moses that he could almost feel the steam rise from his body. He had underestimated Rachel Shetler. She wasn't bright enough to recognize when a man didn't want her, but she knew when to call her daddy.

This blasted leg wouldn't let him go anywhere with ease, or he would have shot out that door and run to the barn where he could yell at Rachel without being heard by anybody.

It took all the strength he had not to lash out at her. *Whosoever is angry with his brother is in danger of hellfire.* Moses did not trust himself to reply just yet. He took a deep breath and looked up at the ceiling. Another deep breath.

"That is the most selfish thing I've seen anyone ever do," he finally said. "You should be ashamed of yourself."

Rachel's face turned various shades of pink before blooming bright red, but her voice still oozed that syrupy sweetness. "Moses, you must understand how concerned I am for Lia's feelings. She is such a dear girl, and if you pay her attention, you'll just get her hopes up. I won't let her be hurt like that. My dat and I both thought it would be for her own good to be at home. And don't you worry about the cooking. I consider it a privilege to take care of all of you." Rachel turned to his grandparents and spread her arms wide, as if inviting the whole world to join in her benevolence.

Heavenly Father, he prayed silently, *please calm my fiery anger and give me patience.*

Now.

Moses's heartbeat gradually slowed from a gallop to a trot. He gazed down at short, little Rachel and suddenly felt sorry for her. How could he not pity a girl who had no love in her heart for anyone but herself?

He looked to his grandparents to see how they bore this kerfuffle. Dawdi sat placidly, eating his runny eggs and pretending not to hear the conversation, a wisp of a smile playing at his lips.

Mammi spoke with an edge of scold in her voice, but her eyes twinkled as if she knew a secret. "Oh,

Rachel, you are such a tease. Besides, Moses, Wautoma is only an hour away by car."

Moses perked up considerably. Of course. The distance to Wautoma was nothing. He often got so caught up in his own little world that he forgot how close things were by car. He could go back to the cheese factory, call a driver, and be engaged to Lia by nine o'clock.

Lia's dat wouldn't like it, but at this point, it might be impossible to gain his approval. Moses could bring Lia back to Huckleberry Hill until they were married in the winter. It was a perfect plan.

His heart soared to the sky and a smile wider than a country mile bloomed on his face.

Not wanting to waste any time, he backed out the door instead of trying to turn his scooter around.

"Where are you going?" Rachel asked, a hint of desperation in her silky voice.

"To Wautoma to bring Lia back where she belongs."

Rachel narrowed her eyes and lost all pretense of sweetness. Balling her hands into fists and stomping her delicate little foot, she said, "I told you—"

"Do you want to come with me? You can pack your things, and I'll drop you off while I'm there."

Moses had to hold his breath to keep from laughing out loud at her expression. She held her mouth open like a trout out of water and blinked her eyes as if she were attempting to fan up a breeze.

He had accomplished something he'd never been able to do before. He'd rendered Rachel speechless.

Moses took her silence as a refusal. "Mammi and Dawdi, if I succeed in bringing Lia back, can she stay with you for a few more months?"

If Mammi's smile would have been hooked up to a

generator, she could have powered the lights in three counties. "What a gute boy you are. You've always been one of my favorite grandsons." She rose from the table again and reached for her secret hiding place. The blue porcelain canister said "sugar" on it, but Mammi used it to hide things from the grandchildren, like after-supper treats or Christmas surprises. Mammi lifted the lid and retrieved an envelope from inside. "Lia wrote you this note right before she left. I reckon you can read it on your way out of town."

Moses grinned at scowling Rachel and took the envelope even as he scooted backward out of the house. "Denki, Mammi."

"Keep your eye out for license plates," Dawdi called. "Wautoma gets more traffic."

By the time Moses hopped down the stairs, Rachel found her voice. "Go ahead," she yelled, "make a fool of yourself." She slammed the door so hard the front window rattled. It was a good thing Moses had installed that glass nice and tight.

With no intention of waiting one more minute to read his letter, Moses rolled to the buggy and leaned against it. The letter could mean the realization of all his hopes. Maybe Lia had wanted to tell him how she felt before her father carted her back to Wautoma.

If Moses was sure of Lia's affection, he could go to Wautoma with less trepidation.

Eagerly, he tore open the blank envelope and pulled out the card, written on the same stationery Lia had used for her note to him three days ago.

Moses,
 I wanted to write a quick note of thanks for all you have done for me while I've been on Huckleberry

Hill. Thank you for driving me all over the county and introducing me to Sarah and eating my meatballs. You have meant so much to me, and I will always remember my summer on Huckleberry Hill as the best time of my life.

Lia

P.S. We are friends, but I don't love you.

Moses stumbled over the last line as if the words had tripped him. He read it again. And again. Forgetting his surroundings, he crumpled the letter into his fist and stood by his buggy, paralyzed by the thoughts whipping about in his head like sand in a dust devil.

We are friends, but I don't love you.

This had to be a trick. Surely this was a trick by Rachel or her fater. Lia wouldn't say such a thing in a letter.

Moses opened his fist and studied the handwriting. It was Lia's, all right. No one else curled the tails of her *y*'s and *g*'s like Lia did.

Still, it could be a trick. Perhaps her dat forced her to write it, hoping Moses would turn his attention to Rachel.

With growing dread, Moses reread the note. As far as he knew, he and Lia were the only two who knew about the meatballs. There was no reason she would include that bit of information if her dat had insisted she write it.

He didn't want to believe she wrote it. It would mean he had no hope left.

He pressed his fist to his chest to keep his dreams from shattering into a million pieces.

Shutting his eyes, he thought of Barbara—so young

and pretty. He'd fallen in love with her enthusiasm. Her quitting the community was, to Moses, like dying by degrees. He sensed her withdrawal from him a little more every day, and he'd felt powerless to do anything but watch her go.

Her leaving had cut deep. Even three years ago, he probably knew without saying that she would not return, but he held on to the hope because he didn't want to deal with the crushing pain. He'd been such a coward—recoiling from what Barbara might do and afraid of being hurt—that he'd let her drag it out.

Everybody knew that it was easier to rip a bandage from the skin rather than prolong the pain by peeling it back slowly and deliberately.

He should have let Barbara go. He would have gotten over the pain and been ready to sweep Lia off her feet when she finally came into his life.

Too late he'd realized how much he loved Lia and how little he had shown it.

Moses glanced at the house. Rachel stood at the window, smiling and waving as if she hadn't just slammed the door in rage.

With a sinking heart and no idea what to do next, Moses shoved his scooter into his horseless buggy and grabbed his crutches. He shouldn't have unhitched the horse.

He would go home.

Moses halted in his tracks.

Go home and wallow in self-pity for three more years?

Suddenly he saw himself more clearly than he ever had before. He'd been using Barbara as a crutch. A crutch so he wouldn't actually have to face rejection and heartache and life. Moses looked at the crutches tucked under his arms. It was time to quit hiding behind his fears and be a man.

He couldn't lose Lia.

He refused to lose her.

For God has not given us the spirit of fear, but of power and of love and of a sound mind.

Moses had the power to seek for God's will and do it. The power to go to Lia and prove himself to her.

He could think and act for himself instead of accepting the role of a victim. He'd played that part with Barbara. Never again would he excuse himself for someone else's choices. He had his own choices to make.

His love for Lia almost overpowered his ability to think straight. He wouldn't throw that love away simply because of a little discouragement from her. With every ounce of his strength, he would fight for her. He'd fight harder than he'd ever fought for anything in his life.

With more resolve than he had ever been able to muster with Barbara, Moses made up his mind.

And if he couldn't make Lia love him, then he'd accept the pain as God's will.

But at least he had to try.

By wildly swinging his crutches in front of him, Moses rushed to the barn for the horse. Once the horse was out of the stall, Moses abandoned his crutches and on one foot, hitched Sammy into place. He had no time to waste maneuvering with his clunking crutches.

As he leaped into his buggy, Rachel emerged from the house with her lips forced into that weird smile. She must not have been mad at him anymore. That girl could change moods faster than a bat could change directions in flight.

"Have you decided against going to Wautoma?" Rachel said sweetly.

Moses didn't even look at her as he jiggled the reins and got Sammy going. "What I do is none of your business."

Undeterred, Rachel kept her smile in place as she waved and yoo-hooed and chased the buggy halfway down the hill.

Anna and Felty stood on the porch and watched Moses practically race down the hill in his newfangled buggy. They grinned as Rachel jogged next to the buggy waving to Moses until he went too fast for her to keep up.

"Persistence is that girl's best quality," Anna said.

Felty put his arm around Anna. "Well, Annie Banannie, you got what you wanted. Moses is miserable. Absolutely miserable."

Anna smiled smugly. "Of course he is. Nothing makes a man more miserable than thinking he's lost a girl he should have married months ago."

"And it's all your doing."

"Thank you for the compliment, but I can't take all the credit. You allowed Lia to come live with us."

"And now they're both miserable."

Anna patted Felty's hand. "They love each other. Moses will put things right eventually. But I hope it doesn't take him too long. I'd like to get rid of Rachel by maple syrup time."

Chuckling softly, Felty hugged Anna tightly and gave her a big kiss. "Maple syrup time."

They held each other and listened to the birds chatter in the trees as Rachel hiked back up the lane.

"Do you remember David Eicher's daughter Lily?" Anna said.

"A sweet little girl, for sure."

"Wouldn't she be just the thing for our grandson Aden?"

Felty groaned and squeezed Anna tighter. "Don't you start, Banannie. Don't you start."

Chapter Twenty-One

Perhaps the cumbersome cast was God's way of telling Moses to take his time, to take action only after careful thought. The cast and scooter were certainly teaching him patience. He wanted to be by Lia's side right now, immediately, flirting with her, gazing at her beautiful features, cajoling her into loving him.

Moses's heart skipped a beat. The thought that she might never love him sent his heart plummetting to his toes. Moses shook his head. He wouldn't bend his imagination in that direction. It only made him feel worse.

That's why he'd brought his backpack. He might have to be in Wautoma for several months, because he wouldn't leave without a fight. He'd do whatever it took to win Lia's love.

Roy Polter carried Moses's backpack to the Shetlers' front porch while Moses hopped up the steps with his scooter.

"I'll go make some deliveries and be back here in two hours," Roy said.

"I don't know if I'll be going home tonight."

"Will you be spending the night here?"

Moses surveyed his surroundings. Not another house in sight besides the Shetlers' place. "If I'm not welcome here, I might find a nice field to camp in."

Roy grimaced. "Let's hope you don't get rained on."

"Rain's the least of my worries."

With the way Moses's life seemed to be going, Lia's dat would probably answer the door and refuse to let him see Lia. Then Moses would spend the next three months living under some bridge subsisting on berries and roots, waiting for a chance to catch a glimpse of the woman he loved.

He pictured himself sneaking around Lia's house in the middle of the night and rapping on the windows until he found the one with Lia behind it. Moses smiled to himself. He remembered stealing around Mammi and Dawdi's house and knocking on the bathroom window in hopes that Rachel wouldn't see him. He wasn't sure why he had picked the bathroom window that day, except that Rachel didn't clean bathrooms, and Lia was more likely to be the one who discovered him.

Moses squared his shoulders and knocked on the door. No fear. Love gave him power to face whatever might come.

To Moses's relief, not Lia's dat, but a middle-aged woman, a remarkable copy of Rachel, answered the door. Sparse strands of gray mingled with her golden hair, and she stood even a little shorter than her youngest daughter. She wore a pale blue calf-length dress without a bertha. Her eyes, punctuated with shallow wrinkles, were Rachel's, except that their lake blue depth revealed kindness instead of disdain.

She looked up and smiled at him as if he were an old friend instead of a stranger.

Moses stuck out his hand. "Hullo. I am—"

"Jah, you are Moses Zimmerman. I would know you anywhere. You are as tall and handsome as they say. Please come in. You are very welcome in our home."

She held the door open for him and Moses rolled into the front room, feeling more than a little anxious.

"My name is Eliza. I am Rachel's mamm." She motioned for him to sit, but he was too agitated to relax.

"Nae, denki. I can stand."

"I heard how you broke your leg. Rachel wrote that she almost fainted."

"So did I." Despite his distress, Moses tried to appear easy and carefree, even if at any minute they kicked him out of the house.

"I suppose you are wanting to talk to my husband."
No, anything but that.

Eliza's eyes danced, and she seemed to burst with excitement. "Rachel wrote weeks ago to expect you."

Moses squirmed. Spending a week on Barbara's roller coaster would be more pleasant than this. Eliza thought he came here to ask her husband's permission to marry Rachel. All three were about to be very disappointed.

He'd be tossed out by supper for sure.

"I came to see Lia. Is she home?" The inviting aroma of homemade bread wafted from the kitchen. Jah, Lia must be here.

Eliza's countenance fell and a look of puzzlement flitted across her face. "Are you sure? I can go fetch Owen."

"Nae, I'd like to talk to Lia."

"Lia is out to the barn." Still unsure, Eliza pointed to the back of the house. "You can go through the mudroom."

"Denki," Moses said, rolling his scooter awkwardly down the hall.

Eliza called after him. "Owen will be home from work in a few hours, but I will fetch him early for you."

"No need," Moses said.

"And you must stay for supper."

Moses didn't reply. If Lia rejected him, no one would want him to stay for supper, including himself.

Lia accidentally clanked the bucket of oats against a pole in the barn and spilled half its contents onto the cement floor. "Blast!" She seemed to be growing clumsier with every passing hour. Why couldn't she snap out of her gloom?

She'd been home less than three days, and she moped around as if her life were the most tedious in the world. Why had she ever left Wautoma? Before she met Moses, she had been perfectly content to live her perfectly dull life.

Things in Wautoma carried on as if she had never gone away. Mamm gladly turned the meal preparation over to Lia, and all her regular chores waited for her. The only change was Rachel's absence, so there was no talk of gatherings or singeons or potential husbands. Her mamm had spent all her enthusiasm on Rachel and never had an inkling that Lia might be interested in such things.

And Lia wasn't interested. She loved Moses. Why spend time with any other boy?

Lia sighed as she brushed the fallen oats into a pile with her foot. Who else would think of her height as an advantage? Who else would buy her a book because he knew how pleased she would be? She remembered the pained but good-humored look on Moses's face as he popped the first, then the second, and then the fifth of Lia's scorching-hot meatballs into his mouth. She thought of his bright red scarf and the time they stood under the trees and he compared their heights. It had been then that Lia knew he was something special. A man to admire. A man she couldn't help but love.

Moses, so unselfish and eager to make everyone happy, had struggled to be plain about his feelings for Rachel. He must have sensed that Lia was fond of him and didn't want to hurt her feelings. Rachel had said as much.

I am grateful that I have arms to help Dat with the chores. I am grateful that I can be such a blessing to my parents when all their other children have left them. I am grateful that Rachel has found a gute husband so the boys will no longer get their hearts broken by my insensitive sister.

Dear Lord, I shouldn't have used the word "insensitive." Rachel cannot help that she is pretty any more than I can help that I am tall. Moses can't help that he loves Rachel instead of me. And I cannot help that I love Moses more than I could ever love anybody else.

Lia snatched the broom from the hook and swept the oats in earnest. She must convince Fater to let her study midwifing again. These menial tasks left her mind free to wander where she did not want it to go.

"What a gute sweeper you are!"

Lia heard that voice in her dreams every night. Try as she might, she couldn't prevent her heart from leaping into her throat and her hands from shaking at the sight of him.

Moses smiled tentatively. She adored that smile as she adored Moses. Hopelessly, without reason, and forever.

Her lips curled automatically just being near him, and she swept with such vigor that the oats in her pile went flying in every direction. "I thought you didn't like my sweeping."

Gripping the handles of his scooter, Moses studied her face. "I have always loved the way you sweep. I wish you would come sweep at my house. It's very dusty."

He rolled farther into the barn on that clunky scooter with one wheel that squeaked. She couldn't place the expression on his face. Fear? Uncertainty? Sheer panic?

Lia peered out the open barn door. "Is Rachel with you?"

Moses pressed his lips into a hard line. Had she said something to upset him? "Nae. I came to see you. You left while I was in Minneapolis. I didn't get to say good-bye."

Lia's heart fluttered like a butterfly. "You came all this way to say good-bye?"

"I'd rather not say good-bye. I want you to come back to Huckleberry Hill."

Sorrow pressed its heavy hand on her chest. "You don't mean that, Moses. You know it is better if I am away."

A shadow passed across Moses's face. "Mammi gave me your letter."

"I'm sorry if it made you uncomfortable." Lia stood up straight and gave Moses a relatively convincing smile. "But you need not worry. I am happy here, and I wish you all the best."

"What are you talking about?"

"Rachel says I am making a fool of myself. I'm determined not to be a bother to you ever again."

Moses scowled and scooted closer. She wished he wouldn't. He smelled like newly oiled leather. Manly and irresistible. "You have never, ever, been a bother to me."

"Why should you have to humor the troublesome older sister when it's plain as day that you love Rachel?"

His scowl deepened until it looked to be permanently etched into his face. "Is it?"

Lia lowered her eyes and stared faithfully at her pile of oats. "I'd just be in the way."

"Lia, look at me," Moses said with a determined edge to his voice. "What makes you think I love Rachel?"

Lia met his gaze. That dimple on his left cheek momentarily distracted her. "You said something to my dat . . ." Best not bring that up. She shouldn't have been eavesdropping. "You had your arms around each other after the picnic."

"Her idea, not mine. She's clever. Didn't wear shoes to a picnic in the woods. She is your sister, and I knew I should help her. But if I had my way, I'd have left her to fend for herself."

Lia refused to believe it. Once again, he was trying to make her feel better. "She said you tossed my pie on the floor because you were tired of the way I threw myself at you all the time."

Moses lifted his hat, shoved his fingers through his hair, and growled. Actually growled. "You've lived with Rachel all her life and yet still believe the things that come out of her mouth? Lia, you're smarter than that."

A light went on in Lia's head. "You . . . you didn't throw my pie on the floor?"

"At this point, I think I would give my right arm for one of your pies. I am dying to taste one of your pies. Everybody in Bonduel has tasted one of your pies but me. Rachel saw how excited I was about it. She turned red as a beet and dumped it on the floor."

Lia fell silent and tried to make sense of the world. "Do you love Rachel?"

Moses growled again. This time he sounded more exasperated than angry. "I've always tried to be plain with you, Lia. I told you before. I don't even like your sister. You're accustomed to everybody fawning over her and ignoring you, so I suppose I can understand how you came to believe that I liked her. But to be honest, I'm annoyed with you for jumping to that conclusion."

"You are always annoyed," Lia said cautiously, but church bells chimed inside her head and her feet wanted to do a happy dance right here in the barn. Moses didn't love Rachel.

"Annoyed and insulted," he continued. "Insulted to know that you don't think very highly of my intelligence." He shook his head. "For you to believe that I would pick a girl like Rachel . . ."

Lia put her hand to her mouth to stifle a giggle. "Her face turned red as a beet?"

Moses's somber mood seemed to melt in the blink of an eye. He studied her as his eyes began to twinkle. "I've never seen the veins in her neck pop out like that before. Then she stomped on the pie for good measure and left a trail of berry juice all the way down the hall. Mammi made her clean it up."

Lia truly pitied her sister. "Oh, poor girl. That wood soap chafes her hands."

"She wore gloves."

They laughed in unison. Moses got so carried away that he snorted and made Lia jump. That prompted the laughter to continue for another minute. Finally Lia cleared her throat. "We shouldn't. It is uncharitable to make light of Rachel's misfortunes."

"Her misfortunes are of her own making." Moses changed moods faster than the horse could swish her tail. "Can we sit?"

Lia looked around and retrieved the two milking stools. She tried to support Moses's arm as he sat as carefully as he could. It was a long way down for him, and his knees bent awkwardly as he braced his foot and cast on the floor. A look of annoyance camped on his face. What else?

Lia sat facing Moses and wrapped her arms around her knees. Dread pulsed in every nerve. That look of annoyance often accompanied a declaration that he was not looking to marry. She braced herself for yet another rejection.

But why should it hurt? She had already accepted the fact that Moses was not interested.

He pulled an envelope from his pocket. "I want to talk about this letter you asked Mammi to give me."

Lia couldn't breathe. Jah, a rejection was coming. She remembered every word of that letter she'd written three days ago.

You have meant so much to me. I will always remember my summer on Huckleberry Hill as the best time of my life.

She had been too plain with her feelings in her good-bye note, and he wanted to deflate her hopes gently.

He fingered the folds of the envelope as he studied her face. "Lia, you have always been honest with me. Did you truly mean what you wrote?"

She didn't want to make him uncomfortable, but he was right. She had always been honest with him. "Jah," she said breathlessly, "I meant every word."

Moses looked so unhappy, Lia wanted to weep for him. He slumped his shoulders and buried his face in his hands. "Is there nothing I can do?"

"What do you mean?"

He sat like that, perfectly still and silent, while Lia held her breath. He slowly reached over and took her scarred hand in both of his. "Lia, can you find it in your heart to give me a chance?"

A flicker of hope shimmered in the back of Lia's mind like the first star on a clear summer night. She looked down at his hands—strong, calloused hands, big and able. The warmth of his touch spread through her entire body. "I don't understand."

He handed her the letter and gestured for her to take it from the envelope. "Did you say those things to let me down easy or because you thought I loved Rachel?"

His piercing gaze left Lia unable to catch her breath. Growing more flustered, she pulled the card from the envelope if only to have something to do with her embarrassment. Her gaze traveled to the bottom of the note.

P.S. We are friends, but I don't love you.

Her heart jumped to her throat.

"I think I could bear it if you haven't completely decided against me," Moses said, "if you can see fit to give me even a speck of encouragement. I'll do anything to win your love."

The words flew from her mouth like a bird escaping from a cage. "I didn't write this."

Moses raised his eyebrows and riveted his attention to her. "What?"

She couldn't talk fast enough. "I wrote this note, but I didn't write this last part—about not loving you. It's in my handwriting, but I didn't write it."

Moses's whole face seemed to come alive. "You didn't?"

"I would never write that," she said, her voice trailing off as she looked at him. The pure joy in his expression left her speechless.

"Rachel must know of Mammi's secret hiding place," he said, as if it were the best news in the world.

Lia nodded, bewildered and overcome with emotion.

He put a hand on her knee and locked his brilliant blue eyes with hers. "Do you love me, Lia?"

There was nothing to do but be blunt. "Jah, more than I can ever say."

In one swift movement, Moses stood on his good leg, braced his cast on the milking stool, and pulled Lia with him. He wasted no time in wrapping his arms around her and tugging her close to him. She thought she had died and gone to heaven as every nerve in her body seemed to come alive and tingle with happiness. "Don't let go," she whispered, sliding her arms around his neck. "If you let go, I might wake up from this blessed dream."

He nestled his mouth close to her ear. "Did I ever tell you how much I love tall girls?"

She giggled softly. "Do you?"

"Oh, Lia, I love you so much I think I will float away."

He stared at her lips until she tilted her face closer to his. He took the hint and kissed her hungrily. She kissed him back with all the emotion she'd bottled up for so many weeks.

"Oh, Moses, I've loved you from the day I laid eyes on you."

"Then marry me?" he said, his lips barely half an inch from hers.

"Have you changed your mind about not wanting to marry?"

He pulled away slightly. "Have you changed your mind about refusing to have me?"

"Yes," they said together.

Moses transferred his bad leg to the scooter so he could get a better hold of Lia. Squeezing the stuffing out of her, he kissed her again and again. If they kissed a million times a day, she still wouldn't grow tired of it.

Lia knocked Moses's hat off his head and intertwined her fingers through his thick hair. She was on fire.

A groan came from deep within his throat, and he relaxed his hold on her. "I promised myself I would only kiss you three times, but I find it impossible to resist you."

Lia grinned at him. "I am not inclined to think that is a bad thing."

"Only because you don't know how fast my thoughts are galloping," he said, releasing her completely and nudging her away from him.

Lia thought it was completely unnecessary. She reluctantly took a step back, surprised at how out of breath she was.

Moses picked up his hat and grimaced. "I wasn't going to ask you to marry me in a barn. I got carried away."

"The barn is a very romantic spot. I never knew this much happiness existed in the whole world, let alone in my barn."

"Me either." As if it pained him to separate from her, Moses slid his scooter backward. But after only a few seconds, he rolled next to her and laced his fingers with hers. Lia felt quivery all over.

"Truthfully, I can't bear to be more than a few inches away from you," he said.

Lia giggled like a schoolgirl as delight and joy overflowed from her heart.

Moses stroked the back of her hand with his thumb, and the corners of his mouth quirked upward. "Is there any hope that your fater will give his permission?"

Lia slumped her shoulders as her excitement collapsed. "He will be furious for Rachel's sake. What are we going to do?"

A sympathetic smile sprouted on Moses's face. "Would you consider coming back to Bonduel without his permission? Mammi and Dawdi will take you in until the wedding."

Lia let out a breath and shook her head. "I don't see any other way."

Moses took her by the shoulders and knit his brows together. "Is that what you want? Because I'll do anything you say. If you want to stay here, I'll camp out in the field and work your farm until I win your dat's approval. It might kill me, but I'm willing to wait."

Lia slid her arms around him, leaving him no choice but to enfold her in an encompassing embrace. "You already have my dat's approval. It's me who is lacking."

He nudged her closer and gently kissed her forehead. "I hate to hear you talk like that. I promise I will always take care of you and that you will never be starved for affection again."

She closed her eyes as he tightened his arm around her waist and took his other hand and slowly traced his warm fingers down her neck and then followed the trail his fingers made with his lips. A sigh escaped Lia's mouth before she felt him withdraw. When she opened her eyes, he had scooted a good three feet away.

Holding up his arms as if to stop her from advancing, he said, "I'm in control now. Complete control." He smiled sheepishly. "But don't touch me."

Lia obediently clasped her hands behind her back.

He regarded her doubtfully. "What do you want, Lia? Shall I set up a tent in the field across the road?"

Lia longed to melt into his arms. Instead, she took a step forward. "I want to go back to Huckleberry Hill."

Lia couldn't help but beam with delight as Moses threw his hat into the air and whooped and hollered as if he were cheering at a horse race. They both erupted into a fit of laughter when his hat got stuck in the rafters.

Unfortunately, the laughing could not drown out the sound of Rachel's shouts. "I told you, Dat. I told you!"

Lia looked around so fast, she almost wrenched her neck. Rachel marched into the barn with Dat close behind, his expression as dark as a looming storm.

With her anxiety rising, Lia glanced at Moses. He smiled reassuringly and held out his hand to her. She seized it like a lifeline and let him pull her close. She fit nicely, tucked under his arm and close to his heart. "I'll always take care of you," he whispered.

Rachel jabbed her finger in Lia's direction. "You see how she throws herself at him, Dat? It's disgusting."

Dat, angry and stern, put a protective hand on Rachel's shoulder. "Lia, you should be ashamed of yourself, deceiving your sister like this. Get away from him."

Lia, who had never been anything but obedient to her fater, would have pulled away from Moses, but he held her firmly at his side and said, "She's not going anywhere." He looked at Lia with a twinkle in his eye as if he didn't understand the seriousness of the situation. Lia's heart swelled as wide as the sky. No one had ever stood up for her before.

Rachel scowled. "Didn't you read the letter Lia left you? She doesn't love you, Moses."

"How do you know what was in that letter?" Moses said, gazing at Rachel like a cat playing with a mouse. "Did you read it?"

Rachel didn't move one muscle in her face except for her eyebrows, which shifted a fraction of an inch higher. "Of course not."

"In truth, you added your own special note," Moses said.

Rachel scrunched her lips into a very unattractive shape. "I never did."

Moses exhaled loudly. "I forgive you, Rachel, because today I am the happiest man alive. But I want you to think about what you have done. You tried to separate us. I could have spent the next fifty years mourning a girl I'd never lost."

"You would have forgotten her soon enough," Rachel protested. "Once you got to know me better."

Moses shook his head in astonishment and pity, and then he winked playfully at Lia. She pressed herself closer to him. "Lia is your own sister, yet you care nothing for her happiness. I'm sorry to say this, but you make me sick. I can't hardly bear to look at you."

Rachel stood like a statue, silently blinking back tears and staring vacantly at Moses.

"Now, now," Dat said, taken aback by Moses's speech. "Rachel is a gute girl. There's no need to be so harsh."

Moses looked down at Lia and twitched his lips. "I probably shouldn't have said that about being sick."

Lia wanted to smile back at him. Instead, she kept her eyes to the ground. Playfulness would only compound Dat's anger.

Dat folded his arms across his chest. "What are your intentions, Moses Zimmerman?"

Moses wrapped both arms around Lia and kissed her on the lips, right in front of her dat. "I intend to marry your daughter."

Dat opened his mouth but Moses interrupted him before he could speak. "The tall one."

The tender way he said it brought tears of gratitude to Lia's eyes. Was there any girl ever as blessed as she?

Rachel snapped out of her momentary remorse. She stamped her foot and squealed loudly enough for every dog in Wautoma to hear her. When she was younger, such a fit of temper would have triggered her violent coughing. Mamm and Lia would have scrambled like decapitated chickens to make Rachel stop crying. Today, everyone stared at her while she dissolved into tears. "Felty said you wanted somebody sweet. Didn't you see how sweet I acted this morning?"

Dat narrowed his eyes. "I don't understand why you would pick Lia over Rachel unless Lia has deceived you."

Rachel was beyond hysterical. "She's done everything she can to steal him."

"What do you have to say for yourself, Lia?" Dat said.

Moses nudged Lia slightly behind him and stretched to his full height. "I won't have you blaming Lia for anything."

Glancing at Rachel, Lia was tempted to feel quite satisfied. Dat always stood up for Rachel. Now Lia had someone to stand up for her.

But was that what she wanted?

She really looked at her sister, who still fussed and fumed. Why had Lia never defended herself against Rachel or Dat? Rachel had grown progressively more selfish every year. Dat had let Rachel get away with bad behavior, but by being so long-suffering, Lia had indulged Rachel too. At first, she had felt responsible for Rachel's getting sick and made excuses for Rachel because she felt sorry about what had happened. Rachel's mistreatment of Lia became a habit, and Lia wore Rachel's abuse like a badge of honor. In some way, she had even come to believe that she deserved her parents' indifference.

The truth struck Lia so forcefully, she almost cried out at the sting of it. All these years, she had been confusing weakness with meekness. If she wanted to be a midwife, she had better be strong enough to deal with life-and-death situations. Shouldn't she be strong enough to stand up for herself? Strong enough to stand up to her unbending fater and spoiled sister?

She swallowed the lump in her throat and nudged Moses's arm. "Wait, Moses. I have something to say."

"You got nothing to say," Rachel said bitterly.

Lia didn't respond to her sister and kept her eyes on Dat. "I didn't want Rachel to come to Huckleberry Hill and neither did the Helmuths."

"What a liar you are. They love me."

"Rachel, be quiet," Lia yelled, actually yelled. Had she ever raised her voice in her life?

In shock, Rachel snapped her mouth shut.

Lia glared a threat at Rachel and turned back to Dat. "When you sent Rachel to Huckleberry Hill, I tried to be obedient to your wishes. Moses and I took Rachel everywhere, even though Sarah was set against her. She was a terrible hindrance when a baby was coming."

"There is no use for you to train with a midwife," Dat said.

"Dat, listen to me," Lia said. She laced her tone with authority. Dat fell silent out of sheer surprise.

Moses gazed at her with admiration. His confidence gave her resolve.

"I made all the food for Rachel's picnic," Lia said. "I stayed away from Moses's room when he recovered from his broken leg so Rachel could have all the time with him she wanted. I have done nothing wrong. But no matter how I tried, Rachel treated me with ingratitude."

Dat frowned. "Rachel is a gute girl."

"You can tell yourself that if it makes you feel better, but in truth, Rachel is a selfish, lazy baby."

"How dare you?" Rachel snapped. She took a step forward and without warning, slapped Lia hard on the face.

Dat called out in astonishment. Moses gasped and stepped quickly forward even as Lia motioned for him to stay back.

Lia pressed her hand to her stinging cheek and blinked back the threatening tears. She would never give Rachel power over her again.

"Rachel," Dat growled, "you shame yourself."

Rachel practically snarled. "You should give her the switch for saying such horrible lies about me. You're on my side, aren't you, Dat?"

With her cheek still smarting, Lia moved close enough to Rachel to tower over her. She pointed to the milking stool. "Sit down, and don't say another word."

Rachel lifted her chin and looked to Dat for support.

"Go, sit," Dat said.

Rachel shot daggers at Lia with her eyes, but she got no sympathy from Dat, which must have surprised her. Her bottom lip quivered as she flounced to the milking stool and plopped herself into place.

"I know you have grand plans for Rachel's husband," Lia said. "She is, after all, so very pretty. But I deserve to be happy too." She took Moses's hand. His eyes brimmed with emotion as he squeezed her fingers in his.

Dad stroked his beard. "Rachel had her heart set on Moses. I did not know that you and Moses had feelings for each other, and I believed Rachel would be a more suitable wife."

"Of course you did, Dat. Rachel is your favorite child. You want the best for her."

Dat grunted in protest. "I do not have a favorite child, but Rachel has so much to offer a man."

Lia ignored the sting of her fater's indifference. She would never be able to talk him into loving her.

Moses knit his brows together and spoke sharply. "You are Lia's fater and know so little about her. Certainly she is an excellent cook, but there is so much more." His expression softened when he looked at her. "Not only is Lia beautiful, but she is tall and graceful and brave. Sarah often brags about Lia's skill as a midwife, and I've seen it for myself. These are only a fraction of her gute qualities. Even though you think little of her, she is my greatest treasure, and I love her."

Lia turned her face to Moses. His expression was a mix of love and concern as he caressed her bruised cheek with his warm fingers.

Lia pulled her gaze from Moses. "Dat, we ask your permission to marry."

Dat looked to Rachel, who sat slumped on the stool

sniffling pathetically. "And what of your sister? Don't you care that she suffers?"

"I would be so pleased to have your permission, Dat, and your blessing, but I will marry Moses whether you give it or not."

Rachel let out an exaggerated whimper.

Dat balled his hands into fists. "If you marry without my permission, I will not allow you in our home ever again."

"At least you will still have the daughter you really care about."

Outrage flashed in Dat's eyes, and he paced the barn floor while holding on to his beard like a handle. His steps gradually slackened, and he stopped to study Lia's face. "I love you as much as I love Rachel, but maybe I haven't shown it as I should." Regret traveled across his face. "I fretted over Rachel, but I never had to worry about you." Dat sat on the stool next to Rachel and put his arm around her. "Rachel, I can see that you and Moses are not well suited, no matter how hard you try."

"Nae, we're not," Moses said, lifting Lia's hand to his lips and gifting her with a feather-soft kiss.

Rachel, her face red and shiny with tears, stood and glared at both of them. "You're tall as a giraffe. Why would I ever want a man whose legs are like telephone poles and whose face is like, is like, a pig?" She spat out the word before turning on her heels and stomping to the house, whimpering and squeaking all the way.

Dat slowly rose to his feet. "Don't judge her harshly. She is a gute girl." He ambled to the door of the barn before turning to look at them. "You have my permission to marry," he said and followed Rachel into the house.

With his hands around her waist and his cast firmly

planted on the scooter, Moses picked up Lia and lifted her high in the air. She squealed in delight.

He set her on her feet and kissed her with so much passion, she didn't know which way was up.

"When do we leave for Huckleberry Hill?" Lia asked, lacing her fingers around his neck.

"My driver will be back in an hour."

"Can you join us for supper?"

"Do you think I can push my luck?"

Lia smiled mischievously. "As long as you compliment Rachel on all her cooking, she'll be fine."

"She got here after I did. She didn't cook a thing."

"Things will go more smoothly for all of us if you just pretend she did."

Moses chuckled and kissed Lia again. "We should have been doing a lot more of this all summer. I can't get enough of you, Lia."

"I have a wonderful-gute surprise for you too. I brought some huckleberries from Anna and Felty's and made a huckleberry pie for dessert tonight."

Moses pulled her close and kissed her again. "And I thought this day couldn't get any better."

The back door swung open so hard that it banged against the side of the house. Rachel appeared with an armload of dresses and aprons, Lia's dresses and aprons, and hurled them one by one into the flower beds, screaming and hissing with each swing of her arm. Rachel quickly dispatched of Lia's entire wardrobe, stepped back into the house, and slammed the door.

Lia and Moses looked at each other in surprise and burst into laughter.

"Maybe you won't have to pack after all," Moses said.

The door opened again, and Rachel came out of the house carrying Lia's freshly made huckleberry pie.

"No!" Moses cried.

But the words barely had time to escape his lips before Rachel turned the pie tin upside down and dumped the pie onto the sidewalk. With a smug glance in Lia's direction, Rachel tossed the tin like a Frisbee, and it clattered onto the roof of the chicken coop. Rachel had a very good arm.

The corners of his lips drooped, and Moses looked as if he were going to cry.

Lia leaned in and kissed the frown right off his mouth. "There are lots of huckleberries still left on the hill."

"And we'll have many summers together to enjoy them."

She nodded and kissed him again. "Take me home, Moses. I want to go home."

Chapter Twenty-Two

Moses jiggled the reins and prodded Sammy into an easy trot up Huckleberry Hill. He had never been so eager to get to the top. Riding horseback would have been faster, but he still couldn't manage it with his bulky cast.

He hadn't seen Lia in four days, not since Saturday when Roy had driven them back to Bonduel after Moses proposed. A busted water pipe at the cheese factory had monopolized Moses's time since he'd been back, and nothing short of a flood could have kept him from Lia's side for so long. He felt as if he would starve if he couldn't see her today. The distance from his house to Huckleberry Hill made him long for November when they would never have to be apart again.

The buggy came around the bend, and he saw her. She waved, and her smile set the trees ablaze and chased the clouds from the sky. Moses had never beheld a more beautiful sight.

She jogged to the buggy and slid the door open. Moses grinned, braced his hands against the sides of the opening, and hopped out. Not waiting for her approval, he swept her into his arms and planted a swift and decisive kiss on her lips. It must have been to her liking, because she kissed him back.

"Moses Zimmerman," she scolded, as she pulled back, "your grandparents are just inside. They would be shocked."

He showed her what he thought of her indignation by kissing her again. The feel of her soft, full lips made his heart pound ferociously. "You're right. We wouldn't want to give my dawdi a stroke," he said breathlessly. But that wasn't the reason he swiftly released her. He could get addicted to those kisses.

Lia straightened her crooked kapp. "So, you got my invitation for supper tonight."

"I'm sorry I couldn't come sooner. We mopped up the rest of the water this afternoon."

"I pined for you," Lia said. "But it was bearable. I pined for you for weeks, but this time I knew you'd come for me."

Moses decided he deserved another kiss for being smart enough to fall in love with Lia. He pulled her close and kissed her one more time. He shouldn't get carried away.

Lia reached into the buggy and pulled out Moses's scooter. "Cum. I will unhitch the buggy."

"I can do it."

Lia wrapped a fist around Sammy's bridle. "Only if you want your supper to get cold. Anna made a surprise, and she won't tell me what it is."

"We wouldn't want Mammi's supper to get cold."

Moses watched as Lia unhitched Sammy and led her to the barn, something that would have taken Moses three times as long on his crutches. While Lia stabled Sammy, Moses reached into his buggy and pulled out a stack of letters. Lia came from the barn, and he handed them to her. "I fetched the mail on my way up the hill. There's one from Wautoma."

Lia shuffled through the mail and pulled a tan envelope from the pile. "It's from my dat." She handed Moses the rest of the stack and tore open her letter. Her smile stretched even wider as she read. "Listen to this. 'I know we've had our disagreements, but we want you to be married here at our home. What about November 17? Seeing as how Rachel is likely not getting married this winter, Mamm has plenty of celery for you. Rachel made a cake this morning. It turned out quite well, and she says she knows what she did wrong and will never mistake salt for sugar again. Maybe she can help wash celery for the wedding.'"

Lia's eyes sparkled with emotion.

"Would you like to be married in Wautoma?" Moses asked.

"Jah, more than anything."

Moses rolled to the house while Lia ambled beside him. "Then we will marry in Wautoma. But I think we should steer clear of Rachel's desserts."

"Agreed."

Lia's lips twitched upward as she opened the door. "I hope you like what I made for dessert."

Moses gasped. Five whole pies sat on the kitchen table, while several tempting aromas wafted into the air. "Oh my."

Mammi and Dawdi stood at the cookstove while Mammi stirred something in a steaming saucepan. She turned and squealed with delight. "Moses, just look at the pies!"

"I wanted to make sure I made at least one of your favorites," Lia said. She pointed to each in turn. "I made butterscotch, apple, raisin, rhubarb, and of course, huckleberry."

"I think I've died and gone to pie heaven."

"And I promised Lia that we could have dessert first, no matter what," Mammi said.

"I didn't want anything to interfere with you getting your pie." Lia pulled out a chair for Moses at the table and handed him a fork and a small plate. "What would you like?"

Moses shook his head and deposited the fork and plate on the table. Then he rolled behind the counter, kissed his mammi on the cheek, and pulled a large dinner plate from the cupboard. "Do you think I could have one of each?"

Lia giggled and nodded. Moses sat at the table letting his mouth water while Lia cut a slice from each pie and slid them onto his plate. Moses sank his fork into the rare huckleberry pie and took a bite. He sighed when the sweet, tangy combination touched his tongue. He had never tasted anything so delicious, and the sweetness of the moment made it the best meal he had ever eaten.

Lia studied his face. "Did I add the right amount of sugar?"

Moses took her hand and pulled her to sit next to him. She looked so worried that he brushed his lips lightly across hers, and in plain sight of Mammi and Dawdi.

Her cheeks turned a delicate shade of pink.

"I've never tasted anything so delicious, Lia. It makes me want to weep for all your other pies I never ate."

Lia glowed from the inside, and her brown eyes became deep pools of chocolate. Moses resisted the urge to kiss her again. There was no limit to his love for her, but there was a limit to Mammi and Dawdi's patience.

Moses motioned for his grandparents to come to the table. "Mammi and Dawdi, bring a plate and come share my pie."

Mammi brought a plate for Lia too, and they each ate at least one slice from all five pies.

"I've always liked rhubarb pie," Mammi said. "My dat used to boil rhubarb in sugar water and eat it like a bowl of soup."

"I love them all," Moses said, taking Lia's hand and caressing her soft skin with his thumb. "But huckleberry pie reminds me of the wonderful girl I met on Huckleberry Hill and the love that fills my life because of her. Huckleberry pie will always be my favorite."

Lia's eyes glistened with tears. "Mine too."

Moses smiled. He would never grow tired of gazing at her.

Mammi scooted her chair from under the table. "I hope this won't spoil our dinner. I've made something special in celebration of your engagement."

Moses winked at Lia. "I always have room for something special."

"Gute," said Mammi, standing up and bustling to the cookstove, "because you are in for a treat."

After donning oven mitts, she took the saucepan from the stove and brought it to the table. Dawdi lifted the lid to reveal a soupy mixture of vegetables and meat that didn't smell particularly appetizing but looked hearty.

"What is it, Mammi?"

"Beef tongue stew."

Moses didn't alter his expression as he leaned close to Lia's ear and whispered, "Run!"

Please turn the page for an exciting sneak peek of
Jennifer Beckstrand's
next Matchmakers of Huckleberry Hill romance,
HUCKLEBERRY SUMMER,
coming in June 2014!

Felty Helmuth took a hearty bite of the mushy concoction in his bowl. "Why, Annie Banannie. This soup is fit for a king. Is this another recipe from that new book of yours?"

Anna smiled and pushed her thick, round glasses over the bridge of her nose. "How kind of you to notice, dear. It's called Indonesian beef stew."

"It's so tender, I can't tell the beef from the potatoes."

"There is no beef. It's a vegetarian dish."

Felty winked at his wife of sixty-two years. "The name ain't quite right, don't you think?"

"Well, the recipe calls for beef, but I didn't add any beef, and I don't think it's my place to change the name of the recipe."

"Right you are, Annie. Was they out of roast at the market yesterday?"

"No, I am learning to cook vegetarian. Aden is a vegetarian, and I don't want him to starve."

"Aden our grandson?"

Anna nodded and looked at Felty as if he were finally in on the secret.

"Banannie, Aden lives in Ohio. He don't eat your cooking more than once a year or so, but I'm sure he'd be pleased to know you are thinking of him."

"Now, Felty," Anna said. "I want Aden to come and live with us, and he's got to eat."

"Us? Why would Aden want to live with us?"

"He's going through a rough patch."

Felty reached over and patted Anna's wrinkled hand. "Don't worry yourself. All boys his age go through a rough patch."

"*Jah*, but most boys don't get arrested three times."

"He can get arrested just as easy in Wisconsin as Ohio."

Anna pursed her lips and scolded Felty with her eyes. "Boys like Aden need a wife to settle them down. A girl like little Lily Eicher."

Felty sputtered and coughed, and Anna stood up and thumped him on the back until he motioned for her to stop. "Not another one of your matchmaking schemes, Annie. I don't think my weak heart can stand it."

"Felty, your heart is fit as a fiddle. Your knees will give out long before your heart ever does."

"Not these knees. They're titanium alloy. The doctor said so." Felty stood and waltzed around the table to prove his point.

"Now, Felty. Sit and finish your supper." Anna served him another heaping helping of Indonesian beef stew, vegetarian style. "I was right about Moses and Lia, wasn't I? Moses is so happy, he's like to float off the ground. That does your heart good, doesn't it?"

"I suppose so, but what it took to get him and Lia together almost gave me an ulcer."

"Our grandchildren deserve our very best efforts.

How will they ever find suitable mates if we don't help them?"

Felty plopped into his chair and kissed his wife on the cheek. "Our grandchildren will get along fine without any help from us."

"Of course they won't. Look at Moses. If we hadn't introduced him to Lia, he would still be pining over that Gingerich girl. And Aden can't seem to stay out of jail long enough to court a girl. He needs to meet Lily." Anna stuck a pat of butter on the top of a corn bread muffin and placed it on Felty's plate. "He's got to come to Huckleberry Hill, Felty."

Felty propped his elbow on the table and rested his chin in his hand. "Little Lily Eicher probably doesn't know how to cook vegetarian."

"I can teach her."

He sighed. "No doubt about that, Banannie. You are the best cook in Bonduel, Wisconsin."